HIDDEN

HIDDEN

A BONE SECRETS NOVEL

KENDRA ELLIOT

Montlake
Romance

Text copyright © 2012 Kendra Elliot
All rights reserved.

Printed in the United States of America.

Published by Montlake Romance
P.O. Box 400818
Las Vegas, NV 89140

ISBN-13: 9781612183886
ISBN-10: 1612183883

For Alexa, Annaliese, and Amelia

CHAPTER ONE

Lacey Campbell stared across the hazy field of snow at the big tent pitched against the rundown apartment building. She inhaled a breath of icy air, letting it fill her lungs and strengthen her resolve.

There. That's where the body is.

Her stomach knotted as she trudged toward the site, carefully watching where she placed her feet. She yanked on the sides of her wool hat and tucked her chin into her scarf as she strode through the fluff, blinking away the swirl of snowflakes. Snow was great, unless you had to work in it. And six inches of new snow covered the grounds of her current assignment. This weather was for skiing, sledding, and snowball fights.

Not for investigating old bones in a frosty tent in Boondocks, Oregon.

Two big boots appeared in her downward line of vision. She hit her brakes, slipped, and landed on her rear.

"Do you live here?" The cop's voice was gravelly and terse.

From her ungraceful, sprawling seat on the ground, Lacey blinked at the meaty hand he held out.

He repeated his question and her gaze flew to his scowling face. He looked like a cop who'd stepped straight out of prime-time TV. Solid, tough, and bald.

"Oh!" Her brain switched on and she grabbed his offered hand. "No, I don't live here. I'm just—"

"No one's allowed near the apartment complex unless you're a resident." One-handed, he smoothly hoisted her to her feet as his sharp eyes took a closer look at her leather satchel and scanned her expensive coat.

"You a reporter? 'Cause you can turn right around. There'll be a press conference at the Lakefield police station at three." The cop had decided she was an outsider. Not a difficult conclusion; the neighborhood reeked of food stamps and welfare checks.

Wishing she were taller, Lacey lifted her chin and then grimaced as she brushed at the cold, wet seat of her pants. *How professional.*

She whipped out her ID. "I'm not a reporter. Dr. Peres is waiting for me. I'm a..." She coughed. "I work for the ME's office." No one knew what she meant when she said she was a forensic odontologist. *Medical examiner's office* was a term they understood.

The cop glanced at her ID and then bent over to stare under the brim of her hat. His brown eyes probed. "You're Dr. Campbell? Dr. Peres is waiting for a Dr. Campbell."

"Yes, *I am* Dr. Campbell," she stated firmly and tilted up her nose.

Who'd he expect? Quincy?

"Can I get by now?" She peered around him, spying several figures moving outside the big tent. Dr. Victoria Peres had requested her forensic skills three hours ago, and Lacey itched to see what the doctor had found. Something unusual enough to demand Lacey come directly to the site instead of waiting to study the dental aspect of the remains in a heated, sterile lab.

Or maybe the doctor thought it'd be amusing to drag Lacey out of a warm bed, force her to drive sixty miles in crappy weather, and squat in the freezing snow to stare at a few teeth. A little power trip. Lacey scowled as she scribbled her name on the crime-scene log the cop held out and then shoved past the male boulder in her way.

She plodded through the snow, studying the old single-story apartment building. It looked deflated, concave along the roof, as if it was too exhausted to stand up straight. She'd been told it was home to seniors on small pensions and to low-income families. There was warped siding on the walls, and the composite roof sported bald spots. Irritation swirled under her skin.

Who dared charge rent for this dump?

She counted five little faces with their noses smashed against the windows as she walked by.

She forced a smile and waved a mitten.

The children stayed inside where it was warm.

The seniors were another story.

Small groups of gray-haired men and old women in plastic rain bonnets milled around in the courtyard, ignoring the cold. The rain bonnets looked like clear seashells capping the silver heads, reminding Lacey of her grandmother, who'd worn the cheap hoods to protect her rinse and set. She trudged by the curious lined faces. Without a doubt, today must be their most exciting day in years.

A skeleton in the crawl space under their building.

Lacey shivered as her imagination spun with theories. Had someone stashed a body twenty years ago? Or had someone gotten stuck in the crawl space and was never missed?

A half dozen Lakefield cop cars crowded the parking lot. Probably the small town's entire fleet. Navy-blue uniforms gathered around with hot cups of coffee in their hands, an air of resignation and waiting in their postures. Lacey eyed the steam rising from the paper cups and unconsciously sniffed. The caffeine receptor sites in her nerves pleaded for coffee as she pushed aside the flap door of the tent.

"Dr. Campbell!"

At the sharp voice, Lacey popped out of her coffee musings, froze, and fought the instinct to look for her father—also Dr. Campbell. The bright blue tarp at Lacey's snowy boots framed the partial recovery of a skeleton. Another step and she would've crushed a tibia and sent Dr. Peres's blood pressure spiking through the tent roof. As she ignored the doctor's glare, Lacey's gaze locked on the bones and a sharp rush surged through her veins at the sight of the challenge at her feet.

This was why she accepted assignments in freezing weather. To identify and bring home a lost victim. To use her unique skills to solve the mystery of death. To put an end to a mourning family's questions. To know she made a difference.

The cold faded away.

The skull was present, along with most of the ribs and the longer bones of the extremities. At the far end of the tent, two male techs in down jackets sifted buckets of dirt and rocks through a screen, painstakingly searching for smaller bones. A huge, gaping hole in the concrete wall of the crawl space under the building indicated where the remains had been discovered.

"Don't step on anything," said Dr. Peres.

Nice to see you too.

"Morning." Lacey nodded in Dr. Peres's general direction and tried to slow her racing heart. Her eyes studied the surreal scene. Bones, buckets, and bitch.

Dr. Victoria Peres, a forensic anthropologist, was known as a strict ball breaker in her field, and she didn't take flak from anyone. At six feet tall, she was an Amazon incarnate. A recovery site was her kingdom, and no one dared step within breathing distance of her sites before she gave her assent. And don't dream of touching anything without permission. *Anything.*

When she grew up, Lacey wanted to be Dr. Peres.

Lacey had worked with the demanding doctor on four recoveries before the doctor trusted her work. But that didn't mean Dr. Peres liked Lacey; Dr. Peres didn't like anyone.

Black-framed glasses with itty-bitty lenses balanced on the narrow ridge of the doctor's nose. As usual, her long black hair was in a perfect knot at her neck. No stray hairs had escaped the knot, even though the doctor had been on-site for five hours.

"Nice you could make the party." Dr. Peres glanced at her watch and raised one brow.

"I had to wait 'til my toenails dried."

A sharp snort came from the woman and Lacey's eyes narrowed. *Wow.* She'd actually made Dr. Peres laugh. Well, sort of. Still, it should give Lacey some bragging rights among the ME's staff.

"What'd you find?" Lacey's fingers yearned to start on the puzzle. This was the best part of her job. A mystery to decode.

"White female, age fifteen to twenty-five. We're pulling her, piece by piece, out of the hole that leads into the building's crawl space. Over there's the guy who found her." Dr. Peres pointed through a plastic tent window to a white-haired man speaking with two of the local police. The man clutched a wiener dog with a graying muzzle to his sunken chest. "He was taking his dog out to do its business and noticed several big chunks of concrete had broken out of the cracked wall. The dog crawled into the hole and when grandpa stuck his hand in to haul out the dog, he got a surprise."

Dr. Peres gestured at the gaping hole. "I don't think the body's been here all that long, and it was skeletal when it was placed."

"What do you mean?" Lacey's curiosity rose to code orange. So much for her idea of someone getting stuck under the building.

"I think the hole was recently made and the skeleton shoved in. It was a pile of bones. An undisturbed, decomposing body doesn't end up in a heap like that." Dr. Peres's brows came together in a black slash. "Bones scatter sometimes, depending on the scavengers in the area, but these look like they were dumped out of a sack and pushed into the hole."

"One skeleton?" Lacey's gaze darted back to the skull. What kind of freak dumps a skeleton? What kind of freak *has* a skeleton to dump?

Dr. Peres nodded. "And it looks pretty complete. We're finding everything—phalanges, metatarsals, vertebrae. But what I don't understand is why it wasn't hidden better. They had to know we'd find it. They left the hole wide open and the big concrete chunks on the ground for anyone to trip over."

"Maybe they were interrupted before they could finish. Cause of death?"

"Don't know yet." Dr. Peres's tone was short. "No obvious blows to the skull and I haven't found the hyoid, but both femurs are broken in the same spot. The breaks look similar to what you see in a car accident where someone hits a pedestrian with the front bumper." She frowned. "A high bumper. Not a car. A truck, maybe."

Lacey's thighs ached. "Antemortem breaks?"

"Either postmortem or just prior to time of death. No signs of the slightest start of healing." The doctor was curt, but bent to indicate several wedge-shaped fractures on the femurs.

Lacey's gaze locked on the cracks as she crammed her mittens into her bag and knelt, automatically slipping her hands into a pair of purple vinyl gloves from a box by the skull. The thin gloves were second nature to her hands.

"Someone hit her with a vehicle and hid the body," Lacey muttered, drawing a look of disgust from Dr. Peres. Too late, Lacey remembered the woman hated speculation on the cause of death before an exam was finished. Victoria Peres voiced only facts.

Mentally cringing, Lacey stood and self-consciously brushed at her knees. She'd stepped out of line. *Not my job to figure out the who, what, where, when, why, or how of the death.* She was here to focus on a minute aspect of the skeleton: teeth.

The dirt-sifting technician let out a whoop and added a patella to a growing pile of tiny bones. Dr. Peres picked it up, glanced at it briefly, spun it in her fingers, and assigned it to the left leg on the tarp.

"She seems small." *Too small.* She looked like a child.

"She is small. She'll be around five feet tall or so, but she's a fully mature woman. Her hips and growth plates tell me that." Dr. Peres lifted a black brow at Lacey. "Her teeth indicate that too. But that's your department."

"Hey, I can empathize if she was that short," Lacey stated, unconsciously shifting onto her toes and stretching her spine. Standing next to the tall doctor, Lacey's petite height was making her crane her neck as she spoke. "Can you tell how long she's been dead?"

Dr. Peres shook her head as she turned back to the bones. "There's no clothing to work with. All that's left is bones and blonde hair, and I won't make a guess. I'll know more after I study her in the lab."

"My father said you'd found some interesting dental work."

Dr. Peres's face brightened a degree. "Maybe that could help give us a time line. It was removable, so I bagged it already." She strode six steps to a plastic storage case and started rooting through a pile of evidence bags.

Lacey's shoulders relaxed a notch. Victoria Peres wasn't one of the people who'd mutter "nepotism" about Lacey's job. Maybe the doctor understood the job was tougher when your father was the chief medical examiner of the state. And your boss.

Lacey pressed her lips together. Anyone who'd worked directly with her knew Lacey was damned good at her job.

"That's a rock, not a bone." One of the techs peered at an ivory chunk on his partner's outstretched hand.

"No way. It's gotta be a bone," argued his counterpart.

Lacey glanced at Dr. Peres, expecting her to referee the dispute, but the doctor's attention was still buried in a storage case. Curious, Lacey carefully stepped over the tiny skeleton and held out a hand.

"Can I take a look?"

Two startled faces turned her way. Lacey stood her ground and tried to look like a competent forensic specialist. The men were young. One dark, one blond. Both bundled up as if they were working in the Arctic. Probably college students interning with Dr. Peres.

"Sure." Acting like he was handing over the Hope diamond, the dark-haired tech handed her a narrow piece, shorter than an inch. He cast a quick look at Dr. Peres's back.

Lacey studied the piece in her hand, understanding their confusion. She couldn't tell if it was bone. She lifted the piece to her mouth and gently touched her tongue to it, feeling its smoothness.

"Jesus Christ!"

"What in the hell...!" Both men rocked back, identical shock covering their faces.

Lacey handed back the little piece, hiding her smile. "It's rock."

Porous bone would have stuck to her tongue. A trick she'd learned from her father.

"She's right." Dr. Peres's close voice made Lacey jump and turn to face her. The doctor glanced at the men over Lacey's shoulder. "I can never shock those two guys. I guess I need to start gnawing on skeletons more frequently." Her eyes narrowed at Lacey. "Don't repeat that."

Dr. Peres's reputation was hard-assed enough without a rumor circulating that she gnaws on bones.

"I'm still looking for the dental work I removed first thing this morning. Why don't you take a look at the rest of her teeth while I check the other bin?"

Lacey nodded and kneeled by the sparse skeleton, the tarp crinkling loudly. She scanned the lonely remains, feeling quiet sadness ripple through her chest.

What happened to you?

The skull silently stared at nothing.

Lacey's heart ached in sympathy. The dead woman was the ultimate underdog, and Lacey was a sucker for the vulnerable.

Whether a long shot in a football game or an injured animal, she instinctively threw her support to the weakest. It was the same with her job. Every victim sparked Lacey's utmost effort.

But this situation felt different from other recoveries. Was it the freezing weather? The depressing location?

This feels personal.

That was exactly it. The examination felt personal.

Was it because the body was so small? Petite like herself? Young. Female. A victim of a horrible...

Stop it. She was projecting herself onto the remains. Lacey mentally pulled back and hammered down her emotions, swallowing hard.

Do the job. Do your best. Report the findings and go home.

But somewhere, someone was missing a daughter. Or sister.

Resolute, she gently lifted the mandible from the tarp and focused. Perfectly aligned teeth with no fillings. But the first molars were missing. Strangely, the second molars behind the missing ones were in perfect placement. She touched one of the empty spots with her little finger. It fit perfectly. Usually when teeth have been extracted, the proximal teeth eventually tip or shift into the empty spaces. Not on this mandible. And the extraction sites weren't new, because the bone had fully regenerated in place of the removed roots.

"Something was keeping the spaces open," she mumbled as she set the mandible down and reached for the skull. She ran questioning fingertips over the smooth, bony surfaces that shaped the head. Definitely female. Male skulls were lumpy and rugged. Even in death, the female form demonstrated a distinctive, smooth grace. She tipped the skull upside down and saw a perfectly aligned arch with all teeth present.

Braces. Or else great genes. The woman's smile had been beautiful.

Large silver fillings covered every surface of the upper first molars.

"She managed to keep the upper set of first molars," she muttered to no one. Lacey squinted as she scanned for any elusive white fillings. "But the bottom set was beyond saving at some point. Something probably weakened her first molars during their formation," she theorized. Lacey eyed the central incisors, looking for any signs of odd development, since those teeth formed during nearly the same time period as the first molars, but her front teeth were white, smooth, and gorgeous.

Lacey touched the bone posterior to the second molars. Bare hints of wisdom teeth poked through the bone. Without X-rays to check the root lengths of the wisdom teeth, she wasn't quite ready to agree that the woman was in her late teens or early twenties, but she hadn't found anything to counter Dr. Peres's premise.

The roar of an approaching vehicle seized her attention.

Her freezing fingers clenched the skull as she watched through a hazy plastic window while a man on an ATV ripped into the snowy parking lot and spun, deliberately covering one group of cops with thick snow.

Lacey jumped to her feet, pushed aside the tent flap, stepped out, and stared, sucking in her breath.

The cops weren't going to appreciate that stupid prank.

The men in blue brushed off the snow, and their disgruntled rumblings reached Lacey's ears. The driver of the ATV gave a shout of laughter as he hopped off and strode toward the incensed group, casually pulling off his gloves.

Was he crazy?

He was tall and walked with confident strides, apparently not concerned with the wrath of the cops. He faced away from her, showing trim black hair below his baseball cap, and she wished she could see his face. To her shock, the circle of cops opened to let him enter, slapping him on the back and shaking hands all around. The knot in Lacey's spine relaxed.

They weren't going to kill him.

Fifty feet away, the rider abruptly turned his head and a laughing, steel-gray gaze slammed into hers. Lacey stepped back at the instant onslaught, her eyes blinking. A solid jaw tensed briefly as he looked her up and down. He gave a deliberate wink and grin, and turned back to his group.

Lust in Lacey's brain jumped up and took notice. *Did he just flirt with me?*

Very nice. Her limbs warmed.

Lacey's fingertip slid into an empty eye socket and she gasped, dropping her gaze to the forgotten skull, terrified she'd crunched a delicate bone. She studied it frantically, searching for fresh cracks. Finding none, she exhaled in a low whistle.

Dr. Peres would have *her* head if she damaged the skull.

CHAPTER TWO

Jack Harper coughed and stumbled forward a step in the snowy powder as Officer Terry Schoenfeld slapped him hard on the back. It felt good to be loved.

The rest of the cops peppered him with questions and greetings.

"You drive that tiny thing all the way from Portland?"

"How's the cushy life?"

"You still owe me fifty bucks from that football game."

"That game didn't count. The refs screwed it up. The whole bunch of 'em got suspended for all those lousy calls," Jack answered Terry, speculatively rubbing at his chin and keeping a straight face as he eyed the circle of cops. The group of men snorted.

Terry's face turned dark pink and he sputtered. "It was the score that counted. The Ducks won. The other team played rotten enough to let them score two touchdowns in two minutes. Lousy calls or not, you still owe me the money." Ropey tendons popped in his neck, and he pounded a gloved fist on his thigh.

Jack laughed, joined by hoots from the other cops. Jack had known the exact buttons to push to rile his friend. The University of Oregon's big ex-lineman would get defensive over any dissing of his alma mater. Jack and Terry had met in high school, then attended rival Oregon colleges before they'd served in the Lakefield police department together.

Before Jack had to leave the force.

The other cops continued to harass Terry, a chorus of male heckling, but a gut-deep instinct made Jack look over his shoulder at the apartment building, and he saw the woman. She stood motionless outside the white tent, intently watching the group. Long, wavy blond hair fell past her shoulders, and the black thick hat she'd pulled down over her ears framed wide, dark chocolate eyes. His gaze locked on those warm eyes, and her cheeks turned pink. *Charming.*

The warm buzz of attraction started in his gut and shot up to his brain. He gave her a wink.

"'Bout time you gave us a visit." A cop with a familiar face spoke, pulling Jack's attention from the striking woman, but Jack couldn't remember the cop's name. It'd been too long.

"He's too busy making money," Terry complained. "They hunted you down, huh?"

"The answering service forwarded the call from the Lakefield police department to me. Luckily I was in town, and only a few blocks away, visiting Dad."

"That's why you're on the ATV."

Jack shrugged. "Seemed right for the weather." He brushed at the snow accumulating on his shoulder and took another look at the tent by the apartment building. The woman had vanished. He twisted his lips. *No matter.* He was here on serious business. Not to score. Jack gestured for Terry to step aside with him. Behind them, the cops reformed their circle and started grumbling about the weather.

He stared Terry in the eye and lowered his voice. "What in the hell is going on over there?"

Terry tightened his mouth. "Resident found a skeleton in the crawl space this morning."

Fuck. The cop who'd called him hadn't been full of shit as Jack had hoped. "What was he doing under the building?"

Terry shook his head. "He wasn't under the building. He was walking his dog when the animal crawled into a hole in the wall of the foundation. That's when he found some bones."

"Are they sure they're human bones?" The words came out of Jack's mouth just as an image of the blonde woman flashed in his mind. She'd been holding a skull.

A skull? How'd he miss that?

Terry nodded.

"So the bones have been there a long time?" Maybe they'd been there before Dad bought the building.

"I don't know. One of the forensic techs was overheard saying the bones were in a pile under the building like they'd just been put there."

"A pile?"

"And no dust like you'd expect from something sitting under the building for years."

"Male? Female?" Like it mattered. A skeleton was under his building. The sex wouldn't matter to the media.

Terry's eyebrows lifted slightly. "I don't know. They brought in a forensic anthropologist to take a look. A real bitch. She bit Darrow's head off when he peeked inside the tent a few hours ago. Darrow also told me he'd signed in another specialist from the medical examiner's office not too long ago."

"No reporters yet?" Jack scanned the street. When had the neighborhood grown so old? The houses looked like they'd been banished to a rest home for old buildings. It'd once been a well-kept, middle-class area. He turned back to the apartment building, heart sinking at the dated architecture and failing roof. It looked like crap. He'd have a firm talk with the manager. No one had told him the building had fallen into such lousy condition. Jack grimaced. He couldn't personally supervise every structure owned by Harper Developing. That's why he hired local property management companies.

"Not yet." Terry paused. "Looks like that place needs a lot of work. Wouldn't hurt to plow the building under and start over."

"I don't think a high-rise of condos would blend into the neighborhood."

Terry chortled and punched him in the shoulder. "That's right. Now your buildings are too snobby for the likes of this hick town."

The words stung.

This little apartment building had been one of Dad's first investments. Back in the 1960s, Jacob Harper had bought several rental properties in his hometown of Lakefield. Property values grew and he bought more. After Lakefield, Jacob had slowly expanded his purchases to the north and south, picking up aging properties and remodeling them into places Middle America called home. Over forty years, he'd created a solid reputation for Harper Developing.

A reputation that'd sat heavily on Jack's shoulders for five years.

"I need to know exactly what's going on. Who's in charge of the scene?"

"You're looking at him." Terry expanded his chest with a deep breath and a frown. "I was here first and cordoned everything off. All the residents have been interviewed. No one knows shit. We've handed the investigation off to state. We don't have the forensic equipment or specialists for this type of crime."

Jack wasn't surprised Terry was the lead cop on-site. Under the big athletic persona was a quick, logical mind. "I don't see anyone from OSP." Oregon State Police often assisted small communities like Lakefield when they needed help.

"I expect a detective team from Major Crimes at any time. They called the medical examiner, who came and confirmed the skeleton was dead." Terry rolled his eyes. "The ME called the anthropologist."

"Well then, that's who I'll talk to. I can't stand here blind. My cell phone's going to be burning up as soon as the media gets wind of this. I need some answers." Jack strode toward the tent.

"Uh, Jack." Terry grabbed at his arm, talking quickly. "That anthropologist isn't gonna tell you anything. She looked at me like I'd crawled out from under the building with the rats. And I'm in uniform."

He shook off Terry's grip. "I'm the owner."

"Don't say I didn't warn you." Terry clamped his mouth shut and followed at Jack's right flank. Silent team support. Just like when they'd played football in high school.

"Here." Dr. Peres emptied the contents of a paper bag into Lacey's hands. Lacey's memory of the man with eyes like storm clouds evaporated as a pair of intricate gold earrings sparkled on her palm.

Lacey's mind snapped into place and her focus sharpened.

No, not earrings. *Bridges.* A pair of old, removable gold dental bridges designed to replace a missing tooth. These bridges had held the mandibular molar spaces open. Lacey could clearly picture them in place on the skeleton's small jaw. They resembled small pieces of jewelry. The delicate spider-leg clasps would connect to adjacent teeth to secure a gold tooth in the place of the missing tooth.

Something sparked and then dimmed in her memory.

"Old dentistry. No one makes bridges like this anymore. And they haven't for a long time," Lacey stated.

"How old?" Dr. Peres peered at the gold. "Could they help narrow a time frame?"

Lacey shrugged as her field of vision narrowed to exclude everything but the bridges. An overwhelming urge to hurl the gold to the ground shot through her.

Something was wrong.

"I can't say. Maybe the dentist was old, not the dentistry. Maybe he practiced old-school techniques. There are hundreds of dentists who don't update some of the methods they learned in dental school. These could be any age."

"Well, that's not a very big help." Dr. Peres glanced at her watch. "I'm going to go steal a cup of the cops' coffee. Want some?"

"I'd kill for coffee. Please. Black." Lacey watched the doctor disappear out the back flap door. She exhaled and relaxed her shoulders, noticing that both techs did the same thing. The three in the tent exchanged a wry look. It was tough to be in close quarters with Dr. Peres for any period of time. Lacey turned her focus back to the gold in her hand.

Déjà vu.

In her mind, Lacey saw the bridges sitting on her palm, but the image wasn't from today. She'd held them before. Or held some bridges that were identical. They'd creeped her out at that time too. But where'd she see them? In dental school?

No, the memory was older than that. Rusty fragments of images poked at her brain.

The front flap door of the tent yanked open, startling Lacey, and she tightened a fist around the gold. Two men stepped in from the snowfall. The first was the black-haired man from the ATV who'd winked at her. Up close, he was taller than she'd expected. His red ski jacket hid broad shoulders, and his jeans indicated well-muscled, but lean thighs. Lacey swallowed dryly.

His eyes were hardened steel. No flirting.

Lacey blinked and tucked a strand of hair behind her ear. Who was he?

She barely glanced at the second man. He was a beefy Lakefield cop with an uncomfortable tightness around his mouth, his brown gaze darting to each corner of the tent.

"Are you in charge?" Steel Eyes asked her. A muscle tensed at his jaw.

"God. No." Lacey touched her hair again. "Dr. Peres is in charge. She went for coffee." She turned to glance at the back flap door. Where was the doctor when she needed her?

"I need to know what's going on." Steel Eyes stepped closer, deliberately leaning toward her.

Ire and annoyance crept up Lacey's back as she stood her ground. It took more than a big man to intimidate her these days. Much more.

"Are you with the police?" she asked. She ignored his statement and attempted to keep her focus on his face.

"No." He broke their eye contact, his perusal slowly wandering down to her boots.

Every nerve ignited. His scrutiny seemed to touch her physically, and Lacey struggled to speak through her instant brain fog. *Jerk.* He was harassing her on purpose. "Then you need to get out of the scene. Now. Or I'll get the police to move you out." She deliberately eyed the cop, but he was looking everywhere but at her. *Big help.*

"I own the building. When a body is found on my property I should be told what's happening." The king of the hill stood his ground.

Lacey glared. Gorgeous man or not, did he think he could bust into a crime scene and expect her to bow at his feet? She took a step forward and placed her fists on her hips. "I don't care if you created the building out of your own flesh and blood," she snapped. "This crime scene is off limits until Dr. Peres clears it. And believe me, you don't want to cross Victoria Peres."

The cop nodded vehemently. "Told ya."

The other man pressed his lips together, his gaze stroking each part of her face.

She wondered if she looked as pissed as she felt. Behind her, the techs were quiet. The constant rustling of their sifter had stopped. The silence in the tent probably lasted only a second or two, but it felt like twenty.

Steel Eyes held his hand out to her. "Jack Harper, Harper Developing."

Lacey snorted. Now he was playing nice? She paused long enough to be rude then shook his hand. She didn't offer her name. He held her hand longer than was necessary, and his eyes flickered. Was he laughing at her? A tent flap behind her slapped shut and the heavenly scent of coffee blew through the air.

"What's going on?" Dr. Peres asked sharply.

Lacey kept her gaze on Jack as the doctor's footsteps moved closer. She heard the doctor set the coffee on a table and then move to stand beside her.

"I asked, *What's going on?*" Dr. Peres repeated.

"Mr. Harper owns the building. He was just leaving." Lacey gave him a smile that didn't touch her eyes. *Get out while you can still walk.*

Jack looked past Lacey to the skeleton on the tarp. His nostrils flared slightly. "Jesus," he whispered. "Is that a child?"

"It's a woman," Lacey corrected. She lifted her chin. "You need to leave. There's nothing else to tell you right now."

Jack nodded, held her gaze for two heartbeats, and turned to leave with the cop. A strange wave of regret flooded her.

"Dr. Peres! Look at this!"

Lacey started at the excited voice of the tech. She and Dr. Peres turned as the young tech edged around the tarp. Jack and the policeman froze midstride.

"It's a necklace, and it's got her name on it. Well, maybe her name." The blond tech's grin nearly split his face above his bulky scarf. "It says 'Suzanne.'"

Dr. Peres slipped a vinyl glove out of her pocket and yanked it on. Breathless, the tech carefully placed the necklace on her outstretched palm. Lacey moved closer to peer at the necklace. Jack and the cop stepped up to look over her shoulder. Dr. Peres was too engrossed to scold them.

It was exquisite. The chain was delicate, with fine links, not cheap loose ones. The name was the centerpiece of the necklace, small handwritten letters crafted of gold. Like the "Carrie" necklace from *Sex and the City*.

Suzanne.

Lacey unclenched her right fist and stared at the two gold bridges. She looked back to the necklace. Then back and forth again.

Suzanne.

Dr. Peres tentatively touched the necklace with a curious finger, preparing to slide it into an evidence envelope. Her lips moved as she spoke to the tech, but Lacey couldn't hear the words. Her stomach felt like she'd ridden the Zipper at the fair too many times.

The roar in Lacey's head drowned out the doctor. A mental connection was painfully materializing between the necklace in the anthropologist's hand and the gold bridges in her own.

Suzanne. It can't be…

The gold bridges glinted in her hand and she knew where she'd held them before.

The college stadium in Corvallis, Oregon, reverberated with hundreds of conversations and cheers. Oregon State fans adored their gymnastics team and the tickets to the meets always sold out.

In her red team leotard, Lacey scanned the throngs from the sidelines, a competitive high rushing through her veins, jazzing up her energy level. The stadium was smaller than her home stadium at Southeast Oregon University, but it shook with the same vitality she'd felt a hundred times in meets across the country. She reveled in the adrenaline, bouncing on the balls of her bare feet. Two more floor routines and then she was up.

"Hold these for me, will ya?"

Suzanne, Lacey's best friend and teammate, grabbed her hand and thrust something into it before she could protest. Lacey flinched at the gold pieces, still warm and slightly wet from the girl's mouth, and thrust them back at her.

"Gross! No way! Don't you have a baggie or something to put 'em in?"

The gymnast held up her hands, taking a retreating step backward.

"I forgot it. And I'm paranoid I'm gonna swallow one in the middle of a routine. I don't trust anyone else to hang on to them. My mom will kill me if I lose one." She tilted her head, gently wrinkling her nose as her manipulative brown eyes begged Lacey. "I'm up. Don't drop them."

Without waiting for an answer, the girl whirled around and marched out onto the springed floor, saluting each of the judges with her usual confident flair. The fans who'd made the lengthy drive from Mount Junction in Southeast Oregon roared as the announcer sang Suzanne's name over the speaker. Her sassy floor routine was a favorite and they screamed their enthusiasm.

"You owe me for this," Lacey muttered, balancing the gold on an open palm as she concentrated on Suzanne's routine.

Lacey exhaled deeply and gulped, her breath steaming in the icy air. Her hand had closed around the bridges again, the gold's sharp points stinging her palm. Her body spasmed and she started to double over. Jack grabbed at her shoulders.

"What the—" He caught her weight as her knees buckled.

It was Suzanne.

It couldn't possibly be anyone else. The age and petite size of the skeleton, the odd dentistry, and now the necklace.

The facts pointed to Suzanne.

And ten miles from this snowy spot, Lacey had helplessly watched Suzanne vanish into the dark night with a killer.

Suzanne had been abducted after a gymnastics invitational at Oregon State University in Corvallis, just south of Lakefield. Suzanne was the ninth victim of the Co-Ed Slayer, the serial killer who'd preyed on Oregon college girls over a decade ago.

With stinging eyes, Lacey stared at the small, lonely skeleton on the ground, and her heart pounded a mournful rhythm. Her body ached to crawl back into bed and pull the covers over her head. Her instincts had been right. This assignment was personal.

Suzanne's body had never been found.

Until now.

CHAPTER THREE

State police. Even at fifty yards, Jack could tell that the two men in regular clothing with the group of Lakefield cops weren't local. Terry had told him that the Lakefield police department was simply too small to handle this sort of investigation on its own. Terry pointed at Jack, and the two outsiders turned to stare his way.

Jack watched Terry and state detectives head toward him through the snow. One was older with the beginnings of salt-and-pepper hair. He was of average height with a rangy, lean build. The cop's black cowboy hat and boots made Jack smile.

Doesn't that hat make him one of the bad guys?

The other was younger, heavier, and carried himself like a serious weight lifter. The type whose arms don't swing as he walks, because too much muscle's in the way. No cowboy hat. Jack could see the starched white collar of a dress shirt and the red of a power tie under muscle man's overcoat. *Snappy dresser.*

"Jack Harper?"

"That's me."

The older detective held out a hand and Jack met sharp eyes as they shook hands. The cop had known exactly who Jack was. He'd asked only as a courtesy.

"Mason Callahan, Oregon State Police Major Crimes. This is Detective Ray Lusco." They both flashed badges and Callahan got right down to business, apparently a no-nonsense straight shooter. "You own the building, right?"

"My company...our company does. My dad and me. I haven't set foot here in at least eight years. We use a property management company to handle it. Personally, I can't tell you much about the place, but I can get the rental records."

Callahan straightened slightly at Jack's offer. Jack knew the cop had expected to argue or get a court order for the information Jack had just handed him. Then the detective's green eyes lightened imperceptibly as he made a connection.

"You were on the force here in Lakefield. You were the cop who got shot."

"Yep. That was quite awhile back." Jack's mouth was tight. *Shit.* Beside him, Terry straightened his back and Jack heard him clench his teeth.

Jack held solid eye contact with Callahan, uncomfortable with the cop's knowledge. Not that it'd been private. Jack's picture had been in the newspapers for a week back then. Lusco didn't speak, but Jack saw an eyebrow shoot up as he made the connection. No muscle for brains there.

"What can you..."

The tall black-haired woman from the tent marched up and stepped in front of Callahan, blocking Jack. Imperious, she shoved a plastic bag at the detective's chest. He made no move to take it.

Jack bit his cheek as he watched the woman actually stomp her foot in impatience.

"You need to see this. Steven just found it beneath the last of the bones. You also need to talk to Dr. Campbell. She's ID'd the victim."

Dr. Campbell? She'd ID'd the vic? Jack shook his head. Ten minutes ago in the tent, he'd grabbed the blonde woman as her knees buckled, and he'd lowered her to a chair. In his arms all he'd noticed was her incredibly small size and her scent. She'd smelled like cinnamon, or vanilla, or something from a bakery. Totally out of place in the death tent. Dr. Peres had shoved the woman's head down between her knees and ordered him and Terry out of the tent. He'd hesitated to leave, but Dr. Peres was adamant and obviously more than capable. As they'd left, he'd caught the blonde woman's name but not the "doctor" part.

Now the detectives stared at Dr. Peres, speechless. Jack reached over and snagged the woman's wrist to pull the baggie toward him. He focused on the oval piece of shiny metal. It was a police badge. He glanced at Terry, whose gaze was glued to the bag, and watched comprehension sweep over his face.

It was a Lakefield police badge.

Jack squinted at the numbers on the badge. He made out the first four digits and his heart plummeted to his frozen toes.

The snow had stopped falling for a few minutes and Oregon State Detective Mason Callahan glanced at the gray sky. It looked ready to dump the white stuff for several hours. Six more inches by evening? Now he believed the forecasters. They claimed it was shaping up to be the worst Oregon winter in decades. *Amen for four-wheel drive.*

He glanced at the apartment building, noting that Dr. Peres and her techs were still inside the tent. What other goodies would they find?

A cop's badge stashed with a mysterious skeleton.

Mason didn't like that one bit.

The Lakefield police badge number was being called in to trace its owner. Jack Harper had sworn he recognized the number and had given the cop's name, but the detectives wanted official word. Harper hadn't worked for Lakefield PD for over five years; he could be wrong.

But until that was cleared up, Mason and Ray were interviewing the little dentist. Dr. Campbell perched on the tailgate of an old Chevy pickup truck in the freezing parking lot that was serving as their preliminary interview room.

The detectives exchanged silent looks over her head. Wrapped up in her jacket and a borrowed yellow parka, Dr. Campbell looked like a teenager. A shiver rattled her every thirty seconds, nearly making her coffee spill each time. She hadn't taken a sip.

She didn't seem old enough to be a forensic specialist, let alone an instructor of dentistry at the prestigious dental school up on Pill Hill in Portland. But the forensic anthropologist had vouched for her, and that lady didn't seem to like anyone, so Mason was taking her reference seriously. Mason had expected days, maybe weeks of searching and following leads to identify the old skeleton. Instead the dentist had presented them with a solid lead right off the bat.

It was too convenient.

Mason rested a boot on the truck's bumper, laid his forearm across his thigh, and leaned in to continue the odd interview.

"So from her teeth and a necklace, you're convinced this is a college friend."

"Yes. For the fifth time." Dr. Campbell spoke like she was instructing five-year-olds with a double dose of ADD. She set down her coffee.

"Suzanne was kidnapped by the Co-Ed Slayer in Corvallis eleven years ago. After he was caught, he confessed to her murder but wouldn't say where he'd left her body." She turned impatient brown eyes on Mason and ticked off the facts on her fingers. "Suzanne had a necklace just like that one. She wore it constantly. There are strands of blonde hair with the bones, the same color as hers. And I know those ridiculous gold bridges. I had to hold them once for her at a gymnastics meet, because she forgot a baggie for them." Her hand movements paused. "Don't you remember the Co-Ed Slayer?" Her voice cracked on the name.

"I'm familiar with the case." Mason was more than familiar. He'd served on the task force to find the killer, and the facts had been forever broiled onto his brain. His gut suddenly rocked. His stomach had been working overtime on acid production since the minute he'd understood this skeleton might be linked to that sick fuck, Co-Ed Slayer Dave DeCosta.

It'd been a big deal a decade ago. A really big deal.

Mason remembered the women who'd vanished from the college campus. Tortured bodies had turned up in dark corners of town. Rumors of the Green River Killer moving south from Seattle. Parents had yanked their daughters out of Oregon State University as school officials tried hopelessly to quash the stampede from campus. Other gossip of witchcraft and white slave trade had flown around the state.

It had been every parent's nightmare.

It had been every cop's goal to solve.

At first, the police hadn't included Suzanne Mills with the victims. Unlike the other women, she hadn't vanished directly from the OSU campus. She'd been kidnapped in the business district, outside the campus, and her body never recovered. The other victims' bodies had turned up within two or three weeks of their disappearance. After his capture, Dave DeCosta had admitted he'd taken Suzanne, and she'd been officially listed as the ninth victim, but DeCosta had refused to tell police where to find her body.

Every cop had blown out an exhausted breath when the killer was caught. Mason had gone home and slept for twenty-four hours, relieved the nightmare was over.

He'd never had another case like it and that was just fine with him.

Photos of every victim shone clearly in Mason's memory. During the investigation he'd examined each picture a thousand times. He recalled the image of the perky blonde gymnast, Suzanne Mills. She'd been a beautiful girl with a wide smile and natural blonde ringlets. Each victim had radiated a fresh energetic beauty, setting them apart from their peers, making them irresistible to a killer. All had been athletes and all had been blonde.

Only in Suzanne's case had there been a witness to the abduction. Suzanne had been with another gymnast, walking downtown, heading for a team dinner at a nearby restaurant. DeCosta had first attacked the witness, but she'd fought off the bastard, suffering a broken leg and severe head injuries. Then DeCosta had turned his attention to Suzanne, knocking her out and carrying her to his car. From her position on the bloody sidewalk, the injured witness had managed to memorize part of the license plate. Later the brutalized girl had bravely sat in court and testified to convict the killer.

The image of the surviving victim was also burned into Mason's memory. She was sitting in front of him. He scanned her distraught face.

"You were there," he stated softly. "You were the one who got away."

Dr. Campbell didn't react.

Out of the corner of his eye, Mason saw Ray's jaw drop. Everyone had known there'd been a girl who escaped, but her identity had been kept out of the newspapers. Now Ray stared at Dr. Campbell, studying her with renewed curiosity and awe.

Ray's thoughts had to be identical to Mason's. *The woman who'd identified the skeleton was also the girl who got away?*

"That was you?" Ray asked.

She nodded silently.

"And you're positive this skeleton is Suzanne Mills."

Dr. Campbell didn't meet Mason's eyes, her gaze fixed on the silent tent that housed the remains of her friend.

"No one would know her better than me."

CHAPTER FOUR

Cal struggled to place the tune as his captor continually hummed.

A rock anthem from the sixties, maybe early seventies. The lead singer had a big hooked nose. What was the band called? The song's name? Cal tormented his brain in the effort.

The insignificant questions gnawed at him.

Cal opened his eyes. Well, one eye. The other had been swollen shut for… How long had he been sitting here? The room had no windows, no clock.

Nothing to measure the passing of time.

His bladder had emptied as he'd sat tied to the chair. That'd been a long time ago, and he'd held it forever before giving up.

Twelve hours? Twenty-four hours? Days?

He didn't know how long or, more importantly, *why* he was here.

It was freezing in the room. And it stank. At first it just smelled of mold and musty disuse, but now the sharp ammonia of urine nauseated him.

He figured he was in a basement because of the low ceiling and dirt floor. Its walls were built with big bricks of concrete that gave the room an impenetrable, underground feel. Someone had taken the time to paint an American flag that covered one entire wall. Its colors were fresh and crisp.

Cal hadn't missed the irony of being tortured in front of the symbol of freedom.

He remembered he'd been nabbed in his garage. He'd just driven in and stepped out of his truck. A powerful blow to his head had cut off the rest of his memory. Then he'd woken up here, suffering from the stepmother of all headaches. And that was when he felt good.

Closing his good eye, he tipped back his head to rest on the wooden chair. The humming continued to stab at his brain. It was the same damned song over and over. He ached to tell the hummer to shut the fuck up, but he'd already made that mistake. And now he had one functioning eye as a result of his temper. He'd never use the injured eye again and he wanted to keep the good one intact.

He kept his opinions to himself behind the foul gag in his mouth.

"You like to hunt, Cal?" The humming had stopped.

Cal didn't answer.

"I know you do. Elk, deer, ducks. People."

Cal's head lurched up off the chair back. His eye opened again.

"You didn't like that? People? I know you've hunted people. That's what you did for thirty years. Right? Isn't that one aspect of a cop's job? A big aspect?"

The hummer stood behind him. Cal couldn't see his face. He didn't need to. It was rammed deep into his memory. He wouldn't forget this guy. Ever.

"Ever kill anyone?" The hummer paused. "You don't have to answer that. I know you didn't. I checked. You were involved in four shootings in your career but never snuffed out a life. You ever wonder how it'd feel? To take a life? Would the guilt destroy you? Eat away at your brain? The way it did Frank Settler?"

Cal jerked in the chair, his wrists and ankles straining against their bonds. Frankie'd been dead for over twenty years. A suicide. A fellow cop, he'd accidentally shot a kid and couldn't handle the mental and emotional aftermath. Frankie's pain had haunted Cal for years.

Who was this guy?

"Frank must've been a wimp. He showed a dire lack of internal control. That's what separates the men from the boys, Cal. You've gotta have power over your emotions and actions. A man can achieve whatever he wants with self-discipline. But you've got to exercise it, develop it."

What the fuck?

"Ted Bundy started with firm willpower, then lost it. He made careful plans but didn't stick to them. That's the key to every success: *stick to the plan*. Bundy could've eluded police forever if he'd kept his head and controlled his lust."

Disappointment rang in the man's voice. Obviously Bundy had been a huge letdown. The fucker probably mourned after Bundy's execution.

The hummer stopped at an Eisenhower-era folding table in front of Cal. Alarm spiked up Cal's spine. It was a table of torture. It looked like the hummer had walked through his garage and randomly picked items to spread on the table. Hammers, rakes, a wrench, a long hose. With horrific, inspired ways, the man had adapted them to create pain.

Except the shotgun. Cal had recognized it immediately. It was his own, taken from his personal collection of guns. His heart rate spiked as the man's hand stroked the barrel, lingering. He passed over it and moved to another item. Cal watched him open a small pink shoebox and his stomach heaved with bitter fear.

A headband?

The hummer lifted out a girl's blue headband and gently caressed it. A soft smile graced his face and his eyes developed a distracted look of sweet memory.

"I kept this one. But I can let go of it whenever I want. It can't control me. I'm a slave to nothing and no one." He dropped it back in the box, crushing the lid into place.

The sweet look was gone, replaced with angry determination. *He's fucking crazy.*

"Thanks for telling me where your badge was."

You're welcome, asshole. Thanks for leaving me two usable fingers.

"This is just the beginning of my plan. I'm going to make the cops tear around like starving mice in a maze, searching for the cheese as I move it from corner to corner." His eyes widened as he paced rapidly in front of the table, using Cal as his audience. "They'll think they're closing in on me and then I'll vanish. They won't have enough intelligence or control to keep up. And you and your badge are just the beginning. Well, actually you're the second stage. I set the first stage with your badge where they can't miss it."

The man's eyes took on an icy, empty cast as he halted and studied the tools on the table. Cal stiffened. He knew that look.

Humming again, the man chose the black rubber mallet, hefted it in his hands, tested its weight, and turned toward Cal.

CHAPTER FIVE

By early evening, the police badge from the Lakefield skeletal recovery had led the detectives to a fresh murder scene.

Retired cop Calvin Trenton was dead. He'd been tortured brutally.

At the brick Oregon State Police building in downtown Portland, Detective Mason Callahan sat at his desk, deep in thought. His body, his mind, and his heart were exhausted. Mason picked at the desk's peeling paint as he stared at the grisly photos of Trenton, letting his anger fuel his determination to find the fucker who'd committed this act of evil. Evil was the only word to describe the murder. The bastard had tortured the cop, broken his legs, and then strangled him, dumping the dead body back in Trenton's own bed.

And neatly pulled the covers up to the victim's chin.

It was as if the killer was taunting the police. Mason jammed a pencil in his automatic sharpener, let it whir, and then pulled it out. A perfect point.

He studied the fresh tip as the smell of wood and lead touched his nose. What would happen if he shoved it in the killer's eye?

One of Trenton's eyes had been destroyed.

Calvin Trenton had been off the job for five years. Divorced for twenty, he'd lived with his current companion, a big Rottweiler mix. Police had found the protective dog camped under Trenton's bed. The dog had snapped and growled at anyone who'd tried to approach the body. Animal control had to be brought in before anyone could reach the corpse.

Two of the responding cops had shed tears as they gaped at Trenton in his bed, unable to act because of the sharp teeth of the dog. Trenton just lay there, obviously dead, and the cops couldn't do anything but stare.

Mason didn't like coincidences, and this new case had too fucking many. He liked his cases to be neat and tidy, but that was usually the exception instead of the rule. This case was pureed clam chowder.

He tipped back in his chair, tapping the pencil on the edge of his desk, and studied his big dry-erase chart for the tenth time in ten minutes. Suzanne Mills's name sat directly in the center in blue ink with red arrows pointing out from her name to four other names. Green arrows made connections between the names on the periphery. So far he knew:

One of the forensics workers, Dr. Lacey Campbell, knew Suzanne Mills and identified her at the recovery site.

Mills was a victim of the Co-Ed Slayer, Dave DeCosta, a decade ago.

Dr. Campbell nearly became a victim of DeCosta a decade ago.

Jack Harper owned the building where Suzanne Mills had been found.

Jack Harper just happened to be standing there as the anthropologist walked up with Trenton's police badge.

Jack Harper recognized Cal Trenton's police badge.

Years ago, Jack Harper had partnered with Calvin Trenton on the Lakefield police force.

The chart was a mess of colorful crisscrossing arrows. But nothing made sense.

Why had Cal Trenton's murder been purposefully linked to Suzanne Mills's bones?

Mason eyed Lacey Campbell's name. He dropped his pencil, grabbed a dry-erase marker, and drew a green dotted arrow to Calvin Trenton and stared at his work. His gut told him there was a connection. He just had to find it.

He needed to interview Dr. Campbell again.

Mason's stomach churned. He'd put the Co-Ed Slayer case to bed years ago, and now it was trying to crawl out from under the covers.

He deliberately pulled his strained gaze from the drawing and glanced at his partner, who was deep in concentration in front of his computer screen. If Mason said a word, Ray would never hear it. The man had extreme linear focus. One thing at a time was how the detective worked, but damn, Ray was thorough and sharp. Ray's big shoulders strained the seams of his suit jacket, his power tie askew—a sure sign the precise man was as frustrated as Mason about the case.

Mason glanced at his watch. Seven o'clock on a Saturday night. Ray's wife, Jill, should be calling any second. Too often the job of a detective demanded a cop put his work first, but Ray managed a healthy balance. His wife and two kids were the priorities in his life, and Ray made sure they knew it. Secretly, Mason envied Ray's marriage and family life. He'd watch Ray and Jill as they finished each other's sentences or silently communicated with eyes and facial expressions. He'd never had that type of connection with a woman. Especially his ex-wife.

Mason discreetly studied his partner. If Ray ever discovered how he felt, he'd have his wife setting Mason up with blind dates every weekend.

Jill invited Mason over for dinner at least twice a month, but he rarely went. Lusco's preteen kids were cool, easy to tease, and kicked his butt at every video game on the market, but Mason hated the depression that slapped him in the face each time he left their warm home. The kids made him want to see his son, Jake, who was almost seventeen...*shit. Jake was almost eighteen.*

Had it been seven years since his marriage went down the crapper? Frowning, Mason counted back on his fingers. He'd dated here and there, some even seriously, but it'd never lasted. Now he was forty-seven and still single. His wife...ex-wife... had had two more kids with the new husband, a CPA. Jake lived with his mom and stepdad. The man kept banker's hours and coached Little League and soccer, all while maintaining an active social calendar. He always had a grin and handshake ready for Mason.

Mason hated him.

Mason tossed the dry-erase marker onto Ray's keyboard and it clattered across the keys.

"Damn it! What was that for?" Ray glared, swiped up the marker, and hurled it back. Mason easily ducked. Ray was rather predictable.

"Go home, Ray. Eat the dinner your sexy wife made for you. Then pull her into the bedroom and—"

"Shut up." Ray glanced at this watch. "Look at the time! Fuck. I gotta get out of here." Ray stood and slapped his papers into piles and binders.

Mason rubbed at his chest and watched Ray wrestle on his overcoat.

"Aren't you going home?" Ray stopped with his arm halfway in his coat sleeve, his pale eyes probing and his brows narrowing into concerned lines below his blunt military haircut.

"Naw. I'm right in the middle of something. I'll go soon."

Ray looked away and finished pulling on the thick overcoat. "All right." He wrapped a black scarf neatly around his neck. "You'll be over for the game tomorrow? Jill's making that nacho dip you like."

"Wouldn't miss it." Mason picked up his pencil, twisting it in his fingers. "See you tomorrow."

"Later." Ray sped toward the door but glanced back. "Go home, Callahan."

"I will, I will. Get out of here."

Ray vanished around the corner, and Mason blew out a sigh. He sank deeper into his chair and swung it around to face the white board. The chair creaked and complained as he leaned back, cracking his knuckles as he studied his artwork, directing his mind back into the case.

What the fuck was going on?

CHAPTER SIX

The dental school, on the hill overlooking Portland, occupied a tiny bit of the sprawling Oregon Health Sciences University campus. Inside the aging gray walls, every dental chair held a body with an open mouth.

Hovering beside a male student, Lacey watched him remove the decay from a little girl's tooth. From Nick's raised eyebrows and wide eyes Lacey knew he couldn't believe the size of the cavity. She agreed. The cavity looked like a moon crater. Ten years old and the child had never been to the dentist. At least she was holding still while Nick worked. Some of the pediatric patients wiggled like...*damn it!* Lacey stepped closer and spoke in Nick's ear.

"If you prep any deeper, you're going to be doing a root canal instead of a filling."

At her voice, Nick whipped the handpiece out of the child's mouth and straightened his back. Lacey watched a flush shoot across his face and she silently grinned. She always flustered the male dental students. Nick swallowed dryly and Lacey saw his Adam's apple bob below his blue mask. The little girl's confused eyes blinked at Nick.

Good girl. Very patient with her wannabe dentist.

Lacey glanced at the clock, praying clinic hours were nearly over for Monday. Two hours left. She winced at the surging headache behind her eyes, inflamed by the bright fluorescent lights of the ancient clinic.

And aggravated by the stress of her weekend.

It wasn't every day she discovered the missing skeleton of her best friend. After hours of being grilled by police on Saturday, she'd slept away the entire next day.

Tranquilizers deterred her nightmares.

She'd broken her cardinal rule by taking the tranquilizers. They were too easy to use for escape.

She'd been on an emotional seesaw since Saturday morning. A heartbreaking ride she hadn't experienced since her mother died. Lacey rubbed at her temples. The emotions she'd carefully bottled were threatening to explode.

She'd avoided the phone all weekend. Her father had left several messages, but not nearly as many as Michael. She figured Michael had heard about Suzanne early on Saturday, a perk of being a newspaper reporter. Michael knew all about Lacey's history and Suzanne's. Every twisted bit of it.

Lacey wasn't ready to talk.

Michael's last phone message had said he'd come bang on her door if she didn't answer the phone. That call had come in Sunday at 2:00 a.m., and Lacey knew he wasn't bluffing. For an ex-boyfriend turned close friend he was way too protective. She'd sent a text message, "NOT NOW." The phone calls stopped.

She should have talked to Michael. He would have warned her about today's front-page newspaper article on the recovery. With her coffee in hand, she'd picked the paper off the front porch and felt her throat close as she read the headline. "Remains of the Co-Ed Slayer's Final Victim Found in Lakefield." Her throat had eased when her gaze found Michael's byline. She'd immediately tossed the paper in the recycling, unread, knowing Michael would cut off his hand before he put her name in one of his articles.

In the crowded clinic, Lacey scanned the bustling mass of dental students, patients, and instructors. Not seeing any panicked students trying to catch her eye, she headed for the staff lounge. The bottle of Advil in her purse beckoned.

Making tracks for the clinic door, she stopped at the sight of fumbling fingers in a senior citizen's mouth. Sighing, she slapped on a pair of gloves and placed her hands over Jeff's to take control of his weak attempt at an impression of the woman's lower teeth.

"Pull her lip out. Get the goop down into the vestibule and plant the tray firmly, or your impression won't look anything like her teeth." Lacey's fingers deftly maneuvered the lower lip out of the way and settled the metal tray full of alginate impression material into the correct position. Jeff's brows were tight in concentration and he glanced at his watch.

"How long should it take to set up?"

"Don't look at your watch." She tapped a gloved finger on the sticky pink goo oozing over the woman's lip. "Just test the texture every twenty seconds or so. When it's no longer sticky and feels firm, it's done. It won't be more than a minute or two."

Jeff seriously nodded and proceeded to test the alginate every five seconds. Lacey tried not to roll her eyes.

Lacey forced herself to wait with him until the impression was finished. Trying to ignore her blistering headache, she glanced at the Panorex film on the view box, and her gaze flew to the handwritten date on the edge.

"That's a current film? You took that today?"

The film revealed the patient was edentulous on the maxilla—no teeth on top—and the remaining eight lower teeth each had barely six millimeters of bone holding them in place. A fraction of what it should be. Decades of gum disease had destroyed the bone support, and now the teeth were very, very wiggly.

Jeff nodded, concentrating on checking the sticky goo. "I took it this morning. I need an impression of her remaining teeth before her appointment next week, when we'll extract them and get her prepared for a lower denture."

Lacey bit her lip, trying not to grin. She looked around for another instructor, wanting to snag a witness. *Darn it.* No one was close.

The alginate was finally firm, and Jeff tugged halfheartedly at the tray in the woman's mouth. Strong suction was keeping it firmly in place.

The patient had an odd look in her pale eyes, but Lacey knew what was about to happen wouldn't hurt. "Slip a fingertip under the edge to break the seal, then lift." Lacey mangled the words as she fought to keep her laughter in check. Jeff gave a strong yank.

"Holy crap!"

Jeff dumped the tray in the woman's lap and sprang out of his chair as his shout rang through the noisy clinic. All eyes turned in their direction. Five bloody teeth smiled at him from the pink goop in the tray.

The patient didn't budge.

"You OK, hon?" Lacey asked, laying a hand on the woman's shoulder.

The woman wiped at some alginate stuck to her lip and raised a brow as she took in the mess in her lap. "Didn't feel a thing. Easiest tooth pullin' I've ever had." She touched the remaining three teeth in her mouth. "Can you take these out that way too?"

"Hmm." Lacey tapped a toe, feeling her headache evaporate. "We'll see what we can do. But definitely no charge for those extractions today."

CHAPTER SEVEN

"You seen today's paper?" Terry Schoenfeld didn't bother with a greeting when Jack answered the phone.

"Yeah, that article and yesterday's."

Jack leaned back in his office chair, awkwardly propped up his right leg on the desk, and reread the morning's article for the fifth time. Focusing on the list with the names and ages of all the victims.

"You remember all that from those killings back then?"

"Is that supposed to be funny?" Jack snapped at his friend.

Terry was silent for two seconds. "Sorry, man. It just isn't something I think about, I guess. I'd forgotten that they'd never found the remains of the killer's last victim. And how that one gymnast had the shit beat out of her when she witnessed her friend's kidnapping. And then she testified against the killer. They never did release her name, did they? I wasn't caught up in it like you were. Christ. I almost choked when I saw Hillary's name listed along with the other victims. I'd forgotten that you'd dated her."

Jack grimaced. He couldn't forget. Six hours of questioning by the police after the discovery of Hillary's body was rather memorable. He'd been questioned along with all her other ex-boyfriends. And there were a lot of them. He'd been a little dismayed to be a number on a long list of boyfriends. And acutely distressed to be questioned in a murder case.

Mutual friends had introduced him to Hillary. He'd just graduated; she'd been a freshman. They'd dated for a few weeks, no more. He'd been attracted to her. She was pretty, athletic, and into running, but they had absolutely nothing in common and drifted apart. Not a match made in heaven.

He hadn't seen her in several months when he'd heard she'd been murdered. Hillary had been victim number two.

He needed to get her face out of his mind. "The article doesn't say anything about Cal Trenton or his badge they found."

"State police haven't released the info about the badge. They're holding it back to sort out the crazies who call in to confess to dumping the skeleton. Trenton's murder made the local paper down here, but it wasn't in *The Oregonian*. The press hasn't made the connection to the skeleton yet, and we're not gonna help 'em make it."

Jack was silent.

"Trenton was one of the good ones," Terry offered.

"You don't have to tell me," Jack said.

"How many years did you ride with him? Two? Three?"

"Two and a half."

"He could be a royal asshole…"

"…but he was doing it for your own good," Jack finished Cal Trenton's oft-repeated line with a wry smile. The senior cop had taught him the ropes when he'd been fresh in the department. He swallowed hard as he remembered Terry's description of Trenton's death.

The old man hadn't deserved that. No one deserved that.

Jack scratched at his right leg. The skin was tight, itchy. Why did it itch if the nerve endings had been obliterated? The old scar bothered him at weird times, usually when he thought about the Lakefield police.

"I'm hearing that the doctor at the discovery site was the anonymous witness this article is talking about." Terry's voice was low.

"That tall Amazon? She was a gymnast?"

"Fuck, no. Not the black-haired one. The little blonde. The specialist who figured out who the bones belonged to and almost fainted. They're saying she was the one who was there the night Mills got abducted."

Jack swung his leg off the desk and sat up, mind spinning. "You mean Dr. Campbell." The woman had been at the abduction and then ten years later at the discovery of the remains? "That can't be right. That's too weird."

"Seriously. I've heard it from two different sources. They say she admitted it to the state detectives on Saturday."

Jack scanned the newspaper. "Then why isn't her name in the paper? Why keep her anonymous?"

"Shit. You should know that. Who wants that kind of publicity?"

After the phone call, Jack eyed the byline at the top of the article. Michael Brody.

Jack pushed out of his chair and strode to his office window, gazing down at the winding Willamette River, the bright sun warming his face. Many years ago, his life had suffered a big upheaval when Hillary died. This time the upheaval could be more than big; it could be huge.

He had to prepare to see his name in print again. The facts that he'd dated a Co-Ed Slayer victim and a skeleton had been found on his property would be too juicy for any reporter to pass up. Wait until Cal Trenton's badge and death were brought into the mix. What would the media print when they discovered Jack had partnered with the man?

What the hell was happening? First the body found on his property and now Cal? Was someone trying to set him up? For fucking murder? *Why?*

The chance to take shots at Harper Developing was something the media would jump on and relish. They'd ripped at him two years ago in a huge front-page feature about the poor recycling practices of some Portland companies. It wasn't that Harper Developing didn't recycle, but that his company could have recycled more.

Jack had admitted the issue, hired the biggest recycling guru he could find, and set up a committee to improve the company's practices.

Only in Portland was it unforgivable not to recycle efficiently.

Harper Developing had been the big, bad, thoughtless business for two solid weeks in the headlines. Jack had been slammed on the editorial page by dozens of letters. He shook his head at the memory. Wasn't like he'd dumped raw sewage in the Willamette River.

His successful company was a target. The public was fascinated by stories about serial killers, and reporters were going to dig into every aspect of his background, tying his name with the Co-Ed Slayer.

He threw the paper in the garbage can, swore, and then hauled it back out and tossed it in a recycling bin. He raked his hands through his hair. He and his company were going to be dragged through the mud. Over nothing. And he couldn't hire an overpriced guru to time-travel into the past and change whom he worked with and dated.

He'd worked hard to make a good name for his company... their company. His dad started it, but Jack had built it and expanded it into the mini-empire it was today. With his father no longer active in the day-to-day decisions, Jack had paved his own way, wanting to be among the biggest and best developers in the city. And he'd done it.

No one else could've brought that level of success to the Harper name. He gave money to the right causes, built affordable quality housing *and* his luxury high rises, and got his picture in the society pages with the right people.

Now it was threatening to implode.

He wouldn't let all his hard work be for nothing. He wouldn't let his father's legacy crumble under whispers and rumors.

Why was the skeleton in *his building*? Jack rubbed at his eyes. If it'd been in the apartments across the street from his building, today he'd be skimming the front page of the newspaper, then flipping to the sports section. Not pulling his hair out.

Oh, Lord. His breathing froze. He'd forgotten about Melody. He glanced at the clock. She must be sleeping in, since she hadn't called, demanding an explanation. His older sister was going to be mad as hell. One of her nosy friends was bound to let her know Harper Developing was in the news. Melody managed the philanthropy and public relations aspects of the company and wouldn't appreciate the published link to murder. Make that serial murder.

He had to do something before it got out of hand. But what?

He felt like he was trying to hold on to a fish as it squirmed and wiggled. Things were sliding out of his control, and he was in an unfamiliar position. Powerless.

Who was doing this to him?

Jack paced the perimeter of his office, hands deep in his pockets as he concentrated. He needed more information. Some big pieces of the puzzle were missing. He was tempted to call the reporter, Michael Brody, but he knew better. The timing couldn't be worse. Besides, anything he asked Brody about would turn up in the man's next article.

He thought of Lacey Campbell and her dark brown eyes. The one victim who escaped the killing hand of DeCosta. She was as deeply involved as he was. Maybe she could answer some questions. Like why Trenton's badge had been with the Mills remains, and why both were hidden on *his* property.

His mind was a mass of confusing, tightening knots.

He had to fight back, make a stand. But how?

He needed to go back to the beginning, to over a decade ago, when this mess all began. The best source was the person who'd been there. Hopefully, Lacey Campbell had some insight about the past, and why it was colliding with the present. He knew exactly where he could track her down. His questions for the protection of his business were the only reasons he'd seek her out.

Not because her brown eyes had been haunting him for two days.

The two dead girls were severely burned. Caught in a fire while sleeping in an abandoned, decrepit Portland house that had pulled in runaways like a magnet. Cheap barbeques had been used for heat while ten to thirty kids slept on the dirty floors each night. It was a well-known location to score every imaginable drug. Each week police cleaned out the house, scattering kids and drugs, but both always came back. Boarded-up windows and doors were nothing to determined teens searching for a place to escape the freezing temps.

Lacey paused before hitting the auto button on the double door to one of the bright, sterile autopsy suites of the medical examiner's building. *Burn victims.* Her legs shook slightly as she squeezed her eyes shut and sucked in deep breaths. She'd rather do floaters than burns. She shoved two cotton rolls up her nose under her mask. The scent of burned flesh had a freaky way of making her stomach growl that just seemed wrong. Clutching her clipboard to her chest, she hit the auto button with a hip.

Her father's silver head bent over a body. The smell seeped through her cotton rolls and she stopped just inside the door.

"Hey, there. You want to take a look first? Jerry already took the films for you." Dr. Campbell straightened and twisted his back with an audible series of cracks.

"I'll be quick." She nodded at Jerry, her dad's assistant, who recorded weights and measurements on a chalkboard as her father called them out. She commanded her legs to cross the room.

Standing next to the metal table, her digital camera tight in one hand, she studied the length of the pale body that contrasted with the blackened skin of the head. The hands were as severely burned as the head, but the rest of the body wasn't too bad. Clothes and shoes must have offered some protection. The girl's hair was mostly gone. Its color not readily obvious. Looked black, maybe Goth. Maybe simply burned.

"Smoke inhalation?" Her voice sounded high.

"Probably. I'll know soon."

Soon was right. Dr. Campbell drove through autopsies like Jeff Gordon. He was incredible to watch. His hands steady and sure as he whipped through the Y-cut and peeled back the flesh. He snapped the ribs with pruners identical to the ones Lacey used on her trees and sliced up each organ like the tomatoes on the Ginsu commercial, checking for abnormalities. Every body was handled with dignity; every body was given his best work. Her father was a physically and emotionally skilled examiner.

He opened the jaws of the burned girl for her. Lacey flicked on the digital recorder clipped to her waterproof gown and pointed a tiny, powerful flashlight into the gaping cavity.

Just look at the teeth.

"You need a shield," her father stated.

Jerry reached over and slipped the band of a clear face shield onto her head, the plastic covering her from forehead to chin. He grinned and winked through his own shield. She already had on protective glasses and a mask, and now she felt like she was in a hazmat suit. She didn't complain. Dead bodies could expel freaky things at surprising moments.

She quickly took pictures of both arches while her father pulled lips and cheeks out of the way, burned skin tissue peeling and flaking at the movements. Using a dental mirror, she did a quick check of the palate, tongue, and soft tissues, looking for any abnormalities. Her stomach settling, she rattled off the restorations into her recorder.

"Six through eleven have veneers." Her eyebrows rose. "Same with the anteriors on the mandible. Twenty-two through twenty-seven. No other restorations, but victim had had obvious orthodontics. Posteriors show decalcification on the posterior buccal surfaces in the shape of ortho brackets. Probably used the veneers to cover the scarring on the anterior teeth." Her heart dropped. "Somebody spent a lot of money on this kid's teeth," she whispered.

Her father nodded. "Coat and boots were expensive too."

Eleven antemortem dental charts lay on her desk back in her office. Charts requested for comparison to the current victims in the morgue by grieving parents with runaway teenage daughters. Lacey hadn't looked at the charts. She liked to complete her postmortem workup and then compare to the charts. But she had a hunch this was the daughter of the big software executive. The girl had run off two months ago. Her perky picture and wide perfect smile had been plastered on the five o'clock news for a week.

She studied the skull, not seeing any resemblance to the lovely school photo she remembered from the TV. Her lips pressed together, and she stopped her gloved hand before it rubbed at her shielded forehead. She blinked hard.

"Where's the second one?"

"Next door. I've already finished her." Her father picked up a scalpel and raised a brow at her.

That's my cue to leave.

Her stomach churning, Lacey spun on a heel and headed for the door, stripping her vinyl gloves and dropping them in the hazardous waste bin.

One more.

Lacey moved down the quiet hallway to her office, filling out the postmortem dental record as she walked, her mind comparing the two nameless bodies. How long would it take to place a name on the charts in her hands? The second girl had been burned to the same degree as the first. Lacey had easily seen where her father had peeled back the scalp to open the skull and remove the brain. And when she opened the mouth of the burned girl, the tongue was already gone, removed along with organs from the neck. Her father had noted the tongue was pierced with a metal barbell.

The teeth on the second girl had a scattering of small white composite fillings in the posterior teeth. The lower anteriors were crooked, and she demonstrated a class two bite with severe overjet. That girl had never had braces.

The human body was fascinating. Every autopsy taught her something new. But the ones on kids and teens made her angry. Life wasted. It was wrong, but she simmered with anger at the girls for taking risks and at the parents for losing control of their kids. When she had kids, they would never...

She halted and grabbed at the doorframe to her office as her gaze locked on the back of the man who sat at her desk. He was tilted back in her seat, nearly enough to topple the chair over, balancing himself with one foot hooked under the bottom drawer of her desk. She fought the urge to tip him over.

"You're in my chair," she snapped.

For a split second she thought he'd lose his balance as he twitched at her voice. He caught himself and spun in the chair to face her, his compelling gaze locked with hers.

Her stomach lurched at the gray eyes. She identified them instantly. Jack Harper. Over the weekend, those eyes had popped into her brain all too frequently.

She couldn't speak.

The big man lurched out of her chair and she took an instinctive step back into the hall, papers clasped to her chest. She saw a flicker of embarrassment flash across his features as he realized he'd startled her.

He was tall. She'd forgotten how tall, and she took another step back, her gaze glued to his. Hints of turbulence bubbled under his surface. Her heart pounded in her chest, but she wasn't scared. Just caught off guard.

"Sorry." Jack Harper grimaced. "I'd been waiting for a while and then got distracted by your parade of photos." Both of them looked to the computer. He'd been watching her screen saver. An assortment of snapshots of her family. He lightly snorted as the screen morphed to a picture of her and her father bending over brown bare bones on a metal table; her nose six inches from the remains. Lacey scowled. The image wasn't funny. They'd been at the Central Identification Lab in Hawaii. Where the unknown military dead go to be identified.

She studied the picture, remembering back six years. The bones had been a mix of two different men. Believed to be a chopper pilot and his copilot downed in Vietnam. She'd been deeply disturbed by the cold jumble of fragments. It'd added fuel to her desire to become the specialist she was today.

A snapshot of her and her buddy, Amelia, on a beach in Mexico filled the screen. Lacey pressed her lips together at the sight of the two skimpy swimming suits. It was her favorite picture of the two of them. Amelia's head was thrown back in impulsive laughter as their arms tightly circled each other's shoulders, blue tropical drinks in hand.

"Nice pictures."

Jack was still eyeing the beach shot, the start of a smile at his lips. *Jesus Christ*. She glared at his profile, annoyed that he'd managed to both startle and embarrass her inside of ten seconds.

He jerked his gaze back to her, smile fading. "I'm Jack Ha…"

"I know who you are."

He blinked and straightened his back. "Why are you in my office?" She didn't need any reminders of their first meeting. Her irritated gaze dropped from those steel-gray eyes to her chair. "And in my chair?"

"I wanted to talk to you…"

"Who told you where to find me?" The words came out in a rush, harsher than she'd intended. The receptionist had strict instructions to announce all visitors. Lacey had jumped on her case before. She couldn't believe Sharon would direct a strange man to Lacey's office. Sharon knew her bad history.

He drew a hand through his hair.

"Don't get mad at anyone. I told the desk I was from the dental school." Her face must have grown furious, because his eyes widened. "It's not her fault. I'm a good liar and very persuasive." His gaze flickered from one of her eyes to the other.

She snorted and his whole stance relaxed, a slow tentative grin spreading across his handsome face. She had no doubt he was persuasive. Poor Sharon hadn't had a chance.

Loud voices floated down the hall to them. Lacey glanced toward reception, hearing the high shouting voices of distraught women and the lower, angry tones of a man.

"What's that?" Jack frowned as he looked down the hall, stepping in front of her.

Lacey knew immediately. She slapped her papers on her desk, moved around Jack, and jogged toward the racket. The female voices grew louder, more frantic.

Lacey took a breath and pushed opened the door to reception, hitting Sharon in her back with the door. The woman was blocking the entrance and was one of the loud voices Lacey'd heard.

Sharon jumped to the side. Her eyes wide, sweat on her lip. The fifty-something receptionist was thoroughly rattled. "Ohh. Dr. Campbell! They want…I just was…" She wrung her hands.

"Dr. Campbell?" A tall, gray-haired man rested his hands on a crying woman's shoulders. Her body shook with loud sobs. His eyes were dry, but red. And his face was pale, stress aggravating the lines around his mouth. He was working hard to keep some dignity. "You're Dr. Campbell?"

Oh, Lord. Not right now.

"One of them. Dr. *James* Campbell is the medical examiner. Is there something I can help you with?" She kept her voice low. "You're looking for someone." It wasn't a question. She crossed to the couple and took the woman by the hand, guiding her to sit down on the couch. Still holding the woman's hand, she snatched the tissue box from the end table and thrust it at her, her eyes sympathetic.

Lacey understood.

The crying woman pressed a tissue against her nose. "They told us you have two unidentified female teenagers back there. Our daughter, Madison, has been missing for two months."

A chill shot up her spine as Lacey's gaze returned to the husband and she recognized him. *The software executive.* "You're the Spencers." Both nodded, eyes hopeful.

"Is one of them Madison? We sent in her dental chart a month ago when that female body found in the river was brought in." Mr. Spencer shuddered. "It wasn't her."

Lacey slowly nodded, remembering the ghastly floater. "I'm doing the dental comparisons on the two girls. I've looked at them but haven't compared my findings to the charts." She paused. "I've got eleven different charts from missing teenage girls to evaluate."

"Eleven?" Mrs. Spencer broke into fresh tears. "So many missing girls."

"Madison had braces when she was younger. And she's got porcelain veneers on all her front teeth." Mr. Spencer's hands were digging into his wife's shoulders as his voice rose. "Did either of...the bodies show that?"

Lacey froze. The first body now had a name. Rules stopped her tongue; she'd nearly blurted it out. The chance of another missing Oregon female teenager with that type of expensive dental work was infinitesimal. But she had to double-check. She wouldn't make a mistake.

"I'm not finished..."

"You said you'd already looked at the two girls. Did one have teeth like that or not?" Mr. Spencer's gaze raked her face. Mrs. Spencer looked up at his ruthless tone, glancing from her husband to Lacey. The woman looked fragile, like the lightest touch would shatter her skin. What hell had this couple lived in for two months? Purgatory. Limbo. The pain of the unknown, the wondering.

"Did they suffer?" Mrs. Spencer whispered. "I can't imagine being caught in a fire and..." Her hand clutched at Lacey's as her face crumpled.

Lacey shuddered; she didn't want to imagine. Five minutes ago she'd been angry with these unknown parents for not keeping better tabs on their child. How dare she judge them? Now they had faces...and no daughter.

Lacey swallowed hard. "I haven't finished my work. You'll be the first to know my findings." She gave Mrs. Spencer's hand a tight squeeze and headed blindly for the exit, trying not to run. She slapped her hands on the door, pushed it open, and plowed into a forgotten Jack Harper.

He grabbed her upper arms and she kept her gaze on the floor. It blurred. The door closed behind her with a firm whoosh, and Mrs. Spencer gave a high-pitched wail.

The mother knew.

"Are you all right?"

She shook her head, pushed past him, and blindly dashed down the long, empty hall to the ladies' room.

He was in her chair again.

Lacey had spent a good ten minutes with a cold, wet towel on her eyes in the bathroom, trying to get the sound of Mrs. Spencer's pain out of her head. Now the red and swollen tissues around her eyes were gone. Along with most of her makeup.

She stopped in her doorway. This time Jack sat facing her with his forearms on his thighs, his hands rubbing together, and his concerned eyes studying her. She felt him take in her freshly washed face and coolly met his gaze. He looked tightly strung, and her gut tightened in reaction. Why was he here?

"Do you want to get something to eat?"

She blinked. *Food? Now?*

He rubbed at his cheek and she heard his short stubble scratch against a rough palm. "Stupid. I know. But...I think we should talk about what happened last Saturday morning. And ten years before. We're both a part of what happened..."

Jack wanted to talk about Dave DeCosta? *And that day?*

His lips rubbed together and he dropped his gaze to the floor. "Back then I was questioned in the disappearance of Hillary Roske. We'd dated. Now, somehow I'm being pulled in again this time. My property and my old partn—" He raised his gaze to hers. "Obviously my timing's lousy today, but I don't think it's going to get any better. Is the deli across the street any good?"

She stared at him. He had a point. He'd been involved in the case back then and now.

Just like her.

Saturday's memories crashed through her brain. She shook her head. She couldn't do this right now. "No. I don't want…"

"Please." His eyes pleaded with her as his hands clenched in fists. "I've got to figure out why this is happening right now. You were there when it started long ago. And you were there on Saturday. Why is that?" He looked like he wanted to stand but stayed sitting, probably in deference to her height. "Have you heard about the murdered cop?"

He knew? Lacey studied his face as she nodded. When she'd spoken to Michael on the phone that morning, he had briefly mentioned the death of the retired cop. The state police had asked him not to print anything yet. *How did Jack—?*

"Cal Trenton was my partner before he retired. Lakefield Police."

Jesus Christ. Jack Harper was in as deep as she was.

"You know people with the Lakefield Police?" she asked.

He nodded.

Maybe he could get more information on what'd happened at Suzanne's crime scene and the connection to the murdered cop. Her one phone call to the department had been cut short. The police weren't talking to anyone. But maybe they'd talk to Jack Harper. Get her some answers. She owed it to Suzanne.

Lacey glanced down the hallway, seeking a distraction. The last thing she wanted to do was rehash a nightmare with this stranger, but she desperately needed to get out of the building, away from those mourning parents. Urgent work was on her desk, but right now she couldn't focus. She wanted her head on straight before going through those charts; she had to do right by the victims. She made a decision. "I can give you thirty minutes, and then I have work to do."

Lacey inhaled the delicious scents, wiping the smell of burned flesh from her nose. She was used to most of the odors of the ME's office. Disinfectant and death. She rarely noticed them anymore, but the burned smell had been harder to shake.

The tiny deli was a regular haunt of hers. She'd enjoyed their panini and clam chowder since she was a teen and used to meet her dad there for lunch on the weekends. Lacey blew on her hot chocolate, put the two burned teenagers and one set of grieving parents out of her mind, and covertly studied the man across the table.

They'd effortlessly made meaningless small talk as her mind spun.

She'd checked him out on the Internet over the weekend. Her curiosity had been piqued by the man she'd met under odd circumstances Saturday morning.

Jack Harper had made a fortune with his family company in a relatively short period of time. To her amusement, she'd found an article from *Portland Monthly* naming him one of the city's top ten eligible bachelors. It featured a picture of him wearing a hard hat and flashing a cocky smile in front of the bare-bones structure of a growing office building. Those damned eyes grinning at every available female in town. He probably had women tearing down bridges to get at him. Scanning his features, Lacey admitted he was very good looking. He had a rugged maleness that the female in her instinctively responded to. His eyes were the cool, sharp gray she remembered from Saturday morning. How would he look in a bad mood? She'd hate to be on the receiving end of anger from those eyes. The strong jaw and two vertical lines between his brows told her she'd accurately pegged him as strong-willed.

Fascinated, she watched him eat. He'd put away half his sandwich in three bites and rhythmically emptied his bag of potato chips without looking like a pig. He was in constant motion as he ate and talked, moving his hands and arms without seeming nervous. It was probably how he burned off all those calories.

She hadn't eaten like that since she left college and ended her daily six-hour gymnastics workouts.

Lacey looked at the hot sandwich in her hand. She'd had two bites, and Jack was nearly done. Setting it down, she realized she wasn't hungry. Thinking about DeCosta and Suzanne did nasty things to her appetite. Eating after autopsies didn't bother her. Never had. But this was different.

Jack eyed her sandwich with a scowl, highlighting those vertical lines between his brows. She didn't know if he wanted to finish it or was annoyed that she'd eaten so little.

"How often do you deal with situations like that?" Jack asked.

"Like what?" *Serial killers?*

"Back at your office. The parents."

"Oh." Lacey was silent for a moment, remembering Mr. Spencer's tight face. "Only a time or two. It's not my job. My father usually handles it."

"One of those burned girls was their daughter, wasn't she? The fire was on the news last night."

Against all rules and regulations, Lacey nodded and took a tasteless drink. "She was one of them." A memory of the odor of burned flesh touched her nose, and her stomach churned. She wondered what Jack saw as he studied her. *An emotionless doctor?*

"You were really great with the parents."

Until I ran out the door. She shook her head, eyes down. "I didn't do anything."

Silence grew thick and dense between them.

"What happened that night?"

Lacey picked at the seam on her hot-chocolate cup, avoiding his eyes, knowing he didn't mean last night's fire. Jack was going back to the original reason for his visit.

"Why do you need to know?" She forced herself to look at him. Why had she agreed to this?

Steady eyes met hers. "My name is being sucked into a growing snowball of dead bodies and I need to know why. I need some history of the situation to get a bigger picture of what's going on. I figured you were the best person to give it to me."

She nodded slowly. She could see his reasoning. It'd been years since she'd related the events of that night to anyone. Several psychologists, her parents, and two close friends were the only people she'd told the story. So much time had passed. A ridiculous urge to dump her burden in his lap coaxed out her words.

"Suzanne and I were on our way to the restaurant to meet up with the rest of the team after the meet. It was only a few blocks from our hotel. The coaches didn't care if we wandered around town, as long as we were in pairs."

She swallowed hard.

"We started to cross in front of the alley that was behind the hotel when a car came up. We stopped to let him turn out of the alley, but he waved us on. It was pretty dark. I couldn't see much of him except for a silhouette and his hand waving at us. We crossed in front of the car and kept going toward the restaurant."

"You never saw the guy in the car?"

"Not 'til I heard the car door open. I glanced behind me because it struck me as odd that the motor was still running." She expected to see pity in Jack's eyes. Instead, she saw intense concentration and attention.

"He rushed at us and tackled me first. I was on my stomach, with him on my back, when I screamed for Suzanne to run. She didn't." Lacey wiped abruptly at her eyes, angry at the uncontrollable wetness. "She started kicking him and pulling on him, yelling for him to let go of me. She was so stupid! She could've gotten away and got help or something!"

"Is that what you would've done in her shoes?"

She shook her head slowly, locked on his serious gray gaze. It'd taken months for her to accept that she would've stayed and fought for Suzanne. But that didn't lessen the pain. Or the blunt anger at her dead friend for her foolishness. Blotting at her wet nose with a napkin, she pushed on as her insides churned.

"He grabbed her by the ankle and tripped her. He was so big; he could hold me and knock her down at the same time. I managed to twist to my back, and I bit his arm and tried to knee him, but he crushed his knee into my chest and punched me in the nose." She winced. "I can still hear the horrid crunch it made. Then I couldn't breathe because of his weight and the blood going down my throat. I don't know what Suzanne did to him right that second, but it pissed him off. He crawled off me and grabbed her by the hair. I rolled onto my side and just lay there, trying to breathe."

Stalling, trying to get a grip, she took a shaky sip of her drink. "I don't know if I can…"

"Keep going." The voice was firm, but compassionate.

She inhaled and felt strength from his calm.

"I was gagging and spitting blood. I could hear her scream-ing, but I couldn't move. No one had ever deliberately hit me before," she whispered, eyes on her cup.

"Suddenly, Suzanne stopped screaming. I mean, really stopped. She went from ear-piercing screams to utter silence. That got my attention. I rolled to my stomach, flung out blindly with both hands and grabbed at whatever was closest, catching her ankle. He was trying to lift her up and she was totally limp. I couldn't even tell if she was breathing or not. I just knew I had to hang on or else she'd be gone. It turned into a tug-of-war. I pulled her foot to my chest, squeezing with all my strength, and shut my eyes. My gut told if I let go, she'd be dead." She glanced up.

Jack's eyes were wide.

"He kicked me in the face. Really hard. And more blood filled my mouth, and I was coughing and hacking to get it out. It tasted so bad, and it was thick and gross. But I wouldn't let go. I ducked my face into her leg and held on tighter."

"Then what did he do?"

"He kept kicking me in the head, trying to make me let go. I don't know how many times. When he stopped kicking, I thought we'd made it. He was leaving and we were safe, but I still wouldn't let go. Then my leg erupted with pain. The abso-lute worst pain I'd ever felt. Worse than my smashed face, worse than the time I broke my collarbone. He'd stomped on my knee and I let go."

She inhaled unevenly, feeling the phantom twinges in her leg. DeCosta had shattered the tibia up near her knee. She noticed Jack was pale and rubbing at his thigh, unable to look away.

"He heaved her up over his shoulder like she was a doll and dashed back to the car. I remember seeing her arms flop down his back like broken tree limbs, but I don't remember anything after that. They said I repeated the license plate over and over in the ambulance. I don't remember that either."

Her nerves were quivering, fighting the adrenalin in her system, trying to hold still, not let him see how reliving the memories had shaken her core. She'd said she didn't remember any more, because she couldn't articulate the absolute terror and failure she'd experienced as her eyes had strained in the dim light to lock on Suzanne, trying to pull the girl back through sheer brainpower. Lacey couldn't describe the black curtain that had finally fallen as the car spun its tires, leaving her with a glimpse of a shimmering license plate and red taillights. Like evil eyes in the dark.

That black curtain still lurked, slithering over her skin when her guard was down.

She stared out the window at the tall firs, sucking in their icy beauty to chill the memories and cool the heavy guilt.

Why had she let go?

Jack didn't ask if Lacey was going to finish the sandwich. He knew she couldn't. It was a good thing he'd eaten before she started talking, or his sandwich would still be on his plate too.

Jesus Christ. What she'd gone through.

Worse. What she imagined her friend had gone through.

He knew exactly what it was like to be helpless and see someone in a life-threatening position. Frustrating, guilt-producing, keep-you-awake-at-night blame game.

He stretched a hand across the table and laid it on her wrist as she clutched at her hot chocolate. Startled eyes flashed to his and she jerked her arm away, sitting straighter.

"Are you all right?" *Stupid question.*

She nodded, lips closed tight, eyes still startled.

What was he thinking by touching her? *Just talk to her. Distract her.*

"I told you I dated Hillary Roske. One of the first victims."

She gave another stiff nod of assent.

"We met several years before she vanished. I was hauled in for questioning along with a dozen of her ex-boyfriends." He smiled wryly. "The timing wasn't great. I was trying to get hired with the police department. They weren't thrilled to have me questioned in a murder case."

Her wide mouth turned up at one corner, but he wanted to see the entire smile. It wasn't easy to pull his gaze back up to hers and away from those lips. He relaxed as he noticed her eyes had lost the rattled look. He was doing something right.

"It came to nothing, though. I followed the case and cheered when they caught the killer." *There was her smile.* Nearly too wide for her face, but incredibly appealing. His chest warmed and he wanted to see more. "Now I know they caught him, thanks to you. But I'm back in the thick of it again. Between the apartments, Hillary, and Cal, I feel like I'm in the hot seat."

"Who do you think killed him?"

"Who? Cal?" Jack shook his head. "I don't want to leap to conclusions, but I assume it was the same person who dumped your friend's remains. Someone deliberately left that badge there to lead us to him." He paused. "Did you know Cal Trenton?" It was a wild shot, but he had to ask.

"No."

"Do you know who would have wanted your friend's case out in the open again? Or why they would leave a police badge with her skeleton?"

She rubbed her lips together, and he watched her concentrate. His questions had distracted her from her disturbing story—one of his reasons for asking them.

"I can't think of anyone. Or why someone would do that. It just doesn't make sense to me. DeCosta's gone. Dead. It's over. Why would someone stir it up deliberately with…Suzanne? Do you think it's a coincidence that Suzanne and the badge were together?"

"Hell, no. I don't think it's a coincidence. On my property? With my ex-partner's badge? DeCosta may be dead, but someone knew where to find her body. And someone wanted some big fat arrows pointing at me."

They both sat silently. Jack felt a quiet pull toward her, his original attraction from Saturday hadn't dimmed, in spite of the horror of her story. The attraction was stronger. Now he knew Lacey was smart, sharp, and compassionate. And as tough as hell. Anyone who'd gone through…

He wanted to see her again. Jack blinked in surprise at the sudden emotion. Why now? He hastily scrambled for the negatives. Lacey Campbell had a boatload of emotional baggage, and he was facing a war with some nasty press. Why an attraction now?

People don't date under those conditions.

His cell rang and he mumbled an apology to her as he answered the call from his secretary. He listened silently to the unsurprising news as Lacey pushed away her plate and picked up her drink again. His eyes locked on her mouth as she sipped the drink, and a thick piece of blonde hair fell over one cheek, hitting the cup. He reached to push it back, remembered how she'd reacted to him touching her arm, and turned the movement into a reach for his own drink. He tapped his fingers on the glass bottle, not drinking as he studied her downcast eyes. Gorgeous thick dark lashes. She wasn't wearing eye makeup; he didn't think she needed it. Her eyes were big and expressive. He ended the call. "State police want to talk to me again tomorrow." He rubbed his hand over his scratchy chin. "I guess I was expecting that."

"I'm sorry." Lacey grimaced. "I did that on Saturday. It wasn't pleasant."

Her eyes met his in sympathy and the quiet moment stretched. He wasn't ready to let her go. He shifted on his chair as his irrational mind scrambled for an excuse.

"Can I call you? If I think of some more questions?"

"Ah...sure. I guess so." Her words slowed as if she was carefully considering each one. "Why don't you let me know what the police have to say? And if you hear any more from the Lakefield PD." She gave him a half smile, and his heart skipped a beat.

"You can count on it."

Satisfaction flowed through him.

CHAPTER EIGHT

He wanted to run. Feel the icy air pump through his lungs. Feel the endorphins send a high rocketing to his brain.

Everything was going according to plan. The wheels were in motion and the rats were confused, flustered by the maze he'd dropped them in. People were tearing around like rodents as he stood at the head of the table and hid the cheese. *Excellent analogy.* Grinning, he tucked his hands behind his head on the pillow and took a rare moment to rest his brain, organize his thoughts.

Things were just getting started.

What was next? He consulted a page in his mental notebook and crossed off Calvin Trenton, focusing on the name below it. All the years of planning, reviewing, and revising on paper had carved the plans into his brain. It was simple to visualize the page he needed.

The woman next to him shifted in the white sheets, and he repressed an urge to place his hands on her throat. It would be easy, a simple twist with his hands. No one would miss her. She was a simple hooker from the streets. He'd bought her for the entire night, tempting her with a posh hotel and expensive food.

The hotel was lavish and extravagant, and had cost more than he expected. But he deserved it; he'd planned and worked hard. The room and the whore were his rewards. After each successful stage of his plan, he rewarded himself. Positive reinforcement. He eyed the petite blonde beside him. Wouldn't killing her be a nice bonus?

He shoved the thought from his mind. She wasn't part of the plan, and he refused to deviate from it. Closing his eyes, he breathed deeply, fighting the impulse. Control. It was all about internal discipline. He wouldn't give in to his body's foolish whims.

He'd thought sex would take the edge off, relax him, but he still felt an exhilarating pounding in his veins. *What a rush.* Who needed drugs? Why pollute your body with chemicals when there were so many physical things you could do for that high?

He needed to clear his mind and focus on his goals. The whore was a momentary rest stop in his path, nothing else. He'd spent a good chunk of his life training and planning for this, he wasn't going to fuck it up now with an unimportant impulse.

He mentally stretched and relaxed his clenched hands. *Control.* A wave of power swept through him, reminding him of the first time he'd understood what mental discipline could achieve.

He couldn't have been more than nine or ten when he'd tied the dog to the tree, deep in the woods, far behind their home. And then he'd watched.

Watched as the dog had grown weak from lack of water and food. Watched as the dog had chewed on the rope until its mouth bled. Watched as its eyes had become sunken, dull and lifeless.

When it was over, he'd studied the body, debating doing some dissection, but was repulsed by the condition of the creature and the putrid smell. It was a mess, covered in dirt and blood, full of raw sores where the setter had chewed on its flesh. The dirt around the corpse had been full of holes where the dog had frantically dug, trying to escape. *Stupid animal.*

He'd been so proud that he'd mastered his impulses the entire time. No matter how badly he'd wanted to let the dog go, he stayed strong, quelling his instincts. Releasing the animal would have been an act of weakness, failure. The power of success was a rush.

It was his first kill.

His father never married his mother. He'd spent her money and had lived in her house, using her and her kids as personal servants. *Get me a beer, get out of my sight.*

One day his father had vanished. Leaving behind his clothes and old truck. He'd hated the man and couldn't comprehend why the desertion had stung so deeply. Soon after his father left, he'd killed the dog.

"Are you all done, sweetheart?" The whore's sleepy voice broke into his musings, plucking him from the past.

"No. I'm not nearly done yet."

A half smile toyed at his lips, he had lots to do.

CHAPTER NINE

"You've got to stay away from Harper. He's knee-deep in crap with this case and the police are investigating him," Michael steamed.

"He didn't kill anyone! All he did was date a victim," Lacey countered.

"And get questioned for it and *then* have another victim's body show up on his property? And there's the badge. How convenient is it that his murdered partner's badge was under his building?"

"Not convenient at all! You think he'd place it there to turn the police's spotlight on him? He's not an idiot."

Lacey sat on her kitchen counter, nose to nose with Michael as he pressed his point. She knew there was no point in arguing with him. He never gave in. Even when he was dead wrong and he knew it. But she wasn't ready to back down. Her ire was further fueled by his use of the wussy word "crap." He always toned down his coarse language around her.

Like she would wilt at the F-word.

So she used it as much as possible around him.

"You need a fucking haircut," she said, glaring at his hair. "Do I have to make the appointment for you?"

The lanky man pulled away and stormed around her kitchen. Tall with dark blond hair that was always too long, Michael looked like an artist. Or poet. The fact that he'd spent two years in a nasty motorcycle gang in Los Angeles didn't show under his casual veneer. A veneer that hid the body of a man of surprising stealth and strength.

He was probably the smartest person she knew. He was also sharp, shrewd, and reckless. Sometimes not a good combination. He'd been writing a series of articles about the gang experience, so he joined. He'd wondered how it felt to climb Mount McKinley, so he did it. (And claimed it wasn't worth the freezing, sweaty effort.) He'd tried triathlons, skydiving, and paddling down the Amazon. He was never concerned with his own safety or skin; he was concerned only with the pursuit of answers for the questions in his mind or the compulsion for a new experience. He'd wanted to run with the bulls, but Lacey had convinced him he had the wrong dates and he arrived too late. For two weeks he hadn't spoken to her.

She didn't care. At least he'd returned in one piece.

They'd been lovers, but it hadn't worked. She was mostly a conventional woman, and he was definitely not a conventional man. He had too much fire, and she needed stability. He hovered and bossed while she strained to exercise her independence. He'd wanted to shield her from life's abscesses. He didn't understand she needed to face the ugliness, prove she could stand alone. Before they broke up, he swore he'd change. But then he wouldn't be the passionate Michael she loved. He'd brooded for months after she'd broken it off. He'd disappeared to Alaska to work on a crabbing boat, where the women were few and far between. He'd nearly died, barely surviving an accidental twenty-second plunge off a boat deck into the icy Bering Sea.

Very slowly, he'd given in to the friendship concept and had evolved into a type of protective older brother. She loved him fiercely and considered him family. And they argued like brother and sister.

Lacey knew Jack Harper was raising red flags in Michael's gut. Jack was refusing his calls and his name was popping up in every aspect of the case. It stroked Michael's unending curiosity as an investigative reporter. If something seemed fishy, Michael would poke, push, and prod until he got his answers. He'd exposed pedophile priests, Internet child stalkers, and a kickback program in the Oregon prison food system.

He opened the cabinet door next to her sink and rooted through the little pill bottles. "Do you have any ibuprofen? My head's killing me."

"All the way in the back."

She watched as he subtly checked the labels of the other bottles. Did he think she wouldn't notice?

"Anything stronger for pain?"

"No," she snapped, "you know there's not." She blew out a breath. *He cares. He asks only because he cares.*

In a sudden move that made her brain bounce, Michael changed the subject.

"I got the medical examiner's prelim on Suzanne today."

How did he do it? She wasn't going to get a look at it till tomorrow. The man had sources everywhere. Annoyed, she looked at him expectantly.

"Her identity hasn't been completely verified, you know," Michael stated.

Lacey shook her head. "It's just not been officially announced. I have absolutely no doubt it is her. I did the odontology report. I had her previous dental films, and everything matched up perfectly. I know it's her. They might run some DNA testing, but even her mother will know it is her by her distinctive dental work."

"Something's bugging me." He was pacing again. Back and forth over her wood floors, running his fingers over every kitty knickknack in her kitchen. "You didn't tell me both her femurs were broken," he said.

"It was the same MO with all the victims, right? They were all found with broken femurs. Why should Suzanne be any different?" She swallowed hard.

He pinned her with an unblinking stare, making her feel like she'd done something naughty.

"*Think*, Lacey. What other gymnast do you know who had her legs broken?"

She did know one.

"But that was an accident... They said the roughness of the river and the rocks probably did it. Amy died in a car accident, Michael...she wasn't murdered. And that was in Mount Junction, years before Suzanne died." She stumbled over the words and slipped slowly from her perch on the counter to a barstool, her mind awhirl. Suzanne and Amy weren't linked. There was no way. Amy Smith, a gymnastics teammate, had accidentally driven her car into a river. Her body hadn't been recovered for several weeks. "All DeCosta's victims had broken femurs. Are you trying to tie Amy's death to all the others?"

"She was a gymnast. She was blonde. Her legs were broken in almost the same place. She's dead. That's four too many coincidences for me. I'm gonna check it out." He was on a mission. It was in his eyes. The man wouldn't stop until he had his answers.

"Did you tell the police about this?" She was still stunned. *Not Amy.*

"Not yet. It's just speculation on my part. I'm going to Mount Junction to look at it personally. Now, what did you tell Harper?" With a calmer voice, he pulled up a stool and sat in front of her, knees to knees. Those green eyes pinned her again.

She blinked, her mind still focused on Amy. How did he change directions so fast? "Why?"

"Christ, Lace. It's a simple question."

She shrugged. "He wanted to know about the night Suzanne and I were attacked. We talked for only a few minutes." She looked anywhere but at Michael.

"So you made plans to talk later."

"What of it?" she snapped at him.

"He dated one of the victims."

"I know that." She looked away. "I'm tired. Can we talk about this tomorrow?" He glanced at the clock and immediately hopped off his stool. It was after midnight. "I'm sorry, Lace, but you need to know the type of guy you're dealing with."

Michael laid a gentle hand on her shoulders and tilted her chin up to him, kissing her softly on the mouth. "I'll call you tomorrow." He studied her face, frowning at the dark shadows under her eyes.

She knew Michael had a need to look out for her because he believed she wasn't doing a good job by herself. And maybe she wasn't. She'd started talking with a man who had strong links to Suzanne's case.

But talking with Jack Harper was the first time she'd felt a stirring of interest in a man in forever. After years of shutting people out and being numb, it'd felt good to experience that spark. Jack couldn't be involved with Suzanne's reappearance. Jack Harper was one of the good guys. She could sense it.

She walked Michael to the front door and he frowned at the single locking bolt, twisting it back and forth. "Why haven't you got a security system yet? Do I need to make some calls to find one for you?"

"Not tonight, Michael. I can't argue with you anymore. And get your hair cut. Please." She stretched up to kiss his cheek. His gaze rested on her face for a brief second, and then he jogged down her porch steps, determined energy radiating from him.

Lacey walked back to the kitchen, her brain spinning with thoughts of Suzanne, Amy, and Jack Harper.

CHAPTER TEN

Mason Callahan recognized big money when he saw it. And this guy had it. The décor of the Harper Developing offices was understated, but the kind of understated that cost a fortune. The colors were Northwest colors, strong gray-blues and earthy browns with fir-green accents. The office didn't shout how successful the company was; it murmured it. Even Ray had been silent for thirty seconds, gaping as they waited for Jack Harper to spare a moment of his time.

The view was stunning. Mason held his cowboy hat in his hand as he looked out the east windows in the conference room and wondered if Harper had ordered Mt. Hood to pose for his guests. The white peak looked icy proud and crystalline behind the city. With a sky that blue and clear, it was hard to believe the temperature was twenty-five degrees outside.

Harper swung open the door, "Sorry to keep you waiting. What can I do for you? Is the apartment manager in Lakefield giving you what you need for your investigation?" He managed to shake both men's hands, circle the table, and pour three cups of coffee before he finished speaking. The man controlled a room by simply entering it.

Efficient was the adjective that popped into Mason's head. And *smooth*. He took a close look at Jack Harper, taking the offered coffee cup, reluctantly liking what he saw. The man's eyes were honest and direct, his manner welcoming but businesslike.

Mason and Ray had been hard at work turning the man's past inside out. Every person they spoke with sang the man's praises. Except for a few ex-girlfriends, but that was to be expected. It was disconcerting that every rock of Harper's they dug under, they found another connection to Dave DeCosta or some other aspect of their ever-widening case.

It wasn't logical that Jack Harper was involved, but they had to take a look at him.

Ray started. "The apartment manager is fine. You must have put the fear of God in him, because he's bending over backward to make us happy." He snorted. "He even offered to get me a deal on the dent I've got in my rear fender."

That brought a flash of a grin from Harper. "His brother owns a body shop. He's actually quite good. I've used him myself."

Mason saw Ray sip his hot coffee and unsuccessfully hide that he'd just burned his tongue, but the man managed to throw out another question. "We wanted to know what you were doing in Lakefield the morning the skeleton was found. You live here in Portland, right?"

Harper's face closed. "I was visiting my dad. He doesn't live too far from that complex. I'm often down there on the weekends."

"We couldn't find an address for your father in the public records. Jacob Harper, right? Is he renting?"

"No. Well, sort of." Harper took a short walk to the window and stared at the mountain. "He's in adult foster care."

"In what?"

Reflected in the window, Mason watched impatience flash across Harper's face. "A care home. A small, privately owned home specifically for the elderly with special needs. He lives there with four other men and a caretaker or two." Harper's voice was stiff, the words clipped.

His face reddening, Ray opened and closed his mouth, completely blindsided by what was obviously a personal and painful answer. Mason stepped in.

"I thought your father was still active in the company."

Jack shook his head. "His name's on the letterhead. That's it. He doesn't remember that he started this company, let alone have any input."

"Alzheimer's?"

Harper turned from the window and stared directly at Mason. "Yes. Most of the time he doesn't remember that he has a son either."

"That must be a bitch for you. It's a shitty disease."

One brow tilted slightly on Harper's forehead. "What else do you need to know?"

"What else can you tell us about Hillary Roske?"

"We dated. We broke up. Long before she vanished. Didn't you read the paper this morning?"

Ray pretended to write something on his little notepad, as if Harper had provided a vital detail. Harper's history had been splashed across the front page today, and the article accurately matched the facts Mason had uncovered so far.

"Do you remember what you were doing or who you were with the night of Suzanne Mills's abduction?"

Disbelief struck Harper's features. "You're kidding, right? It's been over a decade! You remember who you were with that night?"

"Give me one name. A roommate or girlfriend you would have been hanging out with." Mason pushed the issue.

"Dave Harris was my roommate. He lives in Bend now."

Ray made a real notation this time.

"I understand you've contacted Dr. Campbell about this case. And apparently you already knew of her narrow escape eleven years ago."

"What about it? What'd she say to you?" Harper's back straightened, and he looked at the detectives with defensive eyes.

"I haven't talked with her since then. This came from a third party."

Ray looked up from his notebook and both detectives studied Harper curiously. Something about the little doctor bothered the man. He'd almost broken a sweat when Mason mentioned her. Exchanging a look, both detectives intensified their focus.

"How'd you know she was the one that got away from DeCosta? Her name's never been in print."

Harper rested a hip against the conference table. No one had bothered to sit down. "You were there that day. You saw her reaction to finding her friend's dead body. I'd heard some of the rumors flying around the Lakefield PD that she'd been the one. I'm surprised that it hasn't been in the paper. The reporter covering the story has exposed every other fact."

"Brody?"

"Yeah, that's the one."

"He's been pestering us. Nosy bastard. Only interested in making the front page."

"Tell me about it. My entire life has been front-page news for the past few days. I'm starting to take it personally. The guy seems to have a personal grudge against me just because I refuse to answer his questions."

"You don't think he's curious because you dated a Co-Ed Slayer vic, owned the building where a Co-Ed Slayer body was found, and partnered with a murdered cop whose badge was found at the Mills scene." Catching his breath, Mason waited for the man's reaction.

Harper's jaw locked. "I think I'd like my lawyer present next time you want to talk to me." He pushed off from the table and strode to the door. "We're done here."

He left the two men in the room and marched into the hall.

"Show the detectives out," Harper angrily tossed the words over his shoulder to the wide-eyed receptionist as he stormed by her desk. The thin woman slowly stood and hesitantly stepped toward the conference room like she expected to find two corpses.

Jack barely caught himself before he slammed the door to his office. He shut it gently and leaned his forehead against the wood. *Shit, shit, shit.* When would it end? Who in the hell was doing this to him? And why? First he was dissected in the papers. Now with the police. He hadn't handled the interview well.

But he had to get out of that room before he grabbed Callahan's cowboy hat and shoved it down the cop's throat.

He straightened his spine, determined to find something to distract him. *Get back to work.* He had a company to run. *Get back in control.* Jack picked up the stack of phone messages from his desk and shuffled through them.

Christ. Maybe he didn't have a company to run.

Three clients had cancelled crucial meetings.

Steaming, he thrust the messages into his shredder. His office door swung open without a knock and his sister, Melody, blew in. "Bryce said you were talking with police detectives. What did they want? They don't believe that crap in the paper, do they?"

Her gray eyes were hard. She stood in front of Jack's desk and ground her heel into his floor. His older sister was tall, perfectly made-up with expensive power suits, and was as tense as a threatened mother tiger. But Jack knew she was just unnerved by the police visit.

"What's been printed in the paper is true, Mel. They haven't made anything up." *Now he was defending Brody?* "It's just the presentation that's bullshit."

"Then why were they here?"

"'Cause they found a dead body on our property. And I used to work with Cal Trenton. They're just doing their job."

"But you're the president of this company! How can they come in here and…"

"That doesn't give me some special immunity. They're trying to find a murderer, for God's sake. Of course they're gonna talk to me."

Now he was defending Callahan?

Jack ran a hand through his hair. "I know the publicity sucks. Believe me, I hate it as much as you do, but until it blows over you should be working on spinning it our way. Not bitching at me."

"If you hadn't…"

"If I hadn't what? Had a girlfriend in college? Partnered with Cal? You're out of line, Mel." He turned his back on her and stared, unseeing, out the window.

"So what do we do?" Her voice dropped ten decibels.

Jack knew it pained her to utter those five words. They might argue a lot of the time, but deep down their cores were solidly built of love for each other and their father's company.

"You do your job, I do mine. We show everyone nothing has changed at Harper Developing, and this police investigation has nothing to do with how we run our business."

He thought of the phone messages he'd just shredded. No way was he going to mention them. She'd hit the ceiling.

Melody was silent a minute. In the reflection of the glass, he could see she was scared, but didn't want to admit it. She spun on a heel and left his office. Jack blew out a breath. Together, the two of them would get through this.

CHAPTER ELEVEN

He balanced the golf club across his palm, smiling, liking the feel of the weight. He knew little about golf, but knew these clubs were top-of-the-line. It was a heady rush to hold a toy worth so much money. A wealthy man's status symbol. Wrapping his hands around the grip, he took a practice swing and swore. The damn things were too long for him. He hurled the club onto the bed.

What did he expect? The lawyer was a tall man. And he wasn't.

It'd been a monstrous obstacle all his life. Society preferred height on a man. He hated not being tall. He never used the word *short*. Or *shrimp*. He'd heard them too often throughout his life. And not in kind tones.

But he'd show everyone. Soon they would look on him with awe, his height insignificant.

He crossed to the window, peeked through the blinds, and checked the dark street. No cars. He'd honestly thought the man would be home before now. It was nearly 1:00 a.m. How long did a retirement party take? Hopefully, he hadn't hooked up with some slut and was romping the night away in her bed.

Bored, he decided to snoop some more. He'd already found six pornos, a small stash of weed, and over $2,000 in cash. He pocketed the DVDs and cash but left the pot. He didn't contaminate his body with that kind of garbage. It dulled the mind like a fine blade dragged across asphalt.

The home was some sort of bachelor's paradise. The owner had been divorced for five years and liked to express himself through electronics. High-end stereo equipment and razor-thin big-screen TVs garnished every room. More video games, DVDs, and Blu-rays than in a Blockbuster Video store lined the shelves of the theater-like screening room. The garage housed a Porsche and a Mini Cooper. The owner apparently driving the Mercedes 4WD tonight.

He wandered through the immaculate closet again, mindlessly humming an old Black Sabbath tune. He counted twenty-two suits, nine pairs of dress shoes, and what seemed like a million ties. His hand stopped on a gray suit jacket, liking the style and fabric. It was inviting to his fastidious sense of touch. He pulled it off the hanger and slipped his arms into it.

He couldn't see his fingertips.

Ripping off the coat, he threw it on the floor like a spoiled preschooler hurling a broken toy.

His height. It always came back to haunt him.

His mother had told him he was a slow grower and later he'd catch up with everyone else. The bitch had been lying, as usual.

He'd concentrated on his brain in school, taking advanced classes and even college courses as a high school freshman. There wasn't anything he could do about his height, but he could tower over everyone else in a different way.

Intelligence.

To him school had been a tool to be exploited. He'd targeted teachers, librarians, whoever he'd thought could be of value to him, whoever could teach him a unique skill, whatever it took to get ahead. He learned to be a smooth talker, a manipulator, a salesman.

But he'd hated the students. Especially the other males. They'd tripped him, thrown away his notebooks, and made him the butt of every nasty joke in an evil high school handbook. He'd ached to blow them all away. He'd fantasized about revenge on the assholes who'd made his teen years so miserable.

When the high school shootings suddenly cropped up around the country, he'd been glued to the TV. He'd understood those kids. He'd understood the anger and rage that provoked them to kill. A sense of admiration and a touch of jealousy had stolen over him as he watched the endless news coverage. *They'd actually done it.* He'd thought and dreamed and wished. But never followed through. What a legacy those kids had left; no one could ever forget them.

A smile toyed at the corner of his mouth. He would achieve that level of fame. It was only a matter of time. A very short time, if he stuck to his time line. A painstakingly developed time line he'd honed and sharpened over the years. It couldn't fail.

But he was considering following one unexpected tangent.

He hadn't expected the appearance of Lacey Campbell so soon. What kind of amazing fate had placed her at the recovery of the Mills girl? He shook his head in disbelief for the hundredth time. He'd expected her later, when the corpse had arrived at the medical examiner's office. Even if she hadn't been a part of the examination, she would have heard whom the bones belonged to early on. Her early entry into the game was a powerful sign, but he needed to be cautious with its interpretation.

What did it mean?

Was he to follow his original blueprint? Or fight against his desire to toy with her? Had higher powers decided to move up her place in the time line? Giving him more time with the lovely woman. Was her presence a gift?

A gift? That was an idea. Surely he could simply send her a gift without affecting his plans. He needed to consider carefully what to send her. He set the thought aside for when he had time to weigh the possibilities.

Happier now, he sifted through a box of cufflinks, picking out the gold pairs. Unaware that he hummed as he sorted. The music was always in his head; he didn't notice when he brought it to life.

He squinted at one pair of cufflinks with good-sized diamonds in them. Were they real? He pocketed them.

God, he was thirsty. Heading for the kitchen, he wondered what this lawyer stocked to drink in his fridge. Designer water? Microbrews? He'd just opened the door and happily picked up a Coke when he heard the low buzz of an automatic garage door opener.

Damn it. Why now? He eyed the cold soda in his hand, annoyed he wouldn't have a chance to drink it before he started. He tossed the can back in the fridge and slammed the door.

Where was that golf club? He stalked back to the bedroom, clamping down on his thirst. There was a busy night ahead of him.

The Coke would still be there in the morning.

CHAPTER TWELVE

Callahan and Lusco were trying to make their second personal call of the day. They'd already been lost once on the curving, sloped streets in the West Hills of Portland. Frustrated with the snowy weather, Mason was thankful he'd switched to his Blazer, leaving the useless rear-wheel-drive government sedan at home. A good decision. Several of the snow-packed, narrow streets were steep and treacherous. At least the sanding crews had made a pass through the area.

"God help them if they ever have a fire up here, they won't be able to get out, let alone get a fire truck in." Ray was grumbling, riding shotgun as navigator. He glanced up from his crumpled MapQuest printout. "Over there. That's it."

Mason stared at the big home. "Are you sure?" Dr. Campbell didn't have a private dentistry practice. She just taught at the dental school and took on forensic cases. How'd she afford a home like that?

The house was old Portland. Mason estimated that it had been built around 1900, give or take twenty years. Multiple gables and a wraparound porch gave it an open, friendly look. Impeccably maintained, the two-story house showcased a velvet lawn of snow, manicured landscaping, and pure white siding. Tall, stately old firs added to the prestigious aura of the neighborhood.

People who lived up here didn't have big box homes with three-car garages and pools. No evenly spaced snout houses where the sole difference was the shade of the exterior paint. That wasn't what these homeowners wanted; they wanted quality, history.

Mason pulled up behind a Land Rover at the curb. He noted all the cars parked on the narrow street, a few blanketed by nature like they hadn't budged since the first snowfall a week ago. Most of the homes had a narrow driveway leading to the back of the house, where gardening tools probably filled the old single-car garage.

Ray stepped out of the Blazer and eyed the expensive vehicles lining the street. Mercedes, Lexus, BMW. "How do these people sleep at night with their cars parked on the street? Do they have invisible force fields to keep out the car thieves?" Mason knew Ray locked up his two-year-old Chevy in the garage every night.

Through the snowfall, Mason noticed a square sticker on the rear window of the freshly parked Land Rover. It was a parking permit for *The Oregonian.*

"I don't think she's alone."

Michael Brody was trying to take over the interview. The tall man was intense, nearly rude. Mason bit his cheek and kept his temper in check. He'd allowed Brody to sit in once the man had agreed to be there exclusively as support for Dr. Campbell, not as a reporter.

"Is it possible the wrong man was put in prison a decade ago? Or maybe Cal Trenton was a copycat murder?" Brody asked.

"I'm not going to speculate. We're looking at every angle." Mason had already repeated the same line three times. The damned reporter had a mind that never stopped hypothesizing and scrutinizing. Mason had checked out the man after reading his front-page coverage of the case. Everyone had said the man was obsessive when he was sniffing out a story and brutally honest in his writing.

Mason purposefully turned to Dr. Campbell, hoping Brody would shut up for a minute. She tensely perched on the edge of the couch in the huge formal living room. A room that looked straight from a snobby decorating magazine. Dark hardwood floors gleamed, white baseboards and crown moldings set off the designer wall paint.

Dr. Campbell wore a red ski sweater and jeans. With her hair pulled back, she looked eighteen. If you didn't look in her eyes. They were cautious, measuring, and guarded. She exuded a professional, calm control that reminded Mason of a skilled surgeon during a routine tonsillectomy. If he hadn't seen her struggling to hold herself together last Saturday morning, he'd believe nothing could rattle her.

Brody hovered over her, sitting on the arm of the couch, coiled to attack if something threatened her.

He reminded Mason of a hawk.

"Are you sure you've never met Calvin Trenton before?" Mason asked again. He was still trying to find a connection between Trenton's badge and Suzanne's remains.

Dr. Campbell threw up her palms. "I cross paths with hundreds of patients every year. I don't keep track of names. Plus, I've worked with several police departments in investigations, including Lakefield and Corvallis. I wouldn't be surprised if I'd met him."

Ray's cell phone rang. Glancing at it, he rose from his chair and stepped into the kitchen for some privacy.

Pausing the interview until Ray returned, Callahan searched for polite small talk. Something he was lousy at. "Nice house."

She grabbed at the offered branch. "Thank you. It belonged to my parents. This is where I grew up."

"Your parents don't live here anymore? Just you?"

Dr. Campbell shook her head. "My mother died several years ago. Dad couldn't bear to live here any longer, and he couldn't bring himself to sell it. Now it's mine."

"Your father's the chief medical examiner of Oregon." It wasn't a question.

"Yes." She didn't expand.

Brody cleared his throat and silently communicated something to Dr. Campbell as she glanced his way. She gave him a tiny shake of her head.

Mason felt shut out.

These two were tight. Their body language spoke of intimacy, but they didn't act like a dating couple. "How do the two of you know each other?"

They exchanged another look. Brody shrugged and pulled out his iPhone, giving it his attention, letting her answer the question.

She gave the reporter a glare, but turned polite eyes on Mason. "We met downtown. I didn't have a ride home late one night, and Michael offered to drive me."

She accepted a ride from a stranger? Mason didn't think so. His expression must have reflected his disbelief because she hurried to clarify.

"I was having a problem with my um...date, outside a restaurant. He'd had too much to drink, and Michael stepped in when things started to get...rough."

From the shuttered look on her face, Mason figured "rough" was putting it mildly. With grudging respect, he took an appraising look at the hawk on her right.

"I broke his nose." Brody mildly tossed out the comment. He was still focused on his iPhone. Before Mason could comment, Ray appeared.

"Mason." Pale, he spoke from the doorway to the kitchen and jerked his head for Mason to join him.

"What's happened? What's going on?" Brody interjected.

Out of the corner of his eye, Mason saw that the hawk had scented something. Brody had finally looked up from his cell, and his gaze tracked Mason as he strode to the kitchen.

Ignoring him, Mason's eyes locked with Ray's. Whatever Ray had to tell, it wasn't good.

"They've found another murder they think is related to this case," Ray whispered.

"Who? Where?" *Damn it, Ray, spit it out.*

"Joseph Cochran."

Mason searched his memory and came up empty. "Who?"

"Former DA from Benton County. He's been in private practice in Lake Oswego for a while."

"Benton County. That's Corvallis, right?" Mason's brain was making leaps he didn't want it to do.

"He was the prosecutor in the DeCosta case," Ray stated.

"And that coincidence makes it part of ours? Just because we've got a DeCosta connection with the Mills girl?" Mason could picture the tall man now. Joseph Cochran had publicly sworn on television that he'd nail the "demented killing bastard." Then he'd gone after DeCosta like a shark after bloody chum. And succeeded.

Ray cleared his throat and shifted his eyes to the kitchen doorway, checking for listeners. "There's a baggie of hair with the body."

"Whose hair?"

"Short, gray. They're gonna test it, but it's a visual match to Cal Trenton."

"Christ." They had to get to that scene. Mason started back to the living room to excuse them, but abruptly swung around to face Ray. Something nagging at the edge of his brain. Why would Cal Trenton's...?

"Trenton. Was he involved in the DeCosta case?"

Comprehension spread across Ray's features. "He had to be. Somehow. Shit. Why didn't we look into that earlier?"

Mason had an idea how to get instant confirmation on their theory. His pounding boots entered the living room, startling Dr. Campbell and Brody, who had an ear to his cell phone.

"Dr. Campbell. You testified at the DeCosta trial. Do you remember any of other people that testified against him?"

"I guess." She looked reluctant to dig up painful memories. "Why?"

"I think the name Calvin Trenton might make a connection for you now."

Staring at him, Dr. Campbell's eyes widened, and Mason could see the mental click. "He was one of the cops who arrested him. I remember now," she whispered. "There were at least a dozen cops who testified in the trial, but his testimony was the important one. He nearly cried on the stand as he described DeCosta's torture chamber and weapons. I had to leave the courtroom." She swallowed hard, and Mason worried she would be ill.

The memories were coming back to Mason. As a member of the task force he'd encountered a hundred cops while working on the Co-Ed killings. At Dr. Campbell's description, he also remembered watching the tough cop nearly crack on the witness stand.

"Joseph Cochran's been murdered." Brody slid his phone back in his pocket.

Three pairs of eyes turned to stare at him. One confused and two annoyed.

"Damned press," mumbled Ray.

Brody gave Mason a slow predator's smile. "That's right. You can't keep your secrets for very long. There's always someone who likes to talk."

"I know that name. He was the district attorney in the DeCosta trial." Dr. Campbell broke the tension between the men. "What's going on? Who's killing these men? DeCosta's dead. Right?" She pushed up off the couch as her voice rose, seeking confirmation from Mason's eyes.

"That's right. The man is dead." Mason could tell his words didn't assure her. The dentist was visibly shaking. He turned to Ray. "I need the name of every person involved in putting DeCosta in prison."

"Shit." Brody stood and firmly wrapped one hand around Dr. Campbell's upper arm. "Lace. You're one of them."

Dr. Campbell paled, her gaze locked with Mason's. "My testimony put him away."

Mason held her gaze, flashes of Cal Trenton's tortured body flashing through his mind. *Fuck! Was she on somebody's kill list too?*

Mason turned to eye the big windows. "You got a security system?"

"I'm calling right now." Lacey was already dialing her phone.

CHAPTER THIRTEEN

No fresh snow had fallen that day, but the wind was icy, freezing the old snow at the edge of the sidewalk into dangerous piles of ice. Lacey shivered as she stepped carefully through the Portland street crowds and pulled her thick collar up around her neck, wishing she had a scarf. Stuart Carter, a dental student of hers, had a sculpture showing at one of the smaller galleries, and she'd promised to stop by, not ready to isolate herself completely from the regular world until necessary.

First Thursday was a monthly downtown Portland event where the public mobbed the Pearl District to view art and artists alike. Locals set up crude stands on the sidewalks, selling homemade creations, while the art galleries threw open their doors to tempt the public to drop big bucks and eat organic appetizers.

Jack had caught her by phone in her office just seconds before she'd headed downtown to the galleries. He'd sounded relieved when she answered the phone, but he wouldn't elaborate on his police interview when she asked. He'd wanted to talk to her in person. Tonight. She hadn't mentioned yesterday's visit from the police on the phone, suddenly feeling awkward about Michael's insinuating articles and not ready to explain her relationship with the reporter, who was surely on Jack's shit list.

When she'd told him of her commitment downtown, Jack had asked to meet up and she agreed, not sure why she was doing so.

This was not a date with Jack Harper. She repeated the refrain again.

He simply wanted to touch base with her, tell her what happened in his police interview. That was all. Lacey's mind shifted to the new murder she'd heard about yesterday. Did Jack know about Joseph Cochran?

Who was killing the men from DeCosta's prosecution? Starting with the discovery of Suzanne, everything pointed back to the DeCosta case. Suzanne, the arresting cop, the district attorney.

Am I in danger? How much? Lacey's fingers grew numb as if their blood supply had suddenly been severed. She drew a deep breath and appreciated the masses of people crowding the sidewalks. Safety in numbers.

Finding the street corner where she'd agreed to meet Jack, she stopped to stare through a window at an ugly watercolor, a clashing chaos of browns and grays, and her mind spun back ten years. Dave DeCosta had been evil. Closing her eyes, she could see him at the trial, lounging back in his chair, stretching his long legs under the defense table, watching the proceedings with casual, bored eyes. Like he was watching a scoreless football game on a Sunday afternoon.

She had never seen any emotion in his eyes. As if a nugget of his soul had been missing. His family had sat silently in the row behind him. Their faces expressionless. Their mental states and thoughts hidden from court observers.

She'd spent long days in the courtroom, listening to the parade of witnesses, horrified at the testimony of those who'd discovered the remains of his victims. Graphic descriptions and photos of torture, sexual abuse, and corpse abuse. DeCosta had sat unaffected and aloof while Lacey's stomach fought to keep its contents. She'd picture Suzanne in his hands and mentally collapse under the blistering guilt of being the one who escaped.

Survivor's guilt, her psychiatrist had called it. Common in people who survive ordeals where others died.

Lacey's eyes opened as the pace of her breathing sped up, and she refocused on the watercolor, seeking distraction.

It didn't matter what the psychiatrist had called that hellhole. It had been the blackest period of her life. After leaving the hospital following her brush with death, she'd stayed in bed for days, sometimes weeks, fighting back the nightmares that toyed with her sanity.

It had been a catch-22. She'd wanted to sleep. Just sleep for long blissful periods of nothingness. But the horrors came to life in her dreams. Tranquilizers helped keep the horrors away but affected her sleep quality, making her exhausted. Leaving the sanctity of her house had taken superhuman effort. Even a simple trip to the grocery store had taken mental coaxing and preparation.

She would've stopped eating if not for the efforts of her parents, friends, and doctors. Food hadn't been important. She didn't eat because her body no longer created impulses of hunger.

Because she'd let go, Suzanne was gone.

Guilt had dragged her down to a point where she stockpiled her Vicodin. Every night she'd stared at the growing number of pills, nervously fingering them, counting them, arranging them into piles, and finally putting them back in the bottle, screwing the lid on tight, hiding them from her mother. It went on for months, even after her physical pain was gone. For some reason, just knowing she could resist the drugs had given her a tiny sense of control in her life.

One year to the day that Suzanne vanished, she'd stood staring into the toilet, watching as if from a distance, as she dumped the Vicodin into the bowl and flushed them away. Every last pill. It'd made her feel strong. She'd been given a second chance. Something a lot of people never get.

She'd never looked back at that dark period. Until now.

She'd managed to keep control this time. Her nights were still hellish, but staying busy at the dental school helped with distraction. Wallowing in a bowl of ice cream or simply talking with Michael also helped. She ached for the comfort of her mother, but considered herself lucky to have close friends. Some nights she wanted to beg Michael to sleep on her couch, but she wouldn't allow that crutch. She could get through this on her own.

DeCosta was dead. He couldn't reach her.

Lacey lifted her chin. She wouldn't live in fear from police theories and hunches. It would take a lot more than that to disrupt her life. She didn't hide. She directed her life; not her faceless fears. She had pepper spray in every coat pocket and a brand new kick-ass security system in her house.

Her stomach tightened and her throat burned as she turned away from the watercolor, finally comprehending it was a painting of a graveyard. She wrapped her arms around her middle, guarding against the wind and memories.

"Are you cold?"

She jumped, her hand instinctively moving to her purse, then stared up into questioning gray eyes. Jack Harper. Warmth flowed through her and pushed away the threatening shadows quicker than a venti coffee. Death and graveyards faded. She studied the tall man. He looked good. Nice slacks and a thick jacket couldn't hide the fact that he was…What was the right word? Built. Well built. His black hair was trimmed short, slightly spiky on the top, making her fingers want to drift through it, testing the texture. She shoved her hands into her coat pockets.

Simply put, the man was hot.

Being around him was warming her up, stirring up her insides into a very pleasant eddy. And the way he looked at her… as if he had intimate ideas to mix up more heat between them.

What was she thinking?

He was so wrong for her! He must have women literally falling at his feet. The top-ten bachelor article had hinted he enjoyed playing the field, that he was a man who didn't form commitments. She refused to be a toppled domino in the long line behind him. Besides, he just wanted to talk to her. He wanted information, not drinks and dinner. Or more. *Right?*

She found her voice. "No, I'm not cold."

He reached out, took her hands, and rubbed them furiously, frowning.

"You're like ice. We should've met inside."

His warmth seeped into her hands and leaped to her belly, igniting a low blaze. Startled, she pulled her hands back. She couldn't get sucked in by his charm. "I'm fine. But let's get out of the cold."

He firmly took back one of her escaped hands and started into the gallery with the ugly watercolor in its window. She dug in her heels, eyeing the creepy painting, and pulling back on their clasped hands. His brows briefly narrowed.

"Not this gallery. Let's head down the street."

He'd kept a firm hand on her most of the evening.

It was her size, Jack rationalized. Even in high-heeled boots, she barely reached his shoulder, and it was bringing out the protector in him. He'd already shouldered one slightly drunken klutz to keep the idiot from plowing her over. Or maybe it was the cold. He'd had a brief moment of guilt when he first spotted her on the sidewalk, with her collar up around her neck and hugging herself like she was frozen. He should have insisted they meet in a restaurant or bar.

Lacey stopped their progress to study the name over an art gallery door. "Damn it. Stuart told me which gallery his sculptures were in, but now I can't remember." Glancing at a small green street sign, she exhaled in frustration. "We're on the right street. Hopefully we'll stumble across him, because I promised I'd come see his stuff. I had no idea there are so many different galleries. How many art galleries does one city need?" she muttered.

That was perfectly fine with Jack. He didn't mind wandering. It gave him more time to talk to her, study her, get to know her. They'd rapidly discovered they had one thing in common; the art scene wasn't the place for them. Pushing crowds and pontificating gallery owners and buyers ruined the enjoyment of simply studying the original pieces. He hadn't brought up his police interview yet, putting it off as long as possible. The longer he delayed it, the more time he had to be next to her.

She used her hands when she talked. And her eyes. Her brown eyes sparkled in rhythm with her hands when she was happy. He tried to keep her talking, talking about anything. Her voice was warm, and she frequently sounded like she was about to laugh. He liked it.

They pushed through the doors of a coffee shop, stomping the frozen slush from their feet. He watched her run a hand over her hair, almost absently. Not frantically searching out a mirror, like some women would after the wind. She looked perfect. The cold had turned her cheeks pink, and her brown eyes were bright. She'd left her hair down and loose tonight. Before, he'd only seen it pulled back into a ponytail. It was long and gently wavy, with all shades of blonde from dark honey to polished gold. His hands ached to touch.

"I'm dying for coffee. I don't care what it tastes like as long as it's hot." She shivered.

He moved the two of them into the line, happy to wait. From the length of the line apparently the rest of Portland needed coffee too.

He stood behind her, subtly resting his hands on her shoulders as he studied the board. He stiffened slightly. There was that scent from Saturday morning, and it wasn't from the lattes and mochas. He bent over slightly to sniff at Lacey's hair and closed his eyes. She smelled like a bakery. Cinnamon, vanilla, and honey all tickled his nose. *Delicious.* It suited her.

His eyes popped open as her shoulders jerked. Had she caught him smelling her hair?

Lacey's focus was on a couple leaving the front of the line with their drinks. They were midthirties and dressed for the cold. The woman was blonde and angular with a sour expression. The man with her was the same height, but he had an anxious look that suggested years of tiptoeing around his mate's moods. Jack watched the man's steps slow as he spotted Lacey; his expression darkened as he moved his gaze over her head to meet Jack's.

Lacey sucked in a sharp breath, and Jack felt a quiver travel up his arms from where his hands rested on her. He tightened his grip on her shoulders, reacting to the challenge in the other man's eyes.

Who the fuck was that?

Lacey couldn't believe it.

Three hundred coffee shops in Portland and he had to walk into hers. Well, to be honest, he'd been here first. But the amended movie quote stuck in her head. She'd lasted more than a year without running into this man. Why tonight of all nights?

Jack tightened his fingers on her shoulders, and she thanked the stars for his presence. This was a confrontation where she needed a hot guy at her back. A tall, hot guy. And his possessive hands on her shoulders were perfect.

"Dr. Campbell." Frank spoke like she were filth.

Some things never change.

Anger flared, but she gave a cool smile.

"Frank." She turned to the scowling woman at Frank's side. "Celeste." The other woman said nothing, ignoring Lacey as she sized up Jack. Her sour expression faded into a simpering, admiring smile. *Dream on.* Lacey didn't know which one of the couple she disliked more.

Out of the corner of her eye, she saw Jack briefly stare at Celeste then turn his gaze back to Frank. He said nothing.

Perfect. Lacey sucked in a breath. "Oh, this is Jack." She turned adoring eyes to Jack, trying to signal him with her brows. Confusion briefly flashed across his face but he recovered and gave the couple a formal nod. "Jack, meet Frank and Celeste Stevenson."

No one offered a hand. Jack kept his hands firmly on Lacey's shoulders and pulled her slightly closer. Frank's face clouded.

"Have you been enjoying the artwork? We've had a lovely time browsing—"

"Shut the fuck up, Lacey," Frank spat.

She felt Jack start to push her aside to get at the shorter man, but she grabbed his right arm tight to her chest and held on, pulling his body tight to her back. Frank paled and stepped slightly behind Celeste. *Coward.*

Lacey wished she could see the expression on Jack's face. According to Frank's reaction, Jack looked ready to grind him into hamburger.

"Now, Frank. There's no reason to be rude." Adrenaline pumped through her veins. After all the things this asshole had done to her...

Frank pushed a furious Celeste toward the door, giving Jack and Lacey a wide berth. Celeste's expression twisted to hate as deep lines formed between her brows.

"No reason? I could come up with several million, you sneaky bitch." Frank had the last loud word as the door slammed shut.

The boisterous chatter of the shop abruptly halted. Every person in line, every person behind the counter, and every person seated at the tables stared at Lacey.

Lacey closed her eyes, listening to her heart pound. That didn't go too badly.

"Wow. Who was that?"

She'd nearly forgotten Jack was there. She still had his arm clasped tightly against her breasts and could feel his heat against her back, through her coat. Embarrassed, she dropped his arm and turned to face him. She should've let him pound on Frank a little. By the look in Jack's eyes, he'd have done it with pleasure. She forced a weak smile, trying to meet his intense gaze.

"*That* was my ex-husband."

CHAPTER FOURTEEN

Jack escorted Lacey from the coffee shop in silence. They'd decided to skip the coffee, and he had a feeling coffee was something she didn't pass up.

She'd been married. To that ass. *Wow.*

He shook his head to get rid of the tightening of jealousy that'd seized his throat. Where did that come from? It wasn't like they were dating or something.

Or something.

His gut wanted to start something. Under that bulky coat, she had a body that was burned into his brain. Petite, but curvy in all the right places. She'd had scrubs on at the ME's office yesterday, and he'd had a rough time keeping his eyes off her well-sculpted arms. She'd been an athlete and still kept things hot and tight.

His mind spun as he silently walked her to her car. It was dark in the city and only every other streetlight was on, creating areas of deep shadows next to the wide spots of gold light. They'd left behind the bustle of the art crowd and moved into a quieter section of town. He kept his hands to himself. Lacey's stiff posture was sending out loud and uncomfortable vibes that screamed not to touch her.

He was clueless as to what was in her head. When they'd left the shop she'd seemed proud that she'd stood up to her ex, but then she'd become silent, and now anger simmered around her. Jack hadn't ventured a word. Let alone a question. What was their story? It couldn't be a good one. Obviously, the marriage had split on very bad terms.

Lacey stopped by a big SUV and dug in her purse for keys. Jack eyed the black vehicle, wondering if she could see over the steering wheel.

"That's a big truck."

She whirled on him. "Are you going to jump on me about carbon footprints? 'Cause I get enough of that from my friends. I have to get up the hills to my house when it snows. And I ski a lot." Her eyes claimed she was ready to do battle.

He backed off, holding his hands up in defense. "Whoa. Slow down. Actually, I've got one just like it. Well, a few years older than yours."

"I'm sorry. I didn't mean to snap at you. It's just that..." She waved her hands in a circle and gestured toward the way they'd come. "I'm sorry you saw him make an ass of himself."

"It seems to come very naturally to him."

A small smile crossed her lips and his breath caught. It'd completely transformed her face. He mentally cast around for something else witty to say, wanting to see her smile again. In silent frustration, he stepped in front of her and leaned casually against the SUV's door, feeling anything but casual. His skin was on full alert. Every sensitive cell tuned into the woman in front of him. He felt like he'd had a couple of shots of espresso and couldn't come down from the buzz. He couldn't let her go.

"How long were you married?"

"Two years." Her smile faded.

"How long ago?"

She counted on her fingers. "It's been over for about seven years."

"Jesus. And he's still bitter? After all this time?" Who holds a grudge that long? Of course, Jack didn't know why they'd split, but he'd bet it was the dickwad's fault.

She shrugged and tugged deliberately on the door handle, which wouldn't open because of his weight against the door. She wouldn't look in his eyes, not ready to tell him the story. But he couldn't let her leave when she looked upset. He didn't move.

"I hope you managed to run him through the wringer before you split."

She gazed at him with a wry grin on her lips. "I'd say I was squeezed as much as he was, but I might have stomped on his ego a few times."

"Ouch." Jack slapped a hand over his heart with a grimace and silently celebrated her grin. "Some women seem to have a real knack for that."

Lacey looked at him sharply. "Been stomped on a few times have you?"

"What poor soul hasn't?"

"*Poor soul* isn't the phrase that comes to mind when I think of you."

He gave her a grin and leaned close to whisper. The steam from his breath touched her cheek. "What does come to mind when you think of me?"

"Stubbornness." She yanked at the handle again.

"I knew you'd been thinking about me."

She laughed, but guilt briefly flashed across her face.

She had been thinking of him.

He stepped away from the truck, opening the door and offering her a hand up to the seat. When he didn't let go, she tugged her hand back with a questioning look. He leaned closer, holding her amused gaze.

"Can we do this again?"

"Do what? Freeze? Or fight with my ex?" Lacey's tone was light, but her dark eyes were serious.

Her mouth caught his attention. Her lips were parted slightly and the tip of her tongue moistened her lower lip. His body hardened at the sight. Her breath caught as her eyes registered his reaction.

"Lacey…"

He couldn't finish. She'd understood exactly what he'd asked her. He watched a struggle cross her face and his heart tripped a beat.

"OK." She whispered the single word.

He'd won out over her common sense.

He placed a foot on the running board, cupped her face in his hands, and covered her lips with his. His fingers sank into the blonde hair he'd been aching to touch as he kissed her hard and long on the mouth. After her initial surprise, he felt her soften and lean into the kiss, opening to him. Blood roared in his head. Her mouth was soft and warm, and she gave a small moan in the back of her throat. He felt her hand move to his shoulder, and he wished away his heavy jacket. He wanted to feel the heat of her hand. He wanted to feel her hand slide along his skin and...

She pulled back, her hand still on his coat.

"This isn't a good idea," she whispered.

He held still, fighting the flood of arousal through his limbs. "If I'm going to make a mistake, I like to make it a big one."

Her eyes widened.

He hit the lock button on her door, stepped back, and pushed the truck door shut. She stared at him through the window, her fingertips touching her lips. Her stunned look faded, and he saw the edges of a smile behind her hand.

"Go." He made a shooing gesture. "Go home."

Lacey started her engine and shifted into drive. She looked at him again, lifted one side of her mouth, and winked at him, laughter in her eyes. Just like he'd winked the first moment he'd seen her. She'd remembered. His heart double-thumped, and she stepped on the gas.

He stood in the street and watched until her taillights disappeared.

With a fresh mug of coffee in her hand, Lacey glared out her front window the following morning. Her newspaper lay on the sidewalk. A good forty feet from her porch. During the night, freezing rain had covered the old snow with a dangerous layer of ice. To get her paper, she'd have to dash out in her robe, try not to slip on the ice, and risk breaking her butt. She loved the Sudoku puzzles. Her day couldn't start until she'd mastered the damn things.

She set down her coffee, tightened the tie on her robe, and slipped her feet into boots, Then caught her reflection in the hall mirror. *Christ.* Hair a disaster, ratty green robe and ladybug boots. If Mr. Carson across the street spotted her, she'd never hear the end of it. The crotchety man didn't believe she was a dentist. He'd told his wife Lacey was a dental receptionist.

She looked a little closer in the mirror, trying to finger-comb her hair. Her lips looked swollen. Running a finger across them, she decided they were definitely sensitive, even though it'd been only one kiss. One very hot, electrifying kiss last night that'd kept her awake until three in the morning.

Why'd she agree to see Jack again? Michael's warnings echoed through her head. Mentally she agreed with Michael. Nothing good could come out of seeing Jack Harper. She had enough problems with her own memories of the past. She didn't need his perspective too.

She wasn't thinking with her brain. She was thinking with a part of herself that hadn't had a real date in over a year, a part that craved a man's rough touch and ached for a strong shoulder to support her. A part that craved a man to hold her tight in bed and make her feel like he couldn't live without her.

Lacey bit her lip and admitted the thought she'd been avoiding. *She was lonely.* Filling her time with work and teaching tumbling at the gym. Avoiding men like a piece of gum on a hot sidewalk.

Why him? Why now?

Something about this man had slipped under her defenses. She'd briefly dropped her guard and he'd snuck in, breaking out emotions and memories she'd locked firmly away. And physical needs.

Surprise from last night still lingered about her. As Jack had kissed her, she'd heard that *click* that occurs when the right people come together. It was plainly audible. And she knew Jack had heard it too.

Lifting her chin, she reached for the doorknob but paused, eyeing the mass of hair in the mirror again. Grabbing a clip out of her pocket, she pulled back her hair, twisted it, and clamped it securely.

Now, who cares what Mr. Carson thinks?

Shivering, she cautiously crossed the porch and nearly broke her butt as she slipped on the first icy stair. Her teeth snapped together as a sharp jolt shot up her spine and out of her limbs.

OK. No paper today.

She inched her way back to the door and spotted a small package propped beside the doorframe. "DR. LACEY CAMPBELL," was handwritten in capital letters.

What the hell?

No address, no postmark. Someone must have dropped it by yesterday. Squeezing it, she felt the outline of a disc. She frowned. Had someone at work told her he had a DVD for her?

Ripping the package open, she relaxed as she entered the warmth of her home and inhaled the scent of strong coffee. A silver video disc popped out into her hands. No label. Curious, she picked up her coffee and headed for the TV in the family room.

She popped the disc in the player, grabbed the cat circling her feet, and sat on the sofa, scratching Eve under her chin. The TV screen was showing nothing but grayish snow. *Crap.* Was it blank?

The screen abruptly cleared, revealing an image of a concrete-block walled room. The camera shakily panned, displaying a crowded mess. Dented cardboard boxes stacked in corners leaned in short towers. Old wooden chairs, broken pieces of tables, and a roll of stained carpet filled the tight space. The images were grainy, as if the tape was old or had been copied over several times. The camera moved to a small iron twin bed, and Lacey felt her chest contract as the camera focused on the blonde woman tied to the headboard.

Suzanne.

Eve squawked, and Lacey let go of the cat she'd suddenly choked. Eve leaped off her lap and shot out of the room, her claws skittering, searching for traction on the wood floor.

Lacey held her breath.

Suzanne's face came into focus. Her eyes were half-closed, but she shot a brief arrow of hatred directly at the camera before her expression grew blank. She didn't wrestle with her bonds, the fight seemed purged from her system. Her hair was unkempt and long. Longer than Lacey had ever seen it. And it was straggly, even greasy. Suzanne's head turned to the camera again, making eye contact with Lacey, then looking away, her chin dropping. The camera rudely traced down her body, which was clothed in a tattered T-shirt and sweatpants.

Oh, my God.

Lacey stared harder, focusing on the bulge under Suzanne's T-shirt as her own hands searched blindly beside her for the remote on the sofa cushions. Her eyes never left the screen. If she looked away, the image might vanish. She had to pause the DVD! Where the fuck was the remote?

Dear Lord. Suzanne was pregnant.

There was no mistaking the distinct protruding belly. As Lacey watched, she saw a ripple of movement under the T-shirt. Her hands froze in their search. The baby was moving.

What happened to the baby? Where was Suzanne's baby?

Not a baby. A child now. Possibly nine or ten years old.

The image vanished, returning to dirty snow. "No-o-o!" Lacey screamed.

Tearing her gaze from the screen, she spotted the remote on the side table and grabbed it. As she turned back to the TV, ready to hit rewind, new images cut across the screen. Darker and sharper this time. This scene was shot outdoors, a city at night.

Standing, she pointed the remote at the screen, her finger hovering over the rewind button as she squinted at the dark images of parked cars and trucks. The camera scanned from vehicle to vehicle. She caught sight of a Ford Mustang. A new one. *A current body style.* Her breath caught. This part of the disc had been shot recently.

For a desperate second she believed Suzanne could be alive and pregnant somewhere.

No. Lacey felt her chest deflate. Suzanne's body had been found dumped under an apartment. Lacey had held her bones. Tears burned in her eyes.

Lacey sucked in a shuddering breath and stared at the screen, trying to get the sudden vision of Suzanne's lonely skull out of her mind.

Then she saw him, and Lacey collapsed back on the sofa. Jack Harper. He was leaning into her truck as he gave her a long kiss and then slammed her door shut. Lacey stared at her own stunned face through the truck window. The camera jerked, and she heard the shooter curse explicitly under his breath.

Lacey gagged, stumbled off the bed, and dashed into the bathroom, heaving over the toilet. Sweat beaded across her face, and dark clouds threatened her vision.

That kiss wasn't ten hours old.

CHAPTER FIFTEEN

He fussed with his latte. It wasn't sweet enough, and he'd already taken it back once. The barista had scorched it the first time, and that nasty taste still lingered in his mouth. She'd made a new drink and had given him a coupon for a free latte next time. At least she'd taken care of his complaint. If you're going to do something, do it right.

His knee jiggled as he waited at the little table. He scanned the other patrons in the coffee shop and hummed along with the store's music, until he realized it was Willie Nelson. He hated country music. It triggered images of his father.

Outside, the day was crispy blue and sunny, but twenty freezing degrees. The wind was the worst. It had that biting, icy chill that froze your nose within five seconds of venturing outside. Only the brave gambled with driving on the slick roads.

Driving in snow and ice didn't bother him. He'd grown up with that sort of weather. But in this town, the long cold snap was unfamiliar. In a typical Portland winter, a half inch of snowfall would close down the city as wrecks jammed the freeways and side roads. Portlanders were clueless when it came to navigating in snow. Thank God, he'd grown up where driving in the snow was necessary.

Had Lacey liked his present? At first, he hadn't planned to include the clip of her and Harper, but it'd pissed him off when the man had kissed her.

He'd been jealous.

The woman had struck an unexpected chord in him.

Now what? How did this affect the plan? He mapped out alternatives in his mind, sipping the hot coffee. Lacey had been a loose factor in the master plan. From the beginning, he'd never fully decided on her fate. He frowned. He'd developed a precise, cut-and-dried plan for everyone else. Why not for her?

Subconsciously, had he known she would be special?

Suzanne had been special. A fond smile crossed his face, bringing an answering smile from the attractive woman at the next table. The woman tried to catch his eye, and he looked out the window, ignoring her. He had serious planning to focus on.

He hadn't watched that old bit of video in years. His throat had welled up as he viewed the film. Suzanne had been so lovely, blossoming as her belly grew with child. Out of all the girls, she'd been the chosen. He remembered running his hands along her swollen stomach, feeling the child kick. It'd hurt him deeply to kill her. He'd almost changed his mind, but he'd had no choice. She would've spent her life fighting to escape him. He couldn't allow that, so she'd followed the fate of the others.

If you're going to do something, do it right.

He pulled his mind back to the problem at hand. Lacey Campbell. For a second he pictured her in Suzanne's position on the old bed, her stomach big. His insides tightened and he caught his breath. Could he risk it again?

The woman at the next table purposefully caught his eye this time and smiled again. He looked down into his latte, not wanting to encourage her. Women used to avoid looking at him. He'd been a scrawny geek as a teen. Braces, zits, glasses. If it was nerdy, he'd suffered from it.

But now he took careful preparation with his appearance. His clothes were neatly ironed, his hair styled, and his teeth freshly bleached. There was no reason to look like a slob. Too bad he couldn't do anything about his height. The football coach had once stopped him in the high school halls. The man had scanned him from head to toe and had shaken his head over his size. "Good thing you're smart."

Damn right he was smart.

The football coach never knew who took a bat to the head-lights of his precious Firebird during the homecoming game.

Follow-through was very important.

His first human kill had been a disaster, but he'd forced himself to finish the job. He didn't realize humans would fight so much harder than animals. No species had a deeper will to live than humans. He'd witnessed it several times and never made the mistake of underestimating his target again. He was never overconfident and always in control.

Not like Ted Bundy. Bundy had lost control at the end and that weakness had killed him. He'd gotten cocky, believing he wouldn't get caught and that jails wouldn't hold him. He'd escaped custody twice and had planned to try again before his execution in Florida. When he died, Bundy had been fit and tan from sunless tanning lotion and working out in prison. He'd probably planned to escape and blend in with the sun-kissed Floridians. He didn't succeed.

Tapping his fingers on the table, he wondered about his own end. It was a black hole in his plan. He couldn't precisely picture the finale, but he wanted people to know *he'd masterminded this.* He hungered to experience the admiration and astonishment. There had to be a way. But to bask in the limelight he had to go public. How could he go public and not get arrested? He chewed on his lip, staring out at the snow. He could confess and then commit suicide. That would reveal his genius to the world and avoid the hell of prison. He knew a half dozen different ways to kill himself, some needing no instruments.

Prison scared him; death and suicide didn't. He'd stood face-to-face with death, and it was peaceful. When his victims had glimpsed the magic beyond the physical world, their faces grew serene. What did they see waiting for them?

The concept of his death didn't disturb him, but the mess death brought along with it did. Disgusting, smelly, unsanitary.

His plan needed more thought.

He glanced at the coffee-cup clock on the wall. He'd wait for five more minutes. No more.

Bored, he looked at the woman, willing her to glance his way again. She did. Her right eyebrow lifted a little, her expression warm and open. She was quite lovely, he decided, studying her details, a little older than he liked but well groomed. That was important. He frowned at her brown hair, wishing it golden. Flirting, she tossed her hair, flicking dark strands over a shoulder with her hand. He focused on the hand. A wedding ring.

Disgusted, he looked away. Cheating wives sickened him. Deciding he'd waited long enough, he rose from the table, ignoring the questioning look from his admirer. He headed for the door, dropped his full coffee cup in the garbage and pulled his coat tight against the expected wind. He politely held the door open for the man coming in and watched him stomp the snow off his boots. He grinned at his good luck.

Just the victim he'd been waiting for. It was going to be this man's unlucky day.

CHAPTER SIXTEEN

Detective Mason Callahan stopped the DVD and briefly hit rewind. He ran his fingers in a rhythmic beat on the table as he deliberately watched the bit with the kiss again. He looked at the two people sitting at the table with him and raised a curious brow. The tension in the station interrogation room ratcheted up ten notches. Dr. Campbell turned pink and looked away, but Harper stared right at him, his eyes cool.

"You two move fast, don't you?" Mason tipped his head at the TV, keeping his gaze locked with Harper. "And someone didn't like watching the two of you go at it. His cussing at the end says a hell of a lot."

Harper continued his glare, saying nothing. The tall man deliberately leaned back in the cheap chair and crossed his ankles under the table. Despite the relaxed pose, his body vibrated with intensity. Dr. Campbell sat next to Harper with her hands clenched together on the table, her lips pressed in a tight line, her gaze glued to the screen. Her eyes were wet, but not spilling over. Yet. She hadn't said a word since the DVD had started.

The narrow room in the state police building was drab. Only a conference table, a few chairs, and a TV/DVD unit on a rolling cart. The room needed a paint job. The dingy-white walls showed scuff marks and gashes from careless chair backs. The ceiling bulged in one small section from an old water leak no one had bothered to repair, and Mason's chair squeaked shrilly every time he shifted his weight.

"I think we can easily assume someone is following Dr. Campbell." Detective Ray Lusco spoke evenly and quietly from his position against the wall. Mason knew he was trying to put a lid on the ego contest threatening to boil over at the table. Ray folded his arms across his wide chest, biceps bulging under the white dress shirt.

"What about Suzanne? This isn't about me." Dr. Campbell waved a hand at the TV. "What happened to Suzanne? Did he keep her tied up long enough to deliver that baby?" Her pitch was off, her wet eyes angry.

"This is about you," Harper turned to her. "Suzanne is dead, but you're alive and someone who knows what happened to Suzanne is keeping close tabs on you. I don't like it." The last sentence was delivered to Callahan, who nodded in agreement.

"I don't think we're jumping to any wild conclusions by linking your follower to the murders of Trenton and Cochran.

Suzanne is the primary link we have between DeCosta and the other dead men. Everyone was involved with the DeCosta case somehow, and now these people are paying for it with their lives. We talked about this the other day at your house. If this creep continues in this pattern, you could be on his list. Maybe even next."

"But why'd he send the DVD to let her know she's being watched?" Harper muttered.

Mason shook his head at Harper's question. "Your guess is as good as mine. He's definitely making a statement about something. We need to figure out who shot the video. DeCosta was caught within twenty-four hours of Suzanne's abduction, so he didn't shoot the first part, but it was obviously someone close to him. Close enough for DeCosta to trust with his victims. We're going to look at his family and close associates. It's very probable that the same person shot both pieces of the video." He met Dr. Campbell's curious gaze. "And it's someone who knew where you were going last night or else followed you from work."

"This guy apparently knows of your strong connections to Suzanne," Ray added. "He's sending a message, wanting you to know that he knows about it. He's also telling you that he's the one who initiated current events."

"Current events?" Dr. Campbell rubbed a palm against her forehead.

"Trenton's and Cochran's deaths. Finding Suzanne's remains." Harper's words were clipped.

"Any ideas who it could be? Have any strange men approached you lately? With the ego we're seeing here, I wouldn't be surprised if he's come close or even spoken to you." Mason watched Dr. Campbell's face pale a shade lighter.

"It might not be a stranger to her," Ray interjected. "It could be someone from her past. She brushed shoulders with a lot of people involved in DeCosta's trial."

Callahan nodded. "Any recent connections with old contacts, people you don't see that often?"

At the alarmed look Dr. Campbell shot Harper, Mason straightened in his noisy chair. "What? What happened?" Dr. Campbell was shaking her head, her eyes locked with Harper's, disagreeing with his nodding scowl.

Harper exhaled. "We had a run-in with her ex-husband last night."

"Last night?"

"Before...that." Harper nodded at the TV screen. "About ten or fifteen minutes before."

"What kind of run-in?"

"Nasty." He flashed an apologetic glance at Dr. Campbell. "He called her a lying bitch in front of fifty people. Loudly."

"Name?" Ray was calmly taking notes.

"Frank Stevenson," Harper stated rapidly before Dr. Campbell could speak.

What kind of creep had she married? Mason studied Dr. Campbell as she continued to shake her head.

"It can't be Frank. He's an asshole but not a killer."

"When were you married? Did he know about DeCosta and Suzanne?"

She nodded. "Frank and I dated during college. We got married the year after...Suzanne disappeared." She swallowed hard, but her eyes projected control. "We all hung out together. Frank traveled with the team to most of the meets. Everybody knew him."

"Was he at the meet in Corvallis?" Mason asked.

Anger flashed across Dr. Campbell's face. "I saw DeCosta's face that night. I saw him take Suzanne. It wasn't Frank!"

"I'm not saying it was. I'm just establishing where he was during certain events. From that DVD, we now know there were at least two people involved back then. One in prison and one who shot the video." Mason's gut burned. He'd missed something a decade ago. He'd stupidly thought it was over the minute they'd arrested DeCosta. And now, seeing proof that Suzanne had been kept alive for months after DeCosta's arrest, he knew someone else had a hand in Suzanne's kidnapping. "So your ex-husband knew where you were last night, and I assume he knows where you live?"

She nodded with a condescending gaze. Dr. Campbell clearly thought he was chasing a dead end. But at this moment, every man who came in contact with her was a potential suspect. Especially the weird ones.

"He couldn't have been the one to shoot that video," Harper spoke up. "I saw Stevenson last night. He was shocked as all hell to run into her. I doubt he followed us out to her truck. Especially with his current wife in tow." His words were firm, but Mason saw a flicker of doubt waver in Harper's eyes.

Mason gave Harper a narrow look. "You might be in this creep's sights now too. Whoever it was sure didn't like that kiss."

Dr. Campbell sucked in her breath.

"Are you saying our suspect's got some sort of freaky attraction to Dr. Campbell?" Ray screwed up his face in thought. Mason could hear the wheels spinning in Ray's head. "Maybe that's to her advantage."

Mason heard what his partner didn't say out loud. *If the guy had the hots for Dr. Campbell, maybe he wouldn't kill her.* Not right away anyway.

"Like it was to Suzanne?" Dr. Campbell spit out the words. She'd caught Ray's meaning too. "Look what his attraction did to her." She slammed both hands on the table. "Where's the baby? How come I'm the only one concerned about the baby?"

"First of all we aren't positive there is a baby. And second, that pregnancy scene on the DVD is old. The threat to you isn't old. *The threat is right now.*" Mason fought the urge to point his finger at the dentist.

Dr. Campbell ignored his hints about her safety. "Maybe the DVD isn't old. Maybe he held her captive for years before she got pregnant." She was grabbing at straws.

Mason shook his head. "I briefly talked to the ME last night and he suspects she's been dead close to a decade."

"Did the report say she'd given birth?" asked Lacey. "The bones from her pelvic girdle would indicate a pregnancy."

"They would?" Mason wasn't too surprised. It never ceased to amaze him what anthropologists could tell from a pile of bones. "I don't remember if it said anything about pregnancy." He mentally reviewed the recent report. "I'll double-check."

He fixed his gaze on Dr. Campbell. "I want you out of sight until this settles down. This sicko has an unhealthy interest in you. Get away for a while, go on vacation or something."

"Vacation?" she sputtered. "You want me to go on vacation while people are dying? Go lie on a beach and drink mai tais? I'm not going to hide! I've got a normal life that I worked long and hard for! I'm not going to let a ghost scare me back into a closet." Her voice cracked and Mason glimpsed a hint of the hell she must have suffered through a decade ago. She'd probably jumped at every shadow for years.

"I'm not going anywhere."

Mason studied the new glaze over her eyes. It hadn't been there a minute ago. She projected a strong front, but an old crack in that wall was starting to widen. Mason didn't want to see what she'd buried behind it.

Harper touched her arm. "He's got a point. You should get out of town."

She yanked her arm away, her face dark. "Don't tell me what to do." Harper jerked back at her bitter words, his face reflecting the irritation Mason felt.

She stood and wrestled into her thick coat, grabbing at her purse.

"I'm done here." She headed for the hallway, avoiding all eye contact, and Ray opened the door for her. "Keep the DVD. I don't want to see it again."

Mason listened to angry boot heels click down the hall.

"She won't go far. I'm her ride." Harper stared at the door, his jaw grinding in frustration. He leaned in to Mason. "Is there anything you can do for her?"

"You mean protection?"

Harper nodded, his gray eyes grim. "He could yank her off the street or snatch her out of bed at any time." He paused, bringing Ray into the conversation with a harsh look. "You both know he wants something from her." Looking back at the blank TV, his tone dropped. "Can you imagine the hell her friend went through?"

Mason could easily imagine. And he could easily project Dr. Campbell's face onto Suzanne's swollen body.

"There's not a lot we can officially do. This is all conjecture. But I feel like she does need to be watched 24-7. We can't do that." Mason held Harper's gaze.

Harper slowly nodded back.

Jack's breath caught as he stepped out of the police building and discovered he couldn't see Lacey. He looked up and down the quiet city street. He couldn't be more than thirty seconds behind her. Jack jogged through the packed snow toward the parking lot where he'd left his truck, hoping she'd blown off her steam as she waited for him. He glanced at the sky. Three more inches of snow were predicted in the next twelve hours. If he was going to convince her to leave town, now would be the time to do it.

Why was he making her his business? Didn't he have enough on his plate?

He needed to focus on his company, save it from publicity hell. He didn't have time to play big brother. After all, he barely knew the woman. Her wide smile popped in his brain, and it fired his lungs like a blowtorch. Whom was he trying to fool? Christ. There was no logic to his feelings. Attraction doesn't follow logic. He only knew what he felt in his gut. He'd wanted to shield her from that damned video, hide her face against his jacket, and sink his hands into her hair. He couldn't stand the pain and vulnerability he'd seen in her stricken brown eyes.

He wanted to hit something. Someone.

Jack rounded the corner of the brick building and spotted a small figure next to his truck. Thank God. He wasn't going to let Lacey out of his sight again. His stomach calming, he fought the urge to shake some sense into her.

Lacey wouldn't respond if he tried to manhandle her. She'd just shove back harder, be more contrary. If he was going to watch out for her, he had to be subtle, make her think his ideas for her safety were her own. He stepped closer and, seeing the fresh anger on her face, he promptly dumped his reverse psychology plan in a snowdrift. The woman would do whatever the hell she wanted.

Her greeting to him confirmed it.

"You and those cops aren't going to tell me what to do." Lacey leaned against his truck, her eyes hard. "I've worked my butt off to put that nightmare behind me, not let it control my life and now you're all telling me I have to hide."

"Not hide. Just get out of his path."

"Damn it!" She stomped a heel. "This psychopath is turning my life inside out again. I got through it once, but now...I can't live and be constantly looking over my shoulder. Even if I left town I'd still be doing that."

Jack stood still, letting her vent. He wanted to touch her, calm her, but he knew she wasn't ready. He said nothing and shoved his fists in his front pockets. Tension locked his spine in place. *Wait.*

She suddenly stilled and her hands flew up to cover her mouth as her eyes widened. "Where's that baby? Suzanne ripped a hole in my heart when she vanished and now seeing that she was pregnant, the hole's doubled in size. I feel...I feel like I lost a baby. I know this doesn't feel remotely close to a mother who's truly lost her child, but I've got to look for it. I have to at least try. I owe Suzanne that much...I shouldn't have let go that night. None of this would have happened if I hadn't let go." Lacey faltered and her gaze grew haunted. "Do you think the baby's father is the killer? Oh, God. Does he still have the child?"

Her brown eyes turned darker in her pain, and he took that as his cue.

He drew her into him and pressed her tight against his body, wanting to absorb her grief. She buried her face against his coat and drew jagged breaths. Tentative arms slipped around him inside his jacket, and he felt her heart thud against his chest. He hung on, wrapping his arms around her shoulders and gently resting his chin on her hair, breathing deep of her female scent. He closed his eyes against his stir of arousal and he wished away her pain.

How many years had it taken to heal from the emotional anguish of her attack? Her scab had been ripped away today, exposing vulnerable nerves. Jack thought of Cal and swallowed hard. Cal had been more than a friend and mentor to him. And he'd died brutally at the hands of a killer. Possibly the same person stalking Lacey.

His arms flexed tighter as he remembered the video clip of the kiss. He spun around, holding Lacey tight, scanning for a camera, a body, anyone. He felt eyes watching them. Callahan was right. Jack had to get Lacey somewhere safe. Hawaii, Fiji, Antarctica, he didn't care.

Jack clenched his jaw as anger flushed through his veins. He would keep her safe. He didn't have a choice. His heart was overpowering his head.

And he'd find that baby for her.

Ray and Mason watched the couple from the second-floor window.

"Fuck!" Ray spun away and kicked his chair, sending it crashing across the room. "We can't do a thing for her." His voice dropped an octave. "That's such bullshit. Why can't we stick her away somewhere until this is over?"

Mason remained silent at the window, leaning on one hand against the sill as he ignored the rare tantrum. Ray's question was rhetorical. They didn't have the manpower or the money. They both knew it.

Mason watched as Harper spun around to check his surroundings. *Good man. Maybe you are the right person to watch over her.* If she couldn't have a cop for protection, an ex-cop would do. Harper bundled her into the truck, took one last scan of the parking lot, and sent snow flying with his tires.

The possessive vibes Harper was giving off rivaled Mason's mutt's behavior with his favorite chew toy. Harper would do his damnedest to keep Dr. Campbell safe. If she let him.

But what about that reporter...Brody? Mason pictured the blond man who'd hovered over Dr. Campbell like a vigilant mama bear. The man had emitted a subtle aura that hinted at a turbulent, explosive side. Mason remembered from Harper's first interview that he'd agreed Brody was a pain in the butt.

Where'd Brody fit in this cozy threesome?

CHAPTER SEVENTEEN

"Damn you, Jack."

Lacey swore as she rooted through the folders on her desk at the dental school, searching for the student status reports she needed to finish. After leaving the police station, she'd convinced Jack to drop her off. He'd protested but relented when she demonstrated the tight security system, showing how she had to swipe her key card to get into the building and pointing at the nearby security vehicles. He needed to stop at his office and had made her promise to be at the school's parking-garage elevator in a half hour. "Exactly thirty minutes," he'd growled.

Jack had kept urging her to leave town, but she'd refused. She'd compromised and had agreed to check into a local hotel.

He insisted on driving her to the dental school and then back to her house to pack. *It's just a hotel. Just for a few days.* Lacey wasn't leaving Portland, and she wasn't about to abandon her job. Jack had muttered that she needed a bodyguard. She inferred he'd hired himself for the job.

We'll see about that.

She yanked open her bottom desk drawer. *There they were.* Now she remembered quickly dropping the files in the drawer yesterday and slamming it shut, as a student had stopped by to question her about his grade. She blew out a breath. She couldn't concentrate. What she really needed was some space from all that testosterone. Between Jack and the detectives, she'd had her quota for the month.

She grabbed her lab coat off the back of her chair and headed for the women's locker room. The dental lab at the school was silent as Lacey passed through. She was surprised no students were using the evening hours to finish lab projects. God knows she and Amelia had spent enough stressful late nights in the dreary place. They'd get loopy after a while, guzzling caffeine and popping chocolate, trying not to break down and cry over a crown they'd spent hours creating and totally screwed up.

Sometimes someone had sneaked in a six-pack. That's when most of Lacey's dental mistakes were made. She'd quickly learned not to cast crowns and drink beer at the same time. But tonight the lab was empty. Apparently, the current students were caught up on their projects or deep in procrastination.

She tossed her lab coat into the locker room laundry hamper with the rest of the dental gowns and scrubs. She glanced at her watch. She had five minutes to get to the garage and meet Jack.

Lacey sped down the silent hall then slammed to a stop. "Oh, crap." She reversed direction back to the locker room. She'd forgotten to check her lab coat pockets. One time she'd accidentally left lab keys in a pocket. The laundry company claimed they never found them. Grabbing her coat out of the hamper, she squeezed each pocket. She felt a small, hard lump in the breast pocket, slid her hand in, pulled out a ring and stared.

"What the..."

She'd always kept the ring at home, tucked away in an old jewelry box in a deep dresser drawer. Lacey turned the ring over in her hand, deep lines crossing her forehead, an odd spinning starting in the center of her stomach. The single red stone was set in gold with inscriptions on the thick band. It was one of her NCAA championship rings. She'd never worn either of them. She couldn't even remember the last time she'd looked at them.

How did it get in her pocket?

She held the ring up to one of the lights, turning it to see the year of the championship and the school's logo, and suddenly brought it closer to squint at the initials engraved on the inside of the band.

This wasn't her ring. It was Suzanne's.

Her stomach seized. Her lungs froze.

Get out.

She dashed out of the locker room and down the hall to the elevator, anxiety ripping up her spine. She waited for three long seconds in front of the closed metal doors before whirling about for the stairs and tearing up the stairwell. While she was running down the fourth-floor hallway, her mind chanted over and over in time with her footsteps. *Not my ring. Not my ring.*

Her brain wouldn't think beyond that.

The dental school felt dangerous, too deserted. Ice gripped her stomach as she ran by each classroom and office door. Glassed-in displays of extracted teeth caught her reflection, causing startling movements out of the corner of her eye, making her sprint faster. Someone had been at her desk. In her things.

What if he was still in the building?

Who'd do this?

Twenty feet away the double fire doors of the long, enclosed skybridge crossed from the dental school to the parking garage. Her panic dropped a degree and her steps slowed. She'd make it to the garage. Jack would be there and everything would be OK. At this second, Jack Harper was synonymous with safety in her mind.

She hit one of the heavy double doors with both hands, flinging it open. The long stretch of windowed hall was empty; the garage elevator was at the other end. With a sigh of relief, she took three steps down the hall and caught a flash of movement from the corner of her eye. Spinning around on clumsy feet, she faced a man leaning against the fire door she hadn't pushed open.

"Frank!" Her shocked breath shot out at the sight of her ex-husband and her spine loosened a notch. He was a creep, but he was a creep she was relieved to see. But…

"How'd you get in here?" Her heart slammed rhythmically.

He gave a glimpse of a key card in his hand. "I still have your card."

Jesus Christ. She'd given him a card when she was a student. He'd kept it all this time? And it still worked? She needed to have a serious talk with building security.

"You shouldn't have kept that. You shouldn't be in here." Her dismay morphed into anger, and she grabbed at the card he whipped out of reach. Her eyes narrowed at him.

"What're you doing here?"

"Looking for you."

"Why? What for?"

He gave that slow smile she'd learned to be wary of. Her palms started to sweat at the sight and her pounding heart skipped two beats. Years ago, that smile meant he had a plan, and it usually wasn't one she liked.

"I've missed you, Lace." His eyes grew soft, seductive.

"Give me a break, Frank!" Her heart raced as she sniffed at him. "Are you drunk?"

His face grew tight and he stepped closer, sending her scooting backward. He wasn't tall but he was definitely bigger than her. "No! Is that the first thing you think of?"

"Yeah, because it was usually the reason you used to do stupid things. Like this!" She gestured to include the skybridge and backed up another step, her nerves vibrating. He moved closer. Moisture beaded on her forehead. He was herding her into an alcove.

"What in the hell are you thinking by following me?"

"I just want to talk. I've been thinking about you since we ran into each other last night."

"You called me a sneaky bitch and told me to shut the fuck up. You really think some sleazy charm will make me forget that? Or help me forget all the nasty things you said about me in court? Are you stupid, Frank? Go back to your wife!"

Lacey's heart was pounding its way out of her chest and she bit her lips closed, feeling the wall against her back. She was cornered.

Don't piss him off.

He grabbed her upper arms and shook her, his angry face close to hers. "You're a royal, stuck-up bitch, Lacey. You think you're too good for me?" She felt his hot breath whip across her cheek.

Her eyes went wide. It'd been forever since he'd laid hands on her. A flashback of his fist to her mouth scalded her brain, and she twisted her face away, thrusting up her knee toward his crotch. He swung his hips out of the way, laughing at her.

A loud crack echoed through the skybridge and Frank's eyes rolled up and back, showing more of the whites of his eyes than she ever needed to see. He let go of her arms and collapsed onto the concrete floor. Directly behind him stood a janitor, Sean Holmes, with his feet spread wide and holding his mop handle like a baseball bat. He'd unscrewed the thick handle and nailed Frank in the temple.

"Sean..." Lacey couldn't speak as she stared at the young janitor. She started to step forward but felt her knees dissolve, so she pressed her back into the wall. It seemed a good place to lean. Otherwise, she was going to fall on her ass in three seconds. She dropped her gaze. Frank lay motionless at her feet. Silent in his baggy coveralls, Sean stared at her for a few seconds, then at the body on the floor. His lank hair fell forward into his eyes, blocking her view of his face.

"Call security, Sean." She gestured to the white phone on the wall and dug in her purse for her pepper spray, twisting the top to release the safety. Some good it did her buried in her purse. Why hadn't she dug it out the second she found that ring? She clung to it with both hands, pointing it at the body in front of her, trying to slow her breathing. Her legs shook and she fought for balance.

She must have caught Sean's attention as he was cleaning one of the rooms when she'd dashed down the hall. He'd probably followed her, wondering what on earth was wrong.

"He was hurting you." Sean's words were measured and quiet. He raised his gaze to hers, not moving toward the phone. His brown eyes reminded her of a sad springer spaniel.

"Yes, he was." She took a breath. "You did the right thing, Sean. Thank you for that." Her legs still wouldn't move, so she told him again. "Call security now, Sean." Sean had some sort of mental handicap that made him speak and think slowly. The poor man was frequently the butt of student jokes and generally ignored or dismissed by the staff. Her firm command finally registered, and Sean moved to the phone, casting back apprehensive glances at Frank.

A few months back, Lacey had noticed Sean was droopy, not his usually cheery self. When she'd spoken to him, he could barely move his jaw. She'd dragged him to an empty dental chair, slipped on a pair of gloves, and ignored his terrified eyes. Doing an impromptu exam, she'd found a blown-out crater of a molar. He'd had to be in incredible pain. Unable to save the hopeless tooth, she'd numbed him up and extracted it on the spot.

He'd been devoted to her ever since. She suspected he had a childlike crush on her. It was sweet. It'd probably saved her from a black eye tonight. Or worse.

Lacey closed her eyes and took deep breaths. Had Frank put the ring in her pocket?

Near midnight, Detective Lusco sat scribbling frantically at his department desk, the phone tucked to his ear. Mason watched as Ray flipped over a page on his notepad and continued to write. The only conversation on Ray's end was "Uh-huh. Yeah. Where?" The person on the opposite end had plenty to say.

Unable to sit still, Mason pushed out of his chair and paced the quiet room. No one else was working late in the department. No one else had a serial killer file on his desk.

Ray covered the receiver and caught Mason's eye, waving him back to their desks. "It's security up at OHSU. Dr. Campbell was nearly assaulted at the dental school."

Mason froze as a million questions pounded his brain.

"She's OK. She wasn't hurt." Ray's forehead wrinkled and he gave a disgusted snort. "She says the man is her ex-husband." He refocused on the call.

"Stevenson." Same man who'd harassed Dr. Campbell the night before. Mason had planned to contact the man, but it looked like Frank Stevenson would be coming downtown courtesy of the Portland Police Bureau. Good. Mason had some heavy questions for him. He grabbed the binder he'd put together for the case and tore through the pages, looking for the info he'd dug up on the ex-husband. He stopped on a page and stuck a finger on the name at the top.

Frank Stevenson. Married to Dr. Campbell for approximately two years. Originally from Mount Junction. Podiatrist.

A foot doctor?

He checked Frank's date of licensure. It was only four years old. He'd become a podiatrist after Dr. Campbell graduated dental school. The fact gave Mason a sense of satisfaction and he gave a grim smile. Dr. Campbell had showed up her ex in the professional sense. Could Frankie-boy have issues with that?

"A ring? Whose ring? What? You're shitting me. She's positive?" Ray was incredulous. He stopped taking notes, and Mason automatically knew it was something big. Ray recovered and went back to scribbling faster than before.

Reading Ray's notepad upside down from across the desk, Callahan tightened his lips as he made out a few words. *Pocket. Champ-something. Initials.* Ray didn't have the best handwriting. That was an understatement, Ray had crappy handwriting. Only Ray could decipher his overabundance of notes.

Filling out the manual reports usually fell to Mason. He didn't use handwriting; he printed in perfect capital letters that would make an architect proud.

Ray hung up the phone and shook his head. "You're not going to fucking believe this."

"Try me."

Ray relayed a story about Suzanne Mills's championship ring, and he was right.

Mason couldn't fucking believe it.

Jack wanted to kill someone. Specifically Lacey's ex-husband. He would do it with pleasure, making it long and drawn out, using lots of big sharp pins in sensitive little places. He strode through her house, flipping on every light, checking every closet and hidey-hole while she made coffee in her kitchen. Portland police had already checked the house, finding no sign of a break-in. Her house had been locked up tight. But he was checking again. He threw open a bedroom door and stalked to the center of the room, scattering a cat from her king-sized bed. He paused, staring at the bed, grinding his teeth. *How had she talked him into leaving her alone at the dental school?*

It wasn't going to happen again.

He'd nearly blown a gasket when campus security cars flooded the parking garage where he'd been waiting in his truck for Lacey. Four security guards had dashed through the door to the skybridge, and Jack had leaped from his truck and followed.

Seeing Lacey sitting on the floor next to a body had shocked every nerve he had. His hand had moved to his hip even though he hadn't carried a gun in years. It wasn't a scene he wanted to experience again. Ever.

Jack stomped down her stairs, slightly frustrated he hadn't found a lurking ex-husband to pound on, knowing full well Frank Stevenson was spending the rest of the night in jail. He stopped at the entry to the kitchen, studying the woman pouring two mugs of coffee. Her hand quivered. She was hanging tough after a shitty day. She'd been interviewed by campus security and then the police. Jack had been glad she wasn't driving. Lacey hadn't said a word the entire trip home, staring out the window at the dark, icy streets.

Her head shot up as she felt his presence, her eyes widened briefly then relaxed.

"Sorry. I should've said something." *Way to go. Sneak up on the woman.*

Her smile was weak as she held out a mug to him. A pile of jewelry sat on her kitchen counter. Necklaces, watches, bracelets, and a silver baby rattle. Police had asked to see the jewelry box where she'd kept the ring. Jack picked up the tarnished rattle and read the engraving. *Lacey Joy Campbell.* She was four years younger than he was.

Lacey held out a gold ring set with a red gemstone. "I showed this to the police. I'm missing one just like it. The engraved year is different. This is the ring from the previous year's title." She ran her hands through the mess again. "I can't find my other championship ring. The one from the same year as Suzanne's."

Her tone was flat, her gaze on the heap of jewelry.

Someone *had* been in her house. At some point.

"Could you have misplaced it? Or lost it?" His questions were unnecessary.

She shrugged. "Anything is possible. But I haven't pulled that box out in years. All that stuff is old. I don't wear any of it." She blew out a breath and sat heavily on a stool at the island. Jack eased onto the one beside her, his gaze never leaving her face.

Her blue and yellow kitchen was probably a cheery place during the day, but palpable layers of dread and anxiety were ruining the effect. Lacey had made coffee because neither of them knew what else to do at three in the morning. They were both wired. Sleep was out of the question. There'd been no time to check her into a hotel yet. "When did he do it?" she whispered as she wrapped both hands around her mug. "Why would he break in to steal something? I had no clue someone had been in my house."

"He planted Suzanne's ring because he wanted you to know he'd been in your home. He knew you'd go look for your own ring and figure out he's been in your house. Callahan was right. This guy's got an ego and wants you to know what he's capable of. He's trying to shake you up, play with your head."

"He's doing a good job."

Jack fought his instinct to pack her up, throw her in his truck, and simply get out of town.

Instead, they sat sipping their unwanted coffee, heavy silence growing between them.

"Do you think it was Frank?" he asked. "Does he have a key to your house?"

She grimaced and Jack knew she was thinking of Frank and her key card to the school building. Jack and campus security were ticked over that fact.

"He doesn't have a key. I'm positive."

"That doesn't mean he's not the person who took your ring."

She had no explanation for the police when they'd asked why Frank would follow her. Frank didn't volunteer any answers either. He'd shot surly looks at Jack from the backseat of a patrol car as Lacey and the janitor were questioned.

The janitor was a hero in Jack's eyes. Sean had shrugged, and then he shook his head when questioned why he was working at the school so late. Lacey had theorized he was getting his work done when the place was empty. No one was around to harass him.

Jack swore to find the kid a new job. Surely, Sean could do something at one of his buildings.

"Why do you think Frank was at the school?" Jack asked.

He watched her struggle with the question. After several false starts, she finally blurted out, "I think he needs money." She buried her nose in her coffee.

He blinked. *Not the expected answer.*

"Why would he come to you for money?"

Lacey stared at the closed blinds over her kitchen sink. Jack had shut every blind and curtain as he went through the house, aware of how easily someone could see in from the outside. "I've given him money before."

"What? Why on earth would you loan money to your ex?"

"It wasn't a loan."

"You just *gave* him money? What did he do to you to get cash?" *Blacken your eye? Break a rib?* He didn't know if he was more pissed with Frank or Lacey at that moment.

"It's a long story," she hedged, still avoiding his eyes.

He leaned back in his barstool. "I'm not going anywhere."

She shot him an exasperated look. "Frank...Frank wasn't the easiest man to live with," she began.

Jack snorted.

"Do you want to hear this or not?" she snapped, eyes sparking.

He nodded and shut his mouth.

"We met my freshman year of college and dated for the next few years. I thought he was great. As a competitive gymnast, you don't get much life outside the gym and it can be hard to meet guys, but Frank was one of the followers."

He interrupted. "What do you mean, follower?"

"He was one of a group of guys that would show up at every practice, watching, learning the routines, and getting to know the gymnasts. They would travel to all the away meets. It was great to have such enthusiastic support. And it wasn't just college guys. We had a few retirees and rich couples that were followers and lived for the gymnastic season. They flew to the meets, bought us nice dinners after the competitions and cool gifts. Gymnastics was big in Mount Junction, bigger than football or basketball. We packed the stadium every meet and billboards with our faces lined the freeways. Strangers would come up to us in shopping malls or restaurants, recognizing us from TV." She smiled. "The school had a legendary gymnastics program. Consistently in the top three in the nation. I was on a first-name basis with every sports anchor and writer in the state. We were minor celebrities in that town."

"And Frank?"

Her brows shot together. "After Suzanne vanished, he was my rock. He helped me through some really dark times back then. After I graduated, we got married. He'd graduated two years before. It was fabulous. I thought our marriage would last a lifetime."

"I hear a big 'but' in there somewhere."

"But...I don't know. He had been the one who wanted to go to dental school."

"He did?" Jack wouldn't let that guy near his teeth. Licensed or not.

She nodded. "He applied for years, all over the country. His scores just weren't good enough. When I got accepted it really ate at him. He grew...bitter. He truly became a different person. He sort of lost himself. I don't know if it was symptoms of depression that were emerging, but he felt that didn't have another direction to go."

Jack recalled the way Frank had slurred her doctor title that night. Pure jealousy.

"My mother was sick about the same time, and it was hard on both me and my dad. I was getting ready to start school, my mother was fighting breast cancer and my husband was becoming a different person every day. I decided not to tell him about the money that would come to me if my mom died."

Huh? "What money?"

Lacey squirmed on her seat and toyed with her mug.

"My mom left me a considerable inheritance, old family money. And life insurance." Shadows dropped in her eyes and he felt like a prick for making her touch on a painful past.

"What about your dad?"

She waved a hand. "He had his own money. He knew Mom had named me the beneficiary for her life insurance, and she'd set up a trust for me when I was an infant. She came from blue-blooded timber money." A small smile lightened her face.

"Only in the Northwest." Jack understood perfectly. The original timber barons in the Northwest had amassed huge fortunes before the economy and timber industry went belly up. Most had already left the industry with their millions intact before things collapsed. Now he understood why Lacey taught school and worked for the medical examiner instead of owning a dental practice. She didn't need to work. She could do as she pleased. He had a hunch "considerable" was the wrong way to describe the amount her mom had left her.

"So you never told Frank you were loaded. What did he think about your family? Couldn't he see you came from money?"

"I guess not. Frank saw only what he wanted to see. They never flaunted their wealth." She rolled her eyes. "My mother drove the same damned station wagon for twelve years. I hated that car."

"So what happened?"

"We fell apart. Frank was angry all the time. I was at school all the time. He turned into a different person. The responsible, sympathetic man I'd married was gone. He started drinking too much, too often." She coughed, and Jack figured she didn't want to expand on the drinking. Too bad.

"He hit you." It wasn't a question.

She briefly met his eyes and looked away. "Yeah. After I'd been beaten and nearly killed by DeCosta, Frank punching me in the face was a definite deal breaker. He did it only once, but that was enough for me. No second chances. He found out about the money after the divorce. He's hated me ever since for hiding it and denying him anything in our settlement."

Jack briefly closed his eyes, seeing black eyes and split lips on her face. Rage boiled up again, but he fought it down. "The court didn't make you split it?"

She blinked innocently, deliberately. "I was a poor dental student. What was there to split? I'd put the money in my dad's name after mom died. Deep down I must have known it would go sour with Frank."

Smart girl. "That would explain the 'million reasons' he had to be rude to you that night. He was talking about your money."

She nodded. "And Celeste is convinced I cheated her husband out of his due. They both despise me."

"So why did you give him money the first time?" He saw she'd forgotten about his original question.

"He was in debt to some bad people. The money went to them, not him."

"You paid off his loans?"

"I wouldn't call them loans," she said dryly. "They were more like choking nooses around his neck. And impatient people had their hands on the other end."

"He gambled?"

"Nasty habit. Sinks a lot of people. I guess you'd call me an enabler, but it never happened while we were married. This addiction cropped up afterward. I should have let him deal with it himself, but the money wasn't a big deal to me. He swore he wouldn't gamble anymore."

Jack snorted. *Right.* "You think he's in trouble again?"

"Your guess is as good as mine, but I would bet he's deep in debt to someone. He's probably happy to be in jail. He's safe there." She looked thoughtful. "I could have Michael figure out who he owes. He's got tons of sources at the newspaper."

"Who?" Jack's throat tightened. "Are you referring to Michael Brody by any chance?" Jack mangled the words, his tongue not working right. "My buddy at *The Oregonian*? He's a friend of yours? You're not referring to the reporter who's in charge of digging up my past and plastering it on the front page?"

Her mouth opened and then closed as she rapidly blinked. Steam built in his chest, and he was about to press the subject when someone knocked on her door. An angry, pounding knock.

CHAPTER EIGHTEEN

Their eyes locked and they sat motionless. Lacey knew only one person who would show up at her house at three in the morning. And usually he didn't knock; he walked right in, using his key. *Oh, shit. This could be ugly.* Jack's accusations about Michael's articles echoed in her brain. She slipped off her stool, but Jack gripped her forearm.

"Don't answer that."

"You think somebody who wants to hurt me is going to knock on my front door?"

Lacey headed for the door again, but he hung on. She turned to him and was surprised to see the overprotectiveness on his face. *Caveman.*

"Don't."

She shook off his arm. "*I know who it is.*" He really had appointed himself her protector. How much of this could she put up with?

He tailed her to the door, nearly stepping on her heels. "Who? Who're you expecting?"

"I'm not expecting anyone. But I know only one person who shows up on my doorstep anytime he likes. It's gotta be him."

"Him? Him who?"

Was that jealousy she heard? Or just the caveman speaking again?

Peeking through the peephole, she flipped the bolt and opened the door. "Jack Harper, I don't believe you've personally met your buddy, Michael Brody."

There on the porch with his hands stuffed in his jean pockets stood a brooding Michael. He dragged his pissed-off gaze from Jack's truck in the driveway to Jack. Obviously, he'd known she wasn't alone. And he'd probably known who was in her home. Silence settled among the three.

Lacey's gaze bounced from one man to the other as they stared each other down.

They both were tall and well built, but Michael had a lean, whipcord look. Jack was simply solid everywhere. Protectiveness and possessiveness were high on each personality list, but Michael tended to clam up when he was annoyed, and she'd quickly learned that Jack pushed a subject to the edge. Jack projected cop-like confidence and assertiveness while Michael was more of a sly I-can-kick-your-butt-with-karate type.

Without a word, Jack turned around and strode back to the kitchen. Still at the door, Michael scanned Lacey's face, touching her cheek with a gentle hand. "You OK?"

She nodded.

"What happened last night? I had to hear from a police source that you were nearly assaulted." Michael guided her into the kitchen.

Jack had slipped back onto his barstool, relaxed, and sipped his coffee, letting Michael know he'd been there first. Michael ignored him and strode to the fridge, pulled out the orange juice, and drank directly from the carton. Jack stiffened.

Michael proceeded to open a cupboard, grab a mug, and help himself to the coffee.

Startled from her absorption of studying the two men, Lacey blinked at him. "Oh. Frank. You know…being his usual self."

"He cornered her alone at the dental school, threatened her, and nearly gave her a black eye." Jack filled in the important parts.

"I knew it. That asshole." Michael looked at Jack even though he was obviously speaking of Frank. He wrinkled his nose like he'd smelled sour milk. "Did he want money again? I've told you to keep away from him."

"I was staying away. *He* came after *me*. And I didn't get a chance to find out what he wanted." Lacey's words trailed off as she noticed Jack's frozen expression. She followed his gaze. He'd just seen Michael's coffee mug, which read "Michael."

"You've told me to stay away from lots of people, Michael." She tilted her head a tiny notch toward Jack.

"Yeah, you're great at taking suggestions."

Jack snorted in his coffee, and Michael glared at him. "You don't agree?"

"She doesn't listen to anybody. She does whatever she pleases, not thinking about what's safest for her."

Now both men turned to glower at her. They'd found a common ground and had united in worrying about her safety.

She looked at Michael and changed the subject. "I thought you were going to Mount Junction."

"I'm headed to the airport in a couple of hours. I just wanted to be sure you were OK first." Michael drained his cup and set it on the counter, his name deliberately facing Jack.

"Did you tell him about the video?" Jack scowled at the mug.

Lacey inhaled her mouthful of coffee and briefly choked. She'd actually forgotten the video in the events of last night.

"What video?"

Lacey told him the details, thankful she'd left the DVD at the police station. She knew Michael was going to demand to see it. She didn't think she could stomach watching it again.

"Where is it? Do you still have it?"

Did she know this man or what?

"I left it with—"

"I've got a copy on disc," Jack spoke up.

Lacey stared at Jack. When did he copy it? He shrugged at her. "Detective Lusco had made copies before we even watched it. I asked for one."

"I want to see it," Michael asserted.

Jack hopped up and headed for the TV in the adjacent family room.

Oh, God. Lacey dragged her feet, following him. She couldn't watch again.

Jack popped the disc in her DVD player as she slowly sat on the couch. Michael planted himself beside her and sat with his arms resting on his thighs, concentrating on the screen. Jack sat on her other side in the exact same posture.

"Wait." Jack put a hand on her arm. "You sure you want to see this again?"

Lacey shot off the couch. "No, actually I don't want to see it. I'll wait in the kitchen."

She busied herself in the kitchen, putting coffee cups away and wiping down counters that didn't need it. Anything to keep her mind from picturing what was on that disc.

"Jesus Christ."

She flinched at Michael's curse from the living room. An image of Suzanne's pregnant stomach flooded her and tears started to burn. She sniffed, rubbing at an invisible spot on her stove. What had Suzanne gone through back then? Horrors, she knew. Horrors she didn't want to picture.

"Oh, give me a fucking break."

What? Why was Michael…

Footsteps pounded toward her front door, and Lacey stepped into the living room just in time to see Michael step outside. He glanced over his shoulder, his eyes grim. "Stay safe, Lace." And closed the door behind him.

Jack sat on the couch, still watching the disc. On the TV screen, she saw Jack slam her truck door.

Aha. Michael had seen the kiss.

She marched over to Jack, hands on her hips, glaring. He had no idea what kind of friendship she had with Michael.

"*You* are such a jerk." She stated the words firmly in Jack's face.

"I didn't know he was going to react like that," Jack said. "But I'm not upset he saw it."

He really did look sincere, but Lacey shook her head at him and dashed after Michael.

By 8:00 a.m., Detective Callahan had been hard at work for two hours. He slammed down the receiver at his desk, another dead end. The man he'd been trying to locate had died in a hunting accident two years ago, and Mason had just upset the widow by asking to speak to him. He scowled at his list. He needed to run his list of contacts through some sort of death records before he made calls. It would be the polite thing to do. If he could figure out how to do it. Computers and he didn't mesh well together.

Mason was checking every cellmate or close associate DeCosta had in and outside prison, trying to find out whom DeCosta possibly had confided in. Maybe he'd revealed his hunting or killing techniques, or hinted at someone who would be willing to avenge his life sentences. Anything that would point them in the direction of another killer. So far, Mason was striking out. Ray was in charge of finding DeCosta's family; hopefully, he was having more luck.

He rubbed his eyes, tired of staring at the list. What a bunch of losers. The majority of the men were serving time. Several had been released from prison only to end up back in within a year. Each phone conversation had gone like this:

"You're a cop? Why the fuck do you think I'd tell you anything?"

Or a rendition of the same and then slam the phone.

One prisoner had been interested in talking. From his breathy voice and overuse of the word "fabulous," Mason had inferred the man was a flamer with a major crush on DeCosta. He'd blathered on and on how he'd admired the man and how ecstatic he'd been when they were assigned as cellmates. Dramatic sorrow had filled the flamer's voice as he related how DeCosta had ignored his advances. Then he'd continued in a much cheerier tone to describe his current boyfriend's finer points in descriptive details that made Mason flush and feel like he'd rolled in mud.

Overall, the call had given Mason nothing except a desperate need to exercise his heterosexuality. He'd taken a break and dashed down the block to flirt with the baristas at Starbucks. Now back to work and sipping on a venti coffee, he felt cleansed.

Mason eyed a fax from a buddy, Special Agent Jeff Hines, at the Portland FBI office. He'd put in a request for some profiling help on their killer, but the office was backed up and terrorism was number one on their priority list. They couldn't get anyone to him for a month or so.

Mason couldn't wait that long.

As a favor, Jeff had taken a quick look at their two recent cases and gave a general categorization of their killer as "organized." Meaning their killer was of good intelligence, socially competent, and planned the murders carefully. Jeff thought he was possibly highly intelligent with a masculine image. He was possibly charismatic, controlled his emotions during the crime, and probably had a high interest in the media response to the crime. This was in contrast to a "disorganized" serial killer who spontaneously carried out killings with sudden violence and a below-average intelligence.

This was supposed to help? Mason crumpled up the fax.

How about an address for the bastard?

Ray slid into his desk chair and laid his forehead on the closest stack of paperwork. His tie was shoved in a jacket pocket and his cuffs stained with ink. Apparently his search wasn't going any smoother. Mason had given him the shit task of finding the people he hadn't located right off the bat. It entailed a lot of online searching of public records and frustrating busywork, but Ray was more computer savvy than he was. Mason was lucky if he could check his e-mail.

"I can't find his family." Ray's voice was muffled by the stack of arrest records.

"What do you mean?

"They seemed to have vanished out of Oregon and off the planet." Ray lifted his head and Mason cringed at his bloodshot eyes. They looked like a road map. Too much time staring at the computer screen.

Mason thought on the family for a minute. "You checked death records?"

The look Ray shot him stated Mason was an idiot. "Of course. First thing. Why wouldn't I?"

Mason shrugged. "Just checking." He flipped to the copy of DeCosta's birth certificate in his binder.

Dave DeCosta's birth certificate was blank where the father's name should be.

Mason was positive that DeCosta wasn't the result of an immaculate conception.

The blank space usually meant the mother wasn't sure who the father was, hated the jerk, or the bastard had cleared out before the birth. It created a big hole on the paternity side of Ray's hunting list where uncles or grandparents would usually be. "The family's got to be somewhere."

"All dead on the mother's side. She was an only child." Ray raised a brow and said succinctly, "I found the death records of her parents." Mason made no comment and Ray went on. "I've talked with some neighbors. They don't remember much."

"She probably remarried and changed her name." Mason was grabbing at straws. The mother had been an insecure clinger who never looked anyone in the eye and mumbled when she talked. She had always clung to the arm of the closest cop. She'd driven the task force crazy. Mason doubted any man would decide to marry her. Unless a man wanted a woman who looked like the world had chewed her up, spit her out, and kicked out her teeth. All of them.

Lack of teeth was a big turnoff to him.

"If she remarried, she didn't do it legally. I keep hitting dead ends in that area too."

The relatives of Dave DeCosta didn't even come close to the sketchy profile from the FBI. Charismatic? Socially confident?

Churning these facts in his mind, Mason unscrewed his pen, separated the pieces and then reassembled them. His fingers needed to keep moving. "What'd you find out about Suzanne Mills's ring?"

Ray consulted his notebook of bird tracks. "Her mother says it definitely looks like Mills's ring. She had no idea what happened to it after her daughter vanished. She never saw it again and had assumed Suzanne was wearing it at the time." He flipped a page. "No fingerprints on the ring other than partials of Dr. Campbell's. Oh, and Dr. Campbell says she can't find her own ring from that championship year. She's wondering if someone stole her ring out of her home." Ray sighed. "Dr. Campbell has no idea when it could have disappeared. She hasn't worn the ring in years."

Mason rubbed the back of his neck. Two rings. What a mess.

Ray grabbed at his cell as it vibrated across his desk. "Lusco." He paused. "You're absolutely sure?" Ray flipped to a clean page in his notebook and covered the mouthpiece, looking at Mason through strained eyes.

"He's killed another one."

CHAPTER NINETEEN

Police cars jam-packed Barrington Drive. No civilian cars had been allowed into the upscale neighborhood. He surveyed the scene, standing with the group of neighbors and reporters who crowded as close as possible to the yellow crime scene tape. A blue uniform dotted the tape every six feet. How many police did you need when the victim was already dead?

He tucked away his grin. It was the notoriety of the murder that was bringing cops out of the woodwork. Where were they when the victim screamed for two hours straight?

Only murder would keep spectators out on the street in this icy weather. He shivered. Occasional flurries dropped from the gray sky, but mainly the wind pelted and froze the crowd.

He turned to the older woman next to him who wore a red Trail Blazers stocking cap. She was tall and bent with age, but animation filled her narrow face as she scanned the street. She yapped on her cell phone, gushing in amazement that a murder had happened across the street.

"Did you know the deceased?" He liked the word deceased. It sounded professional. According to the phony badge clipped to his coat, he was Jeff Thomas and worked for the *Portland Tribune* weekly newspaper. He gave her a warm smile.

She frowned at his question, annoyed at the interruption, but she glanced at his credentials, his ready pen and notepad. Her eyes grew greedy and she thawed under his interested gaze.

"Gotta go, Shirl. The press wants to talk to me." She slipped the phone in the pocket of the velvet bathrobe she wore beneath her bulky ski jacket and gave him her full attention.

"Did you know Richard Buck?" He repeated the question and watched the woman's eyes sparkle with the need to gossip. What a nice guy. Someone should give him a medal for making the senior's day.

"Of course I did. I've lived across the street from him for years." She pointed at her mini-mansion with the seven bird-baths spotting the front yard. He blinked as he noticed each one had the snow cleaned out and had been filled with fresh water. How'd she keep the water from freezing? Brightly colored bird feeders dangled from every branch of her birch trees.

She noticed his stare. "Someone's gotta feed the birds when it snows. They don't all fly south for the winter, you know," she said sharply.

He doubted she took the feeders down in the summer.

Her ritzy neighbors must love her. The homeowners' association apparently forgot to add a clause about bird feeders and bad taste.

He turned back to her and showed his perfect teeth. "That's very kind of you. Did you hear or see anything unusual in the last twelve hours?"

"Twelve hours ago? Is that when it happened?"

He caught his breath at the slip. "I overheard a cop mention the time frame." He shrugged a shoulder. "I don't know how accurate it is." *Yes, he did.*

"Nope, didn't hear a thing. Did see the UPS man ring the bell early this morning. He dropped off that package and left." She pointed across the street at the cops swarming the mansion. The UPS box still sat near the door. Nearby, two detectives were having a heated discussion, gesturing at the box, their faces tense.

He remembered hearing the doorbell ring. It'd startled him for the briefest moment. He'd peeked through the upstairs blinds and seen the familiar brown truck, its driver jogging back to his vehicle in the icy cold. He'd finished his work and slipped out of the house minutes later.

His source kept talking. "Buck worked on some big cases over the years. He defended that serial killer down in Corvallis. You know, the one who killed all those college girls. He did a good job in that one. Got that murdering ass dumped in prison." She cackled.

He took a second look at the two arguing detectives and recognized them from the previous body discoveries. He made a mental note to get their names and send them a gift for all their hard work. That's what a good citizen would do. The police were vastly underappreciated.

"They say Buck's legs were broken. Just like that old cop the other day and the other murdered lawyer from that same serial killer case." She leaned close and whispered, eyes darting about to check for eavesdroppers. "Somebody's taking revenge for putting that killer in prison." She nodded emphatically.

"Yes, that's what I'm starting to think too." How had the broken legs information spread so fast? As far as he could tell, the police weren't divulging a word about the body to the crowd on the street, but gory details had a way of jumping from mouth to ear.

His chest puffed out and he straightened his back. This was perfect. Exactly what he'd planned. The public was getting sucked in and the police were clueless. He wondered when the fishing supplies would become part of the public's knowledge.

Hard to kill someone with a fishing rod, but he liked to use something close to the victim, something that reflected their livelihood or favorite hobby. He'd done the best he could with the rod and tried to be creative with the fishhooks. Earlier he'd seen three green-faced cops stumble out the front door and heave in the bushes, so he figured he'd done pretty well. He eyed the detectives on the porch who were still gesturing at the box. They probably thought it was a bomb.

Hmmm. He hadn't fiddled with packaged explosives in a long time. At one time he'd been fascinated with them. Mix a few things together, package it just right, and KABOOM. What a rush. Stumps, mailboxes, and even a couple of cats had been victims of his exploding experiments. As he remembered his last explosives victim, his gut churned woozily.

It had been that teenage bitch's fault. The one who'd laughed in his face in high school when he'd offered to help her with a science project. He'd known she was failing the course and thought she'd be grateful for help from the class genius. How wrong he'd been. She'd recoiled from him like she feared catching his nerdiness. Then she'd laughed at him. And told her friends, who laughed. *High school sluts.* They always were strutting around, flashing hints of their bras and panties through their clothing, and then they'd snub and scorn anyone caught by their trampy lures.

He'd planted the explosive on her front porch. It'd been a work of art. He'd been so proud of it and he'd spent hours meticulously putting it together. The goal had been to pay her back for the laughter, scare her a little, that's all. He hadn't known the house would catch fire and her baby sister would die. The slut never came back to school. The rumors said her parents had moved as far away as possible from the memories. Kids at school had whispered behind their hands and given him a wide berth for months afterward. Some had known he experimented with explosives. All knew she'd humiliated him.

Many times he'd visited the tiny grave and stood there uncomfortably, feet shifting, staring at the small headstone, wondering if the baby had suffered. The guilt had surprised him. Back then, he hadn't known he had a soft spot for babies.

"Do you know Tony McDaniels?"

He'd forgotten the old woman and jerked his head back toward her. "Who?"

Her eyes glanced at his badge again and narrowed. The neurons in that brain were sharper than he'd given her credit for. "Tony McDaniels. He writes sports for the *Tribune*. He's my grandnephew."

"Ohh. *That* Tony. Of course. I'll tell him we met." He glanced at his watch. "I need to get going. Thanks for your help." Bits of tingling stress touched the base of his spine. He had to get away before she whipped out her cell and called her grandnephew to tell him she'd met Jeff Thomas. He took two steps backward and spun around.

"My name's Evelyn Wakefield," she hollered after him, shouting out the spelling of her last name.

Not turning back, he raised a hand in acknowledgment, hoping no one was paying attention to his hasty exit down the sidewalk. Was he was moving too fast? He slowed down to pretend to write some notes, looking from the house to his notebook a few times like he was writing a description. He noticed one of the detectives glance his way and then turn back to the package.

He'd pushed his luck. Why'd he detour from the original plan? *Stupid, stupid, stupid.*

The urge to see the aftermath had been too strong. The power still tingled in his fingers. Seeing the cops confused and the crowd excited. *He'd done that.* Everyone wanted to know who he was.

He stopped and exhaled deeply, eradicating the poisonous pride from his system. He had to exercise better control if he was going to succeed.

He wouldn't make a mistake again.

Against his better judgment, Mason had decided to open the package on the site. The bomb squad had x-rayed it and cleared it, and he'd waited until someone who knew what they were doing showed up. He watched the woman photograph, dust the shiny tape, take trace evidence, and then carefully open the box. The UPS label was addressed to the victim. The return address was a PO box in Portland.

He and Lusco had argued about opening it. Lusco had wanted to take it back to the lab. Mason wanted it open here and now. The crime scene tech didn't want to open it at the scene either, but Mason overruled her. The slaying inside the mansion had shown all the same characteristics of Trenton's and Cochran's murder scenes, except for one: a physical connection to a previous crime.

Their guy liked to leave things behind. Trenton's badge at the Mills scene. Trenton's hair at the Cochran scene. Even the video on Dr. Campbell's porch and the ring in her lab coat.

All Mason's senses screamed to rip open the box. He shifted weight from one foot to the other and repeated the movement. Lusco shot him an odd look, probably wondering if he needed to use the john. Mason stopped and twisted his fists inside his overcoat pockets. His breath steamed in the air.

What the hell was going on? This was looking like the third murder related to that damned serial killer DeCosta. Someone was definitely making a point. The broken femurs on each body were deliberately telling the police that the same person was murdering each man.

Had they put away the wrong man back then? Missed an accomplice? And who was next?

The questions were starting to haunt him in his sleep. He clenched his teeth. The little dentist could be next. She'd played a big role in putting DeCosta away. Thank God the presiding trial judge, Stanley Williams, had died a few years ago. At least that was one less person to worry about.

They'd warned Richard Buck two days ago. Suggested he take a vacation or get out of town for a few days. Just like they'd warned Dr. Campbell. But Buck had been in the middle of an important trial. He'd laughed at Mason's suggestion that someone else finish the trial.

Mason bet Buck believed him now.

Finally. The package was coming open. God, she was slow! He ducked his head and flexed his hands. The tech was doing her job and she was doing it right. But damn it, he knew there was something in there.

Several of the neighbors had told the police they'd seen the UPS truck. They'd all thought it looked legit, not fishy at all. The delivery would be easy enough to check on. The company was so computerized, they knew where everything was and when. Mason knew it would check out as a normal delivery, but the return address would be bogus—the package dropped off at a mailing center.

He bent and peered over the tech's shoulder. And felt no surprise at the sight. There was a baggie of hair that he knew would belong to Joseph Cochran, but in the baggie something gold glinted. The tech lifted the bag to eye level with long tweezers.

Mason stared at the gold ring inside the plastic and felt his heart stop. He knew the ring would have Dr. Campbell's initials. Another connection.

Shit.

Pulling out his cell phone, he whirled to the uniform on the porch and pointed. "Get a patrol car over to Dr. Campbell's house. Have him check on her, plant his ass in front of her house, and not move until we get there." He glanced up at the defense attorney's gigantic home as his phone speed-dialed Dr. Campbell. "Tell him we're going to be a while."

CHAPTER TWENTY

Mount Junction was tinted with all the shades between white and gray. White snow covered the surrounding mountain range and dark gray gunk covered the snowbanks along the lighter gray streets. It was the largest town for a hundred miles in the lower corner of Oregon. A town built around its university. The university was the biggest employer in the county, and the rest of the population either ranched or provided support services for the students, like restaurants and clothing stores. Mount Junction's reputation was conservative, a reflection of the school that was proud to be red in the prominently blue state. Michael had noticed immediately that these Southeast Oregonians were significantly more talented at driving in poor winter conditions than Portlanders. Snow was a way of life out here.

·   The heat cranked, Michael sat in his rented four-wheel drive and studied his map. He wanted to get in and get out of this part of the state as fast as possible. He hadn't liked leaving Lacey alone with Jack Harper. Michael shouldn't care whom Lacey kissed, but this guy was different. Harper had inserted himself in her circle and extended an overprotective shield that was Michael's by right. No doubt Jack was going to look out for her and do his damndest to keep her safe, but that didn't mean he had to like the guy.

Damn it, he was getting distracted. "Concentrate," Michael muttered. *Get it done and get back to her.*

Lacey wasn't his anymore. Michael knew that. But that hadn't changed all the dynamics of their relationship. She still fussed at him like a worried sister and he looked out for her like an older brother. But if she ever showed signs of wanting to go back to the way things had once been...he'd be ready. Their short time as a couple had been the most important relationship in his life. There'd been fireworks. In bed and out. It was the fireworks outside of bed that had caused her to put an end to their dating. He'd been steamed, but he'd gotten over it. He'd learned to bite his tongue and wait. But this thing with Harper was different, and it was causing a stir in the pit of his stomach.

Michael shook the map and exhaled hard. Focus.

He'd found a willing contact with the local police who'd agreed to dig up the official report on the accidental death of Amy Smith, the Mount Junction gymnast who'd driven her car into a river. Michael had done his own research on the accident, but had run into a problem trying to dig into her background. Too many damn Smiths in Oregon. The source had promised to e-mail him everything on the case and what pieces he could find of the girl's personal history. Michael especially wanted to see the autopsy report.

He couldn't get those broken femurs out of his mind. Amy's, Suzanne's, and now three men in the Portland area. All with breaks in the same places.

Michael was searching the map for the site where Amy's car had been found. According to newspaper reports, she'd driven into the river and had been washed out of her car into the rough, rocky river. The car had remained, half stuck in the muddy bank until boaters had spotted it the next day. Three weeks later, the body had turned up a mile down the river. The young couple who'd stumbled over Amy's remains at a riverside campsite hadn't realized it was human at first.

Michael wanted to stand on the ground where Amy had vanished and try to imagine what could have happened that day. The campsite where her remains had been found would be next. Relying on photos and hearsay wasn't good enough for him. He preferred going straight to the source, seeing it for himself.

The map led him three miles out of Mount Junction on a winding, snow-packed road to the spot where her vehicle had been found. He could have used directions off the GPS, but he wanted to study the topography of the area and get a feel for the surrounding landscape. Nothing felt better than a real map in his hands.

He parked his truck along the old road and hiked the quarter mile to the river. The snow was a foot and a half deep and he was sweating by the time he reached the bank. He cursed. The accident had occurred in the spring. How was he supposed to picture it accurately at this time of year? Everything was blanketed.

Slowly, he turned in a full circle, taking in the beauty of the site. He eyed the narrow trail he'd plowed from the road and frowned. Amy Smith drove a quarter mile off the road and into the river? Large boulders and clumps of evergreens edged his trail as it meandered to the river. Apparently she'd avoided hitting those but couldn't avoid the water. Had she been drunk? No one remembered seeing her earlier in the day. No one had realized she was missing until her little Corolla had been spotted in the water.

The bank of the river sloped down steeply from where he stood. He estimated the distance from the bank crest to the water as twenty feet. No way could she have gotten her car back up the hill. Maybe she'd tried to get out of the car and gotten caught in the current. Could she have waded to shore if she wasn't hurt too badly?

Looking up at the snowy mountains around him, he realized the water had to be near-freezing temperatures, even in the spring. Plunging into icy water could shock the breath out of anyone. An icy shiver shot down his legs and into his frozen hiking boots. He'd been swept into freezing water before. His body clenched as he remembered his plunge into liquid ice. He'd stupidly hung on to a crab pot as it'd swung from the crab boat deck back over the ocean and then lost his grip. If it hadn't been for the fast-acting crew and captain, he'd be a human iceberg in the Bering Sea. Almost no one survived a tumble into those waters.

He pulled his gaze from the dark water, rubbed his hands together, and fought to slow his heart rate, channeling his thoughts in a different direction. Was this public land or privately owned? On the opposite bank, about a mile away, a barn stood cold and lifeless. A fence had once stood between the barn and river but was now a spotty line of crumbling, rotted wood. He needed to do a property search.

Pulling up the warm collar of his heavy jacket to protect his neck, he trudged back to his truck. Snow started to lightly fall, creating a hazy Christmas card out of the dreary landscape. Stopping, he turned for one last view of the deadly gray river and wondered if he was chasing a ghost.

Michael downed the scalding coffee as he paged through a property search. The heat in his hotel room was turned to the maximum, but he still had icy toes. The trip to the campsite where Amy's remains had been found was a bust. The grounds had been closed and the access road gated for the winter. He'd debated parking and hiking the road to the campsite, but it was nearly two miles to the river from the gate. Besides, the snowfall had surged into heavy curtains of winter white, and he'd been hungry. He made a mental note to check Google Earth. Maybe he could find some bird's-eye photos of the area.

His eyes skimmed through the property search website as he sought to discover who owned the land around the river. He scrolled down through the legalese and spotted the owner's name in the middle of the page. His breath caught and the gears in his brain turned in a new direction. It was definitely not public land. Where he'd stood this morning was part of a 260-acre parcel of private property belonging to Joseph and Anna Stevenson.

Lacey's ex-in-laws.

Never piss off a reporter.

Jack slammed the paper on his desk and tried to call Michael at the newspaper. Jack's secretary, Janice, had uneasily delivered the afternoon edition of *The Oregonian*. She'd run down to a newsstand and bought a copy after her mother had called to say her boss was on the front page.

Brody was working his butt off, digging into Jack's past. The blasted article detailed Jack's long-ago interview with the Corvallis police when he'd been questioned in the original campus murders. All the facts were accurate, but that didn't mean he liked seeing it on the front page.

Brody's voice mail said he was out of town as Jack remembered that last night Lacey had asked Brody about his trip to Mount Junction today. How long was the reporter supposed to be gone? Jack rubbed the back of his neck as he hung up. He leaned back in his chair and glared at the silent phone. Now what? He couldn't do nothing, but he wasn't about to ask Lacey for Brody's cell number. He still felt kind of bad about the DVD incident.

She'd told him to leave her house at four this morning, lecturing him about her relationship with that reporter. He wouldn't have left, but she'd immediately called her father to come stay with her, and he'd been there within minutes. In the first ten seconds of her rant, he'd learned that Michael Brody was one of her closest friends whom she protected like an angry mother goose. A goose might be smaller than you, but when it was ticked off, honking loudly, and coming at you, you ran in the opposite direction.

He'd get back in her good graces. Somehow.

At least he'd learned she and Brody weren't dating or something.

Jack put the early-morning embarrassment out of his brain and refocused on the article. Of course, the paper reported that Jack stated he'd had nothing to do with the body in the foundation of one of his buildings. It also said Jack hadn't been charged with any crime and he'd been cooperating fully with every police request. He should be pleased, right?

But then the paper listed his connections to the old crimes.

It stated he'd owned the old apartment building at the time of the original crimes. Not quite factual, he mused, twisting his lips. Technically his father had owned it back then. Jack had attended OSU at the time of the first disappearances. That was true, but almost a third of the local college grads in Oregon went to OSU.

It stated he'd dated athletes at college. All the women who disappeared were blonde athletes. Brody had dug up a quote from some anonymous source that said Jack had dated blondes exclusively in college. He scowled. *All his girlfriends back then were blonde?* He thought hard and couldn't seem to come up with an exception. That didn't mean he murdered them.

Lacey. Blonde. Athlete. *Shit.* He threw the paper in his trash and turned his chair to stare out the window at the mountain.

He mentally reviewed the article some more. After reading it five times, he'd committed it to memory.

And Hillary Roske.

Jack dug the front page back out of the trashcan and studied her old picture, searching for memories of their time together. He couldn't come up with many. She'd been a pretty girl, sweet. But the relationship wasn't a good match from the beginning.

Her eyes looked back at his, silent, accusing. He remembered being compelled to help find her abductor all those years ago. When he'd worked for the Lakefield PD, she'd always been in the back of his mind. Along with all the other girls.

Now the old cases were back in the limelight and his name had erupted out of the archives like a submerged cork bobbing to the surface. He screwed his eyes shut but still saw Hillary's perky smile.

He'd dealt with a little bad press before, usually just letting it roll off his back. It naturally came with the territory of being a big, visible company. He didn't take it personally. He couldn't if he planned to stay focused on the company. He was proud of the projects they built and proud of where he'd led the business after his father stepped down. If people were jealous of his success, they could get over it.

But this was different.

He opened one eye as the phone rang. He'd told Janice to hold his calls after the third damned reporter had called. This must be important. Janice's voice came through the intercom.

"It's Bill Hendricks, Jack. I thought you'd want to talk to him."

"Yeah, I'd better take his call. Thanks, Janice."

He set the paper aside and ran his hands through his hair, making the short black spikes stand even straighter. Hendricks was a straight shooter and one of Harper Developing's biggest accounts at the moment. He and Jack were deep in planning for a condo tower in the hot South Waterfront area. It was promising to be some of Portland's priciest living space. Jack reached for the receiver. Blunt honesty was always best when speaking with Bill Hendricks. The man could smell a lie from six feet under.

"Morning, Bill."

"Jack! What the hell's going on?" Jack wrenched the phone from his ear at the roar. Yep, no words minced here.

"Exactly what the paper said, Bill. They found a body in one of the old complexes I own down in Lakefield."

"Did you stash that body there?" The old man's voice was powerful. Powerful mad.

"Christ, Bill! Of course not! You think I'd do something like that?" Jack tried not to laugh at the lack of guile in the crusty man.

"No I don't. But I had to ask and hear what you had to say about it." Thankfully, Bill's voice dropped in volume. "I've had three contractors call me already, concerned I'll back out of the tower project based on a few lousy articles in *The Oregonian*. Don't people think for themselves anymore? Anyone who knows you knows this story's a bunch of donkey crap."

Donkey crap? If there was one person he wanted on his side, it was Bill Hendricks. The man's words were as good as gold in this state and could go a long way in spinning Jack's crumbling public image.

Jack hung up the phone after another minute of Bill's monologue, rubbing absently at the deadened patch of skin on his right thigh. If Bill Hendricks was running into people questioning his company's business future, then other people were having doubts. This rotten publicity was going to be a bitch to handle. How much permanent damage had Michael Brody done to Harper Developing?

"Mr. Harper, your sister's on line two."

"Thanks, Janice." He'd forgotten to tell Janice not to put Melody's calls through too. She probably wanted him to make an appearance at some benefit or had a philanthropy check to cosign. No one was better at spending the company money for good causes than his older sister. Reluctantly he picked up the line.

After Melody's call, he sat back in his chair, unable to fight the grin spreading across his face. One of his problems was on the way to being solved. Fate had just handed him a golden opportunity and he was going to take full advantage of it.

He had a fancy party to go to.

In the early evening's darkening hours, Lacey dashed to the gymnastics academy, finally escaping from the cop who'd sat outside her house all day. He'd hung around until Detective Callahan had called back, updating her on the body found that morning. Attorney Richard Buck had been murdered. Another link to DeCosta. Lacey glanced over her shoulder in the dim parking lot as she left her truck. She'd been twitchy all day, but she wasn't going to hide under the bed.

Again, the detective suggested she leave town. She told him she'd spend the night at her father's place. Tomorrow she was attending a fundraiser at Portland's luxurious Benson Hotel. Maybe she'd get a room there afterward.

Callahan told her Frank had been released from jail, and Lacey said again that she didn't want to press charges. She wasn't scared of Frank; she simply didn't want to deal with him. And she had a hunch he'd learned his lesson. He'd never spent the night in jail before, and she knew the memory would stick with him awhile. What would his patients think if they knew he'd been in jail for assaulting his ex?

She might drop that threat in Frank's ear if he whined.

Lacey pushed open the heavy door to the gym and inhaled the distinctive smell of disinfectant and sweaty bodies. Her body relaxed at the odor. There was a harmony, a coherence that calmed her whenever she entered a gym; she was in her element. Tiny muscular girls and boys worked the equipment. Shouts of encouragement and rock music from a floor routine echoed off the walls. Her practiced eye followed a teen on the beam.

Between throwing Jack out of her house that morning, Michael's furious departure, that nasty morning article on page one, Richard Buck's death, and the topper of her ring being found at the new murder site, she'd become a mental mess. She'd struggled to think straight. She hadn't wanted to think at all. Her first instinct had been to crawl in bed and put reality at bay with a few mind-numbing pills. It'd taken a lot of strength not to do so. She'd held the bottle of Xanax in her hand for five minutes before putting it back on the shelf, recognizing the signs of a depressive downswing. She'd known her best bet was to throw herself out of the house and get some exercise, hence her escape to the gym. If she'd crawled into bed, it might have been days before she emerged. Unacceptable. She had to find out the truth about Suzanne.

How could Michael print another story about Jack? She shook her head. The article was accurate, of course. Michael wouldn't print a story without first triple-checking every fact. At least the article had been in the paper's late edition. Its circulation was a fraction of the morning edition. Lacey crossed her fingers that a new flashy story would push Jack's name off tomorrow morning's front page.

Michael had been more than a little irrational when he'd stormed out of her house after seeing the kiss on the disc. She'd chased him out to his vehicle and banged on the window, but he'd simply shaken his head at her, obviously not wanting to talk, and had driven off.

Michael was lucky he was out of state tonight. She was going to throttle him next time she saw him. He was acting like a spoiled kid who didn't want anyone else playing with his toys.

Little arms wrapped around her thighs and Lacey bent down to give Megan a hug. She'd been teaching tiny tot tumbling once a week for three years now and loved every minute of it. Four-year-olds percolated with energy and life. Each week Lacey would create a different obstacle course that involved basic tumbling skills and games. Zealously, her class would tackle the challenge as she spotted them at the trickier spots. Leaping into the giant pit of sponges, jumping on the trampoline, skipping on the low balance beam.

They always made her laugh. It was always the highlight of her week.

"Hey."

Lacey turned to find Kelly Cates regarding her with a touch of trepidation and curiosity. Kelly and her husband Chris owned the gymnastics academy.

"How are you doing?" Kelly's voice was soft as she pulled Lacey close for a long hug. She'd always been a quiet person. Over the years the woman had lost that conditioned gymnast look. She'd rounded out slightly but still had the pixie face and bobbed blonde hair from long ago.

"All right, I guess. I don't know what the hell is going on from one minute to the next," Lacey answered.

Kelly had been on the Southeast Oregon University Gymnastics team with Lacey and had discovered her bleeding on the sidewalk as she'd run to catch up with Lacey and Suzanne. Kelly was supposed to walk to the restaurant with Chris, but he'd changed his plans, so Kelly had been far behind the two girls that dreadful night. She was still one of Lacey's closest friends. Up there with Michael and Amelia.

What would've happened if Kelly and Chris had been right behind them that night? Would Suzanne still be here?

She dropped the thought. *Been there, done that.*

She smiled at Kelly and greeted another child begging for her attention.

Resentment at Kelly and Chris for not being there when she needed them was something Lacey had struggled to overcome for years. Deep down she knew it wasn't their fault, but at one time she'd been looking for anyone to blame.

Lacey was envious of the relationship Kelly shared with Chris. They'd dated all through college, just like Lacey and Frank. They'd had their rocky moments in the beginning of the relationship, but Chris was a wonderful man and their marriage lasted. He worshiped the ground Kelly walked on.

Kelly glanced around and lowered her voice. "The police called me about my testimony in the DeCosta trial." Kelly never saw the attack or the man. All she had testified about was Lacey's condition when she'd found her. "They think I need to be careful. They said this killer seems to be working down a list of those involved in the DeCosta trial." Her eyes dilated and her voice wavered the slightest bit.

"Definitely be careful, Kelly. Don't go anywhere alone and keep your doors locked tight. Might be a good time to go visit your mom in Nevada?"

Kelly nodded. "I'll mention it to Chris."

"I'm having a security system installed as soon as possible and I'm staying at my dad's tonight."

"Aren't you scared?" Kelly asked.

Lacey didn't get a chance to answer. A tall muscular man had snuck up and wrapped his arms around both women's shoulders, squeezing them in a bear hug. "How're my two favorite women?" Lacey stiffened and her breath shot out of her. Chris.

She was jumping at shadows.

Lacey punched him lightly in the chest with a shaky arm. Chris was an affectionate kind of guy. Good-looking with naturally tanned skin and reddish-brown hair, he attracted attention from women of all ages, but he had eyes only for Kelly.

"I guess I need to correct that. Sorry Lace, you take third place behind Jessica."

Lacey was relieved he hadn't notice her start. "I can handle that." Jessica was their only child and was spoiled horribly. "How's she doing? No interest in gymnastics yet?" Lacey knew the fourth grader hated the sport.

Kelly rolled her eyes. "She acts like it's toxic or something. All she likes is soccer. She's taking after her dad."

Chris had played professional soccer for a few years after college. When he blew out a knee, Kelly convinced him to help her open the gym. Surprisingly, he enjoyed coaching a different sport and had an excellent eye for gymnastics. Probably from all the years he spent watching Kelly practice and compete.

"Jess would love to see you, Lacey. Could you come for dinner tomorrow night?"

"I can't. Tomorrow's that fundraiser for the Portland Dental Van project. I can't miss it."

Kelly nodded, but her eyes still held a trace of worry.

"What's your take on all these deaths, Lace?" Chris's brown gaze was unnaturally serious.

"I hate it. The police are warning everyone who was involved in the trial and digging up DeCosta's past, trying to see who might do a revenge or copycat killing."

"What about that guy in the paper?" Chris asked. "The one Michael wrote about? Are they going to arrest him? He's got too many links to the old murders and to the new ones. How freaky is that?"

"Jack Harper hasn't done anything. He doesn't have any motivation and there's no reason to arrest him." Lacey defended him, but her heart sank a little. She'd been caught off guard by some of the revelations in the article. But he'd stood by her as they showed the police that tape, and he definitely had good instincts about her ex-husband. Plus, she felt safe around him.

To her, that carried the most weight.

CHAPTER TWENTY-ONE

Jack ran a finger between his neck and the collar of his tux and tugged. Usually the formal clothes didn't bother him, but tonight was different. He felt out of his environment at this charity event, adrift. He hadn't seen Lacey since she'd thrown him out of her house yesterday for harassing that damned reporter. He knew she was coming to the party tonight. His sister had confirmed her name on the guest list.

Jack had forgotten about the fundraiser. He always forgot formal events until his always-efficient sister would call the day before and remind him. He believed Melody's phone call yesterday was fate offering him a chance to see Lacey on neutral ground. *Damn it.* He tugged at his collar again. He wasn't in control of the situation and was grabbing his opportunities where they came.

He strolled the hotel ballroom, seeking distraction and looking for a certain petite blonde. Melody had done an impressive job as usual. Her fundraising and organization skills were legendary. A miniature orchestra filled one end of the giant room. Swags of silver and black fabric graced the walls and complemented the existing elaborate moldings. Fresh white roses and every other white flower he couldn't name were displayed in intricate arrangements along the walls of the ballroom.

The theme was Under the Moon and the dress code was black and white. Most of the guests had followed the rules, but he saw a few siren-red dresses here and there. Nothing like a black-and-white party for a woman to make a statement.

The party was to raise funds for the Portland Dental Van project. Run by a nonprofit medical organization, the van was actually a pair of gigantic RVs that traveled the state bringing dental care to low-income areas.

Every person he spoke with had perfect teeth. Jack stopped at the bar and ordered a drink.

"Jack. Over here. I want you to meet someone." Melody Harper tucked her hand through his arm and anchored him in place. His sister looked good. At forty-two her figure was slim and her face wrinkle-free. He suspected she liked to cheat nature a little bit. Melody was tall with dark brown hair and eyes that'd charmed many a man. She'd been divorced twice. Both men she'd married turned out to be fortune hunters.

Jack gave a last quick glance around for Lacey and put on a polite face for Melody's guests. The gray-haired man and woman turned out to be the founders of the dental nonprofit. Trying not to stare at the man's crooked, yellowed teeth, Jack rescinded his earlier generalization about perfect teeth and chatted with the Hamptons while Melody preened on his arm, delighted with her success.

He felt Melody tense and lose focus on the conversation. Turning to see whom she had in her sights now, Jack met a glaring brown gaze, fifteen feet away, which flickered from him to Melody and back again.

He caught his breath. Lacey's simple black dress hooked behind her neck, leaving her shoulders bare and accentuating her curves in all the right places. She'd pulled her hair up into a soft twist at the back of her head and her diamond studs looked bigger than Melody's. His gaze traveled down, past the hem just above her knees, and past the toned calves to spike heels that looked sharp enough to maim. Overall, she was stunning, and by the slant of her eyes, he knew she was still annoyed with him.

He didn't care. All he wanted to do was sink his fingers into her hair and release the twist, letting it spill over her shoulders. A flick of his finger at the back of her neck would drop the entire dress to her deadly shoes. He swallowed hard and tried to ignore the electricity that hit his chest, lighting every nerve and tightening his grip on his glass.

Lacey couldn't have known he'd be here. Seeing him must be a total shock. Good. She'd be a little off guard. He couldn't have set the stage for their impromptu meeting any better. Now he just had to whip her away to dance and grovel out an apology. What could happen after that…?

"Ah, fuck."

Lacey had turned away, giving him a startling view of her backless dress. It barely covered her ass and made Jack's hormones stand at attention. But it was the tall man who'd handed her a drink and took her arm that'd staggered Jack.

What the hell? Jack's heart gave a stumbling thud.

The prick held up his glass in a silent toast in Jack's direction. "Who is that? Why's she staring at you like that?" Melody's protective older-sister instinct had been lit.

"I know them," he muttered. Wasn't the reporter supposed to be out of town? The guest list had shown Lacey and her father together. Jack had stupidly assumed they'd come together.

Melody studied the pair with assessing eyes. Jack knew she was estimating the cost of Lacey's dress and jewelry. "He looks familiar. I think he works for the paper. I've seen him before, but I don't know his date." She cast a side-glance at her brother. "Apparently you do."

The Hamptons excused themselves and wandered off.

Michael pulled Lacey toward the dance floor. "God damned fu…"

"Jack!" Melody rapidly glanced around. "Watch your language! What is your problem with that couple?"

Jack closed his mouth. He didn't know where to start. His perfect game plan had just warped into a clusterfuck.

Jack took Lacey's breath away. The sight of that man in a tux was what a bad girl's dreams were made of. His shoulders were wide, his stance self-confident, and those gray eyes burned hot holes in hers. How could cool gray project so much heat? If she was a bad girl, she'd seduce him under his date's nose without a second thought to how the other woman felt. The look in his eyes said all she had to do was crook her little finger and he'd be hers for the night.

What if her date eyed another woman the way Jack was eyeing her? Lacey would be furious. She should've known he dated other women. A man like him attracted beautiful women like hungry bunnies to a fresh carrot.

Where was her brain?

She wasn't a one-night stand kind of girl. No matter how tempting...

She swallowed the sour disappointment in the back of her throat. They'd had what...one unofficial date? A group interview with the police? One kiss? She didn't have any claim to him. Why shouldn't he date? He'd never officially asked her out. *Ah, hell.*

They were simply two people connected by unusual circumstances. That's all.

She felt Michael approach and pulled her gaze away from Jack's. *Who was the woman with Jack?* She was beautiful with an expensive dress and shoes and she was hanging on Jack's arm with the attitude of a woman who knew him extremely well.

Michael handed her some champagne. "Don't look at him," he murmured close to her ear. "Let's dance."

She nodded dumbly and cast one last look over her shoulder as Michael pulled her away.

Why was Jack here? Lacey had been a sponsor of the Dental Van Project for three years, and she'd never seen him attend the fundraiser before. It must be his date. She'd probably dragged him to the fete.

Lacey didn't get a chance to sip her champagne before Michael handed it back to a waiter and spun her out on the dance floor. She caught her breath and smiled weakly at him, thankful for his attention and relieved to move her feet after those uncomfortable long seconds. Michael was one of those unusual men who danced well and actually enjoyed it. His hand on her bare back was warm, and Lacey felt her stiff spine relax.

"Did you know he'd be here?" Lacey couldn't say his name.

"No. But I'm not surprised he's here."

She tilted her head back to look at Michael. "What do you mean?" Had Jack found out she was coming and decided to show up? Her heart rate doubled.

Michael was silent for a second. "His date is one of the premier fundraiser divas in the city." His words were short, clipped.

"Oh." Her shoulders wilted a bit.

They slowly twirled about the floor, neither speaking. With Michael she didn't feel obligated to make small talk. He was always cozy and comfortable. Sort of like her cats.

A dancing couple brushed against them and Lacey glanced up in time to see her father close by with a young woman in his arms. James Campbell looked fantastic in his tux. "I'll see you at the apartment tonight?" her father asked.

Lacey nodded.

Her father looked directly at Michael. "Keep her safe."

"Of course, sir."

Her father spun his dance partner away.

The sight sparked a smile on Lacey's lips.

"He's having a wonderful time."

"He's in his element in a social situation like this." Michael paused as he watched the couple. "Your mother would have hated this place."

Lacey laughed. Michael was so right. Her mother never had patience with glitzy fundraisers. Lacey's smile faded a bit at the memory of her mother.

"Do you want to leave?"

Her chin came up.

"No. Absolutely not."

"Good." Michael stared over her shoulder. "But you better put on a happy face."

"Why?"

"Could I dance with Lacey?" A familiar low voice spoke behind her.

They stopped moving and Lacey felt heat from Jack's body touch her exposed back. Apprehension waltzed up her spine and she slowly turned from Michael to face the source of that heat. Jack wasn't looking at her. His hard gaze was on her dance partner. "No problem."

And she was in Jack's arms. He held her closer than Michael did. Firmer too. His grip was possessive, his touch smoldering on her back. Lacey was speechless for a full thirty seconds.

"Are you enjoying the party?" she asked, floundering for words. She brought her gaze up and was snared by the intensity in his eyes. Still hot and steely gray.

"I am now."

She blinked and focused on the buttons on his shirt, reliving the harsh words she'd thrown at him that morning. She'd overdone it. But he was offering an olive branch.

"Flirting with me in front of your date isn't very polite," she stated. She'd a felt a prick of sympathy for the woman. *A very small prick.*

He didn't answer. But instead, his mouth showed the smartest-ass grin she'd seen on him yet.

She stopped moving and his grin widened.

"What's wrong? *What is so funny?*"

"My sister wants to know where you bought your dress."

"Your what?" she squeaked.

"My sister," he answered firmly. "She likes your dress." His eyes twinkled. "And so do I. Very much." He stepped away from her the littlest bit and deliberately let his gaze roll over her from head to toe.

She moved into him to block his view of her dress and tipped up her nose. "Saks," she replied primly. She was going to say something to Michael later for deliberately not telling her the woman was Jack's sister.

He tossed back his head and laughed, ignoring the glances of the other dancers. Still chuckling, he spun her around in a tight circle and planted a kiss on her forehead.

Lacey's heart leaped.

Melody arched a perfectly waxed brow as she watched her brother laugh. He *did* know the woman. Why had he ignored her when she'd pestered him for the blonde's name? Her gaze slid over the black backless dress, knowing she could never wear a dress like that. Too many moles dotted her back. She'd had the bigger ones removed, but was still self-conscious about the others.

She grabbed the arm of another organizer passing by. "Sheila, who's my brother dancing with?" The heavily diamonded woman stopped and squinted Jack's way.

"I don't know," Sheila murmured and flicked a wrist. "Never saw her before. Oh! Wait a minute." She squinted again as the blonde woman's face came into view.

"I think that's Dr. Campbell. I don't remember her first name. Something about fashion."

A doctor? That tiny woman was a doctor?

"She has a doctorate in fashion? As in fashion design?" Melody stared at Sheila.

"No, no." The woman primped her highlighted French twist, eyeing Jack with a gleam in her eye that put Melody in vigilant big-sister mode. "She's a dentist. It's her first name that escapes me. Something like Calico or Indigo. You know, kinda fancy." She snapped her fingers. "That's it. Lacey. Lacey Campbell. Her father's the state medical examiner. I saw him around here earlier."

Melody watched the divorced woman's interest refocus to finding James Campbell as she flittered away. For an older guy, he'd be a good catch. Handsome, rich, and widowed. Even Melody had eyed him at one time, only to decide the age difference was too much. But Sheila was ten years older than her. *At least ten years.*

Melody watched her brother kiss the blonde on the forehead. Hmm. Jack wasn't one for public displays of attention. A dentist? That explained why the woman was here tonight, but didn't explain why Jack couldn't keep his eyes and hands off of her. Had her little brother finally found a good woman? Melody tipped her head a bit as she studied the couple. They truly did look happy as they danced. Melody caught Jack's gaze and gave him a discreet thumbs-up. His returning grin lit up his face.

Lacey rested her temple against his jacket and smiled. He smelled good. Completely male and warm. His hand slid up her back and down again, stopping lower down than it had before. Any lower and he'd figure out she wore nothing under the dress. She couldn't. Every undergarment she'd tried on showed some sort of obvious line or came up too high for the low back. Thankfully, the dress had built-in support for the front, but lower down was a problem.

He positioned her closer as the music slowed and she let her eyes drift shut, reveling in the sensation of feeling safe and protected. The music was lovely, the man was dreamy, and she was the happiest she'd felt in a long time. Maybe they were on to something good.

A new hand on her shoulder broke open her reverie. Michael.

"Lace, can I talk to you a minute?"

"Later," Jack growled at him.

Michael's shoulders snapped back but he leaned closer to Jack's face. "I need to talk to her *now.*"

Afraid one of these temperamental men was about to throw a punch, Lacey pushed away from Jack and made Michael back up a step. "Knock it off. The next caveman who growls will get my heel jammed in his arch." She crossed her arms and gave her attention to Michael. "What's so important you need to tell me this very second?"

Michael took a deep breath. "I need to tell you what I found in Mount Junction."

"Now?" She was skeptical. "Why didn't you tell me on the way here? I asked about your trip, but you changed the subject."

"I just got a call I've been waiting for."

"Right now? Here?"

Michael nodded. "I managed to convince the police down there to take another look at some old cases. When I told them what I believed about Amy's death…"

"Who?" Jack cut in.

Lacey shushed him. "Just a minute." Her eyes were all for Michael. "What did they say?"

"It wasn't easy to convince them, but I dug up two other deaths down there that had been classified as accidents. In both, the victim was a blonde female and ended up with broken legs. Each time the breaks were attributed to something sorta normal occurring at the time of death. Like saying Amy's breaks were from the rocks in the river or the accident impact."

"Who in the hell are you talking about?" Jack's tone was frustrated.

"A gymnastics teammate of mine." Lacey instinctively put out a hand to stop Jack from moving closer to Michael. "She died in an accident when she drove her car into a rough river in Mount Junction, but Michael doesn't think it was an accident." Lacey's words came slowly. They were hard to say and even harder to believe.

"And now the police believe there are more murders like Suzanne Mills? In Mount Junction?" Jack sounded stunned.

"Yeah. You like visiting Mount Junction, Jack?" Jack lunged toward Michael, and Lacey stepped directly in front of him to brace him with her body. "Stop it! Both of you! Michael, knock it off! That's not funny!"

She ignored the nasty words Jack was muttering under his breath about Michael's parentage. "He's got a condo in Mount Junction, Lace, at the ski resort."

"What?" Her stomach clenched as she caught Michael's line of reasoning. He was way out of line.

"Jack. He owns a condo at the resort. It's been in his family for two decades. Right up the mountains from Mount Junction. He skis there several times a year."

"That doesn't mean a thing." Lacey warned Michael with her eyes.

"No. But it's one more damn coincidence linking him to this mess."

"You sack of shit! What're you trying to say?" Jack spit the words. "Are you going to print it on the front page? Try to insinuate me into another girl's death?" His voice rose to a shout. "Ruin my business? The company my father started?"

Jack stepped around Lacey and strode forward at Michael, who took two rapid steps back and bumped into the wall. Jack pressed him against the wall with a hand on his chest. "Who do you think you are to mess with people's lives?"

Lacey pulled at the back of Jack's tux, trying to get him away from Michael. It was like trying to get a grip on an elephant.

Michael threw up a knee, barely missing Jack's groin. Jack stumbled backward and tripped Lacey. She felt a dress seam split at her hip.

Jack kept his feet and dived forward with a shoulder, caught Michael squarely in the chest and took them both down.

"Michael!" Lacey gasped. Her hair fell out of its clip and swung into her eyes. She yanked it out of the way and checked her dress for any exposed body parts. The ripped side seam revealed six inches of her hip and waist but nothing too intimate.

A crowd gathered around the men, swarming forward like a shark scenting blood. Glittering women shrieked or stared in horror, their mouths forming a stunned "O" shape. Some of the men glanced at one another, looking for a suggestion of whom to side with. Others just grinned and enjoyed the show.

Lacey grabbed two fresh drinks from a stunned waiter and dumped the contents on the scrambling men's heads. Neither flinched. Strong hands gripped her shoulders and set her aside. She stared at her father's back as he latched onto Jack's coat, yanked him off balance, and threw him backward where a couple of men grabbed both his arms. James Campbell planted a firm foot on Michael's chest, pinning him to the floor.

"That's enough!" her father roared. Two hotel security guards shoved their way through the crowd and came to a halt. Seeing everything under control for a second, they glanced at each other, then looked expectantly to the man with one foot on Michael's chest.

Lacey drew in a deep breath and stepped forward, glaring from one dripping man to the next. Jack caught her eye, raised a brow and licked a thin stream of alcohol from the side of his mouth. He didn't look one bit embarrassed. Jack shrugged, trying to free his arms, but the two men holding him gripped tighter. With disgust, Lacey noticed the men wore twin expressions of enthusiasm, relishing their small role in the brawl.

She turned to glower at Michael and noticed his gaze was locked on the tear at her hip. She checked to confirm everything was still rated PG and waved a hand for her father to let him up. Michael pushed up into a sitting position, and his split lip dripped blood mixed with booze onto his white shirt. Lacey snagged a cocktail napkin and dabbed at the blood on his face.

"You are being crazy. This is way out of line. Why in the world are you deliberately pushing his buttons like that? You know he's not a killer. Is this about the other night? Please tell me this isn't some sort of getting back at him. You're bigger than that, Michael."

"Leave it." Michael pushed her ministrations away and moved smoothly to his feet. Giving Jack a stony stare, he turned to the hotel security guard, who was speaking on his radio. "Are the police coming?" At the guard's nod, Michael cast back a smoking glance at Jack. "Good. I'm pressing charges."

CHAPTER TWENTY-TWO

Lacey didn't speak the whole way home. She knew Michael hadn't thrown the first physical punch, but he'd definitely hurled the first verbal one. Her brain was still spinning.

Michael turned his Land Rover onto her street and she stiffened. If he thought he was coming in to her house to talk or apologize, she was going to set him straight. He was going home. She couldn't handle any more testosterone tonight. She watched his headlights play over the other cars parked along her street and steeled her spine for a confrontation.

How dare they fight like boys! Men sometimes acted like idiots but tonight took the cake. She made a frustrated noise of indignation, and Michael turned his head to eye her questioningly.

He had to know she was furious. He better be scared, she seethed. She was ready to let him have it. Jack too, but he wasn't here, so Michael was going to catch the brunt of her wrath.

He parked in her driveway and turned off the ignition. They both sat in silence.

"Lace…" He started hesitantly.

"Don't say a word," she snapped. "I watched two adult men act like little spoiled brats tonight. My hair is a mess and my new, *very expensive* dress is ripped." She touched an earlobe. "And somewhere I've lost a two-and-a-half-carat diamond stud." She was just getting warmed up. "I know this wasn't all your fault, Michael, but you're here and he's sitting in a jail cell somewhere. If I wasn't so damned tired, and needing to get my stuff packed to stay at Dad's, I'd march down there and yell at him too. I thought you were trying to help me. I can't be alone with that killer running around. How can you act like this?"

He had the grace to look ashamed. "I'm sorry, Lace. That guy brings out the worst in me. You know I'd never leave you alone. When I left the other night, he was still in your house and I knew he wouldn't let you out of his sight." He shifted uncomfortably in his seat. "I recognize something in him. It's the same thing I feel. I guess you'd call it overprotectiveness. On one hand I hate that he feels that way about you, but on the other hand I respect it enough to leave town and feel certain you'll be safe with him around."

All the wind deflated out of her sails. "Then why did you insinuate that he had a hand in Amy's death? That was horrible of you."

"I just wanted to see his reaction."

"Well, he definitely reacted. That wasn't your smartest moment, Michael. Why did you press charges? He can't be around when you're gone if he's in jail."

"Why are you so damn logical?" he muttered. "I'll drop the charges and get him out."

"I'm logical because I'm not high on testosterone."

She reached for the car handle and glanced toward the house. *What was that?*

She froze and stared harder into the dark. There it was again. Somebody was definitely crouched in the shadows against the side of the house below her wraparound porch.

"Michael." It was a whisper. "Look." Keeping her hand below the dashboard, she pointed. "Can you see it? There's somebody there." Her voice wavered and she pressed the lock on her door.

"I see it." He was instantly alert. "Stay here." He reached in his console and slipped out of the vehicle before she could say another word.

She'd spotted the gun as he'd removed it from his console, and it'd shocked her into silence. *What was he doing?* He was licensed to carry concealed, but she'd never seen a gun in his hand outside the shooting range.

The person hiding next to her home couldn't miss seeing Michael exit the truck and leave her behind. Michael casually jogged up her steps, yelling back at her. "I'll go grab it for you and then we can leave!"

Her heart rate escalated. The shadow near the porch hadn't moved. She watched Michael unlock her door with a key from his ring and dart inside, leaving her front door wide open.

She blinked. What would Jack think if he knew Michael had a key?

Her eyes widened as she spotted a new shadow on her porch, slinking along the house. Michael. He'd snuck out the back door and was creeping to position himself above the person hiding below.

Her jaw locked and every muscle contracted. Without looking, she dug in her evening bag for her cell and clutched it to her chest. She watched Michael silently move to the top of her porch rail and then drop directly onto the shadow crouching below. She squawked as the two shadows blended into one and rolled roughly onto the driveway.

With one eye on her phone and the other on the two men wrestling in the snow, Lacey dialed 911.

Mason had crawled out of a warm bed on an early Sunday morning to make a special trip to the city jail. It wasn't necessary, but he simply had to see this in person. He drove into the sleeping city, still chuckling at the description the police officer had given of Jack Harper's arrest.

Arrested for assault while fighting over a woman at some fancy shindig. The cop hadn't mentioned the woman's name, but when Mason heard Michael Brody was on the pressing end of the assault charges, he knew the woman had to be Dr. Campbell. Mason strode down the narrow hallway, exchanging greetings with uniforms he recognized, and stopped in front of a holding cell.

Ohhh. Priceless. The surly arrestee sat on a bench, dressed in a tux with a ripped lapel and something sticky dried in his hair. Mason stuck his hands in his pants pockets, rocked back on his boot heels, and soaked in the view. The furious glare directed his way didn't faze Mason one bit. He gave Harper a toothy grin, wishing he had a cigar.

Damn, he forgot his camera.

Too bad Dr. Campbell's ex, Frank Stevenson, wasn't still locked up. Mason could have set him loose in Harper's cell just to watch the fun. It'd be like dumping a lame chicken in a wolf's den. Harper would eat him alive. Mason snickered at the image.

The wolf snapped at him. "What's so fucking hilarious?"

Mason tipped his head, studied the angry man, and shared his analogy. The wolf softened and managed his own half grin.

"Yeah, I wouldn't mind a punching bag about now. Stevenson's face would be perfect," Harper muttered.

Mason twisted his lips. Harper impressed him more and more at each meeting. Cocky, but honest and direct. Passionate about good causes, and Dr. Campbell was a good cause in Mason's book. Harper had probably been a good cop. Too bad about the shooting.

After Harper's first interview, Mason had looked deeper into the incident. Harper had been shot while on the job. The department had said the shooting left Harper emotionally unstable and unable to perform his duties safely. Harper had done his time with the station shrink, but he'd finally left the Lakefield police force.

Harper was king of the hill when he was in his element. Like when Mason and Lusco had visited him at his office. Harper had staked out his territory and reigned supreme. In that job, the man was able to control his environment and the people around him, something nearly impossible to do as a cop. Mason had a feeling Harper rarely lost his temper with his employees. His contractors, maybe. Mason could see Harper taking a bite out of an ass or two that didn't fulfill their end of a bargain.

Now Harper was once again out of his element with the headstrong dentist. Always trust a woman to throw a man for a loop. Like his ex-wife…Mason immediately put his ex out of his head, but it'd brought his son to mind. Mason hadn't seen Jake since…Christmas? February was about to start and he hadn't seen his son since the holidays. Phone calls with the kid, sure, but no face-to-face stuff. Kid was busy. A senior in high school this year. Basketball. Studying. All that crap.

"Callahan."

Mason snapped out of his thoughts. Harper had stood and walked over to the bars. He was standing two feet from Mason and he hadn't even noticed. "What?"

"I asked when I'm getting out of this shit hole. You know perfectly well there's a woman I'm trying to keep an eye on." Jack studied Mason's face. "Not enough sleep last night? Sorry you had to get out of bed so early." He smiled.

"No. I was just realizing I hadn't seen my son since Christmas. Lives with his mom." Embarrassment immediately flushed Mason's face. He hadn't meant to reveal personal facts to a guy he barely knew.

Harper's grin vanished and his eyes shuttered. "That sucks."

Right. Harper hadn't truly seen his father in years. *All that Alzheimer's shit.*

"I'll find out when you can leave." Still flushed, Mason headed down the hallway without a good-bye. He felt Harper's eyes follow him.

"Nine-one-one, what is the nature of your emergency?"

"There's someone outside my house!" Lacey rattled off the address. "And he's fighting with Michael! They're rolling on the..."

"Where are you, ma'am?"

"In the truck! But Michael's got a gun and I'm afraid someone..."

"A gun? Has anyone been hurt? Do you need an ambulance?"

"No! No one's been shot! But I don't know if the other guy is armed or not!"

"Police are on their way. Ma'am, you'd better stay in the vehicle. Are your doors locked?"

"No! I mean..." She hit the lock button. She'd forgotten to lock it again after Michael had got out. "They are now." Why did the operator keep asking about her? It was Michael who was in trouble!

The figures on the ground stopped thrashing and Michael kneeled on the other man's back, twisting his arms up behind him.

"He got 'em! He pinned him down." She yelled into the phone.

"Don't get out of the vehicle, ma'am."

Lacey had already unlocked the door and was halfway down the drive, her phone to her ear. She tottered on the rough, icy surface in her heels, straining her eyes in the dim light for injuries on Michael. Two fights in one night! He was going to hurt in the morning.

"Ma'am. Don't get out of the vehicle."

"It's OK. He's not going anywhere."

"I've informed the police there is a gun at the scene."

"What!" *Had she caused a bigger problem?* "Michael! Where's the gun?"

She spoke to the operator, "Tell the police no one is armed! I can see the gun in the snow. Don't let them shoot! I'll get it out of the way."

"Don't pick up the gun, ma'am."

Lacey gritted her teeth. This exceedingly polite operator was seriously starting to annoy her. "I'm kicking it out into the street. The police will probably drive right over it."

She gently slid the gun a few feet toward Michael's truck. She could hear the operator relaying her message in the background, but she knew it made no difference; the police would respond with escalated caution and readiness. They didn't like being called to scenes involving a gun. It pumped up their stress level tenfold.

She turned back as Michael ground the man's face into the gravel and snow. Michael didn't look hurt, but his language made her eyebrows skyrocket. Somebody was pissed.

She squatted awkwardly at a safe distance to get a look at the stranger's face, hoping he wouldn't look directly at her. He'd get quite the view up her dress. Wailing sirens filled the night.

Panting hard, Michael grabbed the man by his hair and roughly yanked his head back, turning his face toward Lacey. "Know him?"

By the shock and then the embarrassment on the man's face, he'd gotten a personal view up Lacey's dress.

But her shock was greater.

Her voice cracked. "Sean? Is that Sean?"

Michael was kneeling on her janitorial hero.

Jack was collecting his wallet and change at the jail counter when Callahan reappeared. "You might want to stick around for a bit," Callahan said.

"Why in hell would I want to do that?" Jack stated. He needed his bed.

"Some of your friends are on their way here."

Jack gave Callahan his best who-gives-a-shit eyebrow cock.

"A dentist friend of yours."

That got his attention. His hand stalled as he slid his wallet in his jacket pocket. "What? Lacey? Is she OK? She's here?"

"And her boyfriend." Callahan displayed all his teeth.

"That ass wants to keep me from leaving jail?" Jack's chest had tied in knots at Callahan's word choice.

"No. I guess the boyfriend caught an intruder on her property."

Jack felt a hollow thump in his heart. "Was it him?"

Callahan didn't ask who he meant; the detective knew. "I don't know. They're saying Dr. Campbell knows the guy. That it's someone she works with."

"But that doesn't mean he isn't the one." Had the reporter stopped the killer before his next victim?

"I know."

Dead silence filled the air as the two men studied each other.

"He leavin' or not?" the cop behind the counter asked.

Callahan nodded his head at the cop and tugged at Jack's sleeve, pulling him down the hall. "You want to clean up first?"

Jack tugged at his lapels and heard a stitch rip. He ran an inquiring hand over liquor-crisped hair and eyed his stained shirt. *No tie.* He checked his pockets. *Still no tie.*

"Don't I look good?"

"Yeah. You smell real good too."

Lacey's angry voice carried down the hall to where he stood with Callahan. "No! You can't arrest him! He didn't know what he was doing! He...he doesn't think like we do. I work with him and he doesn't understand it was wrong!"

Jack couldn't see her, but he knew she was livid. He relaxed a little. If Lacey was that fired up and steamed then she was just fine. He silently repeated what she'd said, trying to make sense of the words. Who could...was she talking about that janitor? The mentally disabled kid? The one who'd nailed a home run on Stevenson's head with a broom handle?

He'd broken into her house?

Lacey looked out at the dark street from the drab lobby of the police station and crossed her arms on her chest. Michael and Jack were sitting as far apart as possible in the row of chairs along the wall, both of them carefully watching her, taking their guard duty very seriously. The two men wouldn't look at or speak to each other, and Lacey figured that was for the best. She started to pace the room again, worrying about Sean. The boy had been petrified when the flashing police cars pulled up at her house and armed cops emerged, shouting at everyone. Michael had no longer needed to hold Sean down. He'd plastered himself to the ground and stretched out his arms and legs, refusing to move. It'd taken a lot of muscle power to get Sean off the ground and into a police car.

Lacey hadn't been able to get a word out of him. Neither could the cops. They'd checked her house, decided Sean hadn't been inside, and announced they were taking him downtown. She'd protested vigorously, but the cops had claimed they only wanted to talk to him, and she finally relented. Sean wouldn't tell them where he lived or give a name of someone to pick him up. The lack of ID bothered the officers. They wanted to know exactly who he was and where he lived. Lacey couldn't help; she knew only his name.

At the station, Sean had started cowering again. Then a scuffle had started between him and two officers as they tried to move him down the hall. Lacey and Michael had arrived in time to see tempers flare. She managed to calm Sean down and had convinced him to go with the officers. They'd led him to an interview room and closed the door in her face.

Detective Callahan had been a familiar face she was thankful to see. At her request, Callahan was sitting in on the interview with Sean, giving her a small measure of relief. She'd informed Michael and Jack that she wasn't leaving until the police finished with Sean. Jack had refused to leave until she did and planted himself in a chair. Michael had taken one look at Jack's stubborn face and plopped in the farthest chair. Both their expressions warned her not to argue.

The men looked like they'd been brawling all night. Which was nearly true. Michael had ripped his pants wrestling with Sean. His jacket was sloppily tossed on a chair, and he'd torn two buttons off his shirt. He'd rolled up his filthy sleeves and managed to look menacing as he watched her pace.

Jack looked just as scruffy and intimidating. They both still stunk of the alcohol she'd dumped on their heads. The smell of tequila filled the room and several officers gave the men sharp looks as they passed through the lobby.

Lacey's gown was still split. There was nothing she could do without a needle and thread. She'd washed the smeared mascara off her tired face in the restroom and realized her hair clip was lost, leaving her hair hopeless. She'd finger-combed it and tucked it behind her ears.

They looked like refugees from an earthquake at a state dinner.

She sighed. *Six in the morning on a Sunday.* She should be in bed. She should be anywhere but here.

The three of them jumped as her cell rang from her evening bag under Michael's coat. He didn't meet her eyes as he handed her the bag.

The call was from Chris, Kelly's husband.

"Have you talked to Kelly?" He was out of breath.

"No. Not since the day before when I saw both of you at the gym." Concern raced through her; Chris sounded stressed. "What's wrong?" Chris was never stressed.

"Kelly didn't come home last night."

"What? Where is she?" Lacey stopped pacing, dread swarming over her.

"I don't know! She left after dinner to do some paperwork at the gym. When it got late, I tried to call her cell but it went straight to voice mail. I drove to the gym and her car wasn't there. I checked the office and she'd done the paperwork, but now I can't find her. Do you know where she might have gone?" All his sentences ran together.

"I don't know, Chris, honestly. Did you check with her folks and sister?" Lacey's mind whirled as her stomach tightened. *Oh, dear Lord. Please, not Kelly.*

"I called them late last night. I didn't ask if Kelly was there. I didn't want to worry them. I made up some excuse for calling. None of them mentioned anything about Kelly."

"Did you call the police?"

The sound of boot steps coming down the hall grabbed her attention. Detective Callahan had his gaze locked on her, and he didn't look happy.

"Hang on, Chris. I'm in the police station right now. I'm gonna get someone moving on this immediately." She covered the phone with her hand and spoke to the detective. "My friend is missing. Her husband is on the phone. He's frantic. He hasn't seen her since yesterday evening."

"Who? What friend?"

"Kelly. Kelly Cates. She's the one I told you about who had a ring like mine." Her voice trailed off as his eyes narrowed.

"The gymnast? The other girl who testified at DeCosta's trial? Why the fuck did he wait this long to notify us?" He grabbed Lacey's cell and started grilling Chris.

He's got her. He's got Kelly.

Lacey couldn't breathe.

CHAPTER TWENTY-THREE

Jack watched Lacey on her cell. He'd been eavesdropping on her phone conversation and could tell she was worried about a friend. Who were Chris and Kelly? Hell, he didn't know her friends at all except for the reporter at the end of the room. He hardly knew anything about Lacey Campbell and that needed to change. But every time they were together something freaky happened. They were going in the right direction last night until her overprotective bodyguard decided to spout off, and Jack had lost his cool.

Yeah, he owned a condo in Mount Junction. So what? He skied. His sister skied too. Melody probably used the place ten times as much as he did. Their father had bought it years ago for family ski trips, but Brody had twisted it into a black mark against him.

Now the new murders were being tied to old cases in Mount Junction. He shot a sideways glance at Brody. He was following Lacey's phone call intently. Brody probably knew who she was talking about. He probably knew every finite detail about her that Jack craved to know. Like what's her favorite ice cream? What kind of music does she listen to?

As he watched, Callahan grabbed her cell and started speaking. Lacey wobbled and started to collapse. Jack leaped from his chair, lunging for her. The detective grabbed her arms before she hit the floor, but her cell phone slipped out of his hands and shattered. Pieces of phone and the battery skidded across the floor as Jack grabbed her around the shoulders and knees, lifting her effortlessly. Brody had leaped at the same time but was an instant too late. He reached out to take her, but Jack stopped him with a cold glare.

"Stop it. Put me down." Her quiet voice concerned Jack even more.

"What happened?" Jack looked at Callahan, who'd moved to the lobby desk and was snapping out orders at the officer. "What'd you say to her?"

"Nothing." Callahan finished his instructions and barely glanced at Jack. "She's got a friend missing who's probably been nabbed by our man." Callahan turned his back and started punching his cell phone.

Jack nearly dropped her. "What? Who?" He let Lacey's legs slide down to the floor and turned her firmly to face him. He tilted her chin up, searching her eyes. "What's happened? Who's gone?"

Her face was white. Lack of sleep and shock showed in the dark half-moons under her eyes. "It's Kelly. She's missing. That was her husband. He can't find her and she's been gone since last night." Her eyes filled. "Kelly testified in the trial but it didn't mean much. All she could tell them was how she found me," she whispered.

"Found you? Found you when?" Jack shook her shoulders. Lacey's eyes weren't focusing quite right.

"After." She didn't elaborate.

"Kelly was the gymnast who found Lacey after Suzanne was nabbed," Brody answered quietly. He was picking up the pieces of cell phone, deftly reassembling it, wisely not putting his hands on Lacey in front of Jack.

"This other girl was there that night?" Another DeCosta witness was gone?

"Kelly didn't see anything. Just Lacey on the ground. Bleeding," Brody added.

Lacey had told him. Her broken leg, her beat-up face, bleeding.

Looking about for support, Jack saw the anger in Brody's eyes as he glared from the reassembled phone to Lacey's white face. Brody had come to the same conclusion: Lacey was truly in deep danger. Brody looked ready to haul Lacey down the hall and lock her in a cell.

Good. Maybe she'd listen if both of them got on her case.

Jack's gaze widened. Fuck. He'd just aligned himself with the competition. Of course, at this stage he'd align himself with a terrorist if it meant keeping her safe.

Callahan caught Jack's eye and jerked his head.

Jack sat Lacey in a chair and kneeled before her, rubbing her icy hands. "I'll be right back. I need to talk to Callahan." She nodded silently as he stood, and Michael sat in the chair next to her, seamlessly taking over. Jack couldn't worry about the reporter now. If he couldn't be her warden, Brody seemed an acceptable alternative.

"What's going on?" Jack didn't like the look on Callahan's face.

Callahan moved the two of them down the hall, out of hearing range of Michael and Lacey. "I was just about to show her something I'd gotten off the janitor kid when she fell apart." Callahan pulled a clear plastic bag out of his pocket and handed it to Jack. "I don't think this is a good time to show it to her. She's had enough shock."

Jack smoothed the small bag, trying to read the card and small envelope through the plastic. The envelope simply said "Lacey" on the front in block lettering. A delicate bouquet of blue and yellow flowers decorated the card, reminding him of the colors in her kitchen.

"Thinking of you…" was imprinted below the flowers. He frowned and maneuvered the card open inside the bag and read: "I have a special party planned for you and me. In two days, we will commiserate over his anniversary, together."

Jack's lips thinned and his knuckles blanched white as he gripped the plastic. "His anniversary? Whose anniversary is he talking about?"

"In two days is the anniversary of DeCosta's conviction," Callahan stated.

"You got this from Sean?"

"Yeah, Sean claims he was waiting outside her home because he was worried about her. The attack up at the school really upset him. In the interview he kept going on and on about how Dr. Campbell was in danger." Callahan shook his head, eyes grim. "He got seriously agitated when I told him Frank Stevenson wasn't in jail anymore. Was a struggle to calm him down again."

"Sean said she was in danger?" Jack saw red. Lacey had befriended this kid and now it appeared he was a primary element of her trouble.

The detective nodded. "He said a man gave him that card as he waited outside Dr. Campbell's house. The man asked Sean to make sure she received it and then warned him to be very careful because a bad man might hurt the dentist again."

Jack's head jerked up to meet Callahan's eyes. "You think Sean's telling the truth?" *Sean wasn't their man?*

Callahan inhaled and pressed his lips together. "If he's not, then he's a damned good actor. He can't have much of an IQ. Seems honest and truly scared for Dr. Campbell."

Jack sucked in a deep breath. The threat to Lacey was still walking the streets.

"Could he describe the guy?"

"Yeah. A man."

"That's it?" Jack scanned Callahan's face, incredulous. They had an eyewitness, and that was the best description?

"A man with a hat."

"Aw, shit." Jack looked at the card. It seemed so innocent on the outside, but deadly inside. "You printed this already?"

"It's clean. Just the kid's prints on the envelope."

"I don't think he's a kid."

"He's not. I'd estimate him to be around twenty-seven or eight. Just seems young."

"I don't like the message written inside." Jack took a deep breath and calmed the urge to rip up the card and bag. "This asshole's got a big finale planned in two days. With Lacey at the center." Jack met the detective's eyes, sensing the anger boiling just under the cop's cool surface.

"I know. What I don't understand is why he's telling us his next move."

"Could be a decoy."

"Could be. Might not be." The detective looked at him pointedly. "You want to wait around to find out?"

"She needs to disappear."

"I'm with you a hundred percent. Make it happen."

Jack couldn't bring himself to tell Lacey about the card.

He stood twenty feet away in the police station lobby, silently watching Lacey tell Brody good-bye. Surprisingly, his chest didn't tighten as Brody kissed her on the forehead and hugged her tight for five long seconds. The message in the card had desensitized Jack's jealousy. He was too angry to be concerned with Brody.

With that note, the killer had confirmed that Lacey was on his list. God damn, the man was getting cocky. Jack shook his head. No. The killer had been cocky from the beginning. The psycho had broken into Lacey's house and stolen her ring. Then had taken the chance to drop Suzanne's ring in Lacey's coat pocket at work. The man was getting overconfident, arrogant.

Hubris could trip him up.

Jack knew he should tell Lacey about the message. But surely, the situation with Kelly showed her how much danger she was in. If she couldn't see that, then she was blind.

He wasn't taking her back to her house. If she needed something, he'd buy it for her. He'd call one of those animal sitting services to look after her cat. Lacey wasn't getting out of his sight.

Now if she'd just agree.

And the chances of that? He shook his head.

Brody was going back to Mount Junction. He had more digging he wanted to do. He'd seen the card, and Callahan had to yank the plastic bag out of Brody's hands before it ripped. He told Jack and Callahan what he'd discovered about the Stevenson land and the circumstances around Amy Smith's death. No one liked the coincidence about Stevenson, and Brody wanted to meet with Amy's parents. Privately Jack and Brody had discussed what to do with Lacey. She'd be furious if she knew Jack planned to stick to her like glue for the next few days. Or weeks. However long it took for the creep to be caught.

Jack watched the reporter step away from Lacey after a final hug. Brody gave him a long silent stare as he moved through the police station door and out into the snow. Jack evenly met his eyes.

Brody was handing off a costly treasure and Jack silently swore it wouldn't be damaged on his watch.

CHAPTER TWENTY-FOUR

"You can't make me stay here!" Lacey planted her feet on the home's walkway, eyeing the strange house in anger.

"That's right, I can't. But if you know of another anonymous place to stay, I'll be right beside you." Jack tugged at her arm.

"What?"

She didn't budge. He stepped in front of her and squeezed her shoulders with heavy hands, grabbing her attention. "Lacey! Your friend is missing. Three men are dead. Do you really think you should be by yourself?" He wanted to shake her.

"But I don't even know this guy. I don't want to impose on anyone's privacy or lead a psychotic killer to his house." She looked past him to the front door.

Jack refused to take her to a hotel. He didn't know how electronically connected their killer was, but Jack wasn't about to risk his credit card being tracked. There was no doubt in his mind the killer had connected him with Lacey. He'd sent that message via DVD.

"Alex and I go way back. There's no one I would trust more with my life or yours." He held her gaze, silently imploring her to listen to reason. She wasn't one of his employees. He couldn't order her around. She was a stubborn woman who was more worried about a friend who'd died a decade ago than herself.

The front door squeaked as it opened and Jack glanced back, but couldn't make out his friend's face in the shadows. A tall man stood silently in the doorway, the light behind him. Jack's tight grip on Lacey's shoulders relaxed. Good. He needed another male on his side and Alex Kinton took shit from no one.

Lacey pushed around Jack and stuck out her chin. "I'm so sorry. He dragged me here. I don't want to burst into your home. I didn't know—"

"It's all right. If I needed it, he'd do the same for me." Alex's gravelly voice cut her off. The man sounded like he hadn't spoken in a week.

Her mouth closed abruptly. Alex's tone and words were firm.

Heavy silence floated in the nippy air, and Jack crossed his fingers that she'd listen.

"OK. If you don't mind…" Her voice lost its muster.

Alex took a step back, indicating for them to enter. Jack gave Lacey a small push on her back. She reluctantly stepped forward.

Lacey tried to cover her hesitation. Glancing up she got a good look at the man. Drop-dead handsome was her first impression. Emotionless and shuttered was the second. Jack had told her that he and Alex Kinton had been in the same college fraternity and that they'd stayed tight over the years. She gave a weak smile and stepped self-consciously past the big silent man into the house.

Behind her, the men shook hands and slapped each other on the shoulder. Lacey turned in time to see Alex smile, but it was more of an automatic movement of his lips than a smile. Maybe they *were* imposing on him. She glanced at Jack, who was genuinely delighted to see his friend.

"Damn. It's good to see you. How's it goin'?"

"It's goin'."

Male bonding.

Jack steered Lacey into the kitchen area. It looked like a female didn't live in the house. Everything was bare. Counters uncluttered. The absolute basics for furniture. Nothing on the walls. The only personal items she spotted were photos on the fridge. She stepped closer and saw Alex with another man. It had to be a brother. There was too much resemblance with the dark hair and light eyes. Both Alex and the other man had wide grins, but the brother had a bit of a blank look in his gaze. Lacey didn't see any pictures of women.

"Are you guys hungry?"

The last thing Lacey wanted to do was to take food from this man, but she was starving. She and Jack had made a mad dash through a department store for clothing because he'd refused to take her home. They hadn't stopped for food.

"God, yes." Jack apparently didn't mind eating his friend out of his house.

"The fridge is pretty empty. How 'bout I grab some Chinese?"

Lacey's stomach growled loudly in response and both men looked at her. Jack with a grin and Alex expressionless.

"I think that's a yes." Jack put a proprietary hand on her shoulder, which she promptly shook off. She saw a faint glimmer of amusement flash across Alex's face.

"Fine. I'll go grab something." He met Lacey's eyes for the first time. "There's a blue guest room down the hall on the right. There's an adjoining bath if you want a shower or something." His gaze brushed her from head to toe and then dismissed her as he left the house.

She felt like he'd found her lacking, and she touched a self-conscious hand to her hair. Her last shower had been before last night's gala. She'd changed out of her ripped dress into new clothing at the mall, but Alex had looked at her like she wore nasty scrubs from an autopsy.

After Alex left, Lacey stared at the door, looking like a wounded kitten to Jack.

"He hates me."

"He doesn't know you."

"I know. But he didn't even give me a chance to talk with him first."

"He talked to you more than he's talked to any woman in the last year."

"What?" She blinked.

Jack shrugged. "He's kind of a loner. He used to be a federal marshal but left the job a while back. I drag him out for beer and a game about once a month."

"Not married?"

"Divorced. Alex tried to make it work, but it was too much after his brother died."

"His brother died? Is this him?" Lacey pointed at the picture and Jack nodded.

"He was mentally handicapped. Drowned. Actually was murdered by one of his caretakers."

"Holy shit." Lacey couldn't imagine. "He seems so…"

"Quiet? Reserved?"

She shook her head. "Unhappy."

Jack pictured Alex's cool eyes. "He's been like that since the death. It's been a few years and he's never been quite the same.

Lacey stood at the fridge studying the photos. Jack saw her gaze linger on one of Alex and him.

"Let's find your room."

She followed him down the hall. He pushed open the first door on the right and found a room painted blue.

Jack dropped the Macy's shopping bag on the floor and sat heavily on the twin bed. He twisted his back. He'd been tense all day and finally felt like the knots were loosening in his spine. "Alex's got an impressive security system and probably has a gun in every drawer. This place is like a fortress. He likes to be prepared for anything."

"A regular Boy Scout." Lacey sat at a small desk and tentatively peeked in the top drawer. "Looks like he missed a drawer."

Jack was glad to hear her lighten up a little.

"It's safe here. No one but Callahan knows where we are. Do you teach at the dental school tomorrow?"

Lacey shook her head. "But I have a case I need to finish sometime soon."

"Case?"

"A John Doe at the morgue. I already charted and x-rayed the teeth, and the comparison dental records should arrive tomorrow. I need to evaluate them and finish my report."

"How often do you do this?"

"A couple of times a month. There're several specialists around that do the same thing for the ME's office."

"What's it like?" Jack rested his forearms on his thighs and gave her his full attention. He studied her face, liking the way her soft hair framed her eyes. They'd bought some basic toiletries for their stay but she'd passed on the makeup counter, so her face was bare and natural. It suited her perfectly.

He took a slow breath. Today, wearing jeans, she appealed to him as much as she had last night in that black dress.

"I like it. I like being able to solve a puzzle. Bring closure to families." Her lips pressed in a thin line and he knew she was thinking of Suzanne.

He stared at his hands. "Who do you think is doing this? Who's killing these men and watching you?"

She was silent a long moment. "I don't know. I've racked my brain and laid awake at night trying to find a missing piece to this puzzle. Who would want revenge for DeCosta?"

"You believe it's revenge?"

"Don't you? Why else is he punishing the people who put DeCosta away?"

"What if they got the wrong guy in the first place? DeCosta may have kidnapped Suzanne, but obviously someone else killed her. And I think someone else may have done all the other killings back then. These recent murders have been awfully similar to the ones long ago."

"No they haven't." Lacey stood and started to pace the tiny room. He watched the jeans cling to her rear and had to force himself to focus. She was a walking distraction in faded denim and cute cowboy boots. "The legs are broken. That's the only similarity. DeCosta preyed on women. Young women, athletes. He never attacked a man. He never used the type of torture we're seeing now. The women found a decade ago had been sexually assaulted and cut."

What? "What do you mean cut?"

She stopped and frowned at him. "You know. Where they slice the skin. Just for the pain and control over their victims. It wasn't something put in the papers back then. The police had held back the fact for questioning the freaky suspects that came out of the woodwork and confessed. DeCosta knew all about it when they caught him." She started to pace. "These men haven't been cut," she continued. "Callahan told me that they've been killed with their own stuff. Whatever the victim liked to do is what the killer chose to murder with. The first was a cop. So he used the handcuffs and Trenton's own gun. Golf clubs, fishing poles on the other victims. This guy is creative. DeCosta just killed for the thrill." She drew a deep breath and stopped pacing, turning to look Jack in the eye. "Right?" She'd put a voice to his theories. Their killer was someone different. But he had to be someone strongly related to the old case.

"Right. But don't you think he has a connection to DeCosta? Why else is he doing this?"

"Maybe he's just one of those freaks who obsess about serial killers. I've read about them. Some killers confess to idolizing other serial killers. Bundy, John Wayne Gacy. Richard Rodriguez. They have fans. Or maybe he had a partner. That happens. Maybe the partner was never caught and now has decided to pick it up again."

"What about the girl in Mount Junction? Do you think she's connected?" Jack struggled to think clearly. Heavy vibes of attraction were sizzling through the room. They were sucking the breathable air right out of the area. No wonder his lungs felt tight.

"I don't know." Lacey spoke slowly. "It was weird back then. We had to be careful. I've told you how the gymnasts were like celebrities in that town. Continual national championships will do that. The residents were fiercely proud of our school's reputation for gymnastics. Our phone numbers had to be unlisted. People would stop us on the street just to say they recognized us. Professors liked to single us out in class. We were always in the spotlight."

"But?" He was watching her face closely. Something had occurred to her.

"I wouldn't call them stalkers, but sometimes the same guy would show up wherever we went. Several of the girls reported that men would follow them around campus. Not talking to them, just following. I had that happen a time or two. I'd see the same person too many times in different places. I could usually put an end to it by deliberately pointing at him while talking to a professor or campus security. They'd realized they'd been spotted and drop it."

"That'd take care of it?" Jack was skeptical.

"Usually." Her lips widened as a memory hit her. "Suzanne liked to take their pictures. She'd make sure the man had seen her snap one. He'd panic and take off."

"You think she kept the pictures?" Jack's mind jumped ahead. Could there be old photos of stalkers in a storage box somewhere?

Lacey shook her head, seeing what he was thinking. "No. We'd pin them up on the board in the coach's office so everyone knew what they looked like. Eventually the pictures just got thrown out. Nothing ever came of it. No one was arrested or even questioned. They were just curious guys."

"That had to be disturbing." He hid his shock. If he ever had a daughter, she would live at home during college. With her bodyguard.

"Looking back it is. But back then we thought it was annoying and a little funny. No one ever dreamed something could happen to one of us. None of us ever thought Amy's death was more than a simple accident."

"Do you remember if she complained about someone following her?"

Lacey thought hard for a moment and shook her head. "I can't remember. Amy was a few years ahead of me."

"What would DeCosta have been doing in Mount Junction?" Jack thought aloud. "And why was Amy's case disguised as an accident? Michael had said the other related deaths were cases where the body turned up months after the person went missing. That's not what happened in Oregon. Everyone but Suzanne was dumped and found pretty quickly. Right?"

She swallowed hard and nodded.

"She was a good friend." He spoke gently, seeing the pain cross her face.

"We were tight. We clicked the first time we met. You ever had that happen when you meet someone and you just know it's right?"

She didn't pause long enough for him to agree. That click had reverberated through his brain the first time he'd touched her.

"We did everything together. Studied, worked out. We were the same size and wore each other's clothes and shoes. During the summers, we'd alternate back and forth between spending time at my parents' and hers. We were like sisters."

Jack hadn't realized the friendship was that deep. He frowned. "How did you handle her death?"

"Not good."

The room grew quiet. She wouldn't look at him and he waited.

Her voice was subdued when she finally continued. "I was diagnosed with depression afterward. It lasted for years. All I could think about was what could be happening to her. If it hadn't been for Frank back then...I really leaned on him after Suzanne was gone. I'm not sure I would have made it without him."

"What do you mean?" Jack wasn't sure he wanted to hear the answer. But he had to know her demons. He wanted to know everything about her, good or bad.

"I saw psychiatrists off and on for years after Suzanne vanished. Sometimes the guilt was so bad..." She turned away and gazed at the purple curtains covering the window. She didn't speak.

And he knew she'd considered suicide. Maybe even came close to doing it. Sometimes it was harder to forgive yourself for living than to face death. "I almost made you watch that disc again." He thumped his forehead with the heel of his hand. God, he felt like a piece of shit. "I'm so fucking sorry. That must have been horrible for you."

He would destroy his copy. He rubbed his face, feeling the harsh stubble he'd not had time to shave off that morning.

She didn't answer him and sat back down at the desk, keeping her eyes averted as she studied the desktop computer. As he looked at Lacey, every possessive and protective hormone in Jack's body battered at his gates. He clenched his fingers around the edge of the mattress.

Wrenching his gaze from her, he stood and checked the closed door in the bedroom for something to do. Something to break the tension that'd filled the air. It wasn't a sexual tension, now. It was more of an intimacy. Where one person had bared his or her soul and now the other helped share the burden. It was more intimate than their one kiss and was affecting him deeper, confusing him. She'd just told him something horrid and he wanted to throw her on the little twin bed and comfort her with his mouth and hardening body.

The door in the bedroom led to the bath Alex had mentioned. A connecting door was on the other side of the bath. Alex's bedroom? Turning around Jack crossed his arms, tucked his hands beneath his biceps. He wasn't going to touch Lacey. He didn't trust himself.

Her cell phone chirped and he breathed a deep sigh of relief at the interruption.

Thank God for her phone.

The air in the bedroom had grown heavy and dense with surging emotions. She didn't know what Jack was thinking, but she'd been watching him from the corner of her eye. Since they'd stepped in the bedroom, she'd been disturbingly aware of his presence. It was overpowering in the small square footage.

Even a lesbian would react to the raw testosterone that pumped into the air around him.

He'd pushed her to recall and relate a time in her life when her future had looked bleak. Nonexistent. She rarely thought back to those black times. It was too hard to clean out the muck that enveloped her soul afterward. That was what her fences were for. To keep the memories away and protect her from more pain. Jack Harper was tearing them down, board by board.

She felt exposed and raw.

Deep down she wanted his touch, craved for his touch, but it came with a steep price. She didn't know if she could pay it. She wasn't ready to let her guard down. That thick inner wall that protected her heart. Her heart had been crushed by Suzanne and then again by her mother's death. Her breakup with Frank left deep scars on her heart's walls. She didn't know if they'd healed enough to stay strong against what was growing with Jack.

She dug her phone out of her bag, moving slowly against the heavy air in the room. It indicated she'd received a video message. No wonder it had only chirped instead of giving its usual ring. She tapped the screen and watched as the grainy video zoomed in on a man.

He was dead.

No one alive could stand the fishing lures poking through his eyes.

Her lungs wouldn't expand.

"Lacey?"

Dizzy, she glanced up to see Jack stepping toward her. His hands and arms reached out as if to catch something. To catch her. She felt his arms close around her and she pressed her forehead against his hard chest, squeezing her eyes shut. The vision of the fishhooks persisted on the inside of her eyelids. Her shoulders shook. She was so cold.

But he was warm, and she collapsed into him, shivering against his heat.

CHAPTER TWENTY-FIVE

Something wasn't right.

Lacey had disappeared off his radar. Maybe his note had been too much, too soon. He'd watched her leave the police station with Harper. Assuming the two were going back to her house, he'd sped ahead and beat them there. Then continued to wait for an hour. No one came.

Never assume. His number one rule and he'd blown it.

He resolved to be strong. Trust his inner control. No more stupidity. Why did Lacey Campbell always steer him off his course? She caused him to make impulse decisions that had no place in his plan. He had to stay on track.

Why'd he write the damned note? He probably shouldn't have sent that video clip of Richard Buck to her phone either.

He couldn't resist communicating with her, and now he was paying the price.

Where'd they go? He'd driven downtown and checked Harper's condo, sneaking into the security parking garage behind a minivan full of hyper kids. The harried mother at the wheel hadn't noticed a thing. But Harper's vehicle wasn't there. Had he scared Lacey enough to send her into hiding? Surely she'd grab some things from home first. That was where he'd pick up her trail.

So he parked across the street from her house again and waited. And waited.

He'd nearly completed the *New York Times* crossword when a knock on his window made him jump and drop his pencil. An older man with a wiggly black lab on a leash motioned for him to roll down the window. He complied, his brain rapidly reviewing his cover story.

Sharp eyes under shaggy gray brows studied him. "You keeping an eye on the Campbell house?" the man barked at him.

"Yeah, you notice anyone snooping around since the disturbance last night?" He acted bored. A plainclothes cop on a dull duty. Thank goodness his black sedan looked somewhat like a standard government-issued vehicle.

The old man shook his head, loose jowls wagging. "All those police cars and sirens and shouting woke me up. Haven't slept since and haven't seen anyone stop by. What the hell was going on over there?"

"Apparently, Dr. Campbell had a prowler."

The shaggy brows shot up. "And that reporter boyfriend of hers caught him? I see him around all the time. Looks like he can handle himself in a sticky situation." The old man leaned closer in confidence, breath reeking. "She lives alone, you know. Just asking for trouble, an attractive young woman living by herself. Don't know what her father was thinking when he let her live there."

"You know James Campbell?" A neighbor who loved to gossip. What sort of useful information could he squeeze out of him?

"Of course. I've lived across the street from the Campbells for twenty years. Good neighbors, kept to themselves, kept their yard neat. I remember when his wife died." He shook his head pityingly. "Didn't know if James was going to ever get over her. Beautiful woman. The girl looks a lot like her."

"She had any visitors lately that you didn't recognize?"

"Had some other man spend the night a few nights back. Not the usual boyfriend. This one had black hair. Hadn't seen him before. She doesn't get much in the way of visitors." The dog sniffed the front tire and raised a hind leg.

His fist tightened on the steering wheel, but he ignored the dog. His brain rewinding the man's words. Black hair? Overnight? Was Lacey closer to Harper than he realized? He'd seen only one kiss. The bitch had him in her bed already? *Slut.*

"Also saw a police car parked in front of her house a day or two ago."

He nodded at the old man as if that was a fact he already knew. "You've probably noticed a couple of visits from two detectives." He glanced at his watch, getting a hunch the prying neighbor was nearly tapped out on gossip.

"That's what they were? They looked like life insurance salesmen or something. The ties and jackets, you know. Cooper. Sit!" The dog promptly sat and tilted his head to study the car and driver, his wagging tail flinging snow.

He thought about another dog from long ago.

"That's a good dog you've got there. Time for me to get back downtown. I don't think you're going to have any more disturbances around here, Mr…"

"Carson. Jefferson Carson." The neighbor straightened his back, releasing an audible series of cracks.

"Good day, Mr. Carson. Give us a call if you notice anything unusual."

The old man backed away.

He turned the car around in Lacey's driveway, giving the old guy and his dog a careless wave as he left.

Nice guy. Must spend all his free time spying on his neighbors.

Hopefully, I won't have to kill him.

CHAPTER TWENTY-SIX

Amy Smith's father wanted to throw Michael out of his house. Michael was getting that message loud and clear. Janet Smith would touch her husband's hand as his temper started to rise and her simple movement would calm the man down. Michael was fascinated by the interaction. The couple was like two halves of a whole that could read the other's thoughts. Gary Smith was action and emotion. Janet was calm and analysis.

A perfect marriage.

Michael had returned to Mount Junction to interview Amy Smith's parents and then the families of the other "accident" victims in the state. His gut told him he'd made a vital discovery when he connected the Mount Junction victims to the Corvallis murders. And the Mount Junction police agreed. They'd reopened all the questionable investigations after taking a hard look at the similarities Michael had brought to their attention during his last trip. Michael believed there had to be something out here that would point him toward a killer.

"Our lives have been uprooted and torn apart since you decided Amy was murdered." The strained look on the father's face blamed Michael. "Pushy reporters crawling out of the cracks, news crews, and more damned police interviews than *CSI*."

"Gary, it's not his fault the police reopened the cases. Don't you want to know what really happened? I've always felt something wasn't right. We never knew where Amy was headed to when she drove into that river. She was supposed to be shopping miles away."

Janet Smith was the voice of level-headed reason. The small woman looked to be in her early sixties and had a relatively unlined face. Michael could still see the traces of beauty that must have driven Gary Smith wild. The husband was big, linebacker big, and couldn't sit still. His perfectly white hair contrasted with his black brows and mustache. Somehow, this tiny woman had tamed the energetic man. Just being in the same room with him made Michael itchy.

They sat in an immaculate formal living room in the Smiths' silent house. The house had an aura of acute emptiness—a home simply waiting for time to go by.

Janet turned sympathetic eyes on Michael and, for a brief moment, he wished his mother was like her. His career-driven mother was more like Gary.

Hate shone from Gary's eyes. "We don't need to talk to you and answer all your nosy questions. I don't know what Janet was thinking by letting you into the house. If you want to know what we've said, get it from the police."

"Gary, I let him come because he instigated the new investigation. I'm glad he did. I know you aren't happy, but he's done nothing but help." She laid a hand on her husband's arm.

Gary started to speak and abruptly closed his mouth.

Michael focused on Janet. "Now, I know you've been asked this but what can you tell me about the guys Amy was seeing around that time?" He didn't look at Gary.

"She was dating Matt. They'd been together for at least two years. She didn't see anyone else. They'd talked of getting married after they both finished school. We'd pretty much accepted him as a future son-in-law."

Michael consulted his notes. "Matt Petretti?"

"Yes. He did get married about seven years ago. We get Christmas cards from him and his wife. They've got two little boys and a girl."

Michael heard the painful note of wistfulness in Janet's voice. No grandchildren for this couple. Amy had been an only child.

"So you keep in contact."

"He was a great comfort after Amy was found. He'll always be a sort of son to us." This time she looked to Gary and he nodded, still silent.

"I know her apartment was broken into a few weeks before she died. The police report lists a stereo and CDs as stolen. Did you ever remember anything else?"

"Back then we never considered the two could be linked." Gary spoke thoughtfully. "We've had to rehash everything we could remember about that time, but it's been so long ago, we don't remember much. I know they never did find her stuff."

"She had some pictures stolen too. She didn't list them on the police report because they didn't have any monetary value." Janet spoke quietly.

"Pictures. Like to hang on a wall?" Michael imagined the cheap posters that college kids frame to fill up empty wall space.

"No. Photographs. She was missing a whole album of photos."

"New photos? Old? Were they family pictures?"

"They were new. I remember that, because she was upset, she didn't get a chance to show them to me before they were stolen. I assumed they were pictures of friends and gymnastics, or her and Matt. She hadn't shot any pictures at home in years."

Photos. Why would you steal photos of people you didn't know?

Or maybe the thief did know them.

"Did Amy ever complain about getting too much attention on campus? You know, with the whole gymnastics thing?" Michael switched topics, wanting to think privately on the whole stolen photo angle. Could be something, could be nothing.

Gary and Janet exchanged an uncomfortable look.

"Amy had a hard time getting used to being recognized everywhere she went. They do those billboards, you know."

"Billboards? They'd put the team on billboards?"

"No, it was usually one of the girls in some dramatic gymnastic pose. Advertising for the competition season. People around town would complain if the poses were too risqué. Arched backs, bare limbs, that sort of thing. If you're not used to watching gymnastics competitions regularly, the leotards and bare legs are a little too much in a conservative town." Janet stood up. "Amy had a beautiful board one year, but it did draw quite a few complaints. I've got a poster-sized copy I can show you."

Michael nodded as Janet hustled out of the room, leaving it cold and tense. He and Gary were left in silence, sizing each other up.

"My life was better when I thought it was simply an accident." Gary's eyes moved to a portrait of a toddler above the stone fireplace. Amy.

Michael nodded. Understandable.

Silent resentment filtered through the room.

"I found it." Janet bustled into the living room, bringing back the warmth. Pride for her daughter rang in her voice and, seeing the poster, Michael appreciated why.

Amy had been beautiful. It was a profile shot of her sitting on the floor, her body filling the entire poster. She leaned back on one elbow, her head flung back with her chin pointing to the sky, exposing her neck. Her right leg was bent with her foot flat on the floor; the other leg stretched out straight, toes pointed. Her free hand rested lazily on top of the bent knee. She was in a red team leotard that highlighted the developed muscles particular to gymnasts. "Southeast Oregon University Gymnastics" was printed across the top of the poster. Without the college banner, it could have been a layout in any men's magazine. The overall effect was sexual but athletic.

Michael studied the long blonde hair that caressed the floor from her tilted head.

It was just like Lacey's.

Glancing at Gary, he saw the man regarding at the poster with an expression that swung between displeasure and pride. Michael tried looking at the poster through a father's eyes.

Would he want his daughter posed on a billboard like that?

Hell, no.

"She's beautiful." Michael gathered up his notebook and coat, clearing his throat. "Thank you for your time, I'm sorry to bother you."

Startled, Janet pulled her misty gaze from the poster. She'd been somewhere else. Feeling like a trespasser, Michael headed for the door. With his hand on the knob, he turned back to Janet.

"Would you mind giving me Matt Petretti's phone number?"

Twenty minutes after the video had been sent to Lacey's phone, Alex walked in with two huge bags of Chinese food and two local cops at his heels. Rich smells filled the house and Lacey dashed out of the kitchen. She dry-heaved over the toilet, thankful she hadn't eaten all day.

The food was cold by the time the police had left with her cell phone and a report of the incident. The men sat down to eat and pushed food at her, but Lacey's appetite was gone. How could they eat after seeing those fishing lures? Both Alex and Jack had watched the clip several times. Once had been enough for her.

Alex ate quickly and excused himself, saying he had to make a phone call. He disappeared down the hall and Lacey heard the door click as he shut himself in his bedroom. She and Jack sat alone at the table. Several half-full white boxes dotted the table. The men had made a good-sized dent in the food, but Alex was going to have leftovers for several days.

Alex seemed to be warming up to Lacey. He'd responded in anger to the video clip and seemed genuinely concerned for her safety. He and Jack had done most of the talking over the meal, but he had asked her a few questions about DeCosta.

Now in the quiet dining room, she wished Alex back. He'd made a good buffer between her and Jack. Jack was impossible to ignore. He was one of those people who innately demanded attention simply by being in a room. In the tiny room, his male aura clogged every corner. No female could sit across a table from him and not physically feel the impact. A pang of sexual awareness swept through her, startling her. How could that happen, when she'd just seen the most petrifying sight in her life?

The plain truth was she was attracted to him and it scared her.

The man flitted from woman to woman like a kid let loose in Baskin-Robbins. A little taste here, a little taste there. Tired of one particular flavor, move on and try something else. That article in *Portland Monthly* had made it clear: Jack Harper didn't have a commitment cell in his body.

That wasn't the kind of man she needed.

"Don't you like Chinese?"

"I do." She grimaced. "I'm just not hungry anymore."

Jack laid down his fork and gave her an inquisitive look. "What else do you like?"

"Mexican is good or Italian…"

He shook his head. "I didn't mean food. I don't know anything about you. I don't know what kind of music you like, where you went to high school, or how you lost your mother."

She blinked. Jack Harper wanted to know what made her tick.

She studied him, wondering at his intentions. He looked sincere. She couldn't remember the last time someone had asked such personal questions. She'd locked herself off from relationships for so long, she'd forgotten how to create that feeling of intimacy. She'd been too private for too long. Michael and Amelia were the only people who truly knew her. And Kelly.

Tears filled her eyes at the thought of her missing friend.

"Oh, shit. I didn't mean to pry. I didn't think a few questions would upset you. Was it the question about your mom?" Jack looked genuinely distressed.

She grabbed at a clean napkin and pressed it against her eyes, then her leaking nose. Damn it! She hated crying in front of people. "No. It's not that." She tried to gracefully blow her nose in the napkin. Impossible. "It's Kelly. Dear God. What's happening to her?" Her tears cranked up ten notches.

Lacey had been through this before. When Suzanne vanished, she'd swam and struggled in the "what if" ocean for years. Her imagination had terrified her with painful scenarios. Her visions had been fueled by the newspaper descriptions of torture endured by the murdered girls.

"I didn't mean to remind you of her. I'm sorry."

"I know you didn't mean to. It's just that she's one of the few people who know me inside and out. When you started to ask...I realized how few people I let inside." She sniffed through the words, avoiding those prying and sympathetic eyes.

She wanted to unload on him. She wanted to tell him how scared she was for her friend. And for herself. She wanted to tell him how alone she'd felt after her mother's death and Suzanne's disappearance. And why she was afraid to let other people close: It simply hurt too much when they left.

What man could handle her fucked-up life?

Somehow he appeared, crouching next to her chair, one hand on her shoulder in comfort and the other brushing the hair out of her eyes. The soothing touch started the tears anew, but this time her eyes stayed with his, watching him through the wetness blurring her vision. Genuine compassion stared back from those steel-gray eyes. Those eyes that had captivated her fancy at their first meeting.

Her tears weren't scaring him.

She didn't want him to be the solid rock she ached for in her life. It would rip her to shreds when he left. But right now she needed someone to hold her.

She took the risk and leaned in to him, burying her wet eyes in his shoulder. His arms moved around her and held tight. She felt his lips brush her temple. Calming warmth swept through her, quieting her fears and cracking the hard wall around her heart.

Mason Callahan had three dead men, one missing woman, and no obvious answers. The common denominator was Dave DeCosta, and from that center the threads spread out in 360 degrees. He needed to narrow it down. He didn't like wasting time on useless threads of information, but the flip side was that he didn't know a thread was useless until it'd been meticulously investigated. Like the fact that Suzanne had given birth. No one knew anything about a baby. Where was he to start with that one? Had the baby even survived? There weren't any anonymous babies or baby remains that'd been found in the last decade.

He ventured out of his office into the light snowfall and stared at the hazy sky. Several more inches were predicted in the next twenty-four hours. With a big cup of black coffee in his hand, he walked the parking lot, plowing snow paths that crossed and circled around the vehicles. He liked to think outdoors. The crisp air cleared his head after hours of sitting in the office with its fluorescent lights. He kicked at a chunk of dirty ice that'd fallen off a vehicle. It tumbled through fresh snow, making a dark

244 • KENDRA ELLIOT

path. Mason glanced up and spotted Ray watching him from the same window where they'd watched Dr. Campbell and Harper.

Ray would shake his head, stomp around the office, tell every coworker that Mason was psychotic to be out in the cold, and then come join him. They'd put in a lot of miles in the parking lot over the years. It was surprising what progress they could make as they froze their noses. Mason would hypothesize, question, and brainstorm out loud while Ray took notes in his damned book and bounced theories back at him.

Hurry up, Ray.

Mason sipped his cooling coffee and concentrated. He knew the person who'd left a card for Dr. Campbell, shot a video of Dr. Campbell and Harper, and downloaded the grisly video of Richard Buck was his man. His killer.

But who was he?

Had DeCosta done the old murders in Mount Junction? Or did their current on-the-loose serial killer do them back then? DeCosta had never breathed a word about dead girls in Mount Junction. And that was a man who'd liked to talk.

DeCosta had dumped his victims in forested areas; he didn't hide them. Forest rangers or backpackers had easily spotted his girls. Each one had been found within a few weeks of disappearing, bodies tortured and legs broken.

The Mount Junction girls' deaths had been disguised as accidents, and had stayed hidden for months. The car driven into the river. A missing skier who'd turned up when summer sun melted the snow pack. A lone hiker who'd fallen in a ravine. All eventually had turned up, their remains harshly affected by weather or animals. And the femurs—that could be found—had been broken.

The recent three murders all had the same broken femurs. But they were all men.

Damn it. Mason wanted to hit something. There were too many similarities and differences between the cases, and he couldn't keep them straight. Where was Ray with his notebook?

Two killers. One living and one who'd been dead for the past eighteen months. Which man killed which victims?

Who would be the next victim?

Ray slammed the back door and trudged toward Mason with a sour expression on his face. He made a big show of pulling on his hat and turning up the collar of his coat. "This weather is a freak of nature. We've never had this kind of nonstop snowfall and freeze in town."

"Must be that global warming thing."

Ray shot him an incredulous look before realizing that Mason was joking. He snorted and whipped out his book and pencil. "Start talking."

They talked and paced for an hour. The snow and cold forgotten.

"Frank Stevenson has been in both places. He's from the Mount Junction area and moved here after graduation. That puts him in both places at the right time." Ray made bullet points under Stevenson's name as he talked.

"There's no direct DeCosta connection," Mason countered.

"Maybe he's just a fan."

Mason spit out a choked laugh. Frank Stevenson was an ass. He'd proved it the night he attacked Dr. Campbell and then proceeded to mouth off in a jail cell for five hours. The police had wanted to kick him out just to shut him up.

"DeCosta assaulted his ex-wife. There's your connection."

Mason pulled that apart and examined it from all directions. "Weak. Improbable."

"What are you? A Borg? You sound like a computer program."

"Next input, please."

Ray blew out a frustrated breath that floated up and dissipated in the cold air. "OK. Jack Harper."

Mason stopped walking and turned to face Ray. "He's still on your list? The man's appointed himself bodyguard to Dr. Campbell."

"Yeah, convenient access."

"Aw, you're full of shit." Mason started his snowplowing again, but Ray pushed ahead and stopped him with a hand to the chest.

"Listen. He's been in both places. We can place him close by on the night Suzanne Mills vanished, he owns the property she turned up on, and he dated one of the victims. His name's turned up in more places than anyone else's. Plus he's got a hot temper."

Mason knocked Ray's hand off his chest and pushed on.

"Hey, I know you like the guy and I do too, but we gotta keep looking at him."

Mason halted and spun to face his partner. "He's also a former cop with a bullet hole in his leg and he's the head of one of the most successful businesses in town."

"BTK."

"What?"

"The BTK killer was an elder in his church or something. I doubt his neighbors ever thought he was the killer type. For some reason you're not logical when it comes to Harper." Ray eyed Mason with concern. Like he was cracking.

Mason didn't answer, considering Ray's words. The BTK killer had killed over decades, fooling police and family. You couldn't look at a person from the outside and know he was a killer. Mason knew that. Police school 101.

Ray hadn't mentioned it, but Mason knew he was thinking of the short FBI profile. Seemed to fit Harper to a T. Charismatic. Intelligent. Socially competent.

"What have you found on DeCosta's family?" Analyze other suspects for now.

Ray winced. "Still nothing. I can't find them. I did just dig up a previous address for the mother, Linda DeCosta, in Mount Junction."

"During our window of time?"

"For the most part."

"What does that mean?" Mason didn't like half answers.

"Well, it looks like she lived there during the Amy Smith case and one of the other Mount Junction deaths. But not during the other case. The hiker who fell in the ravine."

"Where'd she live at that time?"

"Don't know. Maybe she stayed with family or friends."

"They don't have any family. And I seriously doubt they have friends."

"You know what I mean, somewhere temporary. Maybe even a shelter or something."

"Look into it."

Ray made a note in his book. Mason could see the wheels turning in Ray's mind as the detective considered where to search online. The man had a gift when it came to computers.

"I don't like the big hole DeCosta's family is leaving. For some reason…"

Pencil poised, Ray finished his partner's sentence. "You like the mother and the younger brother."

"Yeah, I do. We don't have much to go with there, but my gut tells me we need to dig some more. Who has better motivation to avenge her son's death than a mother?" Mason said it out loud even though he knew exactly what Ray's counterargument would be.

"Well, for the most part few women are serial killers. And when they do kill, their methods are less…gory. Poison is usually a woman's instrument."

"Usually is the key word there. How about the kid? Maybe the mother is the brains and the kid the brawn." Mason was grasping at straws. "Not that he's a kid anymore. Gotta be in his twenties."

"But why the strange focus on Dr. Campbell? That's got to be a male not a mother instigating that crap, the note card and video surveillance."

"Maybe she's a lesbian." That idea got a chest rumble from Ray.

"Don't laugh. Remember that movie about the female serial killer? *Monster*. Aileen Wuornos killed truckers. She was gay and it affected what she did. Nothing's improbable."

"You just told me Frank Stevenson was improbable."

"He's still on our list, isn't he? I'm not ruling anyone out right now." The look on Ray's face told Mason he was thinking of his partner's illogical view on Harper.

Ignoring him, Mason noticed his hands were numb. "Let's get inside. We've got some threads to tie up."

The two men kicked the snow off their boots, their breath forming misty clouds, and silently went up the station stairs. Mason was sure they'd accomplished nothing except raising more questions.

CHAPTER TWENTY-SEVEN

Jack had exhaled deeply when Lacey headed down the hall to her room. Any more time alone with her and he'd have her in that little bed with her feet over her shoulders. The crying on his chest had nearly undone him. After he'd calmed her down while mentally reciting every baseball statistic he could remember, she left the kitchen for bed and he hit the fridge, searching for a beer.

He downed the entire beer and stared unseeing at her empty chair. Then opened another beer.

"She's really great."

Jack jerked at the voice. He hadn't heard Alex come back in the room. He relaxed and slammed the second beer. "I know."

Alex eyed the two empty beer bottles as he crossed the room to open his freezer. "Try this instead." He set a bottle of Grey Goose and two tall glasses on the table and sat down, pouring a drink for both of them.

"Is it that obvious?"

"You've got it bad. Written all over your damned pretty face."

"She thinks you don't like her." Jack downed the vodka.

Alex said nothing.

"I told her you were the strong silent type and not to take it personally. Conversing with women isn't your strong point."

Alex still said nothing as he polished off his drink and poured them each another. Jack joined him in companionable silence as he thought about the woman down the hall.

What was he going to do about Lacey? The air sizzled when they were together. When she was near, the hair on his knuckles grew and he fought an overpowering impulse to kick the ass of any man who looked at her.

Not a good sign.

He'd never felt this way about a woman.

Had he morphed into a one-woman man? 'Cause that was the direction his thoughts went every time he was with her. Where was fun Jack? The guy who enjoyed a multitude of first dates and rarely asked for a second.

Now he was tripping over his feet to place himself between a woman and a possible serial killer. Definite brain cell deterioration. The man had killed three men in the last few days, and made it crystal clear that Lacey was in his sights.

Maybe Jack just felt sorry for her.

Yeah. And Osama bin Laden hadn't been a terrorist.

A subconscious attempt at redeeming himself? Save this woman, erase the memory of the woman he didn't save? He stared down at his drink, wishing he could pickle his brain in the alcohol. Then maybe he'd forget.

"Weird to see you gooey-eyed over a female. Not the Jack I know." Alex finished another drink. "You tell her why you're no longer a cop?" Alex had an uncanny knack for reading his mind.

"No."

"Wasn't your fault, man. You gotta get past it."

Easier said than done. Jack pressed his eyes with the heels of his hands but the ghosts still came.

He'd been on the force only two years when it'd happened. Calvin Trenton had been assigned to partner him as a rookie. The man had bitched and moaned in Jack's ear, then proceeded to train him to be the best cop he could be.

Jack had admired Cal. The man had a gift with words. He could talk a drunk driver into believing he was doing the cops a favor to let them drive him downtown. Domestic disputes turned into gales of laughter, and scared toddlers clung to his hand. He always knew exactly what to say to put someone at ease.

It'd been a domestic dispute that blew Jack's life to pieces. The apartment complex had been familiar. Jack and Cal had responded numerous times to the place. But that day, the arguing couple was new to them. Neighbors had called the police, complaining of screaming and fighting.

The couple was Hispanic. Maybe there was a language problem somewhere but Jack and Cal had sworn the couple understood them just fine that awful day.

She was upset. Rosalinda Quintero was twenty-two and hugely pregnant. Bruises of many shades on her face and arms had told Jack that someone close to her liked to hit. And he didn't think it was her two-year-old daughter. He and Cal had separated the couple outside the apartment. Jack talking to the woman, and Cal working his magic on the husband, Javier.

Javier was shorter than his wife. Small and wiry, with a thin mustache that made him look about nineteen. But the cocky look in his eye had said he believed he was a big man.

Rosalinda admitted Javier had hit her before, but that wasn't the problem at the moment. It was him "sitting on his lazy ass" watching TV while the toddler screamed and she made dinner. Javier had exploded when she'd hollered at him to take care of their daughter so she could get dinner on the table. The argument had taken root from there. Sprouting into money complaints, dirty shoes on clean floors, and on and on and on.

Rosalinda's voice grew louder as she complained to Jack. He noticed Javier shooting dirty looks their way as Cal tried to talk some sense into the man. Rosalinda began shouting her grievances at her husband. Jack tried to back her into the apartment to put some more space between the two. Cal's voice was low and cajoling, trying to lighten the situation, but Javier wasn't going for it.

Javier cursed long and hard at his wife. Jack had grown pretty good with Spanish in the last two years. but *puta* was the only word he recognized: whore.

Rosalinda's face reddened. She slid one hand under her pregnant belly for support and shook her fist at him with the other as she volleyed back her husband's taunts. Jack nervously watched her bulging stomach, petrified she'd go into labor on the spot.

Neighbors stepped out of their apartments to stare. A couple of the women yelled their support for Rosalinda, pissing Javier off even more. Men shifted from foot to foot, eyeing the tense scene, occasionally putting in their two cents. The generalized murmur of Spanish and English grew louder. Jack caught Cal's eye: The situation was escalating and he feared a mob mentality was about to take over.

"I want everyone else back in their apartments! This is between the Quinteros. The rest of you need to leave." The crowd did not appreciate Cal's directions.

"He hits her! She's pregnant and he hits her!" A teenage girl with Jennifer Lopez beauty spoke up and the rest of the women nodded fervently.

"Shut the fuck up!" An older Hispanic male in baggy jeans backhanded the girl, drawing irate shouts from all the women and some of the men. Small groups surged forward, stepping too close for Jack's comfort. He tried again to steer Rosalinda back into the apartment.

She pushed past him to yell fresh insults at the man who'd slapped the girl. Jack turned a panicked glance Cal's way and saw him speaking into his radio while trying to hold the husband at bay. Thank God. They desperately needed backup. He spotted three young Latinos with cunning expressions inching closer to Cal and Javier.

Before Jack could warn Cal, two graying *abuelas* stepped in front of the three men and chewed them up one side and down the other in rapid Spanish. Guilt and embarrassment filled the young men's faces as they backed off and blended into the crowd. The groups of women cheered for the old women and the men ominously muttered some more.

Cal steered Javier in the direction of the squad car to get the man away from the crowds. Beside Jack, Rosalinda gasped as she saw her husband and Cal move toward the car. She gave Jack a shove. The heavily pregnant woman darted down the concrete steps with amazing agility and fought her way through the crowds. Jack dashed after her.

Jack had thought she was screaming for Cal to let Javier go. From Jack's position directly behind her, all he could hear was Rosalinda's shrill voice in a blur of Spanish. Then he saw the anger on her husband's face and Jack caught enough words to understand Rosalinda hoped Javier got screwed in prison. Jack hadn't believed the man's face could get any redder until Rosalinda shouted that she could now be with her baby's father.

Silence fell. Shock struck the crowd silent. The only sounds were whimpers from Rosalinda's two-year-old.

Those two seconds of silence were as loud to Jack as the roar of the gunshot a second later. Javier pulled a pistol from the back of his jeans under his shirt, aimed at his wife's belly, and smiled.

The crowd roared as the shot knocked Rosalinda to the ground. People rushed at Rosalinda to help and another group rushed at Javier to take him down. Before he was tackled, Javier let his gun arm fall limply to his side. He raised his head to meet Jack's eyes over the crowd. No regret showed in the cocky brown eyes.

The bullet passed through Rosalinda and buried itself in Jack's thigh. He'd already kneeled to help the bleeding woman when he noticed blinding pain in his leg. Sitting back hard, he stared at the blood on his pants, confused that Rosalinda's blood was causing pain in his leg.

At Alex's table, Jack wrapped both hands around his stiff drink, and blocked the facial expression of the dying woman from his mind. He'd blown it that day and Rosalinda had died.

He and Cal had been cleared after an investigation. The situation had simply gotten out of hand too rapidly. Javier now sat in prison and his daughter lived with her grandmother. Her unborn sister hadn't made it.

If only Jack had moved faster.

Alex filled his glass again and clanked it against Jack's in a cheerless toast.

"I've got something."

Mason glanced up from a series of photos of the Richard Buck murder. Ray looked like he'd hit the Powerball jackpot. Twice. Mason had been trying to get a lead on where the fishing lures could've come from, but every phone call was turning cold. It looked like Buck had made the lures.

"What?" Mason was tired, annoyed, and a headache pounded above his eyes.

Ray's eyes glowed. "A religious commune. Well, it sounds more like a cult. Linda DeCosta currently lives on the commune way out in the boonies in Southeast Oregon. Some sort of fanatic place where each man has five wives and twenty kids."

"Yes!" Mason punched a fist in the air and half of his headache dissolved.

"What about her son?"

Ray shook his head. "Nothing on the brother. I only managed to find her through a disgruntled ex-wife of the man Linda's living with now. The pissed-off ex-wife is working with the police down there, trying to put together a case against the leader of the commune. He arranges marriages. I guess some of the brides are as young as fourteen." Ray's nose wrinkled in disgust.

"That's fucking sick." Every step in this case was getting creepier. "Who the hell would marry a fourteen-year-old and fifty-something Linda DeCosta?"

"She's not married. She's a housekeeper or nanny or something. Guess even whacked out polygamists have standards."

"We've gotta get down there." Mason felt energized. Finally a solid lead that could get them somewhere. He stood, stacking his photos and slamming files.

"I dropped a hint to Brody."

Mason froze midshuffle. "What the fuck'd you say?" What was Lusco thinking? "Didn't your mother breastfeed you long enough, Ray? What's wrong with your brain?"

"Brody's in Mount Junction. The commune's pretty close to that town. That reporter is sharp and has more contacts than J. Edgar Hoover. I thought he could check things out in case we're wasting our time." Ray forced his eyes to meet Mason's angry ones, daring him to argue. "Our killer's in Portland, not Southeast Oregon."

Silently Mason ran through Ray's logic. He was right, but his methods weren't right. He was going to get both of them fired. "Don't breathe a word of this to anyone. Find someone local to officially check her out."

"Already done. Closest state patrol office is a hundred miles away, and they're tied up with a couple of missing hunters in Burns. Takes precedent over questioning a witness. Malheur County sheriff's department said they'd try to get to it in a day or two, but this commune is too far out and they're understaffed." Ray gave an understanding grimace. "That's when I called Brody."

"I want him to check in every two hours."

"I told him every hour. He doesn't need motivation to do this right. Brody's emotionally tied tighter than anyone else in this case. He's half-crazy with concern for Dr. Campbell. I'm glad he's out of Portland and out of the line of fire."

Mason disagreed with Ray's statement. He could think of one man tied tighter.

Jack closed the door to the bedroom Alex had loaned him and stumbled into the attached bathroom. Some protector he was. Getting drunk with a buddy when Cal's killer was searching for the defenseless woman in the next room. Actually, defenseless wasn't how he thought of Lacey. She was tough and smart. He knew she carried pepper spray and watched her surroundings with a sharp eye.

There wasn't another place in the world where he'd let himself fall so low, but in Alex's home he knew he could let his guard down. Alex would always have his back. He'd drag Jack up from the floor a time or two when the past got too close. Then he'd pound responsibility back into Jack's spine, and he'd be able to hold his head up. Alex's home had been an oasis he'd escaped to several times since the shooting. He'd brought Lacey here because he had no doubts she'd be safe.

He swayed slightly from the alcohol, leaned his hands on the counter, and looked at his reflection in the mirror. Lacey didn't need him. He just liked to think she did. She only needed a shoulder to cry on every now and then. She could have done just as well with her cats for comfort. *Great.* He'd reduced his bodyguard role to a purring foot warmer.

Someone was feeling very sorry for himself.

This always happened when he thought about the shooting. He'd feel like a sham. Being a cop was one thing he'd truly wanted to do. He wanted to be part of that line that stood between the public and the scum. But he'd failed. And couldn't handle the consequences.

He'd lost his edge that day. He couldn't face another uncertain situation and that was what a cop's life was. Every simple encounter could turn deadly. A traffic stop. A shoplifting. A domestic dispute. Stupidly, neither he nor Cal had checked the young man for weapons, and someone died from that mistake. Jack couldn't get over it and had left the force.

Now here he stood, a drunken idiot, believing he could protect a woman from a killer. He'd finally stumbled across a woman who spun his wheels, and he didn't believe he was good enough for her.

He reached to turn on the faucet, but knocked a hairbrush on the floor instead. He bent over to pick it up, got dizzy, and pitched head first into the shower door. "Fuck!" He grabbed at his forehead and sat on the floor, silently begging the room to stop spinning.

The bathroom door to the other connecting bedroom slid open an inch.

"Jack?"

"Don't come in." She couldn't see him like this.

She pushed the door open farther.

"Are you drunk?"

"I'm pretty sure." He tried to look her directly in the eye but couldn't choose one of her four eyes. He did see the amazement flood her face.

"You *are* drunk. What were you doing?"

"Drinking." She had to ask?

He pulled himself up and lurched out of the bathroom to his bed. He sat on the edge to unlace his boots. It took a while.

Finally, he let them fall to the floor with a thump and lay back on the bed with his eyes closed. *Much better.*

His eyes popped open when he heard a sharp clatter as she tossed the hairbrush back on the bathroom counter. "Sorry," he muttered. *Couldn't even pick up his mess.* His eyelids felt like they were weighted with Buicks and fell shut.

It was too quiet. He pried one eye open and suffered a full body twitch. Her face was a foot and a half away, studying him as she wrinkled her forehead. "What?"

"I've never seen you like this."

"You've hardly seen me." He shut his eyes to stop her face from doing a pirouette. "You don't know nothing about me. Maybe I'm like this every night."

"I doubt that." Her words were soft and he felt himself float away on their weightlessness.

Lacey was fascinated. The big protective man was drunk in his bed. He'd made so much noise in the bathroom, she'd thought someone had broken in. She sniffed at him. *Beer.* Why had he gotten drunk? She was the one with the baggage tonight.

Slightly envious that he'd managed to achieve the delirium she would appreciate tonight, she considered removing his sweatshirt. He'd collapsed on the bed fully clothed. At least he'd gotten his boots off. It'd taken him three minutes but he managed.

She couldn't stand seeing him sleep with a thick sweatshirt on. She hated the feeling of sleeping in her clothes. Jack probably couldn't care less, but she pulled at a sweatshirt cuff and slipped his arm out. She did the same to the other arm and pulled the shirt up over his head. Underneath he wore a black long-sleeve

T-shirt that did good things with his chest and abs. She looked her fill; the man was cut. He was also out cold.

His jeans bothered her, but she wasn't touching those. No way. Looking at him closer, she noticed he needed a shave. With a tentative finger she touched the bristly stubble, delighted she could study him covertly.

His short hair was mussed, making him look sexier than ever, like he'd been rolling in bed with someone all night. The stubble made his rakish air seem stronger than usual. He had a kind of rogue pirate thing going on. At least those intense eyes were closed instead of unsettling her. The thick black eyelashes made her jealous. Women would kill for those.

Her gaze moved lower to the neck of his shirt where the slightest bit of black chest hair showed. Maybe he was one of those hairy-as-a-bear guys. The ones whose backs looked like a rug. That would make up for the eyelashes. She glanced at his eyes to make sure he was still sleeping. He was, but now he wore a smile. Not a big one, but a very content one.

Her eyebrows arrowed in. What was he dreaming of? His last trip to Hawaii? His last fling with a flight attendant? The man was a playboy. She knew that. He was bad news and she should keep her distance.

She raised his sweatshirt to her nose. A touch of beer hovered under the masculine smell of Jack. He didn't seem ever to wear cologne. That was good. She liked that he always smelled like clean, healthy male. She closed her eyes and inhaled deeper this time, letting the scent unsettle the muscles below her stomach. She smiled at the sensation and reluctantly opened her eyes to check Sleeping Beauty again.

He was looking right at her. Her hands froze. Had he seen her sniffing his shirt? His mouth turned up at one corner and triumph glowed in those heavy-lidded eyes.

"I knew you liked me." The words were quiet but not drunken. "Come here."

Before she could shake her head, a strong hand clamped on her wrist and pulled her down. She braced herself with a knee on the bed as he pulled her closer.

"Lay down." He commanded as he struggled to keep his eyes open.

"No. I'm not..."

"I'm not going to jump you. I just want you to lie down. I need to know you're safe. I can't do that if I'm asleep and you're in the other room."

She pulled at her wrist, shaking her head. Get in bed with him? No way. Every hormone in her body escalated to full alert.

"Jesus Christ. I'll leave my clothes on. And yours. I need to sleep. If I can hold you I'll know you're all right and I can sleep awhile."

That sounded logical. Sort of. Stiffly, she lay down on top of the bedspread next to him. He promptly rolled her to her side, facing away from him and spooned himself up against her butt and thighs. One heavy arm fell over her chest and his breath was warm at her ear.

"That's better."

She felt his muscles relax as he instantly fell asleep. *Well, goody for him.*

She was wide awake.

Lacey's eyes blinked open and she glanced around the bedroom in a panic. The warm body next to her felt comforting, but the surroundings were wrong.

Alex's house. That's right. She relaxed back into the pillow. That intense, silent buddy of Jack's with the sad eyes. And a drunken Jack had coaxed her to lie down next to him. Stretching, she felt her legs rub together.

Bare legs?

Jerking upright, she yanked the covers up to her chest. At least her shirt was in place. She was greeted by the sight of the smooth skin of Jack's back as he slept on his side. Her lungs stopped, even as her brain registered that he didn't have a fuzzy bear back. But he'd *had* clothes on when they fell asleep. And both of them *had* been on top of the covers. Not under them.

She slid over a tentative toe to see if his legs were as bare as his back. Her foot popped back. A definite yes. *Oh, crap.* Her mouth dried up.

Flinging her bare legs out of bed, she grabbed her jeans from a crumpled pile on the floor, noticing his clothes were in the same pile. Oh, shit. She yanked on her pants and perched on the edge of the bed, pressing fingers against her eyes.

"Where you going?" His voice was low with that just-woken-up roughness and he drew the words out, causing little shivers to dance up her spine.

Turning hesitantly to face him, she saw he'd rolled onto his back and propped himself up on two pillows with a hand tucked behind his neck. His eyes were sharp with a deceptively sleepy drop to his lids. And the damned bedspread had slid down to reveal the carved chest and stomach muscles she'd seen outlined beneath his shirt. It was better than she'd imagined. She tried not to drool and kept her eyes on his. Not on that chest.

"I…I'm getting up."

A lazy grin broke across his face and she steeled her own abs to keep from crawling back under the covers. The man was pure sin.

"Maybe you're used to waking up with strangers in your bed, but I'm not," she snapped at him, using scorn as her last line of defense.

His eyes narrowed and silver bolts hit her.

"I don't take strange women to bed."

"Let me revise that to 'women you've known for four hours.'"

The muscles at his jaw tightened and she heard his teeth grind together. It sounded like he was eating rocks.

"Don't do that!"

His eyes widened. "Do what?"

"Grind your teeth. It's not good for your teeth."

After a confused stare, he let out a shout of laughter and pulled her pillow over his face to muffle the sound.

Peeved, she watched her pillow vibrate. She turned her nose up and headed for the bathroom.

"Wait. Wait a minute." He forced the words out between laughs.

She stopped and spun around, planting her hands on her hips, giving her best pissed-off female glare. She couldn't hold in her curiosity any longer. "How'd you get my jeans off? And when did your clothes come off? When I fell asleep we were both dressed and on top of the covers." She winced at her frantic spill of words.

"You don't remember?" His laughter dropped into a silent chest vibration every few seconds.

"No. All I remember is a very drunk man with disgusting beer breath who could barely take off his boots." Actually, he'd smelled warm and wheaty, like a microbrewery.

He let his lips slowly widen and he looked her up and down as if he knew every part of her intimately. "Nothing happened. I didn't try anything."

Disappointment flooded her. "But…"

He shrugged, his eyes scanning the little room. "I woke up in the middle of the night with uncomfortable jeans, and slipped off them and my shirt." The grin slid wider. "You looked hot so I decided to make you more comfortable." He blinked innocent eyes at her.

Yeah, right.

"You shouldn't have done that. You knew I'd freak out in the morning."

Steel eyes locked on hers. "Maybe I was hoping you'd feel something else in the morning instead of freaked." His sizzling gaze said what his mouth didn't. "I didn't touch you."

"But you looked!"

"It was dark."

She knew he was lying. Badly. His eyes had looked at everything they wanted to. Just like hers had. He sat up and started to pull the covers off as he swung his legs over the side. With a squawk, she averted her eyes and dashed to the bathroom.

She locked the bathroom door and stared in the mirror at her messy hair, willing her heart rate to slow. At least she didn't have the usual morning mascara smeared under her eyes. That chest. Those eyes. Jesus Christ. She rubbed hard at her temples, trying to get the hot images out of her brain. The determined look on his face as he started to get out of bed had sent red alerts up her spine. She'd known he wasn't wearing pants, but she didn't know if he had anything else on.

And he seemed like a commando type of guy.

CHAPTER TWENTY-EIGHT

They wouldn't let him in the compound.

Michael paced in frustration outside a tiny rural general store in Southeast Oregon. He'd decided the best way to approach Dave DeCosta's mother, Linda, was to knock on the front gate and charm them with his disarming smile. Too bad a man had answered the gate.

Michael had bailed on his investigation of Frank Stevenson's parents' property. He liked Lusco's angle better. Besides, Amy's old boyfriend Matt Petretti hadn't been much help. He'd been reluctant to talk about Amy in front of his wife, but had quietly answered Michael's questions. The answers got him nowhere.

Michael had been starting to wonder if his trip to Southeast Oregon was a big waste of time when Lusco had called.

Lusco had asked him to check out the location of that murdering son of a bitch's mother. Lusco and Callahan wanted to ask where her other boy, Bobby, was. They were liking him more and more for the murders of the three men the Portland area. And for stalking Lacey.

Lusco was on to something. Michael could feel it in his gut.

The man at the religious compound's gate had let Michael know in plain English and several "French" words what reporters could do with their keyboards. Reflecting back, Michael acknowledged that presenting his business card probably hadn't been the best approach. Americans were fascinated with polygamy and religious cults. Reporters probably hassled these freaks all the time, searching for something to titillate the public.

The tight compound security had reminded him of Waco. High walls, fences, gates. From what he'd discovered with his research, one guy was king inside those walls. Overseeing his wives and children with total authority. A few other men lived there too. Given wives by the main man. One big happy family. Rajneeshees in their red pajamas popped into Michael's mind. It'd been three decades since the cult had taken over the Big Muddy Ranch in Central Oregon and incorporated Rajneeshpuram. Then imploded.

This compound was way off the beaten path, far out in the boonies. It'd taken him an hour of driving to get to the place from Mount Junction. Now it looked like he'd come for nothing. Lusco was trying to get him some cooperation from local authorities but so far no luck. Michael had the feeling he was on his own.

He wanted inside that fortress.

Possibilities rolled through his mind as he paced in front of the store, breath steaming. What next? Waiting for people to leave the compound and following them was useless. He knew they wouldn't talk to him.

How about someone who needed to get in? He rubbed his hands together in the cold. There had to be someone whose services were needed inside. A plumber, or maybe a delivery of some sort. He glanced up at the general store's dusty sign. Did they make their own shopping trips or have food delivered? He shook his head. Probably shopped and grew a lot of their food in gardens. He hadn't found much income traceable to the compound address. Economizing was probably a credo of theirs.

What else would they need from the outside world?

He watched a rusty cattle truck pass through town and a slow smile broke across his face. He'd smelled the livestock as he stood outside the compound. They probably had chickens, cows, dogs. They should need the services of a vet occasionally. He headed for the ancient pay phone outside the store and its dangling phone book that looked like it'd been printed during the disco decade. He swung up the thin book and looked under "V."

He had to start somewhere.

Somewhere directed him to a farrier about thirty minutes from the compound. The vet, Jim Tipton, had hemmed and hawed over the phone when Michael pushed his case. He'd exaggerated a bit about his connections with the state police and was relieved to know the vet remembered the DeCosta killings. He could tell the vet wanted to help, but was uncomfortable with sneaking Michael into the grounds. Tipton was very familiar with the compound and he didn't like the head honcho one bit. Said the man didn't get proper preventive care for his animals and called for his services only when one was hurt or extremely ill.

Tipton also had a low opinion of the lifestyle.

He steered Michael to the farrier, Sam Short. Tipton said the farrier had an even lower opinion of the compound and would probably be thrilled to help. Thrilled? Tipton's adjective stuck in Michael's mind as he parked his rental and stared at the farrier's elegant house with the gigantic horse stable and arena behind it. Why would he be thrilled?

Stepping out of his truck, Michael headed for the main barn and his eyes memorized every detail of the layout. What a setup. Had to be a couple of million dollars' worth of land, buildings, horse hauling equipment, and horses. He detoured to a fenced pasture, leaned against a rail, and grinned as he watched six horses paw and frisk in the fresh powder. A dark horse with two white socks spotted Michael and trotted over to investigate. The horse blew hot breath through its nostrils at the hand Michael held out to him. After gently nibbling at Michael's jacket sleeve, the friendly horse started to scratch his face on Michael's elbow, rubbing his entire head up and down. Enchanted, Michael let him scratch away, patting the big head with his other hand.

"He'll do that all day if you let him."

The voice made him jump. His jump spooked the horse and sent it pounding back to its friends.

"Or not."

Michael took an extended second to examine the speaker. Long wavy black hair was pulled loosely into two ponytails. Her jeans were dirty, along with her red snowy boots, but her fleece-lined royal-blue jacket was pristine. Her eyes matched her coat and he guessed her age to be around thirty. She crossed her arms on her chest and viewed him with suspicion.

"Michael Brody. Jim Tipton sent me out to talk to Sam Short. You know where I can find him?" He gave her his most charming smile, enjoying the colorful picture she made against the white frosty background. *Lovely woman.*

"Sam Short?" Those glaring eyes didn't soften one bit. "You've found *him.*"

Michael's gaze dropped to the embroidery on her jacket. *Samantha Short. Short's Stables.*

He glanced ruefully at his own muddy, snow-covered boots. "Usually when I stick my foot in my mouth I prefer my shoes to be a little cleaner.

Lacey sipped at her triple latte, eyeing the two men in Alex's kitchen nook. Jack hadn't mentioned the bedroom incident and thankfully had worn jeans when he came to breakfast. She was having a hard time looking him in the eye. Talking to Alex was easier. She nervously peppered him with questions about his home and yard, receiving one- and two-word answers in return. Alex had made a Starbucks run, bless him. She was starting to like the silent man. He blew on his coffee as he leaned against the kitchen sink.

Jack finished a phone call with Detective Callahan and sat quiet, staring into his cup. He wasn't showing any hangover signs. In fact, there was no hint he'd been drunk at all. This morning the tension between them had ratcheted up ten notches. He'd wanted her in bed with him. And she'd wanted to be there. The subtle heat low in her belly warmed a degree and she licked at her lips. The two of them were on an inevitable collision course. Why was she fighting it?

She could see the gears rotating in his mind from his talk with Callahan.

"They're following a lead."

"I hope they're following *lots* of leads."

He ignored her sarcasm. "They've located DeCosta's mother in Southeast Oregon. They're going ask her where her other son is."

Lacey tried to call up an image of Dave DeCosta's younger brother from the trial and couldn't. All she could remember was a quiet dark-haired kid who'd kept his head down and stuck to his mother's side. "He was just a kid at the time. Something was wrong with him. I can't remember what the deal was, but the police pretty much wrote him off as an accomplice back then. Seems like the boy was mentally disabled or something. DeCosta worked alone. No family. No friends." Her words were surer than her tone, as she considered the possibility. DeCosta's brother had been younger than her, maybe fourteen or fifteen.

"Callahan has to consider the two of them for revenge kills."

"Two of them? Mother and son?" She blinked. Back then, Linda DeCosta hadn't looked like she could kill an ant. That woman could be a murderer?

Jack nodded, not volunteering any more information.

Lacey studied the set of Jack's chin. He had that granite look about the jaw again.

He didn't intimidate her. At least not when he was fully clothed, she amended. Jack could come across as pretty daunting, but he would never raise a hand to hurt her, she realized as she sipped her coffee. He might chew her out when she pissed him off, but never, never hurt her. A certainty she hadn't had with her ex-husband toward the end of their marriage.

"Did he say anything about Kelly? Have they got any leads on her?" Lacey crossed her fingers.

Jack shook his head. "Nothing new. Hopefully getting to the DeCosta family will also help lead to Kelly."

Lacey saw Alex glance at his watch. Jack stood up and pushed his chair in. He'd caught Alex's time check too.

"Where are we going?" Lacey snapped the lid on her coffee.

"South of Hood River."

"South of Hood River? On the mountain? Up in the snow?" She nearly dropped her paper cup. There wasn't much between the city of Hood River and Mount Hood.

Jack lifted a single brow. "Snow's everywhere right now."

"Yeah, but..." She let the words drop off. She knew by now she couldn't stop him when he'd made a decision. If he wanted to drive for an hour and a half in crappy weather up Mount Hood to even crappier weather conditions, more power to him.

"You going to the cabin?" Alex picked up the Macy's shopping bag of clothing: their single piece of luggage.

"Cabin?" That sounded like no electricity or running water. Definitely not her kind of place. "Why a cabin? Isn't there a hotel or something we could...?" Her question drifted as she caught the determined look in Jack's eye.

"We've got a company-owned cabin up on the mountain. That's where we're going."

"Why?" Finding her backbone, she held his stare. *Please don't mention composting toilets.*

"Do you have a better idea? We both know we can't check into a hotel. I don't want to bring any of your friends or mine into something that could be dangerous." He looked wryly at Alex. "Any more than I have."

Alex shrugged.

"We're going alone?" Her voice cracked. Just Jack and her in a small, isolated space...

Alex coughed. She scowled at him.

Jack leaned close and she caught a whiff of clean male. Her head gave a dizzy spin. He winked at her. "Don't worry. I won't do anything to you that you don't want me to do."

Hot coffee dripped down her hand as she leaned back from Jack and caught her breath. She tightened the lid, more burned by his gaze than the liquid.

What *did* she want him to do to her?

Behind the tinted glass of Sam's truck canopy, Michael bit his lip to keep from whooping out loud. The gate of the compound had swung open for Sam after she batted long, sexy eyelashes at the farmhand. Michael couldn't hear what she'd said, but the farmhand looked smitten. Michael was too.

Sam Short had impressed the hell out of him. Once she'd given him a chance to explain his role in a hunt for a killer and why he wanted into the compound, she was firmly on his side. She'd asked a few sharp questions and made him wait while she placed a call to Lusco. She'd agreed to get Michael into the compound and then led the way through the barn to her truck at a fast pace, explaining that she made regular visits to the compound because of the large number of horses. Maybe the owner didn't seek preventative care for his animals from the vet, but the head man wanted all the horses shod.

She'd kept up a running commentary on polygamy and cults as they walked.

"Blasted idiots. They brainwash the women. Tell them that polygamy removes the pressure on a husband to commit adultery." Sam snorted. "She won't lose her husband or security as she ages because he'll just marry that younger and better-looking woman too. Someone to help out around the house."

"Hmm. Multiple wives. Someone different to choose from every night. Every man's dream," Michael said slyly. He sped up his steps. The woman moved like she would kick ass in a speed walking competition.

"Ha! The men want you to believe that's a hardship. Those men shake their heads and moan about how hard it is to manage such a large family. How hard it is to keep everyone happy. He has to prove he can support all his children equally before he can consider another wife. Boo hoo hoo."

"You seem to know a lot about it."

Sam stopped her march through the barn and turned to face him, hands on her hips. "I should. My dad had several wives." She tilted her head and locked on his gaze, waiting to see what he'd say. Her blue eyes flashed and her lips thinned.

"Uh…" Her father? Foot in mouth again. Michael glanced around the luxurious stables. "How…"

She read his mind. "The stable and business belonged to my husband. Now it's mine."

"Does he have…? Are you…?"

She laughed sharply and spun around to continue her quick strides. "I'm the *only* wife. He didn't believe in it, and neither do I. He died three years ago. Broke his neck in a fall from a horse." She didn't sound too sad about it.

Michael didn't know what surprised him more. Her stack of personal revelations or the fact she was sharing them with a stranger. "I'm sorry."

"Thank you, but I'm not. Maybe he should have tried polygamy instead of ruining our marriage with affairs." Her voice held a tint of restrained anger.

Michael had snapped his jaw shut. Could he say anything else wrong?

Hidden in the back of the truck, he wondered how it'd be to live with multiple mothers. Built-in babysitters, but more kids to watch. Extra hands in the kitchen, but more mouths to feed. More people to help with housework, but more people to clean up after and bigger homes to clean.

Sam grew up in that life?

Her truck came to a stop, knocking his head against cold metal. He peeked out a window and saw ratty barns and fencing that didn't look strong enough to stop sheep, let alone horses. After visiting Sam's beautiful ranch, anything else would look like the first little pig built it.

She opened the door on the canopy and gestured him out, glancing around. "There's no one around right now. I wanted to hide you through the gate just in case the guy you had met earlier opened it. I'll tell anyone else that you're helping me out today."

"If you don't like these people, why do you do work for them?"

She raised an eyebrow. "Their money's green. Besides, the only other farrier around here does a shitty job. For the sake of the horses, I like to make sure it's done right."

A true businesswoman.

Michael turned toward the house. Houses, he amended. Several single- and double-wide trailers were positioned in a staggered half circle around a snowy yard of play equipment. "Any idea where I might find the woman I'm looking for?"

Sam wrinkled her nose. "You said she was about sixty? What was her name again?"

"Linda."

"Linda, Linda," she muttered, pulling her eyebrows together. "That might be the one with the gray braid. She's the oldest around here and doesn't say much. I'd guess she's been here about five years or so. Seems to spend most of her time in the kitchen or taking care of the tiny kids."

"You've been in the house…houses?"

She nodded. "I collect my money in person before I leave. Actually, I collect the money in cash before I do the work. Jed ain't too reliable if I mail him a bill." She shot Michael an impish grin that made his stomach clench pleasantly. "He can't stand seeing me widowed and successful. I've had my share of marriage proposals out here."

"So how do I find Linda?"

"Follow me." She took off at a fast pace toward the biggest home. He'd never met a woman who walked so fast all the time. Excess energy seemed to roll off her. She was confident, sharp, and smart. And gorgeous.

He trotted after her as if led by a carrot.

They hadn't heard from Brody in two hours.

"I thought you told him to check in every hour." Mason watched as his partner tapped at the computer. Mason couldn't focus on his work, pacing the office, overdosing on coffee. He had to know what the mother said. Hopefully, her answers would specify the next step in their investigation.

"I did. On his last call he said he'd found a way to get in to see the mother but mentioned the cell reception in the area was lousy. Said we might not hear from him for a while."

"Shit. I knew we shouldn't have let him do this. If something happens to him…" Mason wouldn't think about the possibilities. All bad. He pulled open his desk drawer and shook an empty Tums bottle. Damn.

"What's gonna happen?" Ray pulled his bloodshot gaze from the screen to glare blearily at Mason. "It's just the southeast corner of the state, for God's sake. You afraid he's gonna get bit by a snake?"

Mason didn't answer. Instead, he eyed his chart of crisscrossed lines. Losing his job and pension was what he was afraid of.

"Wow."

Lacey stared through the windshield of Jack's truck. She hadn't seen anything so gorgeous in her life. When Jack had said cabin, she'd pictured a little log A-frame with an outhouse.

This looked like a rich man's getaway in Aspen. The place was huge. Surrounded on three sides by towering firs, the two-story "cabin" had four gables on the second floor and a wrap-around porch. The pine-green roof and dark wood made the home look as natural as possible, blending into the setting. The fresh snow on the roof and ground was pristine, untouched. This was a cover of *Sunset* magazine

"It's beautiful." Lacey felt socked in the stomach. But in a good way. They were miles away from everywhere. Snow was lightly falling and the sky was growing hazy as a new storm blew in. She could live in a place like this. The beauty of the place momentarily disrupted her heartache for Kelly. She breathed deeply, trying to let go of her stress. She simply needed to let the police do their job and find Kelly. Her worrying wasn't helping them succeed.

"It's gonna be cold," he replied. "No one's been up here for a month and the thermostat is set real low. It's going to take a while to warm up.

"Is there a fireplace? Can we build a fire?" She was having visions of a toasty fire with hot chocolate and richly colored Pendleton blankets. And snuggling with Jack.

Whoa. She could snuggle under a blanket by herself just fine. She shot a look at Jack, who was frowning at the darkening sky, and knew if they were under a blanket he wouldn't settle for just snuggling.

Would she? Her stomach twisted pleasantly and she sighed.

"Yeah, there's a monster of a fireplace. I'll get a fire going. What's wrong?"

She abruptly straightened, her eyes open. "Just tired."

"Didn't sleep good last night?"

Disbelieving, she examined his innocent face.

"As well as I could with a drunken bear snoring in my ear."

"I don't snore."

"Wanna bet?"

"Yes." His smile shifted to a leer and she spit out a laugh. The leer was *so* not him. Her tension evaporated. Still laughing, she threw open the truck door. "I'll race you up the stairs." And took off running. She heard him swear and kick his door open.

She beat him to the stairs and took them two at a time. Throwing herself at the gargantuan double front doors, she slammed her hands on the wood.

"Winner!"

Arriving a half second behind her, Jack snugly trapped her between his hard chest and the solid door, putting his hands over hers on the wood. His head bent down to nip playfully at her ear and she inhaled sharply. Just like last night in bed. But today he was sober and awake.

"Here's your prize." His mouth slid down to her neck and gently kissed and nibbled his way to her collarbone. One of his hands lifted her hair and his lips traced back a slow path to the nape of her neck.

She was melting. It was twenty degrees outside and she was melting.

"God, Lacey." His voice was low and strained. "I've wanted to do this for too fucking long."

She closed her eyes and breathed deep, leaning back against him. The hot rush down her spine settled between her hips and all her defenses floated away. She wanted this. She deserved and needed a break, a temporary escape from the real world. She wanted to shut out everything but the man behind her. Her head turned toward him and he seized the opportunity to move his lips to her mouth and spin her body to face him.

He framed her face with his hands and gently ran his tongue along the line of her lips. She opened with an eager moan, working her hands up around his neck and dragging her nails along his scalp. Hot. Too hot.

She felt his body tighten at the touch of her nails and his gentleness vanished, the kiss turned aggressive. Without leaving her mouth, he slid one arm around her back while the other hooked under her thigh and slid her up to his height, keeping her pinned to the door. Once he had her where he wanted her, he pressed his hips against the vee of her legs, his arousal blatantly obvious.

The man knew how to kiss. And seduce. And arouse. Her legs clasped around his hips and she ground against him, speeding up the rush of blood to that delicious spot between her legs. She settled in to enjoy the mouth she'd been staring at for the last few days. The kiss grew stronger, deeper. The sensation of his tongue sliding against hers was heavenly. It was like she'd never been kissed before.

And she hadn't. Not like this.

He kissed like a starved man. Starved for her.

She wanted this. She wanted this more than anything she'd ever wanted. Every part of her was in sync and screaming *yes*!

She felt him pull at the waist of her sweater, lifting. His hands slid under and…

"Ouch!" She jolted and Jack jerked back.

The man with the hot mouth had hands of ice.

"Did I hurt you? What's wrong?"

He'd nearly dropped her when she jumped, and his lust plunged several notches in his shock.

"Your hands are cold!"

He stared blankly at her. "That's it? That's what shocked you?" He thought he'd poked her with his keys or crushed some tender part of her body. Her legs were still wrapped around his waist. He moved his hands to the outside of her sweater. "Better?"

She nodded but had a wary look in her eye that told him she was overanalyzing the situation.

"Stop thinking." He pressed her against the door again.

Her lips turned up slightly. "Then distract me."

She didn't need to ask twice. Thank God, she was ready for distraction. Lacey had been through too much, and he wanted to make all her thoughts of Kelly and killings vanish for a short while. He dove for her lips, intending on kissing her senseless. She opened on contact and he took full advantage. Her nipples hardened through her sweater as she vibrated in his arms. He wanted that sweater gone. But not out here. He felt in his pocket for the cabin key.

"Damn it. It must be in the truck."

He untangled her legs, dropping Lacey back to her feet. She leaned heavily against the door. "If you tell me you left the cabin keys at home I'll strangle you."

He backed away, locking gazes. "Don't move." He dashed to the truck.

He balanced the Macy's bag and two bags of groceries in one arm as he wrestled the cabin key into the lock. His hand was shaking. *Jesus Christ.* He didn't know if he could wait to build a fire, get the heater going, and put away the groceries. She might change her mind.

He pushed the door open and shoved her in. She took two steps and stopped, staring at the interior. He had to sidestep to avoid knocking her over.

"I thought the outside was incredible but this is amazing." Her gaze followed the rustic trusses across the high ceiling, appreciating the huge river-rock fireplace that touched the highest point in the room. The fireplace separated the great room from the kitchen, and as she bent over to look through the fireplace, he knew she could see into the big kitchen. Overstuffed chairs and couches in rich warm hues filled the great room. Wool throws with Indian patterns were tossed on each chair. He watched her run a finger over a sunset-colored throw and mumble.

"What'd you say?" he asked.

"Pendleton. It's a Pendleton throw."

He looked at the blanket. "Yeah." He paused. "Is that all right?" She had an odd little grin on her face.

"It's perfect." This time her smile was warm and her eyes glowed as she faced him. She grabbed the grocery bags. "I'll put these away if you'll get the fire started." Peering into the bag, she asked, "Did you bring hot chocolate?"

She wanted something to drink? Now? "There's some in the kitchen."

"That's perfect too."

He watched her sway to the kitchen with the groceries, thrilled to see her smile. Hopefully she'd relax for a while. Shaking his head, he took the long matches off the mantel, striking one and holding it to the stack of kindling and wood. Number one rule at the cabin. Before leaving, clean out the hearth and have a fire ready to go for the next visit.

He checked the thermostat and cranked it up. Then turned it up again. He didn't want her cold once he got her clothes off. He chuckled as he listened to her rooting through his kitchen. Her clothes were definitely coming off. Soon.

CHAPTER TWENTY-NINE

Sam knocked on the front door of a double-wide and gave Michael a reassuring smile. His insides tightened. He was jazzed about confronting whoever opened the door; it was in his reporter's blood. But he was also getting jazzed by the woman next to him. She was a go-getter. And he liked it. Sam knocked again, frowning this time.

"There has to be someone home. There's always someone home."

He noticed she was studying him out of the corner of her eye.

No one answered and she started to tap a rapid boot toe. Michael heard some thumping inside and the door opened.

"Hey, Sam." The greeting was from a gangly young teen who'd hit that difficult age where his height outpaced his body mass.

"Hi, Bruce. Your mom around?"

The kid pushed the door open. He studied Michael with unquestioning eyes as they stepped into the cramped entry. "No, she went to town."

"Who's watching the little kids today?"

"Lila. Over there." He pointed across the commons to a smaller mobile home.

Sam spun on a heel and pushed Michael back out the door. He stumbled back a half step, nearly losing his balance. Her eyes looked past him and he blinked as he caught...a flash of fear? No way, not from her. She barreled down the stairs, not waiting for him.

Bruce hollered as she darted away. "Hey, Sam, Dad said he wanted you to stay for dinner the next time you came out."

"Not today." She tossed the answer back over her shoulder and nearly broke into a jog.

Michael pulled alongside her, grabbed her arm and yanked her to a stop, bringing his face close to hers. "Hey! What was that about?"

"What do you mean?"

He studied her, his gaze flicking back and forth over her face. She stared back at him blankly, but her pupils dilated the slightest bit and she shook off his hand.

"I mean, why did you plow me over to get out of that house? And start to run when the kid invited you to dinner?"

"I didn't run." She looked away.

He gave a grim smile. "Maybe it wasn't running to you, but to any person who walks at a normal speed, it was running."

Sam met his gaze and her chin lifted a little. She looked like a little kid standing up to a bully. "I don't like it here. I don't like to be in their homes."

He eased back a little, considering her words. He hadn't cared for the cramped, stifling feel to the space either, but he knew there had to be another reason to her rapid escape and she wasn't ready to tell him. He changed the subject. "Who's Lila?"

She relaxed a little, tossing errant bangs out of her eyes. "I think that's who you're looking for. Older lady."

"Linda, Lila. She probably changed her name. I would if my sons were serial killers."

"Sons?" Black brows shot together.

Fuck. He'd told her he was looking for the second son and mother, but hadn't mentioned the police suspected the second son to be a killer too. His breath steamed in the snow. How much should he tell her?

"The police are considering that her other son could be on a killing spree in Portland, killing the people who put away his brother. Revenge killings. That's the real reason why I need to talk to the mother." Would she change her mind about helping him?

Regal eyes considered him. "Sounds personal."

He straightened. Had he sounded that involved? He gave a small nod. "Could be."

"Well, let's see, then." She marched up the rickety stairs to the smaller mobile home and fiercely pounded on the door. On this side of the commons, the wind was whipping through the compound. She tucked her chin and nose into her jacket collar as Michael stood two steps down and kicked the snow off his boots, smiling to himself. Obviously, he'd picked a good partner for his mission.

An older woman in a faded, floral housedress opened the door a few inches and peered at Sam with tired eyes. Instead of a greeting, she just nodded and stood silently, waiting for Sam to state her business. Michael studied the woman and Sam glanced back at him. With the quirk of a dark brow, she silently asked if this was the woman.

She was older and more tired, but she resembled the woman he'd seen in the DeCosta archives. His gut told him he'd nailed a bull's-eye.

He nodded.

"Lila, this is Michael. He's giving me a hand today. Could we come in for a minute?"

Disinterested eyes took one glance at Michael and dismissed him. "There's no one here."

"I think you could probably help us. It'll take only a minute," Sam coaxed.

The woman paused, considered, and opened the door wider.

She looked as if life had made her run a daily marathon under hot sun. Her mouth had that munched-together look indicating she didn't have teeth. A feature Detective Callahan mentioned several times. Had she changed her name?

He followed Sam into the home. The pungent odor of dirty diapers smacked him in the sinuses. The home was too hot. Between the odor, heat, and small space, Michael felt sick. He swallowed the sour lump in his throat and saw Sam do the same.

This better be quick.

Lila led them to the kitchen, but there was nowhere to sit. Every chair at the table held a toddler's booster seat, and the eating surface was overrun with dirty cereal bowls. Three ancient high chairs lined one side of the table. The woman leaned against the stove and looked expectantly at Sam. She ignored Michael.

Soap opera music came from a TV in another room. If there were children in the house, they were silent. Maybe it was naptime.

Sam's blue gaze was on him, waiting.

He decided to be blunt and handed the woman his business card. He saw her eyes widen as she read it, and he swore she turned a shade paler than her already prison-shade pallor.

"As you can see, I'm from Portland and write for *The Oregonian*." He paused. "Do you know why I'm here?"

Her head shook back and forth and she shoved the card back at him. He didn't take it.

"You are Linda DeCosta, right?"

She shrugged.

"I have some questions about your son."

"Dave's dead." Her words were a little difficult to understand without teeth.

"Your other son."

She tightened her lips into a narrow line and it shortened her face another inch. "What about him?"

"Where is he?"

She looked down at the business card again. She had yet to meet his gaze.

"When's the last time you heard from him?"

This time he didn't even get a shrug. Anger boiled under his skin and he checked his temper.

"Look. Innocent people are dying and your son is a suspect, but the police can't find him for questioning. What name is he using?" His voice was too loud.

"I don't know what you're talking about."

Michael could only describe her look as churlish. *Damn it!* His shoulders and chest widened as he took a deep breath and cast about for the right words to throw at her.

Lila immediately cowered and darted away two shaky steps, raising an arm to protect her face.

Michael's jaw dropped. Anger evaporated. "Jesus. I'm not going to touch you!" What kind of life had this woman led?

Sam touched his hand. "Let me talk to her." Her calm eyes were confident. "Why don't you wait outside for a minute?"

Michael studied her composed face. She believed she could get the woman to talk. He glanced at Lila, who was eyeing both of them with trepidation, and saw her hands quiver. Without a word he strode toward the door.

Outside, he sucked in deep breaths of clean air, but couldn't get the stink out of his nose.

The man studied the computer screen in front of him and tightened his fists. Shit! Where was she?

Maybe he could rationalize where Lacey Campbell went. He squeezed shut his eyes and pressed them against the heels of his hands. *Concentrate.* Last time he'd seen her she'd been with Harper. That old coot of a neighbor had said Harper spent the night. Could she possibly still be with him? Something had occurred between those two. His jaw tightened. It wasn't right, but at the moment that didn't matter. He had to get back on track and find her.

Where would that jerk take her?

He cursed his lack of foresight. He'd placed a GPS unit on Lacey's truck, but not Harper's. They could be in any hotel in the state. Or on a plane.

It wasn't supposed to go this way.

A sour scent swirled around him. The scent of carefully orchestrated plans falling apart. More things were going wrong. Like the recent newspaper article about the missing woman. He bit the inside of his cheek, tasting the metal tang of blood. He hadn't laid a hand on Kelly Cates. That had to be someone else. *But who?*

Maybe the police were planting stories to confuse him. He pushed away from his desk, turning his chair to stare at the blank wall. Maybe the police were trying to draw him in with some convoluted trap involving Cates. But he'd carefully checked out the Cates's residence. A distraught husband and teary-eyed daughter were the only inhabitants he'd seen and their pain seemed real. Would the police use a young, innocent girl like that to trap him?

A brief, possessive anger swept through him.

He calmed, breathing steadily and deep. He couldn't worry about Cates and her daughter now. It was time to track down Lacey Campbell. He settled back at his computer, cracked a knuckle, and ran a search for property owned by Jack Harper or Harper Developing.

The listing of real estate was insanely long. He scanned the screen. What exactly was he looking for? Did he expect a red flag to jump out? Here she is! She's staying here! He made a grunt of disgust and forced himself to read slowly.

Jack Harper owned three private residences in three different counties in Oregon. Even one in Mount Junction. The man raised his brows. What a coincidence.

He didn't have the time to visit them all. Chances were slim Lacey was at one anyway. He was grasping at straws. Frustration boiled in his gut. He shot out of his chair and stomped into his kitchen. He grabbed a Diet Coke from the fridge and slammed the door shut. Where in the hell should he look for Harper?

Maybe Harper would look for him.

The plastic bottle hovered an inch from his lips as his brain grabbed the thought and held tight.

Make Harper look for him.

He didn't move, afraid the idea would slip away if he shifted a single muscle. What would make Harper hunt for him? His mind kicked into overdrive. He could think of several possibilities.

Fuck, yes! He took a deep drink and enjoyed the sensation of the carbonation on his throat. He dabbed at his mouth with a napkin.

He was back in control.

CHAPTER THIRTY

Jack leaned one shoulder against the big fireplace and smiled, watching Lacey in his kitchen as she poured hot water into the mugs of chocolate mix. He'd stood like this before. In her kitchen a few nights ago. Then she'd been petrified and nervous. Now she had a warm smile as she looked up at him and stirred the chocolate. He stepped around behind her, slid his arms around her stomach, and tugged her back to him.

She'd relaxed as they entered the cabin. All the tension during the drive up had melted away after he'd kissed her. He wasn't getting the uncertain vibes that'd hung about her for several days. She had come to some sort of decision about him.

He hoped it was the same one he'd made days ago.

"That smells great." He wasn't talking about the chocolate.

Lacey lifted a mug and took a sniff. "I know. I can't be in this cabin during a snowfall without some hot chocolate. It puts me in the right mood."

"Good." He nuzzled her hair and felt her relax into him. The sun had set and he watched large snowflakes blow against the kitchen windows. The smell of the fire was drifting through the big room. He flipped off a switch in the kitchen and the cabin fell into a lovely warm light from the flames. She shivered.

"Are you cold?" He wrapped more of his body around her.

"No. Just…a little on edge." She turned her head to look at him and he spotted the lines of tension across her forehead. He kissed them away, lingering on the silk of her skin.

"You're safe here. There's no way he can find you. No one can get up our road without a four-wheel drive and night vision goggles." The cabin road was a winding, twisting unmarked dirt road that even he wouldn't attempt to drive in the dark.

She exhaled and nodded. "It's just that I worry…"

He cut her off. "No more worrying or thinking tonight." He didn't let her answer as he covered her lips and turned her to face him. "It's just you and me. And I want to make love with you right now. More than anything I've ever wanted." His chest tightened as he spoke; it was the truth. He felt her soften against him with a small sound.

He took the hot chocolate out of her hand and boosted her onto the countertop, stepping inside her thighs and pulling her tight against his stomach all while keeping the kiss. Her hands moved up to his neck, lightly stroking a clever spot behind his ear that pumped lightning into his spine.

He pulled back from her mouth, gently framing her jaw with his hands, and ran a thumb across her damp lips. His breath hissed in as she took his thumb between her teeth and touched her tongue to the tip. Her pupils dilated, the flames from the fireplace reflecting back at him. God, she was lovely. She brought out something wild in him. It made him want to toss her on her back, rip off her jeans and take her right here on the kitchen floor. His heart sped up and he lifted a hand to touch the soft hair by her ear. He slowed his strokes, wanted to revel in every long second, imprint the sensations in his memory.

He kissed her again, letting his hands slide through her hair. The rush of sleekness tormented the sensitive skin between each finger. The matching silk of her tongue teased his mouth and he pushed deeper into her. His hand slid to the small of her back and under her sweater, down below the low waist of her jeans. His fingers crossed a band of stretchy lace to the smooth skin of her bottom. *A thong.* His groin surged. He slid his hand as far down as he could into her jeans and cupped her firm cheek, pulling her closer. She caught her breath against his mouth with a small moan and he nearly exploded.

Christ. Two minutes with the woman and he was nearly shooting off like a teenager.

He broke the kiss and rested his forehead to hers; his eyes closed and he breathed slowly. His body screamed for him to rush, but his mind said wait. Since when did he listen to his brain in the middle of temptation?

Being with her was different.

"Jack?" She was hesitant, questioning. Her voice throaty.

He kept his eyes shut but nodded. His forehead still connected with hers.

"Give me a second."

She brought her hands down and lifted his shirt. "I want to see you." The shirt pulled higher. "I want to touch you." There was a bit of brazenness in her low words. "This morning I only got to look. Now I want to touch." She leaned to touch her tongue to his earlobe as her nails ran across his nipples. Icy hot bolts of sensation shot down below his stomach.

Apparently she didn't understand what "Give me a second" meant to a man. He clenched his teeth and ripped the shirt over his head. "I wouldn't have complained if you'd touched." He dropped his shirt on the floor, gave her a fast deep kiss, and pulled her sweater off. "No one was stopping you," he whispered. Her bra was simple and smooth. Her breasts were just right. Not big. Just utterly enticing. He lifted one with his hand and felt her nipple tighten. Her chin dropped a notch and she closed her eyes, arching her back, pushing into his touch.

She was his, giving him permission to do as he pleased, responding hotly to his simple touch. She'd handed him total power.

He unclasped the bra hooks, sliding the straps down her arms and stepping back the slightest bit to look at her in the flickering light. Exquisite. He leaned over and lifted a breast to his mouth and tasted the satin of her skin, catching a nipple between his teeth and scraping lightly. She gasped and leaned back on her hands.

Whom was he fooling? This woman had total power over him.

He kissed his way to the other breast and unbuttoned her jeans, his mind under attack by the memory of lace underneath. He straightened and she weakly protested as he left her breasts. He slid her hips forward off the counter, and she landed on unsteady legs, her sexy cowboy boots rapping the floor. He pushed her jeans down to midthigh and tossed her back up on the counter wearing just that thong. It was hot pink. Breathing hard, she curled her hands around the counter's edge. He put two hands on her boots and slipped both off at once. Her jeans followed an instant later. Loving the surprise in her eyes, he stepped close to kiss her witless.

His mind was spinning. He couldn't wait to get inside this woman and drive her wild.

Lacey gasped as her jeans hit the floor. It'd happened so fast. One minute he had the slowest, most sensual hands she's ever felt, and then the next minute he raced along like a NASCAR driver. She couldn't catch her breath; he kept knocking her off guard. He stepped close to kiss her with a possessive male look that triggered a hot fervor in her groin. She moved against him and grew wet, slick. Why'd he leave her panties in the way?

She unsnapped the top of his jeans, but he elbowed her arms out of reach and kissed her with a fierceness that curled her toes. His mouth was hot and commanding, taking everything she had. She wanted to beat on his back with her fists to make him let her touch him, but she settled for touching his shoulders, chest and biceps. Those cut muscles she'd admired last night were as hard as iron. He had the body of an athlete. Muscle, speed, and length. She outlined his pecs, running her fingers through the soft hair on his chest. His mouth moved up her cheek to her eyelids and back to her ear. As he traced the arc of her ear with a hot wet tongue, his hand slid between her thighs and firmly brushed a spot through her panties that made her spine melt. Then he did it again, and she clutched at his shoulders, digging her nails into his deltoids and closing her eyes. It was a double assault. Her ear and her clit.

She wanted this man. It didn't matter about his past or hers. She'd wanted him from the beginning, but never dreamed she would end up in a snow-covered cabin, making love to him by firelight.

"Ohhh. Jack. I need...you need to let me..." He touched her again and she lost her train of thought. *Jeans. She needed his jeans off now. Now.* She reached for his fly again and yanked before he could stop her, flipping all the snaps open at once. He pushed her back, arching her over his arm, and attacked a breast with his teeth and tongue. She squirmed under the wild onslaught of sensation. He pushed aside the crotch of her panties and ran two fingers through her folds. He slid his fingers up and down, spreading her wetness, and she pushed against his hand, needing more than the delicious friction. She was unbearably aroused, her skin ultrasensitive. Her stomach convulsed. She needed him to do more than touch her.

"Please. Jack. You've got to...please."

"Please what?"

"What?" Her brain was low on oxygen.

"Ask me again." His hot, wet mouth swept to her other breast and bit gently.

"Please. I need. You. Now!" She ended on a gasp as two of those fingers slid home and stroked her from the inside. This wasn't going to take any time at all; she was so close. A talented thumb rubbed at her clit as he stroked her inside and she squeezed her inner muscles tight, sending herself over. Flashes of light danced across the back of her eyelids and she strained her head back in pleasure. Her contractions milked his fingers as she rode the wave. He didn't stop his movements and sent her flying again.

Jack carefully laid her limp form back on the counter and slipped off her panties as his head rested between her breasts. He could hear her heart pound and her lungs grab short gasps of air. Her erotic slickness still pulsated around his other hand as her fingernails stroked his hair. He pressed a kiss against her stomach, dipping his tongue into her belly button, making her stomach quiver. He'd never been so fucking turned on in his life. He'd nearly lost it watching her come.

Taking his hands from her, he pried off his boots and pulled down his jeans she'd ripped open. Lacey pushed up to her elbows, watching him, her legs dangling limply off the counter. Her eyes locked on his hard length as it pointed toward home. She sat up and reached for him with an unsteady hand, and guided him to her. The feel of her fingers blew his arousal over the top and he clenched his stomach, fighting for control. Her fingers wrapped around him and squeezed firmly, running her palm over his head. He watched her, fascinated by the hungry look on her face. When her exploration was finished, she put a hand on his shoulder and pulled him closer, directing him into her. His hands took hold on her hips, bringing her to the absolute edge of the counter. He nudged just inside her entrance and stopped, fighting every hormone in his head that screamed for him to pound into her. He lifted her chin with a hand and softly kissed her mouth. She opened her lips with a quiet sigh, closed her eyes, and he entered with his tongue, exploring her mouth. He pulled his hips back, sliding out and she protested, pushing against him. He slid in again, just the littlest bit, feeling her stretch and shape herself to him. He took a deep breath and exhaled.

"Lacey." He wanted her eyes open. He wanted her to look at him.

Her lids slowly lifted. In the firelight her eyes were dark, their color unclear, but he could read her desire. It was the counterpart to his. With the sense of a fated moment, he clamped his palm on her bottom and slid home with one strong thrust. Her eyes widened and she gasped.

"Feel me. Feel me inside you." She was hot, slick, and tight, and he didn't ever want to leave. He fought his instinct to batter into her and held perfectly still, feeling her pulsate and squeeze around him. He would never forget the sensation. She pulled on his shoulders and shamelessly ground against him.

"Damn you, Jack. Move!" She wrapped her legs around his hips and squeezed, rocking her hips. She lifted her chin and pushed her neck against his lips, demanding his attention. He inhaled deeply, smelling her arousal and the delicious scent that was uniquely Lacey. He grazed her neck with his teeth. She continued to grind against him, small exclamations of frustration spilling from her mouth. He didn't move as she tortured him. Pure bliss, pure torture. He didn't want it to end.

It was time. He wrapped his arms tight around her and lifted her off the counter. She let out a cry of anger as he pulled out. He carried her into the great room where he'd created a nest with thick sleeping bags and down comforters. He kneeled and laid her back, brushing the waves of hair out of her face. The firelight caught her eyes, revealing her desperate need. He positioned his body above her and lowered his head, speaking against her eager mouth.

"Hang on, baby."

She couldn't see. She couldn't hear. All her senses were focused on one spot in her body. Jack had finally let go and was fucking her like he'd waited a decade for release. She rocked against him and clutched his shoulders for the ride. The frantic friction was driving her higher. One second she felt waves of satisfaction and the next second her body screamed, aching to be filled. It was a rocking of emotion and sensation that was threatening to burst her heart. He tensed and increased his pace, shortening his thrusts as he reached between them and stroked her. She felt the quake start at her core. She squeezed him tight, heard him shout, and she tumbled over the crest, dragging him with her.

Lacey lay halfway on top of him, sated and exhausted on the cushion of comforters and sleeping bags. She traced a finger down his stomach, exploring his body, watching each muscle tense as she touched it. He was beautifully made. Solid muscle everywhere it counted. They relaxed in the silence, interrupted only by the occasional crackle of the fire. Her hand moved down his thigh and lingered over a thick knot in his skin. Curious, she pushed up and looked closer. It was an angry round scar.

"It was a bullet." He had a hand under his head, propped against a pillow he stole from the couch, as he watched her explore. At his even tone, she turned to study his face.

"What happened?" She caught her breath as his face closed off and he reminded her of Alex. That vacant emptiness in his eyes. Jack didn't want to talk about it. She moved up his body until she could kiss away the blank face that gave her chills. His silver eyes flickered with the firelight and she felt his heart speed up under her hand. She stayed silent and waited.

He told her a story that sent her own heart racing.

"You could have been killed." She stared in shock.

"A lot of people could have been killed. Neither of us checked them for weapons. Stupid mistake." Anger spat from his eyes.

She spoke slowly. "Is that when you left the department?"

Jack nodded. "I couldn't do it anymore. I wanted to whip out my weapon every time I came in contact with a person. I was a mental wreck. I needed a job where I could control what went on around me. A cop's job has too much uncertainty." He paused. "I had to walk away. It got to the point where I couldn't pick up a gun without getting physically ill. And I haven't been able to touch one since." He stared at the fire. "I couldn't do the job. I thought I was going to hurt someone else."

She sat up. "You didn't hurt that woman! Her husband did."

"I know." She could tell from his face he was lying.

She touched his face, loving the feel of the sandpaper of his cheek. She bent down and breezed her lips across the stubble, the tickle stimulating a new arousal. "It wasn't your fault. You could never hurt anybody. When I'm with you...I feel safe. You wouldn't let anything hurt me." She moved to his lips and he ran his hands up and down her back, kissing her deeply. "I trust you, Jack." The words surprised her as she said them. "I trust very few people and you've become one of them."

In a move that stole her breath, he flipped her onto her back and set upon her with his tongue and rough hands. Heat flared in her veins at his possessive handling. She reached out to touch his face. In his sad eyes she saw his desperate need to believe her as he moved between her legs and claimed her again.

Jack stretched his legs, pushing his feet out from under the down comforter toward the fire. The flames were gone and hot red coals warmed his toes. He needed to toss a few more logs on the fire. Lacey slept curled against him. Turning his face to press his nose into her soft waves, he inhaled deeply. He could smell her vanilla scent and something else. Her hair smelled like she'd been rolling around in bed with a man. But not just any man. Him.

He wallowed contentedly in the possessive surge that swam through his tired body. She'd said she trusted him, believed he could keep her safe. God damn it, he'd prove her right even if he had to lock her in the cabin for a month. His body hardened at the thought, erotic images dancing about his brain. He studied her profile in the wan light, wanting to wake her but also wanting to keep staring as she slept. This wasn't the usual postcoital glow.

She'd sunk into his core and imprinted his heart.

He was hooked.

CHAPTER THIRTY-ONE

"We've got an address."

Lusco snapped his cell shut, scribbling on his notebook. "Brody came through. He found Linda DeCosta and she gave him an address. It's out in Molalla, about twenty miles south of here. Property search says the owner is Robert Costar. That's got to be our man. The mom said she's been in touch with her son periodically. Claims her boy isn't doing anything."

"Yeah, right." Mason was already slipping into his coat. "Call county. Get them to do a drive-by and watch the place. Get their SWAT unit in on this. I'm not taking any chances." His energy rocketed like he'd had a double shot of epinephrine. Finally, a break. And it felt like a good one. The search for Kelly

Cates had turned up nothing. No video footage at her gym, no abandoned car, no sightings. She'd literally vanished. He was ready for a lead like this. The phone on Mason's desk rang and he snapped it up impatiently, tucking it between his ear and shoulder as he struggled with a twisted coat sleeve. "Callahan."

He froze, his coat partially on. "Are you shitting me? You're sure? He's the one who called it in? Why?" He grabbed at the receiver as it started to slip.

Mason's hard gaze locked with Ray's as the voice babbled in his ear. Then he hung up the phone and stared at it. He closed his eyes as he felt his adrenaline jump off a high dive and land in a belly flop. His case was imploding.

"This can't be happening. Too many things at once," he muttered.

"What? What happened?" Ray sounded ready to strangle him.

"Melody Harper's gone. Grabbed late last night." He rubbed a tired hand across his face.

"Harper's sister? Another woman's been grabbed? Are they sure? And they think it's our guy?"

"Pretty damned sure. The kidnapper called it in himself. Told the nine-one-one operator we've been looking for him for the cop and lawyer murders."

"Our guy? Why?" Ray was incredulous.

"Beats the shit out of me. Her maid verified Melody never came home last night and her car is still in the parking garage." But Mason knew their killer was pissed. Dr. Campbell had been removed from his reach and now he was striking back by grabbing other women. First Kelly Cates and then Melody Harper. He must have known the little dentist was with Jack Harper so he struck out at Harper through his sister. Mason needed to call Harper. The man was going to throw a gasket.

Mason slowly finished putting on his coat and set his cowboy hat on his head. It felt lined with lead. "Warn SWAT we might have a hostage situation at the Molalla house. He might have Kelly or Melody there."

Lacey felt Jack stir beneath her. From his breathing she knew he was awake. She kept her eyes closed, indulging in the moment. He'd cocooned her from reality for a few hours, letting her relax and briefly forget the horrors going on in the outside world. They'd made love for hours and it'd been heavenly. The fire, the snow outside, the amazing man.

Too good to be true.

But it was true. He was here in the flesh and she could hear his heart as her head lay on his warm chest. Lazily, her thoughts swept back over the hot night. She didn't care if she was just another notch on his belt. It'd been worth it.

Some female instinct told her the night had been special to him. His eyes had told her as he kissed her, entered her. The wanting, the desire. Lust had shined there, but not exclusively. It'd gone deeper than that. She didn't believe he would break her heart.

But she couldn't help but feel…optimistic?

Stop analyzing. Just enjoy the moment. Her lips stretched into a smile and she felt his chest rumble with a silent laugh.

She opened her eyes, purposefully dragging out the movement to make a point about her utter physical satiation. Gray eyes sparkled at her, relaxation shining from their depths. Silent happy fireworks shot off in her brain.

He was gorgeous. So entirely male. And right now he belonged to her. She ran her nails through the hair on his chest, making his nipples tighten in response and she reveled in the power of being a woman. The power to arouse a man through the simplest things. It was intoxicating. She lifted her head to smile directly at him, considering making him beg.

"Hey."

"Hey, yourself," she whispered back, sinking into those silver eyes. He had the most beautiful eyes. They could shift from the dark gray of rain-laden clouds to the silver hue of sunshine glinting off a lake.

He rolled her onto her back for a deep, arousing kiss, raking his fingers through her hair and crushing her breasts with the weight of his chest. She felt his growing hardness at her thigh. A cell phone rang.

"Shit."

"I don't want to answer it." He tried to distract her with his fingers.

"You need to. It might be important." She reluctantly sat up, pushing back the comforter, exposing her breasts to the cooler air. His eyes darkened and he cupped one, a wicked slow smile on his lips. Closing her lids, she nearly gave in, but the phone rang again, and she shoved his hand away and crawled over to his jacket on the couch.

"How can you expect me to keep my hands to myself when you look like that?" Glancing back, she saw his gaze focused on her bare bottom as she kneeled at the couch. She gave a teasing grin and glanced at the screen on his phone.

Detective Callahan.

Her smile faded as she sucked a breath.

Her face blank, she silently handed the phone to Jack. He'd sat up with a frown as she'd stared at the caller ID.

As Jack listened, Lacey watched his countenance change. He flinched and the healthy color faded from his skin. Anger replaced the shock, his jaw tightened and lines appeared around his mouth. Lacey's heart accelerated at the stress on his face, her breathing forced. Her lungs seizing.

He hung up, his gaze on the fire, his face a mess of conflicting emotions. "He's taken Melody."

Lacey sat hard on the floor. "What? Your sister?"

He's grabbed another one. My God. What has he done with Kelly? He's already moved on to another woman?

With a burst of energy, Jack stood up and strode into the kitchen, returning with his clothes. He dressed with shaking hands, words spilling. "The bastard called to let the cops know he had my sister. Callahan thinks they might know where she is. Your buddy, Brody, got an address from Linda DeCosta. Her son Bobby has a house in Molalla. The police are going in with SWAT in a few hours." He picked up his socks. "The guy didn't mention Kelly."

Pulling her bare legs tight to her chest, Lacey buried her head in her knees.

Me. He was supposed to get me. Not Jack's sister.

The temperature in the toasty cabin felt like it had dropped to subzero and her teeth chattered. This was her fault. The killer was sending a message to her. Hurting Kelly and Melody because he couldn't reach her. He was angry and striking out.

She'd pulled Jack into her chaos of a life and endangered his family. Why'd she let Jack stick around? If she'd brushed him off they wouldn't be in this position. His sister wouldn't be with a killer.

They'd been literally screwing around and this was the consequence.

Her newfound happiness floated up the chimney and vanished with the smoke.

She shuddered and bit her knee, causing little red dents.

He kneeled in front of her, his shirt unbuttoned. "Lacey, get dressed. I want to be there when they go in." He looked at the red spots on her knee in confusion. "What are you doing?" His eyes met hers and understanding dawned. "Oh, God. This isn't your fault."

She couldn't answer, and felt tears burn in the back of her eyes.

"This isn't your fault. I've been dragged into this mess by being in the wrong place at the wrong time too many times. It's not because of you." He stayed on his knees in front of her, his hands gripping hers.

Unable to talk, she shook her head.

"Stop it. It's no one's fault except for the creep who's doing this. And the police are about to stop him. I've got to be there." He lifted her chin to get her to look at him, his eyes intense.

"I chose to be with you, stay with you, knowing some sicko could be after you. And I don't regret a single moment! I want…" His fingers tightened on her face as he fought for words. "Listen to me. *It's not your fault!* This isn't doing any good. Let's get going, all right?"

Her heart tightened, and she knew he meant every word he'd said.

She nodded. He was right. Sitting here, feeling sorry for herself, wasn't helping anyone.

Especially Melody and Kelly.

Melody's teeth clanked against each other.

Her bathroom prison was frigid. She paced circles in the tiny windowless room, rubbing her hands on her sleeves, trying to make some heat with the friction. The pale blue walls were icy to the touch and her silk blouse and expensive skirt didn't offer much resistance to the cold.

She glanced down and saw two damned runs in her pantyhose. Her fingers felt around her right calf and found another. She hiked up her skirt and ripped off the suffocating nylon.

She beat on the bathroom door with her fists. Again.

"God damn it! Get me out of here, you fucking bastard!"

Silence.

Maybe he'd left.

Hands stinging, she kicked at the door, using the balls of her feet, avoiding her frozen toes. He'd locked the bathroom door from the outside with a bolt.

Her prison had been stripped. He'd removed the towel racks and shower rod. He'd emptied all toiletries from the mirrored drug cabinet and the cupboards below the counter. Melody had turned the place inside out in her hunt for a weapon or tool. She'd broken her fingernails as she attempted to unscrew the fasteners on the metal drawer handles. Then she'd yanked on the showerhead, but had only torn a good-sized hole in the wall where the head was attached. She'd done the same with the fan cover in the ceiling. Her efforts didn't yield anything usable, but it made her feel much better.

Ever since she'd woken up on the bathroom floor, she'd been racking her brain to understand what in the hell had happened. She remembered standing in the parking garage, fishing in her purse for her car keys, and wondering if she'd left them on the kitchen counter. A soft sound behind her had caught her attention, but she ignored it, concentrating on finding her keys. Then he'd come from behind, fast and strong.

It'd been like a B horror movie, and she'd starred as the too-stupid-to-live female lead. Something fabric had been placed across her mouth and nose, and she'd held her breath, knowing that to inhale would be dangerous. But he'd pinched her, making her gasp with pain and draw in breaths from the stinking rag. Dark mists had rushed at her eyes as she fought to stay conscious. Turning her head, she'd caught a glimpse of short dark hair.

She couldn't remember past that.

He'd taken her watch, along with her shoes. She had no idea what time it was, or how long she'd been locked in the bathroom.

She kicked the door, angry at herself for being weak and stupid. She'd known better. She knew the warnings for women. Have your keys ready, check your surroundings. Confident in the safety of the well-lit parking garage, she'd let her defenses relax.

Never again.

The gaping hole around the loose showerhead caught her eye, triggering an idea, and she spun to look at the toilet. She lifted the heavy lid off the back of the toilet and struck the mirrored cabinet with it. Crashing shards of mirror flew everywhere. She picked up two of the larger sharp pieces. Weapons. She stuck the counter with one, testing it. It broke on the impact, but created a deep gouge in the countertop and a small slice on her palm.

She sucked at the wound. The shards weren't very strong, but they were sharp. She could do some good bloody damage with them. With a grim smile she eyed the toilet lid again. It was too heavy to use as a weapon. She grasped the awkward lid and clobbered the door with it. It made a satisfying boom but no damage. She did it again. And again.

When her arms were tired, she deliberately dropped the lid in the sink, shattering out pieces of the porcelain bowl. If she couldn't get out, she would create a big, expensive mess for someone to clean up and repair. Ramming the door had made a short crack in the bathroom door by the knob. She ran her finger down it, proud. Her muscles ached from its creation, but it was a start.

She drank water from her hands out of the sink. At least she had water. She could survive a long time on just water. Carefully stepping around the mirror pieces on the floor, she sat down on the toilet lid to catch her breath. She buried her head in her hands, wiped at her tears, and tried not to think of the newspaper articles. The ones about the serial killer. She'd read terrible stories about the torture and murder of the men. *This couldn't be related.* Someone was killing men related to that old Co-Ed Slayer case. He wasn't targeting women. *But there was a woman missing.* She'd heard it on the news in her car. Would she be the next part of the story?

No. This had to be a ransom thing. Jack would pay whatever they wanted, and she would be freed. She pulled some toilet paper off the roll and blew her nose. She eyed the small roll and her eyes teared again. Maybe she shouldn't be wasting it on her nose. Exhausted, she straightened her back and took a deep breath. Her eyes fought to stay open as she stepped gingerly over the shards on the floor and into the tub; the only place safe from broken glass. Lying down on her side, the hard plastic was icy against her skin and she shivered. She pulled her knees up to her chest, wrapped her arms around them, and closed her eyes, leaving the lights on. Unpredictable spasms from the cold shot through her torso, but she finally fell into a light sleep.

A rapid phone call to Callahan allowed Jack through the line of police that blocked the road into the Molalla neighborhood. He pushed past the cops who'd stopped him and sprinted through the fresh snow. Two blocks away the detectives and SWAT were readying to raid a house farther around the corner. Thankfully, Lacey had agreed to wait in his truck. She'd been shaken to the core by the news about Melody the entire two-hour drive. Jack was shook up too. Twice he'd nearly rear-ended vehicles on the highway.

"They found him," she'd muttered over and over in the truck. "It's over." Her head had shaken back and forth as she leaned against the headrest. "I can't believe it. I can't believe it." Her eyes clenched shut.

"Do you think he knows what happened to Suzanne?" she'd whispered once.

Jack had nodded. "I think he knows exactly what fucking happened."

"What about the…" Lacey had turned her head toward the window, but Jack had spotted the tears and read her mind.

"We'll find out where the baby is."

She'd nodded, unable to answer.

Not a baby. A child.

Please, God, let Melody be OK.

Jack had parked the truck and leaped out his door. He jogged round to her door and opened it, but Lacey sat still. Her hands were in a knot in her lap. She wouldn't meet his gaze.

"I don't want to watch. I don't want to see…where he kept her. I can't." Jack hadn't asked any more questions. He'd understood perfectly. For the past two hours he'd been sick to his stomach about what the police might find. Fishhooks and broken bones had haunted him as he'd driven off the mountain. But now they'd found the sick bastard's home. He started to help Lacey out of the warm truck, but she'd shaken her head as he reached for her. He'd paused and glanced around at the dozen cop cars lining and blocking the street. He relented.

"Lock the doors," he said firmly.

Anger flowed through him and he pumped his legs harder as he ran down the street. The bastard had his sister. If he'd done anything to hurt her...Jack wouldn't be responsible for his actions.

Melody had to be alive.

He spotted Callahan and Lusco in a group of cops and headed their way. "What's going on?" Their attention was directed toward a small ranch-style house at the end of the street. A newer Toyota Camry sat in the driveway with fresh tire tracks in the snow behind it.

Lusco glared at him, but Callahan answered. "SWAT is getting ready to pull up front. They've got snipers already in position. They're going in through the front door with the back entrance to the house as their plan B. This could be a hostage situation if he's home, so stay the fuck out of the way." His sharp eyes repeated his words as he gave a tug at his hat brim.

Jack nodded and moved twenty feet away into a position where he could see the house. Callahan abruptly turned back to him. "Where's Dr. Campbell?"

Jack gestured back the way he'd come. "Back at the roadblock in my truck."

Relief crossed the detective's face and he turned back to the group of cops.

Jack watched, unable to keep his feet still, wanting to get in the house and beat the crap out of the man. He closed his eyes and concentrated on Melody. *She's got to be here. If he's hurt her, he's a dead man.*

He tensed as the big military-looking SWAT vehicle roared up to the front of the home and hit the brakes. A dozen armored men poured out and divided. Half going to the front of the house, and half streaming to the back.

A horrific crash jerked Melody awake. She pushed up from the tub with her hands, and then cowered back down. Sounds of shouts and threats filtered through her door. A man's high voice screamed and heavy footsteps sounded, running through the house.

She leaped out of the tub and beat her bruised fists on the door, ignoring the sharp glass that sliced her feet. Loud booted steps came closer.

"Let me out!" What if the boot steps left and let her rot in this damned prison? "He locked me in! Let me out of here!" She pounded frantically on the hard door.

"Who's there?" A muffled masculine voice came through the door, and she leaned her cheek and chest against the wood.

"I'm Melody Harper. He kidnapped me and locked…" More shouting interrupted her words. The man outside the door was yelling at others in the house, but she couldn't make out the words. His voice grew fainter.

She pounded on the door and shrieked, "Don't leave!"

"Stand back from the door."

She stumbled back and tried to squeeze between the toilet and wall. *Was he going to shoot?*

The door rattled and shook as something hammered the outside. She watched the crack she'd created lengthen. The door shook again and splintered by the knob. One more hit had it flying open and a man in a helmet abruptly stepped around the corner with a gun pointed at her. Her legs gave out and she collapsed against the toilet in relief. She didn't need to see his face. The body armor was reassurance enough.

"Damn it." The SWAT vehicle had blocked his view. Jack was moving to where he could clearly see when the front door crashed open and a mass of loud voices shouted to get down. His teeth clenched. Every voice inside his head urged him to get over there and find his sister.

A rumble of voices accompanied a group of SWAT members back out of the house. At the front of the group, a man with his hands behind his back stumbled across the white yard. SWAT shoved him onto his stomach in the snow. Two heavily armored officers stood over him, guns aimed at his head.

Fuck, yes! Got him!

Jack squinted at the form on the snow. The man was shaking in fear and awkwardly whipping his head around to see behind him.

Jack blinked. He knew him. He knew that face. Stepping closer, he cast a glance toward the detectives who wore twin expressions of surprise. They'd recognized the figure in the snow too.

Frank Stevenson. Lacey's ex.

Jack stopped cold, sucking in a deep breath. *Something's wrong.* His intestines twisted. That gutless rat-bastard couldn't be a killer. Stevenson couldn't have done all those… Jack's heart froze.

It was a setup. Melody wasn't here. It'd been a ruse to get him...

Lacey.

He spun in the snow and sprinted back to his truck. His heart made the blood pound through his brain and he ignored the shouts of Callahan behind him.

The detective had figured it out too.

Mason swore. He'd made the mistake letting himself hope the nightmare was over.

"Holy shit! It's Stevenson. It *was* him." Ray was stunned.

"It's not him."

"Yes it is. That's Dr. Campbell's ex." Ray headed closer, eager for a look, but Mason grabbed his arm, feeling his blood pressure rocket.

"No. That's not our guy," Mason croaked.

Ray stopped and opened his mouth, but was distracted by a man tearing away down the street. "Where the fuck's he going?" Mason turned. Jack Harper was sprinting away.

"Harper, check your truck!" Stevenson was a hoax; Harper had already figured it out.

"What's going on?" Ray's confused gaze went to the man in the snow and then back to Harper running in the opposite direction. Before Mason could speak, he saw understanding flash across Ray's face. The detective swore.

"We've been set up." Ray moved to race back to their car, but he stopped and glanced back at Frank Stevenson, unsure where to go first.

Mason grabbed his arm and hauled him toward Stevenson. "We're in the right place, but that's not the right guy. He better fucking know where the right guy is."

Stevenson yelled at the circle of cops standing around him. "I didn't do anything. The door was unlocked." He shouted at the pair of detectives as they stepped up. "I was just looking!"

"What in the hell were you doing in that house?" he snapped, wanting to stomp on Stevenson's head and kick him with his cowboy boots. Then punch him in his yellow gut.

"He told me she was here," Stevenson sputtered.

"Who? Who told you?"

"I don't know." He drew out the words in a wail. "Someone called. Said Celeste was here fucking around with some guy. Said I could catch them in the act."

"Your wife's cheating on you?"

"I don't know!" Red jealousy flushed his face, a sharp contrast to the snow. "I didn't think she was until I got the call. I had to find out!" Mason stood silent, weighing the man's words. God damn it, he believed the asshole. The man wasn't intelligent enough to be their killer.

DeCosta had orchestrated this whole setup.

DeCosta must have tempted Stevenson into his home because he knew the police were coming. DeCosta knew Stevenson would come looking for his wife, and he knew the police would come searching for a hostage.

Bobby DeCosta, a.k.a. Robert Costar, had made Mason look like an idiot. An idiot who'd called out the heavy artillery for nothing.

But *why* did he do it?

A commotion at the house drew his attention.

"Sir, we've got her!"

Melody Harper emerged from the home, leaning heavily on the officer next to her. Her clothes were wrinkled, her hair limp, and she was barefoot. She stepped through the snow without noticing the cold, leaving bloody footsteps. Shock covered her face as she took in the mass of police force. Mason closed his eyes.

Thank you, God. He hadn't totally fucked up.

At least on this aspect Mason's gut had been right.

He strode to the woman, pulled off his heavy coat, and wrapped it around her shoulders, rubbing his hands over her upper arms in attempt to warm her. Blurry eyes looked at him gratefully and then shifted to stare at the man on his belly in the snow.

"He doesn't have dark hair." Her voice was confused. "That's not him. That's not the man from the parking garage."

Mason nodded. "We know."

"Then why is he cuffed?" Curious eyes looked at him. They were the same color as her brother's. Mason stared, seeing the resemblance to Jack Harper in the shape of her face, but on her the effect was startlingly feminine.

"Because he's an idiot."

"Oh." She calmly accepted that reason and started to shudder violently.

"Get her in a car and warmed up." He gestured at a uniform to take her as his cell rang.

"Callahan."

"She's gone. He took her." Harper was out of breath, but Mason heard the fury in his voice. "He's got Lacey."

"Don't touch anything." He'd nearly hung up when he remembered Jack had run off before Melody appeared. "Harper, wait! Your sister was in the house. She's OK."

Silence filled the line for two seconds. "She was there? She's all right? When I saw Stevenson I figured the whole thing was a setup. Did he hurt her?"

"She's OK," Mason repeated. "She wasn't hurt. We're taking care of her."

Jack exhaled loudly in the phone. "Thank you."

"Don't move. We'll be right there."

Mason slapped his phone shut and gestured at Ray.

"We've got another situation."

Mason felt like he'd aged ten years. The emotional ups and downs of this case were going to kill him. He took a deep breath, pulled his hat, and started a rapid walk down the cold street to the roadblock. One phrase ricocheted through his skull.

This isn't over.

CHAPTER THIRTY-TWO

It was too easy.

While the police focused on his house, he'd simply hidden in a house down the street. The owners had asked him to feed the dog while they were on vacation. He liked dogs and the home provided the perfect foil to avoid the police and watch as they surrounded his home. He'd even parked his car in the neighbor's garage.

Thank goodness, his mother had cared enough to call and warn him.

She'd hesitated on the phone, uncertain she was doing the right thing. He'd cajoled as usual, lying about his involvement, claimed the police were trying to pin things on him because he was Dave's brother. He'd convinced her he would talk to the police and straighten it out.

So gullible. All women were.

Even the untouchable Dr. Campbell.

She hadn't blinked when he rushed up to the truck, saying Detective Callahan wanted her out of the street, out of harm's way, and in the safe house. The police at the roadblock had been distracted with the events down the street. They weren't watching behind them and didn't see Lacey get out of the truck and cross to the house. He'd seen the flicker of recognition spark. She'd known him from somewhere, but couldn't place him. He'd worn a navy blue ball cap and windbreaker. Generic police-looking enough. She'd probably thought she'd seen him with the detectives. The momentary confusion had her following him silently as she tried to place his face.

As the two of them stepped through the door, and he laid his hand at the small of her back, she'd known.

He'd felt her twitch the second comprehension dawned. By then it was too late; she was in the house. He'd simply followed the same routine as with the Harper woman. Cloth over the face, make them inhale, and then into his car.

This one had fought. Fought like a furious little cat. She'd knocked two pictures off the wall and broke some sort of Chinese figurine. She'd used teeth, fingernails, and feet to fight him. He gently touched his face. He'd have a scratch on his cheek and bite mark on his arm for a week. Bitch.

The police hadn't glanced his way as he backed out of the garage and drove off. The snow in the street in front of the house had been flattened and messed up by police vehicles and boots. His tracks were indistinguishable.

He downed his coffee and scanned the main room of the cabin. He needed to prepare. Since the police had tracked him to one house, it wouldn't be long before they traced him here, just as he needed them to. Out here in the center of the forest, he was alone. He'd always loved this ramshackle cabin as a kid. He and Dave had spent months here during the hunting seasons. Both animal and human. This was the place where his brother had initiated him into his private, twisted world. He'd felt flattered. Together, the two of them had dug out a cellar, lined it with concrete, and built a heavy door for locking up their women.

He'd realized then his brother was sloppy and careless with his women. No finesse. Dave never concerned himself with technique. Dave simply got the job done.

He'd realized the kill could be so much more. An opportunity to enjoy the chase and relish the power. And develop a signature. The broken femurs. It'd been his idea to break the femurs on the girls Dave took and he'd carried it on with his own kills. Not only was it an incapacitating move, but the femur was the longest bone in the body, one of the strongest bones. To him it was a symbolic gesture of his power over the victim. With his more recent kills, adding the signature of using something close to the victim was unique and distinguished him from the sloppier killers. It showed he'd studied his vics and used some careful reflection. He smiled behind his coffee cup. He'd spent years getting it perfect. The recent three victims had been works of art.

He regretted pushing the Mount Junction girl into the river with her car. She'd been his first kill without Dave's involvement, and he'd worried about trace evidence. So he'd disposed of the girl, covering his tracks. In Southeast Oregon he hadn't had a remote place where he could keep someone for a few days.

He'd had to get rid of her immediately, but least he'd been able to leave his signature with the femurs. No one had recognized it until lately. That reporter from *The Oregonian* had put the pieces together. It was a relief somewhat. He'd wanted credit for his work but hadn't known how to publicize it without exposing himself. *Thank you, Mr. Brody.*

He opened a kitchen cupboard and pulled a photo album off the top shelf, gently flipping the pages. The pictures were starting to discolor a bit. His favorite pictures were curling at the corners from his excessive handling over the years. It was one of those albums with the slightly sticky pages to hold the photos, but the stickiness was long gone. He'd had to add glue and tape to make the photos stick.

He twisted his lips as he studied a photo of Amy Smith on the beam. He still wasn't certain why he'd stolen it so long ago. He'd broken into the gymnast's apartment expecting to find her home, but the place had been empty. He'd been furious; he'd wanted her with a soul-deep longing. He'd spotted her on a billboard along the highway in Mount Junction, and had been hooked by the come-hither pose. He'd started following the gymnasts, trying to place a name with her face, find out where she lived. He finally did and she wasn't home. So he'd snooped through her things, fascinated with the trivia of a college girl's life. Posters of rock bands, cheap stuffed animals from fairs, clothes, clothes, and clothes. The album had been lying on her bed, half-finished. After flipping through the pictures he'd known he had to keep it.

He'd memorized the pictures of Amy, Suzanne, and Lacey until he nearly believed they were his pictures. His friends who laughed and panned for the camera. Tight, revealing leotards, amazing feats of balance and flexibility. His fascination for gymnasts had been locked in from that moment. A few years later he'd visited Dave in Oregon, timing it with Southeast Oregon University's appearance at the gymnastic invitational in Corvallis. He'd shown his brother the pictures, suggested a gymnast be their next victim, and his brother had agreed. The result was Suzanne.

Almost Lacey.

His eyes ran a hand down a rough wall of his hidden nest. No running water, a simple stove for heat and cooking, and silence. Here he felt connected with nature, living the life of a settler from two hundred years ago. Hunting, trapping. He pointedly ignored the generator, grocery store firewood, propane lamps, and can opener.

The police had never connected this place to his brother. Originally it'd belonged to an acquaintance of his mother's who'd let the two boys use it whenever they'd wanted. Years ago, he'd convinced the old man to sell it; after all, he never used it. The two brothers were the only ones who'd stepped foot in it for twenty years.

Now it was his. His mother had moved him from western state to western state, searching for a job or men to mooch from. He'd ached for a place to put down roots. That's what the cabin was. Where he was rooted.

Sometimes it was lonely. He missed his brother, their discussions on bondage, sex slaves, and weapons. When he'd found out his brother was going to die in prison, he'd funneled his anger into planning revenge on those who put him there. The cabin was where he'd created his perfect plan.

Dave didn't breathe a word about his brother's involvement in the college girls' deaths. He'd kept quiet on Suzanne's fate to the police, because she was *his* special project, not Dave's. When he was fifteen, he'd been toying with the idea of having a sex slave. Someone who was ready whenever he wanted her and then disappeared when he was finished. He'd been a frustrated teen. Girls didn't want anything to do with him and he'd started to doubt that he'd ever have sex. Dave had said a sex slave wouldn't work, but he'd still wanted to try. They'd tapped into an online newsletter for people in the sex slave trade, studied their habits, the dos and don'ts. He'd wanted to keep Suzanne for himself forever. All that gorgeous hair and spunk.

His hands tightened into fists as his groin hardened.

It hadn't worked. His big brother had been right. Suzanne had too big a mouth and got on his nerves, fighting him every step of the way. When he'd realized Suzanne was pregnant, he'd been surprised by his desire for a real family. Mommy, daddy, and baby. But Suzanne wasn't docile enough. He'd picked the wrong type of woman. After the baby was born, he'd finished her and buried her deep in the forest. Dave had always left their victims to be found. He'd wanted to keep Suzanne for himself in death if he couldn't have her in life.

His thoughts drifted to Lacey, snug and silent in the cabin cellar. Would things have been different if his brother had caught Lacey instead of Suzanne? Would she have driven him to kill her like Suzanne? Or would they be a family today?

Questions. Questions. He knew better than to play the what-if game.

He'd injected Lacey on the drive from Molalla, knowing the original inhalant wouldn't last long. At least Lacey had been easier to move than the Harper woman. Lacey couldn't weigh more than a hundred pounds.

He flopped into a ripped easy chair, slouching, and pictured Melody Harper. What a waste to leave her behind, but she'd served her purpose as bait. Harper and Lacey had come out of hiding as if he'd called them on the phone. Just like he knew they would. Perfect planning.

It would have been nice to follow through on some of the interesting scenarios he'd dreamed up for Melody. He liked her name. Melody. It turned his mind to musical things. Piano and guitar strings, violin bows and drumsticks. He liked to stick to a theme. It got his creative juices flowing.

He heard humming.

Annoyed, he abruptly stood and threw two perfectly cut pieces of wood on the fire. He took a moment on one knee, watching the red and yellow flames attack the new fuel. Beginnings and endings.

He was nearly done. It felt like he'd put his plan in motion long ago. He'd carefully recovered Suzanne's bones from her burial site and then hid them and the cop's badge in a hole beneath the apartment building. Not everything had flowed exactly as planned, but he was still on schedule and sitting exactly where he'd foreseen he'd be at the end.

He was as far as he'd get on his list of five targets. Three dead, one waiting in the cellar, and one unknown. If only he'd figured out who the fifth person was. The one who'd given Dave AIDS. He would've offed the fag. He had to settle for assuming the fag would slowly die of the disease. Maybe he was already dead.

He closed his eyes. Today was the tenth anniversary of Dave's sentencing. An echo of the pain from when the judge slammed his gavel and sent his brother to his death rattled through him.

The cop, the two lawyers, and the witness. Too bad the judge already was dead. Emphysema. It was a hellish disease to die from, gasping for every breath as the lungs failed and the body screamed for oxygen. Good.

He'd considered adding Jack Harper and Michael Brody to his list. They'd interfered substantially along his chosen path, wreaking havoc here and there. It wasn't reason enough for their deaths. Brody had efficiently covered his quest. Robert had loved reading about his own exploits and the police's confusion. Harper had raised the stakes, made things more challenging, and he'd appreciated the competition. He'd known Harper owned that apartment building. He'd chosen that site specifically to muddle the investigation, because it belonged to a former suspect in the Co-Ed killings. He leaned on a hand against the mantel of the fireplace, scowling. He hadn't dreamed his actions would push Harper and Lacey Campbell into bed.

Kelly Cates had been an unexpected kink in his path. He pressed his lips together. Maybe she'd been scared by the murders in the paper and hid. After all, she was linked to the original Co-Ed Slayer case in her own fucked-up way.

She had a good reason to be nervous.

CHAPTER THIRTY-THREE

She was all right. His sister was all right.

Jack sat heavily on the curb holding his head in his hands, fighting the dizziness. Between the shock of Lacey's disappearance and the relief that Melody was out of the killer's clutches, he was ready to crack. When he'd seen Frank Stevenson come out of that house he'd known Lacey was in immediate danger.

He'd left her alone.

The guilt was crippling him. Why hadn't he insisted she come with him? Why hadn't he grabbed a uniform and planted him at the truck? In hindsight, there were so many things he could've done. A lot like the last time he let a woman down. If only he and Cal had…If only. If only.

He'd told Lacey he could keep her safe.

Instead he'd fucked up and possibly killed her. Rage boiled acid in his throat, and his vision tunneled. *Count to ten.*

She'd blown his mind last night. He didn't know what to think. The feisty woman had crawled under his heart and set up camp. As they'd made love, her eyes had made a silent pledge and he'd found himself doing the same.

Images of his future all floated around Lacey Campbell.

He couldn't lose her. He'd just gotten her.

His breakfast stirred in his stomach, threatening to reappear.

It was twenty-five degrees, and he sat in a melting pile of snow, sweating like he'd sprinted a marathon.

He had to do *something*.

It'd taken the police this long to find this house. Lacey couldn't wait a week for them to find another. She probably couldn't wait a day.

Voices sounded. He wearily turned to see the detectives approach. Callahan looked ready to spit fire and Lusco looked like he wanted to hit something, hard. They were good men; they cared about this case and were doing their damned best to find the slippery killer. Jack pushed to his feet as they approached, wincing as he felt the cold seep through his wet jeans.

He had to pull it together if he was going to find Lacey.

"Now what?" he asked as he watched the men circle his truck, studying it minutely. Were they expecting to find an arrow drawn in the snow? Pointing in the direction she'd vanished? He'd already checked. No discernible footprints. No nothing.

Lusco pulled out his phone and got his pencil ready. Callahan stopped next to Jack and looked him hard in the eye from under his hat. *Probably measuring my sanity.*

"Don't worry. I won't crack this time." He managed a sickly smile.

Callahan studied him again and nodded. He didn't look convinced.

"I've got Ray checking for any other real estate under the same name as this house. Our man is using the name Robert Costar instead of DeCosta. Ray's also getting hold of your friend, Brody. Send him to question the old woman again. See if she knows where her son would go."

Callahan took a breath. "She must have tipped him off." The man was pissed, his mouth tight, his hat low. "Your sister's fine. Just cold and freaked out. They're taking her to the hospital to get checked, but she says he didn't touch her."

Jack ran a shaky hand through his hair. "Now what?"

"We wait."

"I can't fucking wait," Jack muttered.

"I've got the local PD setting up roadblocks around the area. Checking leaving vehicles, but I think it's too late. I suspect he whisked her out of here pretty quick," Callahan stated grimly. Both men watched Lusco burn up his notepad with his flying pencil, his phone tucked under his ear. Jack prayed the man would come up with something.

Lusco glanced up as if he heard Jack's thoughts. He nodded, his eyes bright.

"I've got another address under the name Robert Costar. It's an isolated cabin outside Lakefield. That's our boy's home turf."

"Lakefield," Mason repeated.

Where Suzanne's remains had appeared. They'd come full circle.

"Call Lakefield PD. Get them caught up and find out what they know about the location of that cabin, but I want county SWAT in charge of handling the cabin, not just the locals."

Jack whirled toward his truck, mentally plotting out the shortest route to Lakefield. It was going to take a couple of hours for him to drive there, but if he—Callahan knocked his hand away before he touched his door handle. *What the fuck?*

The detective looked pissed. Reluctant, but pissed. "You can't take the truck."

"What?" Every nerve went on defense.

"It's a crime scene. Your truck's not going anywhere."

Jack's heart stopped. *Crime scene?* He stared at the detective, then at Lusco. Lusco nodded.

"Then I'll ride with you."

Both men shook their heads. "You aren't going with us." Callahan moved his face too close to Jack's. "Keep out of it. You're done here. Wait and we'll call when we know something." He held the younger man's gaze, daring him to contradict him. Jack opened his mouth then shut it, feeling anger rocket through his veins. His hands itched to race off in his truck. He counted to ten again.

He nodded.

He'd figure out something else.

Callahan gave orders to two nearby uniforms, gesturing back at Jack's truck. Lusco was silent, watching Jack like he expected him to jump in the truck and split.

Smart man.

Jack plopped back on the curb, his breath gone again. Grounded. His eyes scanned the cops milling about the street. He searched for a friendly face, looking for any hope of getting to Lakefield as his mind rapidly flicked through options and rapidly rejected them.

How could he to get to Lacey?

Lacey woke in the icy darkness and her head jerked in pain. "Shit."

She didn't remember hitting her head, but she had one hell of a headache and a sharp pain in the right temple as it pulsated against the hard ground. She lay silent, blinking rapidly and trying to catch her breath. *How had she...DeCosta. Fight. The cloth on her nose.* Her body shivered spastically, trying to warm itself on the dirt floor. The cold had seeped through her clothes and cooled her core.

Her eyes slowly adjusted to the dim light and she swallowed hard as she studied her surroundings. Low ceiling, close walls. She smelled damp dirt and musty cold air. A few cracks of flickering weak light shone through the wood ceiling. A fireplace. He'd dumped her under a building, maybe a house. She listened hard for footsteps as she stared pleadingly at the cracks, willing heat to filter through. No sounds. Her foggy breath steamed in the dim light. She was fucking freezing.

Death from exposure could come fast in these temperatures. She had to get moving.

She pushed up to a sitting position and blindly fingered the ties on her ankles. Her feet were bound, and he'd tied her hands in front of her. She couldn't feel a thing with her numb hands. Her fingers screamed with pain as she moved them, reviving the circulation, sending tears down her face.

She'd been *so stupid*.

DeCosta. It'd been DeCosta's younger brother, Bobby.

Too late, she'd realized Detective Callahan would never send someone to move her to safety. It'd confused her that the man seemed faintly familiar. She'd thought maybe he was an officer in plainclothes whom she'd met before. Callahan's hunch about the identity of the killer had been right. The kid had grown up.

If she hadn't been exhausted and sick with worry and guilt over Melody Harper, she might've figured it out sooner. She blinked away tears as she fought her numb fingers.

Fighting back had accomplished nothing. Bobby DeCosta had been surprisingly strong for his size. Her pepper spray had been in her purse, stupidly out of reach as he grabbed her arms. She'd clawed his face, drawing blood, making him howl and slap her. At the pain, his eyes changed and didn't look human. It was like he became a different being, something created from rage.

Lacey forced her fingers to keep wiggling and bit her lip at the burning pain. After a long minute, her fingertips could feel the rough texture of the rope wrapped around her ankles. The knots were tight and swollen, because her legs had lain in a puddle of melting snow. A fingernail ripped as she dug at the damp knots, making her gasp and her eyes water.

Her head throbbed like the bass in a teenager's stereo. A concussion? Everything hurt. An all-over hurt. The kind where you can't focus on one particular pain because all the other pains were just as strong.

When would he be back? She moved her hands faster. He hadn't killed her yet, and God damn it, she wasn't going to let him.

Had Jack lost control when he returned to an empty truck? First Melody gone and now her.

I'm so sorry, Jack. You didn't deserve this.

A knot loosened the tiniest bit. She attacked the ropes, fighting to work through her pain. She'd get the damn ropes off and then she'd find a way out. She squinted at the door; its lock looked fuzzy. She blinked and saw two locks. She closed her eyes tight and opened them again. Only one lock on the old door. Fuck. She'd really hurt her head.

She breathed deep and focused on her fingers. She had to get out.

In the fading light, Jack and Alex flew down the freeway in Alex's old Bronco. At this speed, they'd hit Lakefield within the hour. Jack checked the GPS on the dashboard. He'd gotten a look at Lusco's notepad as he'd printed the address. Their destination was out in the boonies, up the Coast Range a bit. Heavily forested. Extremely isolated. It was going to be pitch-dark when they got there.

Alex's truck was old but boasted every techno-geek gadget available. His friend hadn't hesitated when Jack had called for help. Alex had simply asked when and where.

The speedometer read 95 MPH and Jack gripped the door handle tighter. This could be a wild goose chase. Their killer might be headed for Mexico. Or Canada. They were throwing all their eggs in one basket.

Today was the day. The tenth anniversary of Dave DeCosta's sentencing. Whatever horror was going to happen would happen today. Bobby DeCosta had made that clear in his note card to Lacey. He hadn't written specific actions, but his target was clear.

Jack had thought DeCosta nabbed Melody to take Lacey's place. But now he knew Melody had been a lure to flush Lacey out.

Jack had delivered the quarry on a silver platter.

He was going to get her back. He'd promised her he'd keep her safe and he was going to keep his promise. He couldn't live with himself if he didn't. He put the images of a bleeding pregnant woman out of his mind.

Alex concentrated on the slick roads, not speaking. His mind plotting, Jack barely noticed his cell go off. He ignored it. The ring stopped and then started again.

He hit the speakerphone. "What?"

"He made contact." Callahan's tone was short, tight.

"What? How?"

"He knows we're coming. He spotted county and SWAT setting up outside his property and called the switchboard. They put him through. He wants to deal."

"Deal? How much do you need? I can get the money. What's his price?" A spot of optimism touched his spine. Jack could handle money. He understood money.

Callahan paused. "He doesn't want money, Harper."

"Then what?" The optimism floated away.

Alex swerved to avoid a frozen puddle as he took the freeway off-ramp to Lakefield. Jack swayed in his seat and clutched the cell phone.

"Where are you?" Callahan changed the subject.

"About fifteen minutes behind you."

"Shit. I told you to stay put. Stay the fuck away from this scene or I'll bust your ass. I don't need you getting in the way. I'll have you cuffed if I need to."

"If he doesn't want money, what does he want?" Jack ignored the threats.

"He wants to trade. He says he'll trade Dr. Campbell for you."

"Done," he snapped without hesitation.

Callahan paused. "It's a bunch of bullshit. He's obviously stalling. I don't know why he suggested something so stupid. He knows we won't negotiate with that."

"Then don't. I will." Jack cut off the call.

Alex silently met his gaze in the dim light.

"Did you bring it?" Jack asked.

"In the glove box."

Jack popped open the box at his knees. He reached in, and then hesitated, fingers hovering. Pressing his lips together, he grabbed the two handguns. He handed the expensive Heckler & Koch to Alex. He kept the Glock, reacquainting himself with the weight and feel of the gun, ignoring the sickening thunk in the bottom of his belly. It was the gun he'd carried as an officer. He'd given it to Alex years before.

He inserted the magazine and loaded a round in the chamber.

Mason stared at the phone as it flashed the brief time of his call with Harper. The guy couldn't see beyond his obsession with Dr. Campbell. Bobby DeCosta didn't want Jack Harper. He was screwing with their heads.

"What'd he say?" Ray steered with one hand, took his eyes off the road, and focused on Mason like he was on a leisurely Sunday drive. At one time, the dangerous habit had made Mason nervous, but he'd gotten over it. Ray had supernatural peripheral vision when it came to driving.

"What'd ya think?"

"He wants to go in, white flags flying."

Mason grunted. Ray's big bulk hid a sappy, romantic heart. "SWAT isn't gonna let him near the scene. They've got negotiators lined up and snipers on the way."

"Harper know that?"

Mason paused. "You don't think he'd really try, do you?"

"Haven't you seen the way he looks at that woman? The man is in deep. He can't think rationally. He'd step in front of a bullet for her without thinking."

"He wouldn't do anything stupid," Mason muttered. *Would he?*

Ray was quiet for a second. "You've never been in love, have you?"

Mason rolled his eyes. "Fuck you. This isn't some Hollywood movie."

He fumbled with his phone, pretending he didn't see the careful look Ray gave him. The pity in Lusco's eyes was making his chest hurt.

Lacey fiercely concentrated on the ropes at her ankles. One knot had finally come loose, encouraging her to fight the rest. She stopped for frequent breaks. The feeling in her fingers coming and going. She was so cold. A bone-deep chill kept her muscles moving spasmodically, clattering her teeth and shaking her arms. Like untying the knots wasn't difficult enough.

A wave of dizziness rocked her. She lost her balance and thrust her tied wrists to the side in an attempt to catch herself, but hit her head on the floor. The ache in her head multiplied and a sharp crack had come from her elbow. She lay still, catching her breath, wondering if she'd broken something. Breathing deeply, she slowly righted herself, pain shooting up her arm.

A rustling outside the door made her flop back on the ground, gritting her teeth as she slammed her head again. Playing possum, if he was checking on her. The lock and handle clanked on the rough door and it slowly opened, scraping over frozen snow. The noise sounded ridiculously loud in the arctic silence. She kept her breathing even and tried not to scrunch her eyelids.

Look natural.

As natural as an icy, dumped body can look.

"Lacey?"

Her eyes flew open at that familiar feminine whisper. "Kelly?" she squeaked with stunned and frozen vocal cords.

A flashlight flicked on, its battery nearly dead. Kelly held her fingers over the bulb, letting the barest flicker of orange light touch Lacey's face. Kelly flew across the dirt floor and yanked on the tight cords on Lacey's feet.

Lacey stared at her, immobile.

Kelly was bundled up in a thick jacket with a hood. She was wearing boots and had ripped off her gloves with her teeth to get a better handle on Lacey's knots.

"Kelly! What are you doing here? How did you find me? Did you escape too?" The questions stumbled over her frigid tongue.

"No." Kelly glanced up at the ceiling. "Keep your voice down," she whispered.

"No, what?" Lacey whispered back.

"He didn't get me."

Was her brain numb? "He didn't get you? Then why are you here?" An echo of the pain she'd felt when Kelly vanished ripped through her. "Where've you been? Chris and Jessica have been worried sick."

Kelly made fast progress on the ties and ignored Lacey's questions. "Shhhh. We've got to hurry. Almost got it."

"Kelly." Lacey shook her tied legs to stop Kelly's work. "What's going on?" Kelly pulled the rope loose from her ankles.

Lacey's spine prickled. Something didn't add up here. A fuzzy memory of a younger Kelly talking to a slouching, silent boy outside a courtroom door slid into her mind. She blinked. "Did you know him? From before?"

"Let me see your hands." Kelly wouldn't meet her eyes.

As much as she wanted answers, Lacey wanted out of this prison more. She held out her tied hands and Kelly went to work.

"Damn it. They're wet and swollen. I can't get a grip on anything." Kelly stopped her struggles, breathing rapidly. "Can you walk? We need to get out of here before he comes back." She stood and roughly pulled Lacey to her feet.

"Ouch. Hang on a sec." Lacey wiggled her legs and stomped her feet, trying to get the circulation going. Her feet felt like two concrete bricks. She tipped slightly in the dark and tried to move her feet to catch her balance.

She couldn't.

Kelly grabbed her arm and shoulder to keep her from falling. Pain shot down Lacey's arm and into her wrists, forcing tears from her eyes.

"I can't feel my feet."

"They'll get better as we go. We've got to get out of here!" Kelly begged, leading her toward the door. "Come on, sweetie."

Lacey carefully shuffled her feet. If she fell she was going to break a wrist. "I'm trying." Visions of fishhooks flashed, moving her feet faster.

"Good. That's better." Kelly sounded supportive but continued to pull her frantically toward the door.

Lacey kept shuffling, trying to feel the uneven floor through her shoes. Kelly flipped off the dying flashlight. "Gotta save the light. I know where we're going."

"And where's that, Kelly?" The voice was male and angry.

The women stopped. Lacey felt Kelly's hands shake. She could see the silhouette of a male in the dark doorway, faint light reflected from the snow exposing his dark hair.

CHAPTER THIRTY-FOUR

"You tipped him off!" Michael shouted.

The woman cowered at his shout, avoiding looking at Michael's angry red face. He wanted to shake her. Shake her until she bruised her brain.

Michael and Sam had returned to the compound and cornered Linda/Lila again. Detective Lusco had told him the killer had vanished from the address Linda had given them. And Lacey was missing from the same scene.

Where the fuck had Harper been?

Michael had trusted the man to stick by her. He wouldn't have left the city if he'd known Harper couldn't take care of her.

Michael didn't know whom he was madder at. The trembling woman in front of him or that former pretty-boy cop. Or the bumbling state detectives. Or Lacey for putting herself in danger. He should have shipped her off to Thailand or Norway. Anywhere.

Sam pulled at his arm, urging him to take it easy on the mother of the killers. He glanced at Sam's face, her blue eyes frowning at Lila. Sam was cool and collected. He wanted to shake off her grip, but calmness flowed through her hand and into his chest. He took a deep breath and exhaled.

Sam didn't know what he was going through. He hadn't explained his relationship with Lacey. He didn't know how to describe it. She was ex-lover and best friend all rolled into one.

"You called him," Sam stated.

The woman nodded, keeping her eyes away from Michael's burning green gaze.

"Why?"

She shrugged, glancing hopefully at Sam, and Michael remembered Sam had been more effective with the woman the first time. "He's my son."

Her voice was nearly inaudible, but her statement was firm.

"Where is he now?" Sam asked.

No answer.

Michael exploded. "Did you know he's killing people? Murdering them in some of the sickest ways I've ever seen! And now he's got someone I love!" He took two threatening steps, his calmness gone, his voice rising. "If something happens to her because you're too fucking scared to…"

"Michael!" Sam pulled him back, stepping in front of him, her back against his chest. "Lila. Where else would your son go to hide? Where could he hold someone without the neighbors noticing?" Fury sounded in her voice, but Sam kept control.

Michael held his breath, every nerve rattled. If Sam hadn't been here, he didn't think the old woman would still be breathing.

Lila looked at Sam, pretending Michael wasn't in the room. Her dead, empty eyes had flashed briefly when Sam asked about neighbors.

Michael knew she'd thought of something. "Where, Lila?" he growled.

She licked nervous lips. "You could try an old hunting cabin he's got. I've never been there but I kinda know where it is."

Was she fucking with them again? "That's the only place you can think of?"

Her chin dropped. "It's the only one that's kind of isolated. You know he likes to..."

"He likes to do what?" Michael snapped, pulling out his cell.

"Out there he likes to practice with the weapons he collects."

Michael's fingers stopped before he could dial. "What kind of weapons?"

The woman stared at the floor and Michael had to lean close to hear her. "Anything military or unusual. Old grenades, guns, knives. And he makes his own explosives."

"Like pipe bombs? Homemade stuff?" Sam sharply sucked in her breath.

The woman looked up and an odd look flashed in her eyes like an unpleasant memory. "Sometimes. He likes to make traps. Set up things to trigger them."

"Dear Lord." Sam squeezed her eyes shut and placed a hand on Michael's arm.

"Shit." Michael hit his speed dial.

Lacey stared at the familiar outline in the dim light. She'd seen him before. It was the helpful neighbor in the Molalla neighborhood who turned out to be a killer. Bobby DeCosta.

"Kelly. It's good to see you again. It's been a long time." His voice was disinterested but polite, like he'd bumped into a dull acquaintance.

Lacey turned to stare at her friend. Her two biggest suspicions were right. DeCosta and Kelly knew each other. And Kelly had left Chris and her daughter of her own free will.

Not kidnapped.

Kelly's lips moved silently as Lacey looked at her. *Trust me.*

Lacey's lips opened to ask a question, but turned into a gasp of shock as Kelly shoved her forward, sending Lacey hurtling toward the dirt floor and slamming into DeCosta's legs. An explosion of light splintered in her brain as her knees and wrists caught her weight. She couldn't breathe.

"Oww! Fucking bitch!" The man shouted.

Kelly had swung her oversize flashlight like a tennis racquet at DeCosta's head, catching his temple as he tripped over Lacey. He fell and Kelly vanished out the door.

DeCosta scrambled to his feet, stepping on Lacey's hair and shoulder. He took three angry steps after Kelly, froze and turned to see Lacey thrashing on the floor for breath. "Oh, no you don't." He strode forward and kicked her in the ribs with a heavy boot, tossing her onto her side and slamming her bruised head again. She felt the bile rush up her throat and she vomited on the floor.

"Jesus Christ!" He'd stepped up for another kick but stopped as vomit spread toward his boots. Disgusted, he kicked at her head. She saw the boot coming and twisted away to catch it on the back of her skull. Knifelike pains drove through her waves of nausea. He swore at her again and flew out the door. Lacey heard the bolt slam into place.

She descended into blessed numbing darkness.

The cops weren't going to let him near the scene. Jack knew this. Making a snap decision, he told Alex to take a sharp right turn and hung on as the tires spun on the slick pavement. Jack had patrolled this town and its outskirts. A faint memory of back roads was coming to him. He'd find a different way in to the cabin, avoiding the cops. His cell rang.

"What?" He hit the speakerphone again, temper in his voice.

"Harper?" The connection was shitty.

"Who the fuck is this?" It wasn't Callahan or Lusco.

"Brody. What the hell is going on out there? Where's Lacey?"

"I don't know," Jack snapped back. "He's got her holed up somewhere. We're on our way."

There was a long pause. "You're going too? You're with the police?"

"Not exactly."

"Look," said Michael. "I'll tell you the same thing I just told Callahan. The creep's mom says he likes his toys. Any kind of gun or knife, or things that create fire. And he likes to set traps, deadly explosive ones. You could be walking into a war zone. You've got to be careful. The mom said he spends lots of time up there. Months at a stretch. There's no telling what kind of shit he's got rigged up in the place."

Alex suddenly pulled over and hit the brakes on the deserted dirt road. The two friends stared at each other, Michael's words sinking in. They couldn't go rushing into an unknown situation without thinking it through. And clear thinking was at the bottom of Jack's list of abilities right this second. He felt Lacey fade away from him. His chances of getting her back were dwindling rapidly.

The place might be booby-trapped?

Her legs hurt. The rough jolting of her feet bouncing over the ground pulled Lacey out of her oblivion. Someone was dragging her with hands under her armpits.

"Kelly?"

A laugh barked at her tentative question. "Your friend's gone. Some good friend, taking off and leaving you behind."

DeCosta still had her. The realization smothered Lacey, cutting off her breath, and she nearly wept. Kelly had left. Would she get to the police in time? No one else knew where DeCosta had taken Lacey. She was alone. Alone with him. What was he going to do to her?

The empty eyes of Suzanne's skull floated through her mind, those sad abandoned bones. Would someone stumble across her own bones one day? Lay her out on a blue tarp to try to reassemble? Get frustrated because so many pieces were missing?

At least someone who had loved her had identified Suzanne. Tears tracked down Lacey's face as she remembered the video of Suzanne. And her baby.

"Where's the baby?" Her words shook.

"What baby?" DeCosta dragged her into the main room of the cabin, backing toward the fireplace.

"The baby. Suzanne's baby." He turned her to the fire and she stared at the perky crackling flames. She nearly cried again at the blessed warmth on her face.

"Ohh. *That baby.* She's not a baby anymore." He grunted, maneuvering her beside the fireplace with her back to the wall. Lacey took her first good look at the man who'd kidnapped her.

He was slender but his arms were strong. She had an impression of a lot of trim muscle hiding under his jacket. His eyes were pale, pale blue, striking with his dark hair. Those eyes had been helpful and kind back at the roadblock, but now they were angry, full of hatred and frustration. Hints of Dave DeCosta floated about his face, but Lacey would have never pegged them as brothers if she hadn't known. This man clashed with her memory of a straggly-haired, skinny teenager who'd never lifted his head during the trial.

She? The baby had been a girl? An image of a frilly toddler danced before Lacey's eyes. Was she blonde and beautiful like her mother?

"She's in a good home," Bobby sneered.

"Where? Where is she? Who has her?"

"At least I thought it was a good home. I'm not so sure anymore. The mother seems to be having some issues." He fastened new ropes in complicated knots at her ankles to an iron ring in the floor. Lacey stared at the ring. It looked like something a horse would've been tied to a hundred years ago. Her vision scooted to the left. There was another ring in the floor three feet away. Then another and another.

They were for restraining people.

Oh, dear Lord. What'd gone on here?

She closed her eyes, fighting against the horrid pictures that swarmed her mind. *What'd he just say? The mother?*

"What's wrong with the mother?" She needed to keep her mind off the rings.

Bobby frowned as he stepped away and poked at his fire, tossing another fresh piece of cut wood on the flames. "Well, to start with, she just nailed me in the head with a flashlight."

Kelly? Kelly had the little girl? Lacey gasped softly.

Jessica.

Jessica was Suzanne's daughter.

Now she saw it. The beautiful girl had Suzanne's eyes. Had it been instinct that Lacey loved her so much? She'd adored Jessica from the first time she'd seen her.

Did Kelly know who the little girl was?

Of course she did.

Lacey sagged against the rough wall of the cabin. Relief and despair swamping her feelings at the same time. The little girl had been safe all this time.

Why would Kelly do it? And how could her husband, Chris, go along with it?

Chris had to know where Jessica had come from. Lacey squeezed her eyes shut, trying to remember that jumbled year after Suzanne had disappeared. It was hard to keep things straight. Lacey had been suffering with depression and was often heavily medicated. She'd left school for a term, avoided her friends. And Kelly and Chris had broken up.

And got back together many months later.

The perfect couple had gone through a difficult time. Kelly had headed to the East Coast to put some space between them. She'd returned with an infant. Jessica.

Chris must have assumed Jessica was his. And Kelly's.

But there were still too many unanswered questions.

She opened her eyes. He was smiling, studying her closely, enjoying her confusion and watching the revelations change her expressions. His pale gaze seemed to look right into her ripped-up heart.

"Did Kelly know? Did she know about Suzanne? About what you did to her?"

His face closed off. He stood, kicked at her tied ankles and strode out of the main room, slamming the door behind him.

Lacey cringed as she stared at the fire, the jabbing bursts of pain from her ankles shooting up her legs. Her wrists throbbed in her lap, still tied with their original swollen knots. The only light in the room came from the fire, casting a warm orange and golden glow. She sucked in a shuddering breath and tried to focus.

Now what?

Now what, thought Mason.

One hundred yards away through the dark night, dense evergreens, and boulders bigger than cars, a killer was holding Dr. Campbell.

They had to get her out of there before DeCosta killed her. If he hadn't already.

Mason pulled his coat tighter against the icy snow pellets and focused on the conversations around him. Under the generator-powered floodlights, he stared at the rough map spread on a truck hood. Captain Pattison from county SWAT drew a finger across the map as he talked. Pattison was a former marine, always prepared for whatever situation the police threw his unit's way. Satellite imagery showing the terrain in the rough hills was being passed around in the small group of body-armored men as they listened to Pattison. In the dark and snow, the surrounding area looked completely different. Mason glanced at it, shook his head, and passed it on. Pattison's own precise sketch was more helpful. It showed the cabin, the grounds around it, and three circled Xs where snipers with night vision trained their rifles on the small building.

"The negotiators will work first. See if we can settle this without going in." Pattison shook his head. "I wish I knew what was inside that place. He's a weapons freak, you say?"

Mason nodded silently. A growing sense of lack of control swirled in his chest like something was about to go wrong. Very wrong.

"Likes explosives too," added Ray.

"Shit!" Pattison eyed his men. "Jensen's not here yet? No one else has explosives experience, right?" Negative mutters went round the group.

"Seen Harper?" Mason spoke low to Ray as he scanned the area, squinting against the bright lights, trying to see into the dark.

"Who?" Pattison stopped his lecture with a frown.

Crap. Mason pressed his lips together. "Civilian. Dr. Campbell's his girlfriend."

"And he knows about this place? You told him?" Pattison straightened, snarling as he did his own scan of the area.

"Not like that," Mason grumbled. "Former cop. Our guy snatched Dr. Campbell out from under his nose. I know he's gonna show here somewhere. Earlier on the phone our killer offered to trade his hostage for Harper."

"What? You just decided to tell me this now?" Pattison looked ready to use his weapon on Mason. "Do the negotiators know about that?"

Mason's temper shot hot. "I've been here all of sixty seconds. You've been blabbing about maps, snipers, and hostages since we walked up. When did you want me to say something?" He leaned toward the shorter man, using his height, but Pattison didn't back down. He shoved his nose closer to Mason's.

"When I stepped on this property this became my operation. Get your cheap cowboy hat and your steroid-abusing partner out of my way. You'll be informed on a need-to-know basis."

A red aura flared around Mason's vision and his hands tightened into fists. He felt Lusco grab his arms, physically lift him up, and plant him three feet away.

"Callahan." Ray's warning tone snapped him out of his rage.

Mason settled for shooting an icy this-isn't-over-yet glare at the stiff-necked man with the maps. Pattison's gaze coolly scanned Mason, then dismissed him by turning his back.

"Fucking jarhead. I'm gonna report…"

"Shut up," Ray barked.

Mason snapped his mouth shut, fuming. He wanted to lay into Ray but settled for looking for Harper. He'd have the nosy bastard cuffed and in the back of a squad car if he dared to show his face around here. Harper could jeopardize everything.

"Where is he?" Mason took another careful inspection of the immediate area, expecting to spot Harper behind a tree. "Get that Harper on the phone before he gets shot by a sniper."

Maybe that wouldn't be such a bad idea.

"And get a description of him and what he's wearing to those snipers."

Ray silently studied his partner like Mason was about to dash off and take a swing at Pattison. Mason glared back. Satisfied, Ray pulled his uneasy gaze off Mason, whipped out his phone and dialed.

Jack felt his phone vibrate and ignored it. He squatted in the snow, a thick blind of wild rhododendrons protecting him from the chilling wind that slid through the forest. He couldn't see

Alex but knew he was within twenty yards, watching his back. His little flashlight was nearly dead. Its feeble orange light barely lit the ground at his feet. He was exhausted and freezing. He'd barely slept last night and today'd been the worst fucking day of his life. And it wasn't over yet. His stress level hovered somewhere around the moon. He couldn't stop thinking about the killer's offer to trade Lacey. That had to be a bunch of bull. The guy was screwing with their heads. But if he offered to trade Lacey, damn right he was gonna step up.

The snow changed. No longer fluffy flakes, it'd become stinging pellets of ice in the dark. Tiny sharp pins on his cheeks.

Was Lacey cold?

Maybe she'd called…He checked the face of his phone, hoping to see her cell number as the last call. Instead Lusco's blinked at him, and his heart deflated. Stupid thought. The cops still had her cell from the other night. He didn't need a secondhand lecture from Lusco and shoved the phone back in his pocket.

He wasn't going to screw this up. Brody would strangle him. After Jack strangled himself.

Brushing the tiny pellets out of his eyes, he tried to estimate how far he'd come from Alex's truck. If he was headed in the right direction, the cabin should be another two hundred yards or so. When would he hit the line of police?

Maybe he should've taken Lusco's call.

He hit the callback and watched the signal strength wane in and out.

"Harper?" Lusco sounded tinny. "Where are you?"

Jack aimed his waning flashlight at the rhododendron. "By a big bush."

"Shit. Stay out of the area. There're three snipers trained on the cabin. They'll probably shoot you first and ask questions later."

"Tell 'em I've got on a brown leather jacket and jeans. And Alex's wearing a black watch cap, black jacket."

"There're two of you?"

"How do you think I got here?"

Lusco ignored the question. "Are you carrying?"

Jack paused too long. "No." He touched the shoulder holster he'd strapped on before leaving Alex's truck. He'd also slipped a knife into his boot. Armed for the first time since leaving Lakefield PD. He never thought this day would come; he had a gun in his hand and murder on his mind.

And he was still holding it together.

"Bullshit. Don't even think of coming near this place. Callahan will bust your ass."

"I'll give you thirty seconds to get the descriptions to SWAT before I move." He closed his phone, doubting he was even within five minutes of the cabin. Especially if the terrain was as rough as he'd already crossed.

"Hang in there, Lacey," he muttered.

Cursing that he'd forgotten gloves, he rubbed his hands together. Numb fingers would be a bitch if it came to handling a gun. He had a strong feeling he was going to need responsive fingers. He scrutinized his nerves. They were holding up OK. The weight of the gun actually made him feel better, not nauseous. He felt like he had a chance.

He stepped out of his cover carefully, scanned the orange light by his feet, and wished he had night vision goggles. *The man liked to booby-trap.* Jack's feet held still as his heart pounded in his ears. He needed to watch every step or he might lose his head. Literally.

He hadn't gone far. Lacey could hear Bobby pacing in the next room. She blinked unsteadily as her vision blurred and doubled. She slowly inhaled and shuddered at the stabs of pain in her chest. Probably fractured ribs from his kicks in the cellar.

She carefully stretched toward the fire, trying not to hurt her ribs. Could she reach a burning piece of wood? Too far away. Her gaze scrambled around for something she could light on fire, use as a weapon when he came near. Or something sharp to cut her ropes, or a mislaid gun to shoot him with.

No luck.

She picked weakly at the ties on her ankles. Her hands were useless. All she could do was feebly rub at the ropes. At this rate, she might wear through them in…oh, about a millennium. She tucked her face in her knees. She was absolutely powerless.

Kelly was gone.

Michael was in Southeast Oregon.

The police were standing around an empty house in Molalla.

Jack didn't know where she was.

No one knew where she was except Kelly. *Please. Let Kelly come back with the police.*

How long would it take Kelly to get help? Did she have a cell? A car nearby?

Lacey didn't see any other hope.

The warmth from the fire chased away her chattering teeth and she started to doze, shutting out thoughts of the killer in the next room. Her pants were still chilly and wet but the heat of the blaze pushed through the cold, helping her muscles unwind. Blessed warmth.

I'm sorry, Jack. I didn't mean for Melody to get hurt.

She shouldn't fall asleep. Concussions and sleep weren't a good combination. But it felt so good. She'd just relax for a little while. Who knew how long she'd have the comfort of a fire? It was useless to worry over an impossible situation. She should conserve her energy and strength. She might need it later.

She'd sleep for just a few minutes.

They kept calling him.

Robert answered the first call, chatted with the negotiator a few minutes, and requested four Quarter Pounders and a pint of Chubby Hubby. Told them he didn't have any food and he might listen to them if his stomach would stop growling. He hung up, grinning.

Bought some time. The closest McDonald's was an hour away.

He turned off the vibrating cell after the fourth call. He couldn't plan when he was interrupted every five minutes. He'd answer in a little bit, ask where his food was. Make them believe he would negotiate. If they believed they could talk him out of the cabin, they'd hold off the firepower. He'd string them along until he was ready.

Quietly opening the door to the main room, he checked on his hostage. Lacey was sleeping, propped up against the wall with her head on her knees. She didn't look so hot now. He frowned. She was dirty and muddy. His original attraction to her plummeted.

She had been gorgeous, untouchable the night of the fund-raiser in that sexy black dress. And he'd wanted to touch. Remembering the vision of her exposed smooth back, arousal roared back through his veins. She needed a shower. That was all.

Where'd Kelly run off to? He checked the big room, half-expecting to see Kelly trying to free her friend again. One predictable thing about Kelly. She was loyal to those she loved, like her daughter.

He smiled wryly as understanding dawned.

That was why Kelly had hunted him down. She was afraid he'd expose her daughter.

Her fake daughter. A few words from him and he could ruin her marriage. Crush her husband with the knowledge that Jessica wasn't his. Or hers. Would she try to kill him over that knowledge? How would she do it? Beat him senseless with her flashlight? He shook his head. Kelly hadn't planned at all; she needed to think things through, not react in emotion.

Did her love for Jessica go far enough to kill?

His brow wrinkled. He hadn't thought of that angle. Why hadn't it occurred to him when he'd first heard Kelly was missing? She knew he wouldn't physically harm her; he owed her that much. But she must've believed he'd blab about Jessica if the police caught him for the recent murders. Kelly was going to make sure he couldn't talk.

He gave a snort. Little Kelly thought she could take out a professional killer. He pushed thoughts of Kelly out of his mind and focused on Lacey.

Lacey's hair gleamed in the firelight. Even though it was a mess, he still wanted to run his fingers through it, experience its texture. He'd gotten a quick feel as he dumped her in his cellar. But it wasn't enough. He'd been in a hurry and it'd been dark. Now he could take his time and explore.

He loved textures. All different textures.

How would her soft hair feel draped across his bare thighs?

He stepped quietly into the room, his plans for the police and SWAT forgotten, seeing only the woman slumped by the fire.

Her breathing was steady, slow. It was the sole sound in the room other than the occasional crackle of the fire. No outside noise intruded into his world. The circle of threatening police vanished and there was only him and her.

As he crossed the room, he imagined her head lifting, smiling sleepily at him, eyes soft from slumber. She wouldn't fear him. A small wave of excitement touched his spine. He would untie her. Just a little. And she would be grateful, so very grateful. She'd understand he wouldn't hurt her if she was good.

Standing before Lacey, he waited, savoring the quiet moment. It could all be heavenly from here. Squatting, he reached out, his hand hovering over the golden head and relishing the moment before he touched her with love. He caressed her hair, sliding his fingers into the softness, delighting in the sensation as the hair tickled the sensitive sides of his fingers.

She sighed quietly, drowsily turning her head so he could stroke the area behind her ear. The excitement rocketed through his veins, heating his hands. He'd known it would be fantastic.

"Lacey," he whispered, leaning closer.

Her head lifted the slightest bit from her knees and her eyes drifted open.

"Jack?"

Her gaze met his and she screamed. He fell back, scooting away on all fours as she continued to shriek, wild eyes stared at him in hate and fear, and she cowered against the wall.

This wasn't how it was supposed to be!

Fury barreled through his nerves and red anger tunneled his vision. Pushing to his feet, he strode over and grabbed that hair, yanked her head back and slapped her across the face. Then again.

"Shut up! Shut the fuck up!"

She clamped her mouth shut, but her eyes stayed wide open, fear dancing in their depths. He gloated with satisfaction. If she wouldn't respond to his tenderness, she'd respond to his pain.

CHAPTER THIRTY-FIVE

Callahan saw Pattison slap a hand over his earpiece, his body perceptibly stiffening. The man's face blanked and his lips moved as he replied to the voice in his ear.

Something had happened.

Pattison cut a quick look Mason's way, his hand still covering his ear.

"What happened?" Mason muttered and headed toward Pattison. Tempers be damned.

"I'll find out." Ray stepped past Mason, blocking him from Pattison's sight with his bulk and forcing Mason to stop or else trip over his heels.

Mason fumed behind his partner. His fingers itched for a cigarette, surprising him. It'd been twenty years since he'd smoked.

This stress was going to kill him.

Pattison met Ray halfway and caught Mason's eye, including him. The captain looked ready to tear down a fir tree with his bare hands.

"One of my snipers, Cordova, heard a female scream in the cabin a second ago. Stopped abruptly."

Sweat broke out on Mason's forehead, and his gut felt like it'd been stabbed with a torch. DeCosta had killed her. They were too late. They fooled around with this negotiator crap too long. He clapped a hand to his belly; he wanted to vomit.

"She's all right." Ray was calm, and the men gawked at him.

"DeCosta's here for the glory," Ray explained, his eyes earnest. "He's made that clear. Think about his note and all the elaborate buildup to this very moment. It's not going to end with a private murder in that cabin. It's going to be a big production with him as the star."

Mason stared at his partner. *Ray was right, damn him. He was right.*

But the fact wasn't reassuring.

Jack crouched in the snow, the cabin just feet away.

The terrified screams had sent his blood boiling, but the immediate cutoff of the screams choked his veins with ice. He wouldn't have believed there was anything worse than Lacey screaming, but the empty silence afterward was twenty times more petrifying.

He prayed he wasn't too late.

Lacey was wide awake. Every nerve constricted in fear at the man in her face. Bobby DeCosta was furious. Spit flew from his mouth as he yelled at her and whipped her head back, yanking until she felt hair rip from her scalp, and then he slapped her.

Her head ringing from his slaps, she stared at his teeth, bared in a gloating grin. The lateral maxillary incisors were microdonts. Narrow and pointy in comparison with his other teeth. Up close they looked like short fangs. She couldn't pull her gaze away.

The crash of shattering glass startled a scream from her throat and Bobby released her hair, diving to the floor, protecting his head with his hands. Lacey tipped over sideways, trying to get low, and cried out as she took the brunt of her fall on a damaged elbow. White pain cracked through her ribs.

She shook and waited for more gunshots.

Her kidnapper cursed and she opened her eyes. A large rock had landed on the rough floor across the room, surrounded by broken glass from the window.

Not a gunshot. A rock.

Speechless, she couldn't drag her eyes from the gray mass. Who thought a rock would scare DeCosta off?

It had to be Kelly. Tears prickled. The stupid girl hadn't left. Hadn't gone for help.

"Stupid bitch." Bobby had drawn the same conclusion about Kelly. On all fours Bobby scampered across the floor to the other room, reappearing a second later with a length of rope in his hands.

More rope? What else could he tie her to? She wasn't going anywhere. Exhausted, she turned her face toward the floor. Her muscles were too tired to sit up, and frankly, she didn't care.

Bobby pulled her into a sitting position. She fought to stay upright, weaving like she was drunk. He yanked on the rope tied to the ring in the floor, checking his knots. He nodded, pleased.

He grabbed a piece of firewood and set it behind her, surprising her as he sat on it, leaning her gently back against his shins. Her skin crawled at being so close to him, having him touch her. Something cold and thin wrapped snug around her neck, making her eyes gape. *The other rope!* He was going to strangle her.

She held her breath.

But he didn't tighten the rope. He simply held it in place, his focus on the door.

Now she understood. Bobby was waiting for an audience.

Then he'd strangle her.

I've got a nice surprise for you, Kelly. A little payback for the flashlight on the temple. A smile crept across Robert's face as he sat patiently. Lacey blocked most of his body from anyone at the door. By ducking his head, no one could shoot or hurt him without hurting her first.

Kelly would witness her friend's slow strangulation. She'd rush to help and he'd take her down. Then he'd use Kelly to pull in the police for a grand finale. The cops were still waiting in the woods somewhere. Following stupid textbook procedure. Unable to think for themselves.

"Come on in, Kelly." Robert raised his voice enough to be heard outside. "I've got something to show you." He couldn't keep the laughter out of his words.

His captive gurgled against the rope.

"Rope too tight? That's easy to fix. Twist one way and it loosens." He demonstrated and Lacey sucked in a deep breath.

"Twist the other way and it tightens." Her body shook in pain and he loosened the rope the littlest bit.

He pet her hair like she was a purring cat. She yanked her head away from his touch, gasping hoarsely as the movement crushed her windpipe.

"Ouch. Sounded like that hurt," he said. "Maybe you should relax and let me do as I please." His hand moved to her shoulder and slowly slipped forward toward her breast.

Her head frantically shook.

Angry, he tightened the rope a notch. "I don't think you're in a position to negotiate." His hand shot down, tenderness gone, twisting her breast and pinching until he heard her sob.

He loosened the rope the tiniest bit. It would be great to play with her for weeks.

"Fucking sick bastard."

Robert jerked at the male voice. A shock of delight spread through him at the sight of the tall figure in the doorway with a gun pointed at him.

The situation had so utterly sweetened. It wouldn't be Kelly to watch Lacey die; it would be Lacey's boyfriend.

Perfect.

Lacey stared.

Jack had come for her. He'd figured it out and found her. And forced himself to pick up a gun to defend her. Her eyes burned hot. He looked so good. Tall, handsome, and utterly pissed off, his jaw rock-hard. She briefly closed her eyes at the waves of love flowing through her. "Oh, Lord," her lips silently moved. She hadn't known. She hadn't known she'd fallen in love with the bullheaded man. She hadn't thought she could cry anymore, but two tears tracked down her cheeks.

He was going to get himself killed.

Not now, not when she'd just figured out what he meant to her. She shook her head at him, scraping her sore throat against the rope. Trying silently to tell him to leave. He hadn't shot a gun in years. He was risking too much. Jack ignored her, his focus on the scum at her back.

"The way I see it, I shoot you in the head and we're done, Bobby."

The rope tightened and Lacey saw stars.

"Don't call me that. I'm Robert now." He complained like a spoiled child. Through her haze, Lacey picked up on the immature reaction. Bobby hated his childhood name.

"You shoot and you'll hit her first."

Lacey felt Bobby duck his head behind hers to demonstrate. "You don't shoot, and she dies as you watch. You'll never get her out of here alive." Bobby gestured to the walls of the cabin. Lacey gasped, spotting the tiny wires that crisscrossed every smooth surface.

He'd rigged the cabin to burn.

Jack's eyes widened at something behind her. She turned her head the slightest bit and peered out of the corner of her eye, stretching her peripheral vision. Bobby was holding a small remote control in his hand.

She didn't think it was for a TV.

"Fuck! God damned fucking idiot!"

Pattison's face turned a dark shade of red, and Mason wondered how high the man's diastolic pressure was.

"Your boyfriend just walked in the front door of the cabin. Bold as brass. He's gonna get himself killed."

Mason silently cheered for Harper, the arrogant prick, and then cursed him for his foolishness. Sticking his nose in police business, making the situation more deadly. Thinking with his cock instead of his head.

"Then what happened?" Ray's voice sounded strangled; he was probably thinking the same. Gotta admire the man for pure stupid guts.

"Nothing. No sound from the place. Your civilian was armed too." Pattison turned accusing eyes on the pair of detectives. "You didn't tell me he was packing."

"Didn't know." Mason shrugged. "He *was* a cop."

Mason raised a brow at Ray, and his partner's gaze dropped. Ray'd known and kept it to himself. Mason pressed his lips together. He wasn't going to blast his partner in front of General Patton. He'd blister him later in private.

Pattison kicked the tire of the SWAT truck. "Now I've got two God damned hostages to get out of there. Shit!"

Robert prided himself on being flexible and well prepared. His situation had just taken an abrupt turn and he would handle it. He'd pictured himself in this exact situation, holding a hostage with a gun trained on his head. But he'd always thought it'd be a cop holding the gun. Not a boyfriend.

Well, the man used to be a cop. Cop and boyfriend in one. *Delicious.*

Harper's brows narrowed as he registered the stupidity of his actions. He'd spotted the wired walls and remote detonator. Bet Harper wasn't feeling so smart now. One should always explore and think through every action before implementing it.

Running off half-cocked gets you in deep shit. Like right now.

A rush of power swelled in Robert's chest. He'd outsmarted everyone.

He felt Lacey twist her head, and he tightened his rope the slightest bit. She froze. He had control of the entire situation. His thumb played with the button on his detonator. A very small twinge of sorrow flashed at the inevitable loss of this home. So much had happened here. So much he'd learned here.

He crushed the feelings and smiled at Jack. "Face it, Harper. You can't both get out of here alive. Turn around and leave and one of you survives."

"You'll die too."

Did he think he was stupid? "No shit, Sherlock. But death doesn't scare me. If that's what it takes, then that's what I'll do. Either way I'll never be forgotten."

Jack's eyebrows rose. *Good. He was confused.*

Robert felt Lacey's back relax and she swayed gently to one side. He'd cut off her air and she was passing out. *No!* She had to be conscious for this. He loosened the rope several notches and tried to straighten her with his knees.

Abruptly she flung herself to the left, yanking the rope out of his relaxed grip.

He never heard the shots.

Lacey thought Jack had gotten her message. She'd looked into his eyes, then swung her gaze to the floor at her left five times. He'd slightly dipped his chin in a nod.

She took a deep breath and swayed as if the blood was cut off to her head. She felt Bobby relax the death rope and she dived to the side.

Jack's gun roared twice and the cabin walls flashed as the charges instantly exploded, and the ceiling burst into flames with a deafening hiss.

"Go, Jack! Get out!" There wasn't time for him to get her out. She was still tied to the ring by a mass of knots. Sobbing, she curled up in a ball on the hard floor. She hid her face between her arms and prayed she wouldn't feel too much pain.

"Jesus Christ!"

Jeff Cordova jerked his eye away from the scope on his sniper rifle. Flames had simultaneously flared behind every cabin window and would have blinded him if not for the safety feature in the night vision.

He'd been idly listening through his earpiece as his commander bitched about the dumbshit civilian when the crack of two shots pierced the quiet forest. Before Jeff could pass on that information, the cabin exploded in flames.

"It's on fire! He set the place on fire!"

In his earpiece, he could hear the other snipers yelling, drowning out any instructions from Pattison.

Jeff took two steps toward the inferno and halted. He wasn't prepared to enter a burning building. Scanning the surrounding forest, he searched for the two entry teams who'd been standing by, waiting to storm the place. He yanked out his earpiece. The panicked yelling was deafening in his ear. He couldn't think.

"Noooo! Jack, no!"

At the shout behind him, Jeff swung around. A tall man was racing toward him, his gaze locked on the flames. Jeff brought up his weapon, simultaneously registering the man's black knit hat and jacket. He jerked his rifle down. *The other civilian.*

The man sprinted past, but Jeff leaped on him, taking him down in the snow with an illegal football tackle. The man fought, kicking Jeff in the face. "Let go! Let me go! I've got to get them out!"

Jeff threw his bulk on the man's back and pulled back on the thrashing arms.

"Get the fuck off! I've got to get in there!"

Jeff gave the man's arms a rough jerk up and pushed his face in the snow. "You can't go in there! It's too late!"

The man abruptly stopped fighting, his chest heaving. He slowly raised his face in the direction of the fire. He mumbled, his words sounding wet.

Jeff looked to the fire and his stomach heaved. In fifteen seconds, the flames had already broken through the thin cabin roof. The clouds of black smoke mixed with the falling snow.

No one could live through that.

The eight-year SWAT veteran had never felt so powerless.

Two shots rang through the forest. At base camp, every head jerked toward the trees in the direction of the unseen cabin.

"That your sniper?" Mason shouted at Pattison, who shook his head. A look of fear slashed the commander's face, shocking Mason with its vulnerability.

"It's on fire," Pattison whispered, his eyes wide. He connected astounded gazes with Mason.

"What's on fire?" Lusco yelled.

"The cabin. The fucking cabin. Team one, get your asses in there!" Pattison's face flushed with rage. He was back in charge. "Cordova! Black! Ellison! What do you see?"

Mason ran toward the trees, only to have Ray grab his arm. Angrily shaking him off, Mason whirled on the younger man to lash him verbally, but the furious look in Ray's eyes stopped him.

"What the fuck can you do? You'll just get in their way!"

Mason couldn't speak, his heart in his throat.

Ray was right.

Instead, he stared at the growing golden glow in the forest, closed his eyes, and silently prayed.

Lacey coughed and gagged.

The smoke was thick, painfully drying out her mouth and throat. *Just a minute more. Another minute and the smoke'll knock me out and I won't feel the flames.* She ground her face into the floor and shuddered. The room heated rapidly, the orange flames feet away.

She wailed. She was going to burn. Like those girls in the morgue. Like her most horrible nightmare.

"There you are." Lacey felt strong hands try to lift her. Something was thrown over her face. *Jack!*

He couldn't move her; she was still tied to the ring. She heard him curse and yank at the ropes. She went limp, crying. He couldn't untie her in time. "Get out! Put me down and get out!" she screamed. She felt him jerk the ropes again and she pushed at him with her tied hands, her vision blocked by his jacket on her face. *Get out!*

He dropped her shoulders to the floor and pain shot to her brain. She felt him move away and she exhaled. *Good! He was leaving. He'd be safe.*

Lacey felt a vibration at the rope attached to her ankles. Jack had a knife and was sawing at the rope. The tension on the rope vanished and her legs jerked. The knife clattered to the floor and he scooped her up.

Stupid bastard! There wasn't time to grab her! She kicked and thrashed in his arms, tossing her head to get rid of his jacket across her face.

"Lacey! Hold still, damn it!"

She felt him trip. They fell and he landed on her, forcing the breath from her lungs. She struggled to twist away. *He had to get out!*

"Don't make me knock you out! Stop fighting me!"

His hands lifted her again, this time tossing her over his shoulder like a kid with a backpack. The jacket opened at her face and she breathed deep.

Her throat broiled, searing the tissues as she coughed and gagged. Her vision dimmed and she fought for air. There was none. She floated away on the smoke.

What was she doing?

Jack struggled to keep hold of Lacey, stunned that she was fighting him.

He'd seen his shots rip two holes in the bastard's forehead, and then he'd lost sight of Lacey as a rapid chain reaction of charges ripped across the walls, instantly filling the room with black smoke. DeCosta must have hit the button just before the bullets connected. Dropping to his knees, he'd crawled in her direction, trying to hold his jacket over his nose and mouth. His eyes burned and watered in the potent smoke.

And then he found her. Curled up in a ball, coughing. Not even trying to get out.

She'd given up.

She'd fought him, kicking and swinging her tied hands. Her eyes clenched shut.

He'd sucked in a deep breath and held it, covering her face with the jacket and lifting her into his arms. But she was tied to the floor. He'd yanked at the ropes and panic had swept over him. He remembered Alex's knife in his boot. With a sob of relief, he'd cut her loose and lifted her again. That'd worked until she'd made him trip by thrashing around.

He wasn't going to screw this up.

He took a deep breath, held it, and tossed her over his shoulder. Bent over, he headed toward the door. "What…" A low table bumped against his shins, nearly knocking him down again. His mind scrambled.

Fuck! There hadn't been a table near the door.

He'd lost direction in the smoke and confusion.

Lacey stopped kicking and slumped limp against his back. Lord, no!

Jack blindly turned ninety degrees and pushed through the darkness. His head spun from lack of air. He couldn't hold his breath much longer. He felt his bare arms and face started to blister from the heat. Panic flickered in his oxygen-starved brain.

Where was the fucking door?

Mason and Ray ran through the trees after Pattison. If the commander was headed to the scene, then Mason was too. Generalized chaos was rippling through all the cops. Shouting and confusion reigned in the forest.

They emptied into a clearing. And into hell.

They couldn't see the cabin. It was an inferno. Red and orange flames erupting with black, choking smoke. The heat singed Mason's face through the icy air and he stepped back. And he wasn't that close.

"Dear God," Ray whispered, gaze locked on the fire.

Mason could only stare.

A loose circle of cops and SWAT was forming around the clearing. Everyone staying safely back, avoiding the smoke and sparks. Searching and hoping to catch a sign of life. Any sign.

Mason squeezed his eyes shut and felt the hot glow through his lids. What utter hell were Harper and Lacey suffering through?

A shout went up off to his right and a blonde woman stumbled out of the forest. Mason's heart stopped for a double beat.

She'd made it.

He blinked away the smoke. It wasn't Dr. Campbell. His heart fell into his stomach. *Lacey was in the fire.*

The woman rushed the burning cabin, and three cops grabbed her. She fought against their holds, screaming, but Mason couldn't make out the words.

"Shit. That's Kelly Cates!" Ray shouted over the din.

What the fuck was going on?

More shouts pulled their attention away from the woman. Something was moving in the flames. And it was human.

Mason's jaw dropped as he watched Harper stumble out of the flames with Lacey over his shoulder. Harper dropped to his knees and fell forward, throwing her to the ground and ripping the burning coat from her face. His hair smoked and one arm of his shirt was on fire.

Every man dashed to the couple. Someone threw a coat over Jack's arm and choked the flames out. Mason tossed his own jacket on Jack's head, crushing the flames trying to start in his hair. He caught Jack as he pitched forward. The man's face was black, his hands blistering. He tried to talk but no sound came out.

Officers dragged the victims a safe distance from the fire. Mason plunged Harper's burned hands into the snow. Harper's bloodshot gaze grabbed Mason's and he tried to speak again.

Mason shook his head. "Don't try to talk."

The burned man pushed against Mason, trying to twist to see Lacey.

She lay unmoving on her back in the snow, arms spread out from her sides. Two men administered CPR.

A painful cry came from Harper's burned throat, and Mason grabbed him as the man awkwardly lunged in her direction. Mason wrapped his arms around Harper's shoulders and held on. Through Harper's back, Mason could feel the man's heart pound. He finally deciphered Harper's garbled words.

"Is she dead?"

Mason couldn't answer. The cops were still doing CPR. *Don't let her die.* Harper's shoulders sagged and he leaned heavily on Mason.

The cop at her head gestured for the other to stop his compressions. His fingers were curled under her jaw, feeling for her pulse. His head bent close, watching for the rise and fall of her chest. The pause seemed infinite. Then he grinned and nodded at the other cop. "She's breathing, pulse is steady."

Harper sucked in a huge rattling breath. "Thank you, God," he croaked.

Mason silently seconded that.

EPILOGUE

Jessica plopped a lopsided head on the snowman. The ball of packed snow bobbled, and the girl slapped handfuls of snow about its neck as mortar. Lacey felt as if the winter was never going to end. It'd been four weeks since the fire, and the snow was still thick on the ground.

"Thank you for not telling the police about her," Kelly whispered. "I don't know what I would've done if Chris had found out Jessica wasn't his. Or mine."

Standing shoulder to shoulder, the two women watched the girl play in the snow from inside Lacey's home. Against the white background, Jessica was a cheery sight in her red mittens and hat.

"She *is* yours. Both of yours." Lacey tried to smile. "Suzanne would be happy to know she's with you. No one could love her more than you and Chris."

Kelly's face fell. "It's always there. Like a dark cloud around my head. I try not to think of Suzanne. For several years I nearly convinced myself I'd given birth to Jessica."

"You haven't had more babies." It was a question.

"I can't."

At the sharp pain in Kelly's simple words, Lacey pulled the woman away from the window and sat her on the sofa, giving Kelly her full attention. It was time for some answers. She hadn't spoken with Kelly since that night at the fiery cabin. Lacey had kept her mouth shut when the police brought up Kelly's abduction. She'd told the detectives that the kidnapper had kept them apart, that she'd never known Kelly was there. Said she hadn't believed Kelly was still alive.

Lacey's voice was nearly back to normal. She'd been hoarse for a long time, speech extremely painful. She'd suffered four cracked ribs, a broken radius, and a severe concussion. A few days in the hospital had helped heal her body. The healing of her mind was taking longer. The nightmares were back. Only this time they were about fire and smoke and evil. In them, she was trapped in the cabin, unable to escape from the hot flames. Or Bobby DeCosta.

Without the killer to question, the detectives pieced together the old Mount Junction deaths the best they could. They believed Dave and Bobby traveled between Mount Junction and Corvallis, dealing death for several years, sometimes together, sometimes alone. Their mother claimed to know nothing. And she claimed she never knew about a missing baby.

Lacey cleared her throat. "Why can't you have children?"

"Do you remember when I had a miscarriage in college?"

Lacey nodded, the memory very faint.

"At that time they told me I had a bicornate uterus. Usually not a real big deal but I guess mine was a severe type. That's what caused the miscarriage. They said it was doubtful I could carry a child to term unless I had surgery to repair it. I didn't have medical insurance at the time and I didn't want to get pregnant while I was still in college, so waiting on the surgery was fine with me. I told myself that when I was older and ready to start a family I'd get it fixed one day."

"Did Chris know?"

Kelly shook her head. "It happened was before we dated. Then I couldn't tell him after I'd got Jessica. What was I to say? 'By the way, I need surgery to have children and Jessica was just a fluke?' I just let him believe it was too difficult to get pregnant. We'd try month after month and I'd shake my head in confusion at the difficulty. Finally I started telling him I wanted only one child. How could we improve on perfection?"

"No more miscarriages?"

Kelly dropped her gaze. "I got hormone injections. Still do."

She'd punished herself for having Suzanne's daughter. No more children.

"How did you get the baby?" Lacey whispered.

Kelly shifted and her gaze stayed on her knotted hands in her lap. "He gave her to me. I didn't ask for her. I didn't even know who she was."

"Who gave her to you?"

"Bobby DeCosta."

"You *did* know him. Did you know him before the trial?"

Kelly shook her head, raising pleading eyes to Lacey. "No. I met him during the proceedings. He often sat in the hallway outside the courtroom. He never looked at anyone or talked to anyone. I'd heard he had some sort of mental handicap. That's why I spoke to him."

Lacey nodded, understanding. Kelly's little brother, Patrick, was severely mentally and physically handicapped.

"He never spoke to me but listened as I talked. I tried to be kind because everyone else treated him like dirt. I'd heard he was physically unable to speak, but he seemed bright. I sympathized. Somewhere, in one of our one-sided talks, I'd mentioned I couldn't have children. I was trying to connect to him, that's all. He couldn't talk and I couldn't have kids. I know being infertile doesn't compare to not having a voice, but I was trying to show him that no one has everything.

"Several months later he showed up at my door with a beautiful baby girl. Chris and I had fought and broken up. We weren't speaking and I was horribly depressed and lonely. Jessica gave me my life back, she made me feel whole again, and finally I could look at the future positively. I moved to my aunt's in Virginia and passed her off as my own."

"You didn't ask where the baby came from?" Lacey sat motionless, her voice hoarse.

"I did and for the first time I heard him speak. There was nothing wrong with his voice." Kelly's tone grew derisive for a short second. "He told me a friend couldn't raise her and he wanted me to have a child because I was the only person who had ever been kind to him. He thought he was helping me."

"But what about the legal stuff? Birth certificate?"

Kelly shook her head and looked away. "My aunt took care of it. I don't know how she did it. I didn't care. I wanted to keep that baby."

"Then you and Chris got back together."

"He was shocked to hear I'd had a baby, but once he saw Jessica he loved her."

"You didn't know she was Suzanne's?"

Kelly's head came up and she looked out the window, watching her daughter create a snowman smile from stones. "Not until she was about five. One day I saw her do that head tilt and wrinkled nose thing." Kelly demonstrated, and Lacey held back a gasp. "You know what I'm talking about? It shocked me. I could see Suzanne doing the exact same thing. Then I realized she has Suzanne's eyes. That's when I knew."

Lacey was speechless. How many times had she seen Suzanne do that?

"I realized then that Bobby must have done something to Suzanne. His brother was in jail, so someone must have held Suzanne captive through her pregnancy. I was absolutely sick once I realized what possibly had happened."

"You could have gone to the police!"

"He'd long vanished. He and his mother. And I wasn't sure he'd actually been the one who did something with Suzanne."

"But, Kelly! He brought you a baby that you figured out was Suzanne's! The police should have been told so they could find him and question him about Suzanne!"

"It'd been over five years!" Kelly argued. "I didn't know what to do! Then when…Suzanne's remains turned up and those men started to die, I *knew* he was the one behind it. They were obviously revenge killings. During the trial, I'd seen his devotion to his brother. If anyone was striking out at the people who'd put away Dave DeCosta it'd be his brother."

"Why didn't you go to the police? Maybe they could've stopped him! All of this could have been avoided!"

"I was afraid the truth about Jessica would come out." Kelly turned fierce, stormy eyes on Lacey. "I wouldn't let him destroy my family." Kelly's sweet face blazed with hot emotion.

But you'd let other people die. Maybe even me. Lacey squeezed her eyes shut.

"I know you don't agree with what I did. But you don't understand. You don't have kids—you can't understand. I would have killed him to protect Jessica."

The doorbell rang, splintering the tension in the room. "I need to go." Kelly grabbed her purse, dashed for the door, and threw it open.

"Kelly. Good to see you." Lacey's father stood at the door, a cardboard box in his hands. "I saw Jessica out front. She's growing up."

"Yes, she is." Her eyes wet, Kelly looked at Lacey over her shoulder. She slipped by Dr. Campbell and darted across the porch.

Lacey silently watched Kelly escape, utterly stunned by her revelations. Kelly had held the power to stop everything. And she'd done nothing. Lacey's heart cracked. She knew she'd never talk to Kelly again. Dr. Campbell shot a sharp look at his daughter's face.

"You don't have to ring the doorbell, Dad." Lacey forced a smile and her gaze locked on the box. *He brought it.*

"My hands were full." He held out the box. She kept her arms at her sides.

"Is that it?"

"I went to a lot of trouble to sneak this out. I need it back tomorrow."

Lacey reluctantly took the box. It was about fifteen inches in height and length, and weighed next to nothing. Willing her hands not to shake, she set it on the sofa.

"Thank you," she whispered.

Her father wrapped his arms around her and hugged her tight. "I don't get it."

"I know." She squeezed him back, pressing her face against his coat.

The room fell silent.

"Have you heard from Michael?" He stepped back, his arms slowly letting go. He searched her eyes.

Lacey smiled. "He's not coming home for a while. Something about climbing red rocks and rafting the Colorado River."

"And a woman?" Her father's eyebrows rose.

"I don't think he's doing either adventure alone."

He studied her, searching her face. "He's a good man. I always thought the two of you…"

She shook her head. "Not meant to be, Dad. Michael knows it. And it's OK with me."

Her father looked like he didn't quite believe her, but he changed the subject. "Where's your other young man?"

"Right here." Jack stepped out of the kitchen, his silver eyes twinkled, and Lacey knew he'd heard the last exchange.

Dr. Campbell nodded at Jack's bandaged right hand. "How's it coming?"

"It's doing good. Grafts are coming along." Jack ran a hand over his buzzed head. "Hair's nearly grown out past army length."

His hair had also burned. He'd shaved his head, making Lacey feel like she was dating Vin Diesel. She missed his thick black hair.

Lacey also wore her hair short, just below her ears. Several inches had burned in the flames, and her hairdresser had chopped off even more to give it a bouncy, perky look that framed Lacey's face. She'd never had short hair.

She hated it.

Her father grinned, gave Jack an affectionate slap and squeeze on the shoulder, hugged Lacey again, said his good-byes, and left.

Jack pulled Lacey into him, holding her tight as she rested her head on his heart. She listened to the comforting thumps. "I heard Kelly leave."

Lacey said nothing.

"Were you right about Jessica?"

She nodded against his chest.

"What's in the box? Why does your dad need it back tomorrow?"

She'd wanted to open it alone. But they'd made a commitment to face problems together. Since the fire, only during his surgeries had Jack been away from her side. He'd insisted Michael or her dad stay with her at those times. Twice he'd come out of anesthesia with his fists swinging and her name ripping from his lips. Half-conscious, he'd been inconsolable until he'd heard her voice, touched her face.

Lacey no longer worried about his playboy past or his commitment to a relationship with her. Any other man would have raced away in the aftermath; Jack had stayed, been her rock. He'd told her he wanted to be with her. He'd repeated it a dozen times in the days after the fire, clenching her hands like he might be asking too late, like she might turn him down.

Lacey had understood. She should be dead, but life had given them a second chance and neither of them would waste it. He'd moved into her home and clutched her close every night in their bed.

She loved him.

She picked up the box and Jack followed her into the kitchen. "It'll help with my nightmares." Out of the corner of her eye she saw his shoulders jerk. He'd had a front-row seat to her restless and thrashing dreams. Mentally they both knew the danger was gone, but emotional shadows flitted around the two of them. Shadows of stress and strain, remnants from a night of horror. She set the box on the island and rested her hands on its top.

I don't know if I can do this.

Jack ran a hand over his short hair. "I'm trying to help you with the nightmares."

She gave him a smile, meeting his worried eyes. He so badly wanted to heal her, give her peace, and mend every sad part of her. "You do help. I love waking to find your arms around me at all hours of the night." She knew it helped him too.

Lacey frowned at the box. "This is for closure."

She opened the top of the box and reached in, pulling out a rounded shape wrapped in white towels. Slowly she peeled back the towels and heard Jack catch his breath. "Jesus, Lace."

Lacey eyed the sanitized skull. Two round holes punctured the forehead, an inch and a half apart. A large section of the back of the skull was missing, destroyed by the powerful exit of the bullets. The mandible was also missing, but she didn't need that part. She looked at the front top teeth. Taking a deep breath she touched a finger to the tiny lateral incisors, the ones that looked like small fangs. She rapidly rewrapped the skull, set it in the box, and closed the top with quivering hands. She exhaled, feeling the shadows lighten, the tears threaten.

Bobby DeCosta wasn't coming back.

His arms shaking a little, Jack pulled her tight to his chest and pressed his mouth against her hair. "God, I love you. You know that, right? Right?"

Nodding, she closed her eyes, inhaled his scent, and relaxed, feeling his heat warm her to her toes. No one could take her away from him again.

"I love you too," she whispered.

ACKNOWLEDGMENTS

Some authors say it takes a team to create a book. I'm going to revise that statement: it takes a cheerleading team to create a book. The life of a writer is a series of ups and downs, wins and losses. Every writer needs precious people to believe in them and guide them through the downs and celebrate during the ups. These are my people: My agent, Jennifer Schober, who never gave up on me. My editor Lindsay Guzzardo, who loved my books and my writing enough to get them into readers' hands. My editor Charlotte Herscher, who fine-tuned my books into something fabulous. Head cheerleader Elisabeth Naughton, who taught me to Believe. My biggest thank you goes to my husband, Dan, who pushed his way into my life during a very black time and taught me to laugh, love, and never give up.

ABOUT THE AUTHOR

Photograph © Yuen Lui, 2010

Born and raised in the Pacific Northwest, Kendra Elliot has always been a voracious reader, cutting her teeth on classic female sleuths and heroines like Nancy Drew, Trixie Belden, and Laura Ingalls before proceeding to devour the works of Stephen King, Diana Gabaldon, and Nora Roberts. She graduated with a degree in journalism but went on to become a licensed dental hygienist. Now a Golden Heart, Daphne du Maurier, and Linda Howard Award of Excellence finalist, Elliot shares her love of suspense in her first novel, *Hidden*. She still lives in the Pacific Northwest with her husband and three daughters. Keep in touch with Kendra at www.kendraelliot.com or through Facebook.